A Girl
Next Door

Ups and
Downs

MARY JANE STAPLES

A Girl
Next Door

Ups and
Downs

BCA

This omnibus edition published 2004
By BCA
By arrangement with Transworld Publishers
A division of The Random House Group Ltd

CN 134210

Typeset in New Baskerville by
Kestral Data, Exeter, Devon.

Printed and bound in Great Britain by
Clays Limited, St Ives plc

CONTENTS

A Girl
Next Door

THE ADAMS FAMILY

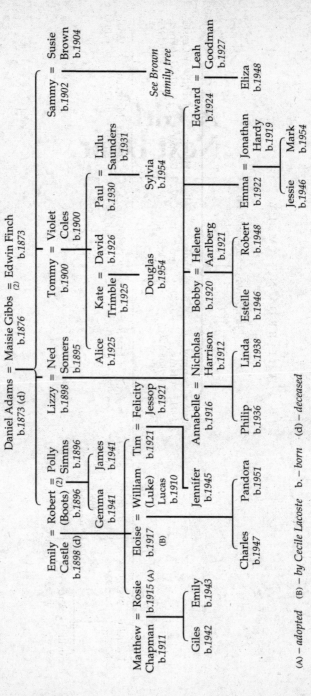

Daniel Adams = Maisie Gibbs = Edwin Finch
b.1873 (d)   b.1876   (2)   b.1873

Emily = Robert (Boots)
b.1898 (d) = Polly Simms (2)
             b.1896   b.1896

Lizzy = Ned Somers
b.1898   b.1895

Tommy = Violet Coles
b.1900   b.1900

Sammy = Susie Brown
b.1902   b.1904

See Brown family tree

Edward = Leah Goodman
b.1924   b.1927

Eliza b.1948

Gemma b.1941
James b.1941

Eloise = William (Luke) Lucas
b.1917 (B)   b.1910

Tim = Felicity Jessop
b.1921   b.1921

Annabelle = Nicholas Harrison
b.1916   b.1912

Alice b.1925

Kate = David Trimble
b.1925   b.1926

Paul = Lulu Saunders
b.1930   b.1931

Sylvia b.1954

Douglas b.1954

Bobby = Helene Aarlberg
b.1920   b.1921

Emma = Jonathan Hardy
b.1922   b.1919

Mark b.1954

Jessie b.1946

Estelle b.1946

Robert b.1948

Philip b.1936

Linda b.1938

Matthew = Rosie
Chapman   b.1915 (A)
b.1911

Giles b.1942

Emily b.1943

Jennifer b.1945

Charles b.1947

Pandora b.1951

(A) – adopted   (B) – by Cecile Lacoste   b. – born   (d) – deceased

THE BROWN FAMILY

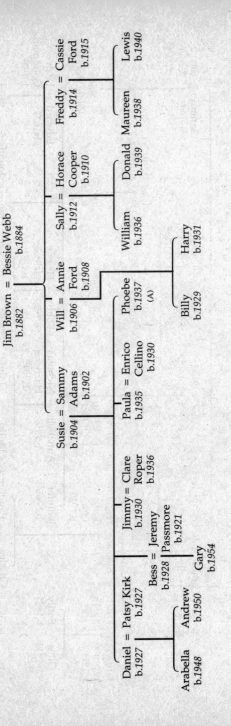

Jim Brown = Bessie Webb
b.1882   b.1884

Susie = Sammy Adams
b.1904   b.1902

Will = Annie Ford
b.1906   b.1908

Sally = Horace Cooper
b.1912   b.1910

Freddy = Cassie Ford
b.1914   b.1915

Daniel = Patsy Kirk
b.1927   b.1927

Bess = Jeremy Passmore
b.1928   b.1921

Jimmy = Clare Roper
b.1930   b.1936

Paula = Enrico Cellino
b.1935   b.1930

Phoebe
b.1937
(A)

Billy
b.1929

Harry
b.1931

William
b.1936

Donald
b.1939

Maureen
b.1938

Lewis
b.1940

Arabella
b.1948

Andrew
b.1950

Gary
b.1954

Chapter One

July, 1956.

The rock and roll movement, born, the public were informed, of the young people's enthusiasm for free expression in music, was reaching a peak of popularity in America and Britain. It has to be said, however, that the singer Liberace, with his jewel-encrusted get-ups, his photogenic piano and his equally photogenic minty-fresh choppers, still commanded a faithful following among older people.

America had something else going on in addition to rock and roll, something that was capturing the interest of all its citizens, young and old, as well as the rest of the world. A programme for exploring space. Heading their scientific team was a rocket genius, Wernher von Braun, the German who had built Hitler's flying bombs. Of course, some people, despite their interest, laughed at the idea of a spacecraft that could reach the moon, thousands and thousands of miles from Earth. And even if it could be managed, who was going to do what with it?

'Don't look at me, I'm up to my ears working on our property company's overheads,' said Sammy Adams, well-known businessman of Camberwell, south-east London.

'Try me,' said his son Daniel, an adventurous type.

'Try you not, honey,' said his American wife Patsy. 'I want you at home. Your granny and grandpa are coming to Sunday tea.'

'How about Edith Hammerglow down the road?' suggested Daniel's cousin, Bobby Somers, to his French wife Helene. 'She's always talking about an urge for faraway places.'

'That woman?' said Helene. 'She'd fall off her broomstick before she reached the rain clouds.'

'Who's going to give her first aid if she lands in our back garden?' asked Bobby.

'Ah, what an idiot,' said Helene, 'but you are still a nice man.'

That kind of dialogue was representative of the fact that in the UK nobody very much gave serious consideration to the possibility of placing a man on the moon.

Far more prominence was given to an event in the Middle East. General Nasser, dictator of Egypt, had summarily nationalized the Suez Canal, much to the anger and dismay of Sir Anthony Eden, Britain's Prime Minister. He was having to consider whether or not he could allow free passage of the Canal to be controlled by Egypt. Since its inception, the Canal had been Britain's lifeline to the Middle East and the Far East, and what was presently left of its Empire in those regions. There were rumblings in 10 Downing Street.

Of interest to the Adams family was the news that in America the police and the FBI were conducting a nationwide manhunt for a young German Jew, Wilhelm Kleibert, who was wanted for the murder of an immigrant Ukrainian doctor, one Paul Rokovsky.

The murder had touched the life of Mrs Felicity Adams who, blinded during a German air raid on London, had been due to consult Dr Rokovsky in New York. An outstanding ophthalmic surgeon, he had restored the sight of several blinded American soldiers of the Second World War. Only a short time before Felicity and her husband were due to take the flight to New York, Kleibert had shot Dr Rokovsky dead.

During interrogation, Kleibert claimed that Rokovsky was actually a German medical practitioner responsible for hideous experiments on inmates of the notorious Auschwitz concentration camp. Kleibert himself had been an inmate, along with his brother and sister, twins. He had survived, his brother and sister had died as a consequence of experimental operations. His escape from police custody had been engineered by two FBI men who held written orders to take him to FBI headquarters. They turned out to be impostors, the orders a forgery.

That had been two months ago. The murder had taken place in December 1954, the trial constantly put back due to the delaying tactics of the defence and the complications of investigations that were mainly concerned with discovering whether or not the murdered man, Dr Paul Rokovsky, really did have a murky history. The defence claimed they had witnesses, concentration camp survivors, to prove he did, that he was actually Dr Gerhard Fischer, a German known to have worked at Auschwitz under Dr Mengele, for whom a hunt was also going on. Both were classified as major war criminals.

The FBI believed the impostors to be agents of Mossad, the Israeli security force, and that they intended to return to Israel in company with Kleibert. Airports and seaports were all being watched.

That murder crushed Felicity's hope of a successful operation.

Chapter Two

On a more homely note, in a house close to the heart of tranquil Dulwich Village, south-east London, Mrs Polly Adams woke up. It was well past nine, but it was Saturday morning and, further, everyone had gone to bed very late. Yesterday her husband, Robert Alfred Adams, known as Boots, had reached the age of sixty, and the celebrations, which had been attended by almost everyone in the extensive Adams families, had lasted until well past one in the morning.

Polly might have had a hangover, but had always escaped that morning-after affliction. During her years as a flapper, friends had known her to be squiffy, but never headless.

Sleepily, she turned her head to find out if Boots was awake, but saw only his pillow. She smiled. Did he have a hangover, and was he suffering it in the bathroom? Downstairs, the sounds of someone at work reached her ears. Her daily maid, Flossie Cuthbert, was busy doing a massive job of clearing up.

Boots, dressing gown over his pyjamas, came in then, carrying a tea tray.

'D'you fancy a cup of hot strong tea, Polly old girl?' he asked, placing the tray on a bedside table and sitting down on the edge of the bed.

'Hot strong tea?' said Polly. 'You old darling, don't you have a hangover?'

'Fortunately, no,' said Boots, and poured the steaming brew. 'There we are,' he said, handing her a full cup.

Polly sat up and took it. She smiled and looked him over. Sixty now, but he showed not a single trace of grey in his dark brown hair, nor any loss of firmness in his features. That, she supposed, made it easy for him to accept his advancing years. But then, he had never quarrelled with old Father Time any more than he had quarrelled with the quirks and perversities of life and people. Advancing years were different for a woman who was as sensitive about her age as she was. She would be sixty herself in September, only two months away. God, how she hated the thought. Boots would have told her she looked nowhere near sixty, and it was true that the piquancy of her looks brought to mind her younger years. Certainly, her hair, as dark as burnt sienna, showed no more grey tints than his did. The whole family thought she and Boots remarkably well preserved. Polly, however, was sure her crow's feet would soon make her look a definite old lady.

6

'How do you do it?' she asked, sipping her tea.

'How do I do what?' countered Boots.

'Keep your wrinkles from showing?'

'Oh, in the same way that you keep yours at bay,' said Boots, 'by the grace of God.'

'Thanks for that sweet notion,' said Polly, who used creams in the reasonable belief that her Maker was far too omnipotent to attend to the wants of foolish individuals and their vanities. What was it about the Adams family that defied time? Boots's sister Lizzy, and his brothers, Tommy and Sammy, were all in their fifties, but looked younger than their years. And his mother, only two months short of eighty, was hardly grey-haired, wrinkled and bent. 'Well, whatever, we both survived a famous party. Congratulations on your stamina, old warhorse.'

'I could say the same about yours,' said Boots. 'What a woman.'

'Is that a compliment?' asked Polly.

'Spoken from the heart,' said Boots.

'Darling, it's been fifteen years,' said Polly. They had celebrated that particular wedding anniversary in March.

'Who's complaining?' said Boots. 'I'm not.' He thought of his long-lost Emily then, his first wife. Fifteen years, yes, that was also the amount of time he had been married to her before she was killed during a daylight air raid. Her image, that of a bright and energetic cockney woman, often took shape in his mind. But he had never regretted marrying Polly. What man could regret marrying a woman who, at the age of forty-five, had presented him with twins as endearing as Gemma and James? He lightly touched her shoulder. 'I'm a fortunate man, Polly.'

'Is that another compliment?' smiled Polly.

'It's well deserved,' said Boots.

Polly asked him what he had thought of the antics of the young people at his party, on the grounds that they had turned it into a rock 'n' roll merry-go-round. Boots said any modern merry-go-round at any man's sixtieth birthday was as entertaining as an old-fashioned knees-up, as long as he wasn't dragged into it himself.

'Wild,' said Polly.

'A knees-up?' said Boots.

'Rock 'n' roll,' said Polly, 'and I must speak to Gemma. It was her record player that started it all.'

'Give her my compliments,' said Boots, 'her record player was a hit.'

'A loud hit,' said Polly. 'The ceiling trembled and the floor shook. If the old people could survive all that, they could survive an earthquake. I must ring Stepmama this morning and find out if she's still alive. And you had better check on the health of your mother and stepfather.'

'I don't think that will be necessary,' said Boots.

* * *

8

In their house on Red Post Hill, his mother, Lady Finch, still known as Chinese Lady to her closest kin, was at breakfast with her husband, Sir Edwin Finch. Neither had a hangover, both had imbibed with respect for their ages. Mind, Chinese Lady did follow two glasses of port with a glass of champagne, but that was out of respect for her age combined with respect for her eldest son's sixtieth.

'Edwin,' she said, spooning marmalade over her buttered toast while thinking about Boots, 'I just don't know how my oldest son can be sixty.'

'Maisie my dear,' said Sir Edwin, 'Boots achieved that in the natural way.'

'Yes, but it seems like only yesterday that he was just a talkative boy,' said Chinese Lady.

'It was his talkative talents and his many questions about life that made him the man he is.'

'If you mean airy-fairy, I couldn't agree more,' said Chinese Lady.

'I mean communicative and wordly,' said Sir Edwin.

'That still sounds like airy-fairy to me,' said Chinese Lady, 'but my goodness, I should think everyone in the family turned up to help him celebrate, as well as lots of friends. All that noise, I never heard the like at no-one else's birthday party. I was trying to talk to Lizzy about when she and Boots were growing up and Sammy was saving all his pennies and ha'pennies in his old

9

socks, but I just couldn't hear what I was saying, and nor could Lizzy.'

'There'll be an even noisier celebration in September,' said Sir Edwin.

'Well, I don't know which celebration you mean, but I do know I couldn't live through a noisier one,' said Chinese Lady, refilling teacups and ignorant, of course, about Polly's reference to earthquake survival.

'I think you'll do very well, Maisie, it'll be on the occasion of your eightieth,' smiled Sir Edwin.

'Edwin,' said Chinese Lady. 'I don't want anyone to fuss about me being eighty.'

'We shall all fuss,' declared Sir Edwin, 'as we will a little later when Polly celebrates her own sixtieth.'

'Well, I can't stop Polly having her kind of celebration,' said Chinese Lady, 'but all I want is just a little private tea party with Boots and Polly and the others, and toasted muffins and a cake.'

'I doubt if the family will let you get away with that,' said Sir Edwin.

'Well, I just don't want no loud noise, nor any dancing like we had last night,' said Chinese Lady. 'What was everyone doing?'

'I think it's called jiving, or rocking and rolling,' said Sir Edwin. 'All to Gemma's record player.'

'Whatever it's called, it's not what I know as dancing,' said Chinese Lady, 'not like a nice waltz or a foxtrot. I could hardly believe my eyes at what some of my granddaughters were doing.'

'Modern young ladies aren't quite as shy or as modest as those of our day, Maisie,' said Sir Edwin.

'Well,' said Chinese Lady firmly, 'I don't mind girls not being shy, but I don't like them doing French dancing. That's what it was, French, showing a lot more than any respectable girls ought to.'

Sir Edwin coughed. True, there had been a profusion of high swirling skirts and an array of pretty, nyloned legs, all to the accompaniment of noisy encouragement from the young men and growing boys jigging in concert with the girls. 'Swing it, baby!' 'Keep rocking, Linda!' 'Go get 'em, Phoebe!' Linda was the eighteen-year-old granddaughter of Lizzy and Ned, Phoebe the nineteen-year-old adopted daughter of Sammy and Susie. And 'baby', no doubt, had been young Gemma herself, she who had introduced her record player and turned the party into the equivalent of a rousing knees-up. Sir Edwin could not fault any of them for their looks or – um – for their pretty legs. However . . .

'I don't think you and I would want to discourage the lively spirit of the young, Maisie,' he said.

'Well, Edwin,' declared Chinese Lady, 'all I can say is that if I do have a large family party on my

11

eightieth, just make sure Gemma doesn't bring no kind of gramophone.'

'Very well, Maisie,' said Sir Edwin, 'I'll take good note of that.'

'Thank you, Edwin,' said Chinese Lady, and reached across the table to pat his hand. Her husband would be eighty-three in September, just before her eightieth, and she was devoting herself to his well-being. If she was still upright in her carriage and firm of body, Edwin was silver-haired, and leaner by the year. It would grieve her to lose him. 'Still, everyone was very complimentary about Boots, which made me feel he's turned out a lot better than I thought he would.'

'Maisie,' said Sir Edwin, 'you can believe me when I tell you you can be very proud of your – ' He smiled. 'Of your only oldest son.'

'Well, it's nice of you to say so, Edwin,' said Chinese Lady, and gave him another affectionate pat.

Her youngest son, Sammy, and his wife Susie, were, like Polly, not yet up. Sammy was awake, but blearily so and wondering what had happened to his head.

'Susie, what went on last night?' he asked.

'You got drunk,' said Susie, sheets and blanket cosily cuddling her.

'Eh?'

'Tight as a lord,' said Susie, coming up to

12

fifty-two and matching Polly in her fight to stay well preserved.

'Eh?' said Sammy, fifty-four and still mentally and physically energetic, except right now, when his whole being felt as if Satan's black angels had been hammering him all night. That included his head.

'Didn't I keep telling you after all that wine and champagne to stop having one more whisky for the road?' said Susie, who had been wise enough to limit her liquid intake, although she did have two glasses of bubbly. 'You must've had six.'

'Suffering cats, I don't remember drinking anything,' said Sammy. 'I only know my head feels like a seasick hot-air balloon, and me mouth feels like it's been down a drain all night.'

'Oh, dear, what a shame, Sammy love, but lucky for you it's Saturday and you can stay in bed and nurse your fat head,' said Susie.

'Susie,' groaned Sammy, 'is someone boiling it? It feels like it.'

'Someone like a cannibal?' said Susie.

'Don't make jokes, Susie,' said Sammy, 'it ain't Christian at the moment.' He closed his bleary eyes. 'Did Boots make a speech last night?'

'Well, of course,' said Susie. 'He talked about what sixty years had done to him, turned him into an old codger, and how he hoped his family would help him totter gracefully through the rest of his days. Of course, he said nice things about

13

Polly, but what I liked best was that he didn't forget to mention Emily and what a wonderful help she'd been to him when he was blind. Polly didn't seem to mind, I think Boots probably told her he was going to include a mention of Emily.'

'Am I hearing all this, or is it disappearing into me fog?' said Sammy.

'Well, you must've heard Boots's funnies,' said Susie, 'because you kept chortling.'

'Well, I'm not chortling now,' said Sammy, 'I'm going to spend the rest of the day doing a slow expiring job.'

'No, don't do that, Sammy love,' said Susie. 'Think of the business. I'm going down to make some tea for us and Phoebe. I don't suppose she's up yet.'

Sammy blinked his suffering eyes.

'Who's Phoebe?' he groaned.

'Your darling daughter,' said Susie, slipping from the bed.

'In my present condition, I ain't up to remembering that,' said Sammy. 'Would you mind telling me who's standing up?'

'Me,' said Susie, out of the bed.

'Well, stay there and keep the light out of me eyeballs,' said Sammy.

In her own bed, their daughter Phoebe was still sleeping the sleep of a young lady who had enjoyed a swinging party that included rock 'n' roll and the heady delights of wine and champagne. Her clothes, scattered over her bedroom floor, testified to her first-ever condition of careless rapture on her arrival home at two in the morning. Well, lovely Uncle Boots wasn't sixty every week.

She slept on, dreaming of Philip, Aunt Annabelle's entertaining son, who was gone on her. At least, she hoped he was. At nineteen, a girl was more than ready to have a bloke as dishy as Philip knocking on her door, especially when he looked smashing in the uniform of an RAF pilot officer.

Chapter Three

'Vi, I don't feel so good,' said Tommy, Chinese Lady's middle son. He also was still in bed, and he also had had one too many for the road. Well, good old Boots stocked good Scotch, and was always generous with it.

'Tommy,' said Vi, who was up and dressed, 'you once promised me you'd never get one over the eight again.'

'I think me promise got interfered with last night,' said Tommy.

'Oh, well, I'll excuse you,' said placid Vi. 'My, imagine Boots being sixty.'

'Sixty?' groaned Tommy. 'Well, I feel like ninety meself.'

'I must say you sound a bit like it,' said Vi. 'Still, wasn't it a lovely party, and there was Boots, not looking half his age, and all that champagne fizzing about while he was making his speech. Did you notice that your mum actually looked proud of him? She told me he'd grown up a good boy, after all. Isn't she funny about all of you? She still says Sammy's heading for purgatory on account of liking money too much.'

'Vi, are you talking to me?' asked Tommy, who, along with Sammy and other related males, really had celebrated in style. In a manner of speaking, it could be said it was the spirits of the occasion that had put paid to his promise. 'Vi?'

'Yes, Tommy,' said Vi, 'I'm talking to you.'

'Well, I don't want to offend you,' said Tommy, 'but would you mind talking to the cat down in the kitchen?'

'All right, lovey,' said Vi.

'I'll come down meself in a while,' said Tommy, 'say in about four hours.'

Smiling, Vi went down to the kitchen. The house was quiet, with Tommy still in bed, and no sounds coming from the room occupied by daughter Alice and her husband, Fergus MacAllister, who were staying for the weekend. Alice and Fergus had been the focus of family interest last year when, at Bristol Crown Court, a gang of four bank robbers had been prosecuted. Alice and Fergus, having tangled with two of the men, the two who had actually done the deed, were prime witnesses, along with the bank clerk forced to hand over the money at gunpoint. The trial proved to be quite straightforward, the prosecution case easily overpowering a flimsy defence, and the four men were convicted and sentenced to long terms of imprisonment.

Alice and Fergus dined out in happy fashion at the end of the trial. Fergus, who had been conducting a subtle, low-key courtship of Alice, became more positive in his campaign from that point on. Alice, who had always felt a scholastic career would be more suitable for her than marriage, found her preference was changing. Fergus had proved himself a stalwart and far less brash than when she had first known him. Her feelings towards him climbed from a modest level to a high one.

She became engaged to him in the spring of 1955 and married him two months later, from her family home on Denmark Hill, much to the pleasure of Vi and Tommy. They had both thought their daughter would end up, in Sammy's sympathetic words one day, as an unmarried spinster.

'You don't have to say unmarried,' said Tommy at the time.

'Why not?' said Sammy. 'A spinster is unmarried, ain't she?'

'Well, yes,' said Vi, 'but – '

'There you are, then,' said Sammy, which closed the brief dialogue. It wasn't much good arguing with Sammy's own kind of verbiage.

Fergus woke up in his in-laws' house. It was nine thirty. He'd enjoyed more than a few wee drams at Boots's sixtieth shindig, but his years of soldiering had given him an armour-plated stomach, and he was quite sober. Sober enough, in fact, to note that Alice's fair hair dappled her pillow with brightness. He lightly touched her shoulder.

'Will you no' come out of your dreams, Alice?'

That woke his wife. She turned. Fergus, beside her, was unshaven, blue-jawed, and eyeing her with a smile. A pirate speculating on his prize captive, she thought.

'Fergus, are you sober?' she asked.

'As a judge,' said Fergus. 'But when it comes to a fine celebration, I canna fault Boots and Polly. D'you have a head?'

'Yes, my very own,' said Alice, looking relaxed. She had slept well, having drunk no more than she knew she could take.

'I'll wager there are some heads that don't feel too clear,' said Fergus. 'I like it fine, Alice, that yours isn't suffering. Will you be wanting a wee celebration of our own just now?'

'What?' Alice gave him a suspicious look. Her piratical Scot smiled. 'Oh, no, you don't,' she said, 'not at this time of the morning.'

'Whisht, my bonny, we'll be as quiet as two bairns in their cot,' said Fergus.

'Well, you have your own quiet time while I take a bath,' said Alice, and slipped from the bed.

Fergus smiled indulgently. Alice still had some reservations, some moments of modesty. But she was a fine wife, and he would not have wanted her to be other than she was, a little different from her extrovert and outgoing cousins. The Adams families lived life exuberantly.

Boots's son Tim was up. He'd been down to the kitchen in his dressing gown. There, Maggie Forbes, the live-in maid, had mixed him the hair of the dog. It took the weight off his hangover. After which, he carried a cup of tea up to his wife, who had a hangover of her own, although only a slight one.

'What's that?' she asked. She was sitting up and peering.

'Tea,' said Tim, close to thirty-five and very much like his father in his tallness and looks.

'Oh, good show,' said Felicity, just thirty-five and a very photogenic brunette. 'Some husbands earn their medals.' She reached for the cup and saucer, and Tim placed the combination in her hand. He had a never-failing admiration for his blind wife, who, having lost out on her arranged consultation in New York with a Dr Rokovsky, due to his violent death, was now exclusively in the care of Sir Charles Morgan, a noted ophthalmic surgeon of London. Sir Charles had become convinced nature was doing that which he confessed he could not do himself by an operation. Felicity was now at a stage where her eyes, which had previously known brief moments of partial vision, gave her longer intervals, although still only of a blurred kind. On those occasions, she saw everything and everyone through a misty fog. But that was more than enough to make her believe the fog would clear one day, and she would see Tim and their daughter Jennifer with clarity and not as misty beings. Sir Charles was encouragingly hopeful about that, especially as her damaged cornea showed signs of natural healing. But he refused to commit himself to a time factor when she asked how long he thought it would take for healing to be complete. Be patient, he said. He wondered, of course, if perfect sight would ever come about.

As for the death of the Ukrainian ophthalmist, Dr Paul Rokovsky, the news that had come out of America suggested there were positive grounds for believing he had indeed been an SS doctor at the notorious Auschwitz concentration camp. Defence lawyers insisted they could call on witnesses who would swear in court that they had indentified his mortuary corpse as such. First, however, the assassin, Wilhelm Kleibert, who had escaped custody, had to be found, rearrested and brought to trial. Until that happened, witnesses could not be brought to court to testify.

With Felicity enjoying the cup of tea, Tim asked, 'What's on your mind this morning?'

'Only the fact that there was a rattling fine get-together of family and friends for your father's sixtieth,' said Felicity. 'If one couldn't see, one could positively hear. And even if I did

21

have a little too much bubbly, I'm wide awake now and ready to take a shower.'

'Need any help?' said Tim.

'None, lover,' said Felicity. She could always cope with the familiar. 'Where's Jennifer?' Jennifer was their eleven-year-old daughter.

'Still buried under her bedclothes,' said Tim.

'I'm not surprised,' said Felicity. 'A two o'clock bedtime for a girl her age was a bit much.'

'No time at all for a girl as lively as all the other young ones,' said Tim. 'Who'd have thought my stepma would have allowed Gemma's record player to turn the happy home into a Teddy boys' dance hall?'

'I think Polly was outvoted by Gemma and James,' said Felicity. 'Listen, lover, isn't it time the American cops caught up with their runaway prisoner?'

'You'd like the trial to take place?' said Tim.

'Yes, I want to know all about Dr Rokovsky's history, and that will come out then, won't it?'

'Good point,' said Tim. 'I'm with you in wanting to know if he really was one of those fiendish German doctors who carried out infernal experiments on Auschwitz inmates. As we've said before, that trial won't take place until the American police do catch up with Kleibert.'

'Send them a cable,' said Felicity, 'tell them to get a move on.'

'I'll underline it,' said Tim, although he thought that if Dr Rokovsky really had been the

German doctor of Auschwitz infamy, then most people would consider Kleibert deserved a row of medals, not a trial.

At ten o'clock in the home of Bobby Somers, his French wife Helene, and their children Estelle and Robert, Helene was downstairs, dressed, Bobby still in bed. So up she went.

'Ah, look at you, you great log,' she said, 'what are you doing just lying there?'

'I'm doing a recovery job from last night's orgy,' said Bobby, 'and that's not lying.'

'What? Ah, I see, another of your terrible jokes.' Helene shook a finger at him. 'Are you still not sober?'

'I'm a lot better,' said Bobby, 'but I'm still not sure about my legs. Where am I, by the way?'

'At home.'

'That should be a help,' said Bobby, 'I don't think my legs would make it here if we were still in France.'

They had returned only recently from a holiday fortnight with Helene's parents, but in good time to enjoy Boots's sixtieth.

'Well, never mind your legs, *chéri*,' said Helene, decorative apron covering her summer dress, 'the children are waiting for you to take them to the park, as you promised. So up, up, Bobby Somers, up, up.'

'Eh?' said Bobby, languid. Along with others, he'd had a great time at the party.

'Up, up,' said Helene, firm of body and firm of intention, and she whipped the bedclothes away. Bobby, pyjamas rumpled, considered that a touch of foul play. And said so. In response, Helene took hold of his ankles, pulled him sideways and yanked him off the bed. Bobby hit the carpeted floor with a bump.

'Strewth,' he said, 'who did that?'

'I did,' said Helene.

Bobby grinned, sat up, reached, took hold of her hands and pulled her down beside him. Helene stifled a shriek.

'Now I do feel better,' said Bobby, 'come here, you French doll.'

'Bobby – oh, you brute – don't you dare!'

'I think your dress is coming undone,' said Bobby.

'Mummy!' Estelle was calling. 'The phone's ringing!'

'Coming,' sang Helene, and jumped up.

'You can call that saved by the bell,' said Bobby, as she ran from the bedroom and down the stairs.

Estelle called again.

'Daddy, when are you going to take us to the park?'

'Give me ten minutes, sweetie,' called Bobby, on his feet, 'and then I'll see if my legs are working.'

While he was shaving, and while his eyes were still a little bleary, he and others of Chinese

Lady's male clan might have said Boots had a lot to answer for in his overgenerous dispensation of wine and champagne. And whisky for the road.

At ten thirty, in a good-looking terraced house in Wansey Street, Walworth, Mrs Cassie Brown turned from the sink as her daughter Maureen entered the kitchen in her dressing gown. Cassie, now forty-one and motherly, was a sister-in-law of Sammy and Susie Adams. Her husband Freddy, Susie's younger brother and a veteran of the Burma campaign, was at work. He'd risen at his usual time in order to open up the Adams clothing store by the Elephant and Castle for Saturday trading. Like Tommy and Sammy, he'd acquired a thick head at Boots's birthday romp. Unlike Tommy and Sammy, and their heads, however, he'd taken his out and about.

Cassie, regarding her daughter, said, 'So there you are, my girl, but not dressed.'

'Oh, man, what a jig,' said Maureen, eighteen and as richly brunette as her mother.

'That's double Dutch to me,' said Cassie.

'I'm talking about Uncle Boots's sixtieth, Mum,' said Maureen.

'Your dad said it would have been a lot quieter if you young people hadn't taken it over,' said Cassie. 'What's more, I must say you went a bit over the top. All that jiving with your skirt flying about, you saucy minx.'

'But the other girls, like Phoebe and Clare,

were doing it as well,' said Maureen. Clare, twenty, was the wife of Jimmy, Susie and Sammy's younger son.

'Never mind that,' said Cassie. 'Me and your dad didn't bring you up to do a French cancan at a birthday party.'

'Oh, but Uncle Boots's sixtieth was great,' said Maureen, 'and isn't he still the sexiest man ever? At sixty, would you believe. I don't know no-one like him at that age.'

Cassie smiled. Neither she nor Freddy would ever do a Victorian act of remonstration with Maureen or their son Lewis. Cassie was happy-go-lucky, Freddy good-natured and tolerant, even if he was never going to lose his acquired hatred of the Japs, whose honourable principles as so-called soldiers embraced cruelty and sadism. His memories of their savagery still gave him nightmares.

'Oh, well, I suppose you'll only be young once, Maureen,' said Cassie. 'D'you want some breakfast?'

'Just some cereal and tea,' said Maureen, her dressing gown concealing a distinctly appealing figure. 'Where's Lewis?' she asked.

'He's gone out to meet some friends,' said Cassie, putting the kettle on.

'What, already?' said Maureen. 'Wasn't he tired?'

'Not like you are,' said Cassie, 'but of course, he didn't go wild like you did.'

'No, well, he was getting really thick with Gemma,' said Maureen.

'Your brother's sixteen now, and he's got a growing boy's natural liking for girls,' said Cassie.

Maureen, filling her breakfast dish with cereal, said, 'Well, Dad liked them when he was only fourteen, so Aunt Susie told me.'

'Girls liked him, you mean,' said Cassie. 'Bless me if I didn't have to pull their hair out.'

'Crikey, Mum, was Dad really your one and only at that age?' asked Maureen, giggling.

'Never you mind,' said Cassie, 'and d'you have to put nearly half a pint of milk on your cereal?'

'It's good for me,' said Maureen. She meant it was good for her figure, of which she was proud.

'All right, love, if you say so,' said Cassie. 'Are you going out today?'

'Not till this evening,' said Maureen, 'then I'm going to the dance hall at Brixton. I did ask Phoebe if she'd like to go with me – '

'Phoebe?'

'Yes, we made friends last night,' said Maureen, pushing back her untidy black hair and spooning milk-soggy cornflakes into her mouth. 'She's ever so nice. But she's going to spend today and Sunday with her cousin Philip, who's on weekend leave.'

'Yes, I know,' said Cassie, 'but what about Billy Rogers?'

'Oh, I'm going off him,' said Maureen, 'he's

always chewing mints and only ever wants to take me to a milk bar or the pictures. He's dead on his feet at dancing. Still, I'll get him to take me to Brixton tonight.'

'Billy's a nice-looking boy,' said Cassie.

'Not much good being nice-looking but only half-alive,' said Maureen.

'Is Phoebe going really steady with Philip?' asked Cassie.

'Well, they were all over each other last night, so I suppose so,' said Maureen. 'He's a smasher. Oh, wouldn't I like him as me steady.'

'None of that, my girl,' said Cassie. 'Hands off, if he's going that steady with Phoebe. And just behave yourself tonight. Don't do Billy down by getting picked up by some fast bloke.'

'Mum, you're just not with it,' said Maureen. 'It's not fast blokes any more, it's groovy guys.'

'Well, never mind what they're called these days,' said Cassie, 'they're all the same, so don't bring one of them home with you, or your dad will make him run a mile.'

Two other people were having a late breakfast, Boots's sister Lizzy and her husband Ned. Lizzy, at fifty-eight, was now indisputably plump, and not even her most expensive corsets could disguise it. Still, she'd reached the stage of not letting it bother her, although she'd cut potatoes and desserts like syrup puddings from her diet. However, she still had a lustrous crown of chestnut hair, and her large brown eyes never lost their appeal for the beholder.

Ned, sixty-one, had thinning grey hair and the look of a man well past his best. He had a troublesome heart murmur, and Lizzy watched over him with long-established affection, never having had cause to find any major flaw in him as a husband and father. Of course, there had been ups and downs, but none of any serious nature or consequence.

She and Ned had both slept long and well after returning home from the rousing party, and it was nearly mid-morning when she eventually released herself from their bed.

'You lie in, lovey,' she said, 'and I'll bring your breakfast up.'

'Kind of you Eliza,' said Ned, 'but that'll make me feel I'm a failing old crock. I put myself in the same class as Boots, who told us all last night he'd reached the stage of being an old codger. I'm that myself, which is a sight better than being an old crock.'

'Still, after a party like last night, I know you must be a bit tired,' said Lizzy. 'I don't know how Mum kept going.'

'Your mum could probably have seen us all off if it had lasted right through to dawn,' said Ned, whose best moments were always after a good night's sleep. His drawn look usually arrived at the end of a day. At this precise moment there was colour in his cheeks.

'Mum's a walking marvel,' said Lizzy, 'and so's me lovely stepdad. Anyway, I'm sure you'd like breakfast in bed, wouldn't you?'

'Breakfast in bed is for the legless,' said Ned, 'and I'll be up in ten minutes.'

'Well, don't rush, love, take your time,' said Lizzy, invariably the guardian angel.

'I'll tell you something,' said Ned.

'Go on, then, tell me,' said Lizzy.

'The best day of my life was the day I married you,' said Ned, which turned Lizzy's eyes a bit misty. Some of the flippant young people of these changing times would have called her a sentimental old biddy.

And sentiment was going out of fashion.

Chapter Four

Late August.

On an afternoon in Beamish Landing, a small American township on the bank of the Colorado river, the phone rang in the sheriff's office. He picked it up.

'Sheriff Gimbell. Who's this?'

'Jack Dodds, visiting from Denver,' said a man's voice. 'I'm at Parker's gas station right now. Listen, man, I've just seen Willy Kleibert.'

'You what?' Sheriff Gimbell alerted.

'Believe me, Sheriff. He was with two other guys, but standing with his back to me while their truck was filled up. It was when they all got back into the truck that I saw his face. Knew him at once. Willy Kleibert, the kraut on the run. They took the dirt road to the freeway. If you're set on getting after him, Sheriff, the truck's a white Ford. I noted the number.' He gave it. 'Sheriff – ?'

Sheriff Gimbell was on his feet, the phone slammed down.

'Ross!' He bawled for his deputy. 'Git your backside outside! We gotta go hunting. Pronto.'

Five minutes later they were on the dirt road, heading fast for the freeway in their patrol car.

'Hey, hold on,' said Deputy Ross, 'what did you say the number of the truck was?' Gimbell quoted. 'Sheriff, that's Barney Flanagan's truck.' Barney Flanagan was a local farmer. 'And I calculate the two guys with him are his sons, Danny and Patrick. And Patrick don't look unlike Kleibert. Sheriff, we got egg all over our shirts.'

'Goddammit!' Sheriff Gimbell, remembering there'd been scores of false alarms in so-called sightings of the escaped prisoner all over the USA, brought the patrol car to a stop and swore violently.

Such incidents were throwing officers of American law and order into confusion, and the FBI had become convinced that these red herrings emanated from Mossad agents determined to land Kleibert in Israel, even if it took them years to get him safely aboard a plane or a ship. And there was little doubt that sympathetic American Jews were helping to lay the red herrings. So all airports and seaports were still being watched.

At Toronto airport, two wiry, brown-faced men were talking to a third man and a woman. The third man and the woman were both young, both twenty-two. They were waiting to board a flight to New York.

'Once more, who are you?' asked the first man.

'Mr and Mrs Joseph Phillips,' said the young man, black hair styled in a Tony Curtis quiff. His nose looked broad and fat, his body looked stout. He had large cotton-wool pellets securely stuffed up his nostrils, and wore a kind of quilted corset next to his skin, stretching from his armpits down to his thighs. His light summer suit bulked. The effects of quiffed hair, fat nose and stout frame completely changed his normal appearance. Further, the nose pellets made him sound nasal. 'We're Canadian citizens, born in Toronto. I'm in the music business and going to New York with my wife to prospect for outlets.'

'Good,' said the second man, 'let us say you've learned your alphabet. Who's got the joint passport?'

'I have,' said the young woman.

'Good. Hang onto it, Leila.'

'Don't take me for an idiot,' said the olive-skinned young woman. She was singularly attractive of face and figure, but steely of character.

'It's a question of no slip-ups,' said the first man. He addressed the young man. 'Remember you'll be met in New York by a friend of ours.'

'Will he know us?' asked the young man, slightly pale of countenance, due to his time in Auschwitz concentration camp. But his nerves were under control.

33

'He'll know Leila. He'll give you your British visitors' visas and the air tickets for an overnight flight to London. You already know all this, but I'm emphasizing it. You'll be contacted at London Airport and taken to your lodgings smack in the heart of south London, where you'll be just two more people in a teeming crowd until you receive new identity documents and air tickets to Nice.'

'From where we'll be ferried across the Med?' said the young man.

'Yes, you know this too,' said the young woman.

'I have to ask these questions to be sure of myself,' said the young man.

'You can be sure of one thing,' said the first man, 'once you're where you belong, you'll be safe for the rest of your life.'

'As well as being received warmly but with no publicity, and privately honoured for that which you accomplished so efficiently,' murmured the second man.

Over the public address system came an announcement that passengers for the flight to New York could now begin boarding. The young woman extracted boarding cards from her shoulder bag, and the young man took charge of their small cabin bag. The two brown-faced men shook hands with them, wished them luck and watched them depart to the flight gate.

Twenty minutes later the plane for New York

roared down the runway, took off, climbed into the sky and disappeared. Among the passengers were Wilhelm Kleibert, wanted in America for homicide, and Leila Herschel, a Mossad agent.

On Monday, Mr Humphrey Travers, senior official at London's Foreign Office, buttonholed his assistant, Bobby Somers, son of Lizzy and Ned Somers. For his distinguished service with the French Resistance movement during the war, Bobby had been offered an excellent position at the Foreign Office, and was now an established and valued official. His wife Helene thought that in his bowler hat and very correct suits, he was most unlike the man with whom she had shared hair-raising dangers in Occupied France. She much preferred him in weekend casuals, such as an open-necked sports shirt and slacks. Then he looked much more like the Englishman she deeply loved, even if he still made idiotic jokes. His bowler hats offended her eye, and she had ruined one of them during a typical fit of Gallic temperament.

'Kindly explain why you did that, my French filly,' Bobby had said.

Helene, predictably, put her foot down on the bowler hat and added to its ruin.

'That hat is not you, it makes you look stuffy, like all the men at your office. I have seen them.' She had been to a reception, the kind to which wives were invited.

'Appearances can be deceptive,' said Bobby, who was never upset by her tantrums. He found them amusing. He found Helene amusing, which made her jump up and down, in a manner of speaking, although she refrained from tearing her hair, thick and dark, with auburn tints. She was much too proud of her wealthy crown to turn it into a ragged mop.

'Appearances? Bah,' she said. 'It is not you, I tell you.'

'Shall I go and live in a London club for stuffed fogeys?' suggested Bobby.

'If you did, I would blow it up,' said Helene. She laughed then. 'Ah, well, you must live with me as you are, your bowler hats also.'

Thinking of that, Bobby looked at Humphrey Travers, a slender man of fifty, impeccable in his grey suit, starch-collared white shirt and grey tie. But stuffy? Yes, people might have thought him so, but there was more to old Humph than that. The Foreign Minister himself knew it.

'Something on your mind?' said Bobby.

'Only that I fancy Kleibert has slipped his leash,' said Mr Travers.

'He slipped it months ago,' said Bobby.

'I mean it's possible he's no longer confined within the borders of North America,' said Mr Travers.

'He's on the outside?' said Bobby.

'It's possible,' said Mr Travers.

Bobby knew from where he'd received that

piece of news. From Intelligence. Old Humph had a friendly relationship with that close-chested fraternity.

'Who's worried?' asked Bobby.

'The Minister,' said Mr Travers. 'Kleibert, of course, will be heading for Israel and the protection the Israelis will give him. They'll turn him into the invisible man.'

'So why is the Minister worried?' asked Bobby.

'Because, my dear fellow,' said Mr Travers, 'of the possibility that Kleibert will use the UK as a stepping stone to Israel. It would be our responsibility to pick him up and extradite him to the USA.'

'Now I see,' said Bobby.

'Yes,' said Mr Travers, 'the public in general are sympathetic to Kleibert, since they've been convinced by the press that the man he shot dead was a classified war criminal of an exceptionally loathsome kind. Should we lay our hands on Kleibert, it'll be headline news and there'll be protests and demonstrations against extradition. And no doubt directly outside our front door and that of the Home Office. Most unpleasant. We simply aren't used to all those aggressive banners protesters get hold of these days.'

'There's one solution,' said Bobby.

'Which is?'

'If Kleibert should be spotted entering this country on his way to Israel,' said Bobby. 'Turn a blind eye.'

'My dear chap,' said Mr Travers, 'what on earth are you thinking of?'

'A quiet life?' suggested Bobby.

'A delightful idea,' said Mr Travers, 'but quite dishonourable, of course, when one is aware that America is our closest ally. And you may be sure the CIA would become acquainted with our blind eye. I wouldn't be in the least surprised if our Intelligence offices themselves were bugged.'

'I suggest we leave these worries to the Home Office,' said Bobby. 'They'll have to deal with any extradition proceedings. And there's always the more likely possibility, that Kleibert won't enter the UK at all. He won't need to.'

'Perhaps not,' said Mr Travers, 'but I daresay Intelligence is keeping an eye open. We – ah – owe that much to our American cousins.'

'True,' said Bobby. He might have mentioned that Kleibert's dramatic public execution of Dr Paul Rokovsky had been a very personal blow to his cousin Tim's wife, Felicity.

However, there was something of a more serious nature concerning the Foreign Office. The Minister was involved in talks with Prime Minister Sir Anthony Eden about the crisis thrown up by General Nasser's nationalization of the Suez Canal. Bobby knew the talk was actually of war.

War against Egypt? We can do without that, thought Bobby. Mr Humphrey Travers had refused to comment. He had a knighthood in prospect, and wouldn't jump one way or another until he was sure his opinion would be regarded favourably.

Meanwhile, the people of London went about their business without giving the Suez Canal serious thought. That wasn't the case at an RAF station in Lincolnshire. The whisper was that a full squadron of fighter-bombers might be despatched to the Middle East sometime or other in the near future.

This was the station where Bobby's nephew Philip, son of his sister Annabelle, was based. His squadron was on standby.

Chapter Five

In the office of his junk yard in Camberwell, Mr Eli Greenberg sighed as he opened up the morning post. At the venerable age of seventy-six, he might have been sighing over his advancing years. Certainly, his beard was liberally sprinkled with white, and his broad-chested, sturdy frame had shrunk just a little these last twelve months.

He was still sighing when his younger stepson, Jacob, arrived.

'Old husband of my mother, do I hear you groaning?' asked Jacob.

'Groaning?' said Mr Greenberg, round black hat rusty. 'I ain't, no, but I vell might be.' His own kind of London English was the same as when he first began to speak it, after the arrival of his family from Tsarist Russia well before the First World War. It was his friend, his communicator, and he rarely used Yiddish. Also, he ignored the example set by his stepsons, Michal and Jacob, who both spoke clear English, if with a slight cockney twang. 'Yes, so I might. Vasn't I up all night vith a sick stomach, and didn't your mother give me a medicine that cured my stomach but did my head no good?'

'Old one, was the medicine out of your whisky bottle?' asked Jacob, solid of body and strong of character at thirty.

'How do I know, my son?' asked Mr Greenberg. 'Vasn't my eyes shut? Ain't I sighing for my head, vhich still ain't in good condition. It ought to be in the sun and air of a kibbutz, vhile the rest of me stays at vork, ain't it?'

'Why not take all yourself there for six months?' suggested Jacob.

'Vhat, and leave the business?'

'It's time you fully retired,' said Jacob. 'Michal and I can cope. Go to Israel for six months.'

'I ain't that old yet,' said Mr Greenberg, 'but I still ain't young enough to put up vith life in a kibbutz. Vhich reminds me that I ain't too happy about the friends you and Michal picked up vhen him and you did a kibbutz year.'

'Good friends, old father, and they've been over once or twice.'

'Don't I know it, ain't I seen them?' said Mr Greenberg sorrowfully. 'Hard noses, hard eyes. Vhich ain't the mark of good men. Vhere is Michal, might I ask?'

'At home with Judith,' said Jacob. Judith was Michal's wife. 'They're expecting friends.'

'Kibbutz friends vith hard noses?'

41

'Friends, just friends,' said Jacob. 'They'll be staying for a little while.'

'I should believe Michal ain't vorking today?' said Mr Greenberg.

'He'll be in later,' said Jacob.

'My life, ain't that kind of him, seeing there's goods to shift and load?' said Mr Greenberg.

'Old man of my heart,' smiled Jacob, 'take an aspirin for your head that's still suffering from my mother's medicine.'

'Now vhere's your respect?'

'Here,' said Jacob, touching his heart.

'Vell, I believe you, my boy, I believe you,' said Mr Greenberg, whose eldest stepson had died for King and country while serving with the Royal Navy during the Battle of the Atlantic. The old boy was proud of the young man's sacrifice, but still sad to have lost him.

'Yes, this will do,' said the young woman, whose smooth olive skin and dark, sultry looks appealed to men who liked that type.

The old-fashioned but good-looking house in Camberwell Grove was roomy, its interior modernized in that there was a tiled bathroom, carpeting had replaced linoleum, well-chosen paint had replaced ancient wallpaper throughout, and gas lighting had given way to electricity. It was situated in the crowded heart of southern Camberwell, South-East London, and although not far from the more open area of Denmark

Hill, its immediate eastern neighbour was densely populated Peckham. Looking for a lost soul in Camberwell or Peckham was on a par with looking for a needle in a haystack.

'Yes, here will do,' said the sultry woman's companion, a young man of lean body, dark hair and pale face. He wore horn-rimmed spectacles of plain glass. He and the woman were on the landing, having inspected the upstairs rooms.

'Good,' said Michal Wirthe, elder stepson of Mr Eli Greenberg. Broad, muscular and handsome, he was in his early thirties and the driving force of his ancient stepfather's second-hand furniture business. The firm of Greenberg and Sons Ltd was the successor to the old rag-and-bone venture, although Mr Greenberg still stabled his horse and cart.

'You'll only be with us for a few days, I believe?' said Michal's wife Judith, a full-bodied woman as handsome in her way as her husband, and grateful to God for her existence as a born subject of Queen Elizabeth the Second. That had saved her and all Britain's Jews from the terrible fate of millions of their European cousins.

'A few days, yes, until a friend arrives,' said the young woman. The conversation was in Yiddish.

'Well, whether for a few days or a little more,' said Michal, 'I thought it was understood we should speak only English, as Judith and I always do, unless Judith gets overexcited at my domestic failings.'

'My life, once a year counts?' said Judith.

'This house has solid walls,' said Michal to their guests, 'but words can still escape.'

'English, yes, very well,' said the young woman, but so curtly as to suggest she did not think much of English people. 'There will be no visitors while we are here?'

'We'll invite no-one,' said Michal, 'but there'll be callers.'

'Callers?'

'The milkman for his weekly payment, the dustmen to pick up the dustbin and the postman to deliver letters and parcels,' said Michal.

'One dustman will come into the house to collect the bin from outside the kitchen,' said Judith.

'Is this a joke?' asked the young woman.

'Not to us,' said Michal, 'we need these services. But they won't climb the stairs. The friend you say will call, is he the man who negotiated with me concerning your stay here?'

'Yes.' The young woman was not given to wasting words.

'He left this for you,' said Michal, and handed her a brown paper parcel. She took it without thanking him. 'Judith and I hope you'll enjoy your board and lodging.'

'Shall we now leave you to yourselves?' suggested Judith.

'Thank you, thank you very much,' said the young man, much friendlier than the young woman.

44

Michal and Judith went down to their kitchen. Judith closed the door.

'Husband,' she said, 'the woman I don't like, the young man I do like.'

'We should let the woman's manners upset us?' said Michal.

'We should hope she won't be here too long,' said Judith.

'If questions come to be asked, remember we have two old friends of mine staying with us.'

'Well, I'm glad I won't have to say the woman is an old friend of mine,' said Judith. 'But there, we must do what we can to help.'

Michal smiled.

'You look after our child,' he said, 'and I'll look after any little problems.'

'Such a thoughtful husband you are,' said Judith, who, at twenty-seven, was four months pregnant with their first child. They had been married for two years.

'Fortunately, there's been nothing in the papers recently,' said Michal.

'Nothing about him?'

'Nothing.'

'Well, everyone is bored by now, including the press.'

'Which takes the spotlight off our guests,' said Michal. 'Look, I must get to work, or my dear old stepfather, who likes to know everything, will begin to ask too many questions. See that my old friends enjoy a good lunch.'

'Is that a request or an order?' asked Judith.

'I should give you such an order?' said Michal.

'You would if you were strictly orthodox,' said Judith.

'If I were, I'd sport a beard,' said Michal.

'Don't even attempt it,' said Judith. She saw him off with a kiss, and away he went to the Camberwell yard.

Upstairs, in the main bedroom, which over-looked the street, Leila Herschel, unfortunately born without a sense of humour, had opened the parcel. It contained a note and a perfect wig of mousy brown hair, together with a matching beard and moustache. The note was for her, the wig and facial adornments for the young man, Wilhelm Kleibert. His own hair was thick and black, symptomatic of his race.

'If I must wear all that stuff, I must,' he had said.

'You must and you will, for the wig alone won't be enough. Your five o'clock shadow contradicts it.' Leila's response had been uncompromising. Her admiration for his deed of assassination was secondary now to the task of getting him to Israel.

'OK,' he said. His acquired English was ex-cellent, with an American accent.

Now she said, 'Let me remind you that the note instructs us to have passport photographs taken.'

'Why do you remind me?' Wilhelm Kleibert

was not a mere cypher, he was a young man of character, and of revived spirit in having avenged his dead brother and sister for all they had suffered at Auschwitz.

'I remind you because it's necessary for both of us to be doubly sure of every step we take,' said Leila.

'So, we're to go looking for a photographer?' said Wilhelm, his unnecessary spectacles now discarded.

'No, to go to a photographer named in this note. His address is at Camberwell Green.'

'And where is that?'

'Wirthe will tell us.'

'Good. I like him. And her.'

'Be careful of your liking for her. She has inquisitive eyes.'

'Must you mistrust everyone?'

'Until we reach Israel, I will trust no-one except our agents here.'

'But we would not be in this house if Wirthe and his wife could not be trusted.'

'You must go along with my instincts, not your own.' Leila was curt. Wilhelm shrugged and glanced around the well-furnished bedroom. The bed, with its colourful counterpane, looked inviting.

'Leila, I need help,' he said.

'You are getting maximum help from our organization,' said Leila, a navy blue dress with white trimmings gracing her fine, firm body.

'I mean a different kind of help,' said Wilhelm.

'Ah? How different?'

'I need the help of a woman to find out if I'm a man,' said Wilhelm.

'That is crazy talk,' said Leila.

'Not when spoken by a concentration camp survivor, one who was reduced to little more than five stone, and lost all sense of being male.'

'I see.' Leila softened a little. 'I'm sorry, my friend, but you are in no position to go out and look for a woman on the streets.'

'My life for the devil,' said Wilhelm, 'am I thinking of that? No, I'm thinking of you. Here is a bedroom, there is a bed – '

'This is my bedroom, and that is my bed while we're here,' said Leila. 'Yours is adjacent. You can forget any idea of sleeping with me.'

'I can't forget you're a woman who could give me the help I desperately need,' said Wilhelm.

'To find out if you're a man?' said Leila. 'That is not for me, that is for a woman you will come to meet in Israel one day.'

'How am I to know I won't disappoint her?' asked Wilhelm.

'That is a worry for you, yes, I understand,' said Leila, 'but iron tablets taken twice daily could prove a simple help.'

'What a cold woman you are,' said Wilhelm.

Leila's face suffused with an angry flush.

'How dare you talk to me like that!'

'You bully me,' said Wilhelm, 'and I would

have smacked your face many times if I hadn't known you to be brave as well as overbearing. Yes, I owe you much for all you are doing for me, but I still think you a cold woman.'

'And I think you pathetic!'

'No, you don't, because you know I'm not,' said Wilhelm. 'But there, I've asked and been refused, and that is the end of it.' He smiled wryly. 'When we go to this photographer, perhaps I'll find a chemist's shop that will sell me some iron tablets, although I don't actually know if I need them or not, do I? I'll go to my room now and unpack.'

He left Leila fuming.

'Michal, my good son, vhy are you so late coming to vork?' asked Mr Greenberg.

'Didn't Jacob tell you Judith and I have some old friends staying with us for a while?' said Michal.

'So he did, so he did,' said Mr Greenberg, cash ledger in front of him. It was one of his favourite pieces of office equipment. His old friend, Sammy Adams, had a similar liking for a cash book. 'But vhy did they keep you?'

'They didn't,' said Michal. 'Out of courtesy, I waited until they arrived.'

'They are friends from the kibbutz?' enquired Mr Greenberg.

'No, just friends.'

'Vell, Michal, I vant you to know I ain't partial to any friends that ain't friendly to our Queen's

49

country,' said Mr Greenberg, who had been very upset by what went on in Palestine immediately after the war, when Jewish terrorists caused the untimely deaths of British soldiers. The old rag-and-bone man was solidly loyal to the country of his adoption. 'You understand, my boy?'

'Believe me, old wise one,' said Michal, 'Judith and I know our true loyalties.'

'I'm believing you, Michal, don't I alvays?' said Mr Greenberg. 'Now help Jacob to see to vaiting customers vhile I keep hold of my head, vhich is trying to float avay on account of your mother's stomach medicine, like I've told Jacob.'

Michal departed from his valiant stepfather's cramped office with a smile. The old boy was supposed to be semi-retired, but wasn't likely to vacate that office and his cash book until he dropped into the arms of heavenly Moses. Nor was he likely to refuse help to a man who had ended the filthy life of a depraved doctor of Auschwitz. But best not to tell him what was happening. He was too old to have to concern himself.

Chapter Six

At mid-afternoon, a car entered the yard. Out stepped Sammy Adams, long-standing friend to Mr Greenberg, with whom he had done more useful business deals than he would ever remember.

Michal and Jacob, with the help of an assistant, newly taken on, and of the driver of a standing van, were loading furniture from a house clearance into the vehicle. The van belonged to a customer who was buying most of it. Good business it was, second-hand furniture, among the working people of south London. Handsome new stuff was expensive and only now were manufacturers beginning to place it extensively on the market. What the war had done to all kinds of manufacturers meant, in Mr Greenberg's eyes, that Hitler still had a lot to answer for, even if the second-hand market was thriving.

'Your dad's in his office?' said Sammy, his suit a light summer grey, his trilby hat jaunty.

'He's in,' said Jacob.

'As ever,' smiled Michal.

'Thought so,' said Sammy, and went on to the office, an old green-painted timber shed with dusty windows. He knocked, opened the door and put his head in. 'Afternoon, Eli old cock,' he said.

'Vhy, if it ain't you, Sammy.' Mr Greenberg, despite his floating head, beamed. 'Vhat a pleasure, ain't it?'

'How's your old self?' said Sammy.

'Vell, I tell you, Sammy, I'm suffering from an upset stomach that Mrs Greenberg cured vith a medicine that vent straight to my head, like Boots's vhisky on his sixtieth birthday. My head, Sammy, it ain't vhat it vas yesterday.'

'Nor was mine after Boots's party,' said Sammy, 'so Susie gave it a friendly tap with her egg saucepan last thing the following night, and there you are, Bob's your uncle, an old-fashioned bump instead of a head complaint. Has Mrs Greenberg got an egg saucepan?'

'Vould I point her at it?' sighed Mr Greenberg. 'And might I mention Mrs G. her very own self didn't recover from Boots's party for many days? Vhat a shindig, eh? It's as vell Boots ain't sixty again next veek. But vhy am I having the pleasure of seeing you?'

'I've got another house-clearance job for you,' said Sammy. House clearances were a very profitable part of his old friend's present business. 'Neighbours of mine on Denmark Hill.

Number forty-one. Mr and Mrs Collins. I've recommended you, so make 'em a fair offer and get Michal and Jacob to arrange the collection day – oh, and tell 'em to wear their best suits. Mrs Collins is a nice lady, but fussy about who she lets into her prime residence.'

'Sammy, vhat a fine day, after all, ain't it?' said Mr Greenberg, head suddenly a lot better. 'You vant commission?'

'No, I want something for Susie,' said Sammy. 'A high-class stone cherub, say about two feet high, for the front garden. You know, one with wings and a big smile. It's to let visitors know they're welcome. Have you got one in stock?'

'Vhy, Sammy, ain't I got the very thing, vhich I'd say is thirty inches high and genuine oriental alabaster?' said the beaming merchant.

'Listen, Eli old cock,' said Sammy, 'if you're talking about a Chinese buddleia – '

'Chinese Buddha, Sammy?'

'Susie's not after one of those, just a good old-fashioned stone cherub,' said Sammy.

'Alabaster, Sammy, is high-class stone, and it's a cherub, don't I give you my vord? Come, I vill show you.'

What he did show Sammy, after Jacob had unearthed it from under a pile of cushions, was, in Sammy's own words, a bit of all right, not half, which would make Susie feel like Christmas had come.

'That is, once I've got the dust off, Eli.'

'Sammy, Jacob vill deliver it shining bright.'

'No, I'll put it in my car boot, and take it home to Susie meself. How much?'

'Say vun green smacker, Sammy?'

'A quid? Eli, I'm not here to rob you. Give you two and a half, how's that?'

'Happy, Sammy, happy, ain't it? Now have a cup of tea vith me, eh?'

Sammy stayed for that, and when he eventually drove out of the yard, the cherub, wrapped in a sack, was in the boot.

Earlier, after a light lunch prepared and served by Judith, Leila and Wilhelm were up in their rooms. Leila had phoned the specified photographer, Amos Anderson. Expecting the call, he was friendly and co-operative in his response, arranging an appointment in his Camberwell studio for three thirty that afternoon.

Leila, gazing thoughtfully at her reflection in the dressing-table mirror, smoothed the dark lines of her dark eyebrows with a moist finger.

Someone knocked. She came to her feet, crossed the bedroom and opened the door to reveal Wilhelm wearing the wig of light brown hair and the matching beard and moustache. She stared in shock, certain at once that his appearance was impossible. She took hold of his arm, pulled him in and closed the door.

'Something wrong with my get-up?' said Wilhelm.

'Everything's wrong,' hissed Leila.

'Well, don't blame me,' said Wilhelm, 'it wasn't my idea.'

'Look at you, you fool,' breathed Leila, 'light brown hair and beard, and eyebrows as black as mine. But that's not the only thing that's wrong. It all is. I see that now. There'll be British security officers at London Airport, you can rely on it, even if not necessarily looking for you. The cold war is throwing up Soviet agents by the dozen. So how do you think airport security staff will regard a man in spectacles and as hairy as you? They'll see everything as an obvious disguise, especially if we do nothing about your eyebrows.'

'Don't think that didn't occur to me when I saw myself in the mirror,' said Wilhelm. 'I've been on the run far too long not to be aware of searching eyes at bus stations, railroad stations and airports.'

'I must phone Stargazer,' said Leila. Stargazer was the code name of their present Mossad contact, the man who had left the note and the wig in the hands of Michal Wirthe. 'I must tell him he's crazy to have thought up such an absurd disguise. London has made him soft and addled his brains. I'll phone him from the photographer's studio.'

'He's another fool, is he?' said Wilhelm, ripping off the wig, beard and moustache.

'Shut up,' said Leila.

'You should stay in London and get yourself softened up in company with Stargazer,' said Wilhelm.

Leila gave him a look. He responded with a smile. Yes, she thought, I'm coming to know why he blew holes in that doctor. He has guts. But I don't like his insolence.

'Despite all I've just told you, bring that stuff with you to the photographer,' she said.

'Oh, sure,' said Wilhelm. 'Sincerely, I'm going to be grateful all my life to you and your colleagues if you get me safely to Israel, but I hope I don't end up working for a female boss.'

'Your gratitude isn't asked for,' said Leila, 'but it's more welcome than your sense of humour.'

Her relationship with Wilhelm, a hero in the eyes of the people of Israel, had changed from being pleasant, if unemotional, to one of distinct coolness. She was still angry with him.

Sammy, approaching the traffic lights at Camberwell Green, slowed as green turned to orange. He stopped at the advent of red. People stepped from the kerbs to negotiate the pedestrian crossing. From the left-hand kerb came three people, a young man and two women, one of whom he recognized. Judith Wirthe. He had met her at her wedding to Michal two years ago. She was what Sammy regarded as a female woman. That is, a woman with looks and a figure, and an entirely feminine rig-out with a fetching hat. No jeans. Sammy considered jeans a blight on fashion. He leaned and tapped on the windscreen as she passed his standing car. Not hearing or noticing, she carried on to the pavement with her companions. They crossed the junction in the direction of Denmark Hill.

Sammy drove forward as the traffic lights turned green. He crossed into Denmark Hill, put himself on the crown of the road and, giving a signal, veered right and pulled up outside the firm's offices. He saw Judith talking to the young man and young woman at the door of a shop a little way down. Then she turned and walked back the way she had come. Her companions entered the shop, the window of which advertised the services of a photographer. It displayed framed samples of his work.

Judith had taken her house guests there herself to make sure they didn't lose themselves.

Sammy went up to his offices by the side entrance of the firm's shop, the shop that represented the beginnings of his now expansive business empire.

No sooner was he seated at his desk than Rachel Goodman, director and the company secretary, entered his office. Rachel, in her fifties, looked as if she was still blooming. Well, she not only owned glossy raven hair and wide velvety-brown eyes, but also a sumptuous figure. She was, in Sammy's eyes, a well-preserved, high-class female woman. So, of course, was his one and only Susie.

'Sammy?'

'Well, Rachel me old friend?'

'I think you'd better have a word with Boots.'

'Might I ask why?'

'He took a phone call from the managing director of Coates an hour ago.' Coates had a West End store and branches all over the South of England, as well as one just opened in Edinburgh. All the stores had been stocking Adams Fashions' superior garments for years.

'Hold on,' said Sammy, 'don't tell me they're thinking of dropping us.'

'My life, Sammy, I should want to tell you that?' said Rachel. 'Far from it. What they do want is to take over our manufacturing factory at Bethnal Green. In fact, they're thinking of acquiring Adams Fashions Ltd if an offer can be agreed.'

'Bloody hell,' breathed Sammy, 'all that's been taking place behind my back?'

'While you were out,' said Rachel. 'As I mentioned, Boots took the call.'

'Well, I hope he talked educated to the saucy geezer,' said Sammy, on which heated note Boots himself walked in.

'You're flushed, Sammy,' he said, his familiar lurking smile suggesting he was the kind of man always ready to find something amusing about life and people.

'Well, pardon me,' said Sammy, 'but I ain't exactly meself right now. What's this about selling off Adams Fashions, which I ain't too proud to say is dear to me heart?'

'Nothing has happened yet, Sammy,' said Boots. 'Suppose Rachel and I take a seat and have a three-way discussion with you?' It was gone four, but that was irrelevant.

'Now you're talking,' said Sammy, 'but d'you mind leaving out any educated stuff? Let's have it plain and unvanished.'

'Unvarnished, Sammy?' said Boots, as he and Rachel seated themselves.

'What I meant was I don't want wordage that goes over me head and vanishes up the chimney,' said Sammy.

Rachel coughed, Boots smiled, and the discussion began.

'Look at him,' said Leila to Amos Anderson, professional photographer, 'is that a disguise or a shout for help?'

'A shout for help it could be,' said Amos, a cheerful Jewish Londoner who had the equivalent of a bedside manner when posing a sitter. He was doing very nicely in this heavily populated area, with its regular weddings and a full quota of girls wishful to be photographed as potential pin-up dollies somewhat saucier than the swimsuit beauties of the war. The modern versions were regularly featured in papers like

59

the *Daily Mirror* and its light weekend companion, *Reveille*, as well as monthly magazines such as *Men Only*. Some archbishops thought this lurid development was hastening the disintegration of the British Empire. So did some rabbis. It hardly kept Amos awake at night; his chubby missus was comfortably relaxing to cuddle up to. 'I know little of plots and plans, don't I?' he murmured.

'It's not important, how much you know and how much you don't,' said Leila.

'Well, I tell you, I'm always ready to help the cause,' said Amos, forty, lean, and well turned out in a blue turtleneck sweater and knife-edged trousers. Sloppiness didn't impress customers dressed in their best. 'I don't ask questions, I do the passport photographs your people want. In fact, the less I know, the better I like it. Now, what shall we say is wrong with your young bloke's hairy look?'

'There's too much of it,' said Leila. 'It shrieks of a disguise.'

'I should consider that my problem?' said Amos. 'My pennyworth for the cause is to take passport photographs on the QT, which I do, don't I?'

'I must phone Stargazer,' said Leila.

'She must phone Stargazer,' said Wilhelm, sighing.

'That secretive cove tells me never to phone him unless trouble's at my door,' said Amos, 'serious trouble. Which I don't want on account of earning myself a legal living. Legal is a happy word. Trouble, I say again, I don't want.'

'There'll be no trouble,' said Leila, 'where's your phone?'

'There, on my desk, under my hat,' said Amos.

'Why do you keep it under your hat?' asked Wilhelm.

'Force of habit,' said Amos.

Leila dialled a number. A man answered.

'Atkinson's, tea merchants.' A pause. 'The manager speaking.' That was his password.

'Indian Moon here.' That was Leila's responsive password. 'You've made a mistake.'

'I never make mistakes.'

'You've made one this time. That wig and beard shriek of a disguise.'

Silence for a while, then, 'You might have a point, but he'll never clear airport security as himself.'

'Tell me something I don't know.'

'Use the previous outfit. Fatten his nose, face and body.'

'Is that wise?' Leila obviously didn't think so. 'The principle is to avoid repetition. Also, the covering passport shows exit from New York. We shouldn't use anything that shows he's come from America.'

'We all know that. Haven't you been told his new passport will show entry into London Airport from Paris as an English representative of the Worth fashion house in London? And that your own will show you as his secretary and assistant?'

'No.'

'You've been told now. Use a black moustache and a small pointed black beard for your man.'

'He'll look French, not English, but he doesn't speak French.'

'Which was why we opted for brown fuzz, more English than French, but I'm willing to believe you find it too obvious. Tell the photographer to get hold of the alternatives.'

'That will mean making a new appointment.'

'Yes, but do it. Your man will be in London for several days, ostensibly on business, and then you and he will be flying to Nice, from where we'll get you both across the Med to Israel. I'll let you have the necessary documents, with the new passports, as soon as possible. Get the photographer to insert the photographs. And take care of our man. I'll see you both sometime, perhaps next week, when I hope I'll be in a position to drive you to London Airport. That's all.'

The phone went dead. It left Leila explaining the necessary adjustments. Amos said he could get the required beard and moustache by Wednesday, and take the photographs of both of them on Thursday morning at nine thirty, if they could manage that. Leila said yes. Wilhelm said as the fatty disguise made him sweat, it would be a relief to stick on only a moustache and a little beard, but he knew nothing about fashions.

'Fashions I don't know about myself,' said Amos.

'Don't worry yourselves,' said Leila.

'She's the boss,' said Wilhelm.

'I don't want to know who's which,' said Amos, 'my commitment is just to supply required photographs, and some hairpieces in this case. Anything else I don't want. See you again Thursday morning.' He shook hands with Wilhelm. 'Privilege to have met you.' He knew about the young man's heroic deed.

When they had gone, he looked at his appointments book. Ah, that was more like it. Four thirty. Maureen Brown. A lovely young lady thinking of making a name for herself in a black corset and black stockings.

Who needed to do under-the-counter passport photographs? Oh, well, a small contribution to the cause from time to time was a small price to pay. How many had he supplied? Only three, all of revengeful Jewish men on the run from West German authorities for assassinating men they claimed were ex-SS officers. This new one, Wilhelm Kleibert, was the bravest of them all for his public execution in New York of a one-time SS doctor.

Chapter Seven

Miss Maureen Brown, daughter of Freddy and Cassie Brown, arrived five minutes late for her studio appointment with Amos Anderson.

'I'm ever so sorry, Mr Anderson, I worked through me lunch hour at the office so's I could leave an hour early, but it took me a few minutes longer.' She worked in the Camberwell Green branch of an insurance company as a copy typist.

'You're not late, Miss Brown, no, not a bit,' said Amos, giving her a smile. 'Five minutes is punctual, fifteen is late. Might I say punctual is a pleasure?'

'Oh, mutual, I'm sure,' said Maureen, eager to impress. She had thoughts of a glamorous career, far removed from the four walls of a boring old insurance office. Certainly, she looked highly fetching in a dress of daffodil yellow with a trim bodice that shaped her figure. The knee-length skirt of the dress was flared, her nyloned legs worth a second look. Further, she was pretty, her skin smooth and unblemished, her hair a shining blue-black. Amos classed her as a perfect example of 'the girl next door' type. Very popular as a pin-up.

'Come this way,' he said, and took her into his studio, the backcloth of which was of an un-relieved creamy-white for this particular sitting. 'There, that's the dressing room, you can change there. Take your time.'

'Thanks,' said Maureen, her eagerness touched with a hint of nervousness. Carrying a suitcase, she took herself into the dressing room, and closed the door.

Amos placed his camera on a tripod. He used a German Rolleifex with a reflective viewfinder and a push-button that operated the shutter and flashlight simultaneously.

It took a while for Maureen to emerge. Amos eyed her entrance with profound professional interest. Pin-up of the month? More like pin-up of the year. Nervous, and slightly pink about her appearance, yes, but that made her all the more delightful. She was worth special attention, faultless camera work and inspired guidance in her posing. In a figure-hugging black corset with built-in bra cups, black panties and sheer black nylons, her sex appeal was undeniable.

Maureen, ambition under attack from the nervousness of a beginner, gulped and said, 'What d'you think, will I do?'

'I'm impressed, and I can't say I'm not,' said Amos, his smile kind but impersonal. One had to be careful with some of these would-be glamour girls from the ranks of the working classes. Eager though most were, too intimate an interest was not what they wanted or liked, unless they were a bit tarty. And he himself had to be strictly principled. 'I think you'll do, Miss Brown, yes, I think you will.'

'I'd like to see meself in the *Daily Mirror*,' said Maureen. The *Mirror* sold in millions under the editorship of its go-getting editor, already a legend in Fleet Street.

'So would I,' said Amos, checking his camera, 'but hairy blokes like me they don't want.' He straightened up. 'Um, sit yourself on that bar stool, Miss Brown.'

The tall bar stool fronted the bright backcloth. Maureen placed her round bottom on it, her long legs stretching, the tips of her high-heeled strapped black shoes touching the floor. The backcloth outlined her black-clad figure. Amos looked into his viewfinder. Blimey, a natural, he thought, except for her hands. She was worrying about where to put them. She tried clasping the back of her neck.

'Is this all right?' she asked.

'Not exactly,' said Amos. She was all elbows and armpits. 'Try clasping the sides of the stool seat with your hands.' Maureen did so, and at once her pose took on a more natural look. 'Great. Great. A smile, say? Lovely.' He pressed the plunger the moment the smile arrived. The flash, bouncing off the ceiling, flooded the studio with light for a fraction of a second.

'Oops,' said Maureen. 'I think I blinked.'

'Not before the camera caught you. Hold that pose, lovey, but lift your chin a little. Look up now. No, not at me, at the top of the wall. That's it. Now, another smile? Fine. Lovely. Gotcher.' The shutter clicked, the flashlight bounced.

He posed her with instructive care, this way, that way, and his sitter, enthusiasm replacing jumpy nerves, fell into line with his every recommendation. And always there were words of encouragement for her.

'Great. Super. Right, just right. Lovely. My life, that's the tops, lovey, hold it.'

And so on.

Amos used two rolls of film, each of twelve exposures, his belief in what the results would be like as high as her adrenalin, for she finished the sitting flushed with excitement.

'What d'you think now, Mr Anderson, d'you think the photos will be groovy?'

'Groovy we don't want, Maureen. Top-class pictures of the girl next door we do.'

'Beg pardon?'

'Groovy is flashy. What they like, the picture editors, are happy pin-ups of what their readers see as the pretty girl next door. It's a question, lovey, of the difference between a professional model who chews gum and a shy amateur who likes ice cream and takes her doggie for a walk.'

'Crikey, I didn't look shy, did I?'

'You did in some poses, and I tell you no porkie. Shy is good, professional ain't rated, not by an discriminating picture editor. You know about discriminating?'

'I know what it means.'

'Well, all Fleet Street picture editors are discriminating about what lands on their desks. Now, get changed, then I'll talk to you in my office, won't I?'

Maureen entered his poky office as soon as she had changed. The rolls of film were already in the developing tank, and Amos was sitting at his desk, using the modern equivalent of a fountain pen, a biro, to fill in a form. He told her to sit down, then he advised her the copyright of the photographs was his, that he himself would submit the best of the selection first to the *Mirror*. If the *Mirror* turned them down, he would try *Men Only* and then, if necessary, *Reveille*. He was confident, however, that acceptance for publication would come from one of them. In fact, he would eat an uncooked camel if that didn't happen.

Maureen giggled.

'A whole camel, Mr Anderson?'

'A whole one would kill me, lovey, so I'm laying my life on the line on your account. Now, I'm paying you three quid for your modelling – '

'You're paying me?' said Maureen. 'But I thought I'd have to pay you.'

'Not when I keep the copyright and take care of the submissions,' said Amos. 'I also pay you twenty per cent of any fees earned for publication, which I'm certain will come about, ain't I? There's papers and magazines all over the country that use pin-ups these days, especially the Sunday papers. Mind, there's not much going on around the synagogues.' Amos showed the grin of an unorthodox worshipper. 'The rabbis ain't in favour of stocking-tops. By the way, do your parents know you want to be the nation's pin-up?'

'I haven't told no-one,' said Maureen, 'but I am eighteen.'

'I should believe your parents might be church-going?'

'Oh, now and again,' said Maureen, 'but they're not prim and proper like – ' She was going to say Grandma Finch of the Adams family. Instead she said, 'No, me parents aren't narrow-minded.'

'Well, you're eighteen, so it's up to you,' said Amos. 'Come in after you've finished work to-morrow evening, and I'll have contact sheets ready for you to see.'

'What's contact sheets?'

'Prints of the negatives, twelve to a sheet, each print two by two. You and me, we'll look 'em over, select the best and then I'll run off whole-plate prints, eight by six. In that size, I'll be sending one or two to the *Mirror* as starters.'

'Crikey, you're getting me real excited,' said Maureen.

'Too much excitement you don't want,' said Amos. 'Cool, that's the word. And self-belief. Now, if you'd sign this form and date it, I'll let you have your modelling fee of three quid.'

Maureen didn't argue. She scanned the form. It concerned the basics of copyright, and quoted the fee due to the sitter. Using the biro, she signed it and entered the date. Amos studied her signature.

'It's wobbly, love,' he said.

'It's me excitement,' she said.

'Didn't I tell you – '

'Yes, stay cool, but I can't just yet. Oh, thanks.' She took her fee of three pounds. 'I'll come in after work tomorrow like you said.'

'Good,' said Amos, and gave her a smiling look. It hit him then, his obvious mistake. There she was, everybody's girl next door in that pretty dress. She'd been that on arrival and so she was now, when she was about to depart. But in between he'd photographed her in a black corset. Every picture editor would see her as a sophisticated night bird. The idea of promoting her as everybody's girl next door, a sure winner, had just flown up his office chimney. He was as much of an idiot as if he'd asked for a ham sandwich at a Passover feast. What had addled his curly noddle? He knew. It was that passport photograph muddle, and the young woman with the steely air who obviously thought he ought to be more involved than was good for any English Jew who had a happy business going.

'What's up, Mr Anderson?' asked Maureen.

Amos, coming to, said, 'Well, I'll tell you, Miss Brown. We're trying to run when, rightly, we should be walking. It's my fault. I want to promote you as London's top girl next door. So, as a starter, a black corset we don't want.'

'But you said – '

'I know, but what I said we don't want, either. What we do want, as a starter, is a pretty girl in a pretty day dress lifting in the breeze. Black corsets are for later. You with me, lovey?'

'Oh, yes, you want me showing me legs accidental, like.'

'Miss Brown, it's me pleasure to be acquainted with a young lady quick on the uptake. That's it, accidental uncoverage and, if I might suggest, a blush or two?'

'How can you photograph a blush?'

'By how you look, can't I? One hand up to your face, other hand pushing at your dress, eyes big, and mouth wide open, like you're saying, "Oh, help, me legs."'

Maureen giggled.

'Mr Anderson, d'you mean stocking-tops?'

'Such, as a starter, is classical for the girl next door. Believe me.'

'But how do we do that?' asked Maureen, willing to go along with anyone who could get

71

her photographs published. Besides, she liked Mr Amos Anderson. He had nice eyes, an easy style and a sort of fatherly smile.

Amos consulted his desk diary.

'If you've got Saturday afternoon free, and the weather's dry, we'll motor into the countryside, find a breeze and pip, pip, click, click, who's a pretty popsie, then, eh?'

'Oh, great,' said Maureen.

'Be here by two next Saturday, then?'

'I'll be punctual again.'

'Punctual is good.'

'In this dress?'

'That is better than good,' said Amos.

'Oh, shall I still come in after work tomorrow to see the photos you've just taken?' asked Maureen.

'We'll leave that until Saturday,' said Amos. There was no hurry. Corsets were for later in her career, he should have thought of that.

'Okey-dokey,' said Maureen, happy that her prospects were in good hands. 'Crikey, I'd better get home, it's nearly six o'clock.'

Amos saw her out, thanked her for everything, told her she was a certain winner and watched her depart. She did so on lithe legs, and the flared skirt of her dress swayed very fetchingly. She was nice, that girl, and he wasn't going to throw her to the wolves.

He thought about that woman agent and the young Jewish man, and the fact that he needed to get hold of a little pointed black beard and a matching moustache. Well, he knew where to find them.

'You're a bit late,' said Cassie when Maureen arrived. 'Your dad's beat you home for once.'

'Oh, I went to see a photographer about having some photos taken,' said Maureen, helping herself to a glass of water from the kitchen tap.

'Photos, what photos?' asked Cassie, preparing a summer supper of sliced ox tongue, hot boiled potatoes that would glisten with a smidgen of butter, and a mixed salad.

'Oh, sort of glamour photos,' said Maureen.

'What?'

'You know, Mum, pin-ups like you see in our *Daily Mirror*.'

'Like what?' Freddy, having had a wash and a brush-up on arriving home from the store, was entering the kitchen. He had changed into a light blue summer shirt and dark blue jeans. The Walworth store, part of the Adams Fashions empire, stocked a wide range of jeans, even though Sammy considered they were only for cowboys. In fact, the Adams factory at Bethnal Green manufactured them from imported denim. 'Like what, Maureen?' repeated Freddy.

'Like in the *Daily Mirror*,' said Maureen.

'Did you say pin-ups?' asked Freddy, forty-two, lean and hardened from years of jungle combat in Burma, but still a bit of a joker and regarded as a sport by his son and daughter.

Maureen, who had had no intention of keeping her mum and dad in the dark about her ambitions now that she was making a beginning, said she'd been to see Mr Amos Anderson at his Camberwell Green studio. She didn't say he'd photographed her in a new and sexy corset, because of what he'd said about it afterwards, making her aware that it was just a bit too sexy for her as a starter. But she did say he was going to take her out on Saturday and photograph her as a girl-next-door type for *Daily Mirror* readers.

Freddy fell about.

'I've got to believe this?' he said, laughing his head off.

'What's funny?' asked Maureen.

'I think your dad thinks you and Mr Anderson are,' said Cassie, smiling.

'Well, I'm serious,' said Maureen. 'I don't fancy working in any old office all me life, I want to have a career that's glamorous.'

'Like being a mannequin?' said Cassie, tipping the hot boiled new potatoes into a colander over the sink.

'Mannequin? Mannequin? Mum, that's as antique as bloomers,' said Maureen. 'You mean fashion model.'

'Let's hear a bit more about you being photographed as the *Daily Mirror*'s girl next door,' said Freddy.

74

'Yes, Mr Anderson's going to get me to pose in a country background with the breeze blowing me dress about and me blushing because of me legs showing,' said Maureen.

'Eh?' said Freddy.

'Honest,' said Maureen.

Freddy roared with laughter. Cassie, with the steaming, creamy-white potatoes in a tureen, was applying the smidgen of butter while trying to keep a straight face.

'Cassie, did you hear what I heard?' asked Freddy.

'I don't know how anyone could photograph a blush,' said Cassie.

'That's just what I told Mr Anderson,' said Maureen, and went on to explain how he would get her to pose so that she looked all shy and blushing. Freddy fell about again. 'Honest, Dad,' she said, 'I don't know why you're going barmy.'

'I can't help meself,' said Freddy, 'I've heard some cock-eyed waffle during me years of living, but that beats the lot.'

'Now, Freddy, don't make fun of your daughter,' said Cassie, although she was trying hard not to giggle. 'If she wants to do pin-ups, well, lots of girls do these days.'

'But our Maureen, shy and blushing?' said Freddy, cackling.

Enter Lewis, Maureen's brother, a thin and lanky young sprig, but passable in looks, cheerful by nature, and, like his dad, a bit of a joker.

'What's going on?' he asked.

'Supper, that's what's about to go on,' said Cassie, 'so call your grandpa, there's a good boy.'

'Oh, right,' said Lewis, and called up from the open kitchen door. 'Oi, Gaffer, come on down, supper's ready!'

'Coming, coming,' called Cassie's good old dad, Harold Ford, long a widower and still living with his daughter and son-in-law. He was affectionately known as the Gaffer from his working days as a ganger with the old LSER, now part of the nationalized railways. Well retired at seventy-two, his hair was grey and his face lined, but he was still sturdy of body and character. Down he came from his room, and entered the kitchen on lively legs. 'Have I been hearing a riot?' he asked.

'Yes,' said Maureen, 'me dad's got – '

'Never mind that now,' said Cassie, 'you can talk about it over supper, so sit down, everyone. Freddy, take that soppy grin off your face.'

Cassie and her family took every meal in the large, old-fashioned kitchen of their equally old-fashioned terraced house. Except Sundays. Sundays, tea was always taken around the table in the parlour, as was the long-established custom with most Walworth families. Television hadn't yet had a bad effect on table meals, but it was only a matter of time. Cassie and Freddy would fight that.

76

Chapter Eight

Over supper, Freddy encouraged Maureen to talk about her intention to become a pin-up dolly. The Gaffer listened to her with his mouth open, his knife and fork at a standstill.

'Eh?' he said.

'Here we go again,' murmured Cassie.

'Gaffer, wait till you hear how she's going to do country poses on Saturday,' said Freddy.

'Country poses?' said Lewis through a mouthful of ox tongue and potato. 'I can't wait.'

'If you go barmy, like Dad did, I'll tread on your model Spitfire,' said Maureen.

'I dunno I want to hear more,' said the Gaffer, recovering enough to put his knife and fork to work again.

'Well, I think you ought to, Dad,' said Cassie, 'it's sort of fascinating.'

Freddy spluttered.

'Come on, tell us, Muffin,' said Lewis. Muffin had been his sister's nickname from infancy to girlhood.

'Well, all right,' said Maureen, keen in any case to talk about her ambitions with her family. So, mainly for the benefit of her brother and grandpa this time, she gave her version of what Mr Anderson, the Camberwell Green photographer, had in mind for her, including how she was to look like the nice girl next door, shy and blushing because of her legs showing.

Lewis went overboard, in a manner of speaking. The Gaffer choked on a potato.

'What's up, Gaffer?' grinned Freddy, highly tickled by his daughter's fanciful hopes. He was not in the least the disapproving dad. 'What's up, eh?'

'I'll tell yer,' gasped the Gaffer, 'in all me years I ain't never heard the like of what I've just heard this very minute.'

'Like our Maureen all shy and blushing?' said Lewis, still a bit over the top.

'Now don't you start making fun, my lad, just because Maureen will be showing her legs,' said Cassie.

'In a kind of accidental way,' said Maureen.

'Accidental?' said Freddy. 'Oh, me aching ribs.'

Lewis went spare again, and, of all things, a grin was slowly dawning on the Gaffer's weathered face. His mouth split, his dentures gleamed, his eyes twinkled, and a throaty chuckle emerged from his tickled tonsils.

'Well, blow me over,' he said, 'it's legs and a blush, is it, young Maureen?'

'Well, yes, Grandpa,' said Maureen, who couldn't raise a blush, even for her much-loved Gaffer.

'So she naturally has to look – well, embarrassed,' said Cassie.

'Mum, if you'd ever seen Maureen at a hop, swinging it, you wouldn't have noticed no embarrassment, nor blushes,' grinned Lewis. 'Just her legs.'

'I saw her swinging it at Boots's sixtieth,' said Freddy, 'and all the other dollies too, 'swelp me, I did. And what's more, even the married ones, like Patsy, Paula and Clare. Not a blush among 'em.'

'Oh, they all looked ever so young and lively,' said Cassie, who, during her teenage years, had kept her own legs very much under cover, which was the proper thing to do in the early Thirties.

'Has everyone said their bit?' asked Maureen.

'Go on, Muffin, get with it, do your stuff as a pin-up,' said Lewis, 'and we'll order six copies of the *Daily Mirror*.'

'Laugh a minute, this is,' said the Gaffer. 'I ain't known the like since Conker Kelly's belt busted and his trousers dropped off.'

'Some young kid, was he, Gaffer?' asked Freddy.

'Not likely,' said the Gaffer, now hugely enjoying his meal. 'Gang foreman at the time, and we was all walking through Woolwich station after finishing a shift. Fell over his trousers, didn't he, arse over tip, in front of a ladies' church outing just coming off the train. They all fainted.'

Everyone went spare then.

And no-one minded about Maureen becoming a blushing pin-up.

Boots, Sammy and Rachel had had a long discussion about how to respond to a possible takeover bid for Adams Enterprises Ltd. Sammy began by saying an affirmative response would be like selling his own baby. Rachel said hardly a baby, Sammy, at thirty years old.

'To me,' said Sammy, 'it's still on Cow and Gate.'

'And I should say you're not still its doting father?' smiled Rachel. 'Never, Sammy.'

'Let's think about what the offer might amount to,' said Boots.

Sammy said he wasn't keen on thinking about anything that might lead to losing their fashion company. Still, money's money, he said, which wasn't going to be exactly peanuts in this case, so what figure did Boots have in mind? Boots said Coates would probably know, for a start, what the balance sheets of the company were like over the last few years. There were ways and means of finding out. That meant Coates would know Adams Fashions Ltd was consistently in handsome profit. And even if they didn't know, they were capable of making a good guess.

'So?' said Rachel, addicted heart and soul to

her position in this family firm of Gentiles dear to her.

'We call in our auditors and get them to estimate the worth of our private company to a corporation long gone public,' said Boots.

'Well, all right,' said Sammy, 'but I asked you what you personally think it's worth.'

'A hundred thousand to a keen bidder,' said Boots.

'A hundred thousand?' gasped Rachel.

'A hundred thousand?' Sammy sat up. 'Would you do me the favour of repeating that?'

'Consider what's on offer,' said Boots. 'Shops, store, stocks, factory, machinery, outlets, goodwill, turnover. Our auditors will make something of all that. I'm making something of it. I'd quote £100,000, yes.'

'My life, £100,000?' breathed Rachel. 'But, Boots, aren't you forgetting the shops, store and factory are owned by our property company?'

'So the property company gets its share,' said Boots.

'Heavens,' said Rachel, quite flushed, 'all that much is money, Sammy.'

Sammy said that kind of money in the bank would be highly agreeable to the shareholders, but they'd be minus a business which he personally had brought up from its East End cradle, and he'd miss it. And how many shareholders were there?'

'We three,' said Boots, 'along with Lizzy, Ned,

Tommy, Vi, Susie, Polly and Chinese Lady.' All these family members now held shares in each of the three companies, Adams Enterprises, Adams Fashions and Adams Properties. Rachel counted as family because her younger daughter Leah was married to Lizzy's son Edward.

'A ten-way family split?' said Sammy.

'With variations according to each one's holding,' said Boots. 'But, of course, we'd up the asking figure to £200,000.'

'Do what?' said Sammy.

'Boots lovey, did you have a liquid lunch?' asked Rachel. 'I mean, my every life, £200,000?'

'Pick me up, someone,' said Sammy, 'I think I've fallen off me chair.'

'I fancy you're still with us, Sammy,' said Boots, and went on to point out that as a private company, the share value wasn't quoted on the Stock Exchange and they could put their own value on the company. Further, he didn't think any of the shareholders would sell if the directors advised against it. If Coates backed off, nothing would be lost. If they actually went for it, then the recipient shareholders could invest their windfalls in the property company. That would give it a capital huge enough to turn it into a major development corporation. There'd be new and worthwhile jobs for Tommy and Jimmy, both of whom were presently running the Bethnal Green factory.

'Blind O'Reilly,' breathed Sammy, '£200,000

capital? We could buy up every undeveloped site for miles around.'

'And wait for the developers to come running when the economy's really on the turn,' said Rachel.

'Or go in for development ourselves by acquiring an established firm of contractors,' said Boots.

Sammy thought long and hard.

'Boots,' he said, after some while, 'I've got a feeling we could be overreaching ourselves. Look at it this way. What we've got now is what we've built up over thirty years. It's all been gradual, and we ain't ever been out of control. Up to now, nothing's ever been too big for us to handle. Then there's the factory and all the staff, all the machinists and seamstresses who've been working for us for years, a lot of them all through the war. I know some have retired, and some are coming up for retirement, but all of 'em are used to Adams management. How will Coates management treat 'em? Not like Tommy and Jimmy do, I'll bet on it. Tommy's their mother and father, and Jimmy's their uncle. Then there's Susie's brother Freddy, running the Walworth store. Didn't know the first thing about shop-keeping when he came back from Burma, but look what he's done for the store. I ain't keen on telling him we might sell it. Boots, we've got to think long and serious.'

'No need,' smiled Boots, 'who wants ulcers? We

can make our decision now. We simply refuse to sell, whatever Coates offer.'

'Boots, is that what you'd like?' asked Rachel.

'I set out the possibilities, I know,' said Boots, 'but I favour the simple option – that what we have we hold. Sammy's right, we're in control and always have been. What are your feelings, Rachel?'

'The same as yours and Sammy's,' said Rachel. 'I love what we have and how it's been achieved. I don't want ulcers and I don't need a windfall. Money, Boots, isn't the same as happiness.'

'A little helps, an excess is for the greedy,' smiled Boots, and Rachel thought how cool he was. She herself had experienced hot little flutters about the proposition and what it could mean, and Sammy had actually shown agitation. Boots hadn't blinked an eyelid. If anyone was in control, he was, always. These brothers, Boots, Tommy and Sammy. She knew no other trio of men quite like them. Not one of them looked his age. She wondered, not for the first time, how their Victorian mother had produced such sons. Their father, the man who, as a corporal in the army, had been killed on the North-West Frontier fifty years ago, had he been as remark-able a character as Boots, his eldest? He must have been.

'Well, Sammy?' she said.

'If I might say so,' said Sammy, looking as if a dud penny had turned into a genuine coin of the realm, 'I'm highly gratified that you two coincide with me.'

'Coinciding we all like, Sammy,' said Rachel.

'I'm particularly gratified that Boots ain't turning me upside down any more,' said Sammy. 'Upside down makes me feel I'm falling ill. D'you know, Susie does that to me sometimes when I'm talking to her. It's the way she talks back. All me married life I've done me best to let her know I'm the one wearing the trousers. And what happens? She turns me upside down, if you get me.'

'I get you, Sammy,' smiled Rachel.

'Knew you would,' said Sammy. 'Anyway, this special board meeting is agreed we give Coates an affirmative negative if they make an offer?'

'A firm negative, Sammy?' suggested Boots.

'Same thing, Boots old cock,' said Sammy.

'I'll put my hand up to the same thing,' said Rachel fervently.

'All agreed, Sammy,' said Boots. 'We three constitute a quorum.'

'Sometimes,' said Sammy, 'I'm in favour of your educated talk, Boots, and you're still king of the family castle.'

'Don't mention it, old lad,' said Boots, 'it's all done with mirrors.'

Rachel laughed. Boots and Sammy, two lovely blokes. How she would have liked to have been the wife of either, if only her religion hadn't compelled her to marry a man of her own race.

*   *   *

Something else went Sammy's way when he arrived home. That was Susie's happy approval of the alabaster cherub. In fact, her approval stretched to the point of giving him the kind of kiss that touched his heart and made his waistcoat quiver a bit.

Bust my braces, he thought. I'm lucky with Susie, and lucky with me well-preserved corpuscles. I wonder if Boots's are still in working condition? You can never tell with Boots about this, that and the other. Mind, if he's still enjoying the other with Polly, Chinese Lady wouldn't label it as proper, not at their ages. Oh, well, I'm lucky all right with Susie.

Next: 'Sammy – Sammy – be your age.'

'Believe me, Susie, you've still got class.'

'Yes, I know, Sammy love, but kindly don't muck about with it in the kitchen.'

Chapter Nine

'Well, old love,' said Polly to Boots that evening, 'I agree with Sammy. Much jollier to hang onto what you've got than give up a large slice of it for filthy lucre. Sammy's one love, outside his family, is the business. And let's face it, old sport, he's been the driving force from the time he opened up that first shop.'

'All of us who benefit from the business owe Sammy,' said Boots.

'As for that shop, grotty though it was in those days, I've tender memories of it,' said Polly. 'It was where I first met you. I haven't been inside it for ages, but it's still sacred to me.'

'Like a church?' said Boots.

'Hardly. You were never a verger, and I was never one of God's heavenly souls.'

'A wild flapper, if I remember right,' said Boots.

They were having one of their companionable evenings, sitting on the swing hammock on their patio and looking out over the garden, the late August evening russet and balmy under the setting sun. They were perfectly relaxed, with no urge to be other than where they were, and no wish to be rushing about in pursuit of excitement. The restless generation these days was that of the teenagers, perhaps the equivalent of Polly and her flappers who had gone on crazy searches for the fruits of victory during the years immediately after the First World War. Those fruits, when found, had been bitter. The fruits of the Second World War had hardly proved sweet, and so the teenagers were creating their own pleasures. These related to music, music, dancing, dancing, and rock and roll concerts featuring up-and-coming young bands. If some austerity still existed, at least there was not the disillusionment suffered by the young people of the Twenties.

Polly and Boots, of course, had reached the age when they could be philosophical about every turn of the tide. The twins, Gemma and James, lived life with all the ardour and eagerness of their teenaged contemporaries. At the moment, they were with Polly's widowed stepmother, who loved having them.

Thinking of that, Polly said, 'By the way, Stepmama would like a photograph of Gemma and James.'

'We've scores of snapshots,' said Boots, 'and she's welcome to take her pick.'

'Snapshots, no,' said Polly, 'a formal photograph, yes.'

'Formal?' said Boots. 'A studio job? Who's going to tie them down? If I do, they'll tell their friends that their father's turned into a Victorian sadist, as per Wackford Squeers. Now mothers, of course, can do no wrong.'

'Mothers, of course, get taken advantage of by backsliding fathers,' said Polly. 'Oh, well, heigh-ho, I'll take them to a studio while they're still on school holiday and still have a Cornish tan.' The family, along with Susie, Sammy and Phoebe, had spent two weeks in North Cornwall and its foaming rollers. 'Stepmama wants a large portrait photograph of the two of them together, and in a large frame. It's to hang on her living-room wall.'

'Happily, Polly old girl, I'll leave it all to you,' said Boots.

'In return for which, I'd like a drink,' said Polly.

'It's a warm evening,' said Boots, 'so would you like a large gin and tonic with a large amount of ice?'

'Love it,' said Polly.

'I'll have one with you,' said Boots, 'and we'll make love to them together.'

'That'll be worth seeing,' said Polly. 'It'll let me into the secret of how a man makes love to a glass of iced gin and tonic. As far as mine is concerned, I'll just drink it.'

She watched him as he rose to his feet and entered the house, his movements still of the same easy long-legged kind as ever. She sighed for the years that had gone, the years that were now pointing her at sixty, the age of a definitely old woman.

Come back, the days of my wild heartbeats, come back.

She remembered again Sammy's grotty shop, and the moment when she first came face to face with Boots, tall, grey-eyed, masculine and whimsical. That was the moment when her first wild heartbeats began.

But there was a bright smile on her face when Boots returned with the drinks.

'Here we are, Polly.'

'Yes, here we are, old scout, two of a kind.'

'What kind?'

'A happy ever after kind,' said Polly, and laughed as she took the glass. 'Out of one of your mother's Victorian novels.'

'Are we as old-fashioned as that?' asked Boots.

'We would be,' said Polly, 'if we weren't about to down our twentieth-century gin and tonics.'

'Here's to you, Polly.'

'Here's to you, old darling.'

After supper with Leila, Michal and Judith, Wilhelm said, 'I think I'll go out.'

'Where to?' asked Leila.

'I thought I'd take in a movie,' said Wilhelm.

'Then you're an idiot,' said Leila, 'you could be recognized.'

'Not in a cinema,' said Wilhelm, 'cinemas are dark, aren't they?'

Leila turned to Michal.

'His photograph has been seen in many of your newspapers, hasn't it?'

'Yes, but not so much lately,' said Michal. 'Why don't you go with him? He'll attract less attention if he's with a woman who could be his wife.'

'I see most films as trivial,' said Leila.

'The trivial can be a form of escapism,' said Judith, 'and we all need an occasional helping.'

'I guess I'll help myself to some this evening,' said Wilhelm.

'You have orders not to show yourself unless by special arrangement, such as going to have your passport photograph taken,' said Leila.

'Look, he's bottled up,' said Michal, 'so go with him to the cinema. I'll drop off both of you in my car. Then neither of you will be seen except by the girl in the ticket office, and not even then if you get the tickets, Leila.'

Judith thought how patient he was with this touchy woman from Israel. It looked as if her responsibilities as an agent at this particular time were making her edgy. Certainly, it was going to be a great coup for Mossad if the man wanted by America for murder could be safely landed in Israel. Michal had been more than willing to help. He had friends in Israel, friends he had made during his sabbatical year in a kibbutz. One of them had been a security man.

'Very well,' said Leila, 'I will go with him, but I hope the film won't be one of those absurd American Westerns, with every cowboy talking out of the side of his mouth.'

'And just saying either "yup" or "nope"?' said Michal with a smile. He thought Leila should show more empathy with America, for America had provided the greatest help to the Palestine Jews in the establishment of their independent State.

'We shall see when we get there,' said Leila. She softened. 'I must thank you and Mrs Wirthe for taking good care of us.'

'Oh, you're very welcome,' said Judith.

'I shall be forever grateful,' said Wilhelm in his generous way.

Michal looked at his watch.

'I'll drive you to the cinema in ten minutes,' he said.

'Come along, bless you,' said Polly's stepmother, Lady Simms, to the twins, 'time for Thomas to drive you home.'

'Oh, can't we stay the night, Grandma?' said Gemma, on her way to fifteen, and an entrancing image of her vivacious mother at that age. Her looks were deliciously piquant, her slender body taking on a convex curvature, and Gemma was very pleased about what nature was doing for her. Well, thin flat-chested girls were just a little bit freakish, poor things.

'Yes, could we stay the night, Grandma?' asked

James, the same age as Gemma, of course, but already taller. Twins they were, with similarities, but just one glance at the pair told the beholder that while Gemma resembled her mother, James was like his father, with his dark brown hair, his grey eyes and his firm mouth. Already susceptible young schoolgirls were sighing over him. Cathy Davidson, who lived with her mother in Paris, wrote regularly to him, frequently reminding him that during their time together in Dulwich they had made promises to each other. James sometimes wrote to say he was too young to make that kind of promise to any girl, but she never took any notice. James had long thought girls were a bit of a problem.

Well, there was Cindy, daughter of Harry and Anneliese Stevens, friends of James's parents. Talk about a girl dynamo. She phoned him frequently, gave him orders about when to meet her and where to take her, and all this while she was beginning to bring other young fellers into her social round. His dad said it was known as playing the field until she settled on whoever she considered was her best prospect. James reckoned she was more likely to settle on being the country's first woman Prime Minister.

Lady Dorothy Simms regarded the twins affectionately. There they were, asking to stay the night after being with her since lunchtime. She loved having them. As a childless woman, she considered herself blessed in her happy relationship with stepdaughter Polly and her loving relationship with Gemma and James, firmly referring to them as her grandchildren. At seventy-six, she was still an elegant, aristocratic woman, daughter of a Yorkshire landowner, and still permanently involved in charity work. She was a rich woman, with a butler/chauffeur, two house servants and a gardener. The butler, Thomas Hillier, had succeeded the previous incumbent years ago, and was devoted to her.

'Darlings,' she said, 'you have no night things with you.'

'Oh, I can sleep in my pants,' said James airily, 'and Gemma can sleep in her knickers.'

'Grandma,' said Gemma, 'can you believe that boy can be so common? Mind, I don't mind sleeping like that.'

'Oh, I think we can find both of you some nightwear,' smiled Lady Simms, 'but first I must phone your parents.'

She phoned. Boots answered.

'Hello?'

'Hello, Boots, dear man. How are you?'

'Fairly normal, but Polly's a little high.'

'High?'

'Yes, she's just finished her second large gin and tonic.'

'I'm astonished she can manage even one after all that which went down our throats at your sixtieth last month.'

'Dorothy, not much went down your throat.'

'Oh, I'm a modest drinker, Boots. Listen, the twins are here, as you know.'

'I do know,' said Boots. 'This house is remarkably quiet. Is yours in need of repair yet? They've been with you since noon.'

'Yes, and good as gold,' said Lady Simms. 'They'd like to stay overnight and have breakfast with me. Do you mind?'

'Not a bit, except they've no pyjamas.'

'I can find them nightwear,' said Lady Simms.

'If you put James in a nightshirt,' said Boots, 'take some snapshots and send me one. Which reminds me, Polly says you'd like a formal photograph of them for framing, so she'll be popping in on a photographer and making an appointment for them.'

'Well, thank you, Boots, and Polly too.'

'Just thank Polly, I'll be ducking out.'

'I can't think why. Gemma and James are adorable.'

'How adorable is adorable if the walls of this house fall down one day?'

'Energy, dear man, allow them energy,' said Lady Simms.

'Could prove expensive,' said Boots. 'Anyway, say goodnight to them for me and Polly.'

'Yes, of course. Goodbye, Boots, I enjoyed every moment of your sixtieth.'

'Polly's of the opinion that if it had gone on any longer, only the fittest would have survived. Goodnight, Dorothy.'

When Boots put the phone down he thought what a splendid woman Polly's stepmother was. He knew she missed Sir Henry, her late old warhorse of a husband, but she was as resilient as Chinese Lady and a figure of warmth and compassion to the unfortunate souls she helped through her charities.

How old was she? Seventy-six, yes. And old Aunt Victoria, living with Tommy and Vi, was seventy-seven. And Chinese Lady was coming up to eighty. Most women outlasted most men. Which suggested that, all in all, they were tougher.

On that reflective note, Boots rejoined Polly, a woman as brightly alive as ever.

It was dark when Leila and Wilhelm left the cinema to find Michal waiting for them in his car. Driving them home, he discovered the main film had not been an American Western but a British comedy, featuring Will Hay as an eccentric and hopeless headmaster of a boys' school.

'Was it funny?' he asked.

'It was to Wilhelm,' said Leila. 'Myself, I didn't understand a word.'

'But you laughed at times,' said Wilhelm.

'At the visual content, not the dialogue,' said Leila. 'However, it was not too bad, no.'

'A small helping of escapism?' said Michal, then drew a breath as a uniformed constable stepped from the pavement and held up a restraining hand. 'Damn,' said Michal, bringing his car to a stop. In the back, Leila and Wilhelm sank in an attempt to make themselves more invisible. The constable advanced and tapped on Michal's window. Michal, noticing a second constable watching from the pavement in the glow of a street lamp, wound his window down. 'What's up, officer?' he asked lightly.

'Good evening, sir,' said the policeman, 'would you mind telling me where you've come from?'

'The cinema,' said Michal. 'A Will Hay film.'

The constable peered at the vague outline of the passengers, studying them for long seconds, then asked, 'What's the number of your car, sir?'

'CYV 853.'

The constable checked, came back and said, 'Would you mind stepping out, sir, and opening up your boot?'

'Is there a reason?'

'Step out, sir, would you, please?' The constable opened the door. Michal shrugged and alighted. In the back, Leila and Wilhelm were tense. Michal walked round the car and opened up the boot. It was empty save for a spare wheel. The constable took a brief look. 'Thank you, sir, you can go on your way now. Sorry to have inconvenienced you.'

'But what's it all about?' asked Michal.

'A break-in. A jeweller's shop by the Elephant and Castle. We think a stolen car was used.'

'I see. Well, good luck and goodnight, officer.'

Michal eased himself back into the car and resumed his drive home. He heard Leila tell Wilhelm in sibilant Yiddish that he'd just been shown how dangerous it was to appear in public. And he heard Wilhelm say they would have to do that when they kept their new appointment with the photographer. In response, Leila told him to muffle the lower half of his face with a scarf.

'It's summer, not winter,' whispered Wilhelm.

Michal spoke up.

'I've told you both it isn't wise to speak Yiddish. It's a foreign language in Camberwell. You must get into the way of always using English.'

'I guess you're right,' said Wilhelm the amenable.

'You need not remind us again,' said Leila the unbendable.

Michal brought the car to a stop outside his home, and they were all greeted by Judith minutes later.

'And how was the film?' she asked.

'Funny,' said Wilhelm.

'A mystery to me,' said Leila.

'We were stopped on the way home,' said Michal, and told Judith of the inquisition.

'Perhaps you were lucky that the constable didn't ask Leila and Wilhelm to step out with you,' said Judith.

'There, you see?' said Leila to Wilhelm.

'I see,' said Wilhelm, 'but the film was still funny.'

'I'll make a bedtime milk drink,' said Judith, 'and offer everyone a slice of my honey cake, the kind I bake for Passover.'

'You are very hospitable,' said Wilhelm.

'Yes, thank you,' said Leila, and since she followed that by being almost mellow over the little bedtime repast, Judith, Michal and Wilhelm felt the long day had ended quite plesantly.

Chapter Ten

'Are you awake, young sir?'

James opened his eyes. The morning of the first day in September was flooding the pleasant bedroom with light, and beside his bed stood Jane Hillier, sixteen-year-old daughter of Thomas Hillier, the butler. The girl was Lady Simms's parlourmaid, three months into the position. In her maid's uniform of royal and blue and starched white front, she was demure in appearance and expression. Not many girls were choosing to be in service these days. The Labour Party had conditioned most young people into avoidance of menial work. That is, slaving for the nobs. In any case, employment opportunities were now improving.

Jane held a cup and saucer as she regarded James with eyes that were not quite as demure as her smile.

'Oh, hello,' said James, dark brown hair ruffled from its night-long contact with the pillow. He looked warm from sound sleep.

'I've brought you a cuppa,' said Jane.

James sat up and she placed the cup and saucer on the bedside table.

'Thanks,' he said.

'Her Ladyship said breakfast in half an hour.'

'Kippers?' said James.

'Kippers? Kippers?' Jane giggled. 'Her Ladyship don't allow the smell of kippers around the house. It's eggs and bacon. My, you're a cheeky boy, aren't you, young sir?'

'Not specially,' said James, stretching his arms. 'I've decided on a serious life.'

'Serious? Crikey, what a one,' said Jane, and sat down on the edge of the bed. She regarded him again. She knew he wasn't yet fifteen, but already he seemed more grown-up than any of the boys she knew. 'Would you like a present?'

'Before or after I've had my tea?' smiled James.

'Now,' said Jane, 'but you've got to promise not to tell no-one.'

'OK, fair's fair,' said James, as airy-fairy as his dad, despite his declared intention to live a serious life.

'Close your eyes, then, and I'll give it you,' said Jane at her demurest.

'All right, try me,' said James, and closed his eyes in the expectation of receiving a dead frog in his hand.

Almost at once an eager pair of rosebud lips connected with his unready mouth. All demureness departed from the young parlourmaid, and

James could hardly believe the kind of kiss it was. Certainly, it was nothing like the boy and girl kisses he'd exchanged with Cathy and Cindy. Even the tip of a girlish tongue pushed into his mouth. This kind of kiss took his breath and his body seemed to flush. The ardent, lingering contact broke eventually. He opened his eyes, and there was Jane, standing up and looking as pure as an unopened rose.

'Don't tell now,' she said, 'drink your tea. My, you're a nice boy, really, young sir.' And out she whisked.

James lay back, eyes blinking, face hot. Well, blow me, he thought, I'm lucky she didn't catch me in the dark. Saucy minx. If Mum knew, she'd yank me back home and pull the drawbridge up. What goes on with girls? Blessed if I know. I thought they were all innocent at her age. Oh, well, not a word to Grandma Simms. I'll just talk about her rose garden over my eggs and bacon.

After breakfast, he and Gemma said goodbye to their loving grandmother, and were driven home by butler/chauffeur Thomas, Jane's dad. Jane herself waved them goodbye, hankie fluttering demurely. Lady Simms, beside her, also waved.

'If you don't mind me saying so, ain't they sweet children, Yer Ladyship?' said Jane.

'Hardly children,' said Lady Simms. 'In no time at all, Gemma will be a young lady, James a young man.'

'Will they be coming to stay again?' asked Jane.

'I hope so,' said Lady Simms.

Her demure parlourmaid smiled the smile of the flighty.

James was thinking that when he started living his serious life, he'd have to pay serious attention to what made girls a puzzle to fellers, or he might end up falling overboard out of sheer ignorance.

Boots, if consulted, would have said, 'James old lad, in certain cases, and at certain times in one's life, ignorance is bliss.'

It was the kind of wrinkle he'd given James during the time when young Cathy's attentions were turning his good-natured son upside down.

Vi's mother, now living with her daughter and son-in-law Tommy, was known to the family as old Aunt Victoria, although no-one referred to Chinese Lady as old Grandma Finch, even if she was senior by two years. The difference, of course, was that Chinese Lady was still comparatively vigorous, while Aunt Victoria kept mostly to her armchair like a woman content to slowly fade away. She was, however, much mellower than in her former years, when her main interest – even recreation – had been finding something to complain about.

She was frail of body now. Her seventy-eight years were showing, her memory faulty. She kept asking Vi where Tom was. Tom, her husband, had died a few years ago. Vi, compassionate, liked to answer in the best way she could.

'Oh, he'll turn up sometime today, I expect.'

'Well, I must say I can't think where he's got to.'

She was no trouble, she really had mellowed, and was quite content with the two rooms Vi and Tommy had put at her disposal. But she was definitely fading.

Vi spoke to Tommy.

'I'm worried about Mam.'

'So am I, Vi, I think our old lady is feeling dead tired,' said Tommy.

Vi said she hoped he didn't mean her mum was tired of living. Tommy did mean that, but didn't say so. However, he did say he'd get Dr Jerribond to call. Dr Jerribond, he said, was the kind of GP who could cheer up someone suffering appendicitis and two broken legs all at once. Perhaps that was what the old lady really needed, a bit of uplift from the kind of doctor who'd go as far as to prescribe a reviving tonic of two glasses of port a day.

'Tommy, are you being funny?' asked Vi.

'On me honour, Vi, no,' said Tommy, 'it's what they call being talked into feeling better, along with a drop or two of your favourite tipple. You and me, we can't talk our old lady into feeling better, because she's listening to us every day. But good old Dr Jerribond, he could do the trick.'

'Tommy, you could be right,' said Vi. 'I mean, it's not as if Mum's really old. Not really old.'

'Just getting on a bit, Vi. I'll phone the doctor tomorrow morning.'

That resulted in the arrival the following afternoon of Dr Jerribond, bright and encouraging, if a bit portly for a medico who was forever busy on his afternoon rounds. Although Aunt Victoria said she wasn't ill, and that her son-in-law was fussing, the breezy GP gave her an examination and a fund of cheerful adjectives, and spoke to Vi on his way out.

'Slightly anaemic, slightly, Mrs Adams, but there's life in the old lady yet. Here's a prescription for vitamin tablets. See that she takes one a day, would you?'

'She's not actually ill, doctor?' said Vi.

'Ill? No, just a little aged, and she seems quite perky at the moment. Let me know – '

'Perky?' said Vi.

'At the moment. Let me know as soon as you feel she needs me again.' That was a hint that an emergency might arise. It didn't register with Vi, simply because she refused to believe her mother's fading condition was terminal. 'As it is, perhaps I'll call in once a fortnight, anyway.'

'Oh, thanks, doctor,' said Vi.

'Goodbye now, regards to Mr Adams.'

'Goodbye, doctor, and thanks ever so much for calling,' said Vi gratefully.

'Don't mention it. Must get on.'

No sooner had he departed than Vi's mum made herself heard from upstairs.

'Vi? Vi? You there?'

'Yes, Mum.'

'Well, I wonder, could you get me a little glass of port, dear?'

When Tommy arrived home, Vi gave him details of the doctor's call, then asked him a question.

'Did you tell Dr Jerribond that a little drop of port would do Mum good?'

'Me?' said Tommy. 'Now would I tell any doctor how to treat a patient, how to do his job? Not much. What makes you think I did?'

'Because as soon as the doctor had gone, Mum called down and asked if she could have a glass,' said Vi.

'Of milk?' said Tommy.

'Port,' said Vi.

At that, Tommy showed a grin from ear to ear. Well, almost.

'Port?' he said.

'Well,' said Vi, 'I told you the doctor mentioned she was feeling a little perky.'

'Well, I'm blowed,' said Tommy, 'good old girl. I'll treat her this evening.'

'What to?' asked Vi.

'Another glass of port,' said Tommy.

*   *   *

On Wednesday afternoon, Mr Geoffrey Piper, a director of Coates, was keeping an appointment, arranged yesterday, with Mrs Rachel Goodman, secretary and director of Adams Enterprises and its associated companies. He sat facing her on the other side of her desk. He was finding her not just a handsome woman, but an intelligent and lucid one.

He was there to lay before her a general outline of his board's possible proposal to acquire Adams Fashions Ltd. So far, Rachel considered his outline not too precise.

'You realize, Mr Piper, that before I submit details to our senior directors, Mr Sammy Adams and Mr Robert Adams, I need to have a clear-cut presentation. You've spoken of your interest in taking over our Bethnal Green factory, and you've also indicated an interest in our store and our shops. Tell me, what exactly will the possible proposal cover? A hundred per cent purchase of the shareholdings, which will give you complete control of the company? Or do you have merely a majority holding in mind? Or an offer that will give you full ownership of everything?'

Mr Piper, an appealing gentleman in his late forties, raised a hand.

'My dear madam, I've no wish to be vague, indeed not, and forgive me if I haven't made myself reasonably clear. This, of course, is a preliminary and informal meeting intended to lead to an official discussion between your senior directors and ours.'

He's sounding me out, thought Rachel. He wants to discover if I'm eager to present a favourable case to Sammy and Boots. Little does he know what a couple of wise old owls they are.

'Carry on, Mr Piper,' she said.

'Shareholding could give us control,' he said, 'but I imagine your board would resist a move that might result in their being voted out. Therefore, I think I should tell you we have in mind outright ownership of the company and its assets.'

'Ownership of our factory, our shops, our Walworth store and all shares?' said Rachel, velvety voice delightfully pleasing to Mr Piper.

'The freeholds of all these properties are yours?' he said.

'Oh, yes,' said Rachel, but refrained from informing him that the freeholds of the factory, the Walworth store and most of the shops belonged to Adams Properties Ltd. Adams Properties was as solidly established as Adams Fashions, so much so that Boots's son Tim, and Sammy's son Daniel, co-managers, were still sold on the idea of building an American-style supermarket in the not too distant future. 'Yes, these freeholds are ours, Mr Piper.'

Mr Piper mused and looked Rachel in the eye. Rachel smiled. Mr Piper blinked. Undeniably, Rachel was still a very comely lady, and Mr Piper probably put her in her mid-forties. Next month she would be fifty-four, the same age as Sammy, but she was very much like Susie and Polly in the resistance she offered to the persistent sorties of Father Time, not a gentleman in the unpitying war he waged on ladies.

'Well, Mrs Goodman,' said the impressed representative from Coates, 'let me be frank at this point and say that we definitely have full ownership in mind.'

'On my life,' murmured Rachel, 'a total acquisition? That's clear-cut indeed. Am I to be informed of what offer your company has in mind, or will that remain confidential until the official meeting?'

'You'll probably understand it won't be made known until then at least,' said Mr Piper, 'when I presume your auditors will supply us with a copy of your latest balance sheet.'

'There's no chance you can whisper a guess to me?'

'I'm afraid not.'

'Well, I can at least let my senior directors know that the official meeting should be extremely interesting,' said Rachel. 'So thank you for coming, Mr Piper.'

'My dear madam, it's been a great pleasure,' said Mr Piper cordially. 'I hope we shall meet again. Um – perhaps over lunch one day?'

'Who knows?' smiled Rachel, and saw him to the door. He shook her hand, said goodbye, put on his bowler hat, picked up his rolled umbrella, and left. The bowler hat and umbrella made him look what he was, a City gent. Rachel, smiling, popped into Sammy's office. Sammy used the house line to call Boots in, and the brothers listened to what Rachel had to say, all of which was highly interesting, and no error.

'All right, it means they're keen,' said Sammy.

'It means they'll make an offer,' said Boots.

'At the meeting?' said Sammy. 'What's the point of going, if we intend to turn down any offer?'

'To turn it down without meeting them wouldn't be good manners,' said Boots.

'Come again,' said Sammy.

'A lack of courtesy, Sammy,' said Rachel.

'I've heard of that, and I'm all for it,' said Sammy. 'I was brought up on showing me manners and keeping me shirt tucked in. So all right, we go, and I daresay we'll get a cup of tea and some biscuits. That's if they don't fall out of their waistcoats and watch chains at hearing our sale price of £200,000.'

'Sammy, we still need Coates's custom,' said Boots, 'they still buy in large quantities from the factory. So let's have the meeting and let's tell them, without mentioning £200,000, that whatever their maximum offer is, we'll give it consideration. Unless, in some way, they corner us and we're compelled to drop a bombshell, our figure of £200,000 need never be mentioned.

In any case, our balance sheet will speak well enough to make them realize we're worth more than a pound of peanuts.'

'Boots,' said Rachel, 'I must point out that the balance sheet won't show the assets owned by the property company.'

'We'll explain that,' said Boots, 'and I fancy they'll ask for them to be included by special arrangement with the property company. It'll be then that we say we'll give the whole proposal consideration.'

'As a matter of courtesy?' smiled Rachel. 'I'm for that, Boots.'

'Agreed,' said Sammy. 'You mean negative consideration, of course, Boots?'

'Yes, as we decided,' said Boots. 'Eventually, we'll come up with the information that at a meeting of all shareholders, the majority voted against the proposition on the grounds that, as family members receiving excellent dividends, they insisted on the family retaining the firm.'

'All that counts as good manners?' grinned Sammy.

'It will allow you and Boots to sound like very courteous gents,' said Rachel.

'Stuff my old socks,' said Sammy, 'when you think what it's done for Boots, don't you consider education highly recommendable, Rachel?'

'Highly, Sammy,' said Rachel.

'I wish I'd had some meself,' said Sammy.

'Sammy old lad,' said Boots, 'what you did

have was a grounding. And in your case, what you didn't have was never necessary. You've been a man of the world since you were fourteen.'

'I'm tickled, Boots old cock, tickled,' said Sammy. 'And might I say, Rachel, what a helpful meeting you had with Mr Diaper?'

'Piper, Sammy.'

'Yes, something like that,' said Sammy. 'Anyway, good on you for your performance.'

'Well, thank you, Sammy,' said Rachel.

'Can't do without you these days,' said Boots.

'Boots, my dear, I'm the happiest of women in all I'm able to do for our companies,' said Rachel.

Boots looked at his watch. Mid-afternoon. Office teatime.

'Rachel, have two extra biscuits with your cup of tea,' he said, 'you've earned them.'

Chapter Eleven

Earlier that afternoon, Patsy, the American wife of Daniel, elder son of Sammy and Susie, came out of her house in Kestrel Avenue with her children, eight-year-old Arabella and six-year-old Andrew. They walked to the bus stop at the lower end of Herne Hill before it joined Denmark Hill. Patsy was taking her children to Lyons at Camberwell Green to treat them to ice creams and milk shakes, a promised outing.

There, waiting at the bus stop, was Emma, younger daughter of Daniel's Aunt Lizzy and Uncle Ned, and the wife of Jonathan Hardy. With Emma were her nine-year-old daughter Jessie and her two-year-old son Mark. They lived close to Patsy and Daniel.

'Hi there,' said Patsy, outgoing and as lively at twenty-nine as she'd been at seventeen, when she'd first met Daniel. 'Hi, kids.'

'Hi,' said Jessie, while little brother Mark stared shyly, and Emma said hello to Patsy's two. Then she addressed Patsy.

'Where are you off to with yours?'

'Lyons, for ice creams and milk shakes,' said Patsy. 'I've told them it'll make them fat, but at their age, do kids care?'

'I'm taking mine to the park,' said Emma, who, like her mother and her sister Annabelle, was a chestnut-haired, brown-eyed brunette. She was coming up to thirty-four, and considered by Jonathan to be a prime example of how to promote continuous sex appeal with the minimum effort. Come to that, Daniel thought much the same about Patsy. Both ladies accepted these compliments as their fair due, and both kept their sex appeal up to the mark with attractive make-up, well-chosen clothes and healthy bodies.

'How's Daniel, Patsy?' Emma asked.

'Believe me, Emma,' said Patsy, with the kids mixing it, 'I'm still waiting for that guy to grow up. By the way, Uncle Boots's sixtieth was just great, wasn't it?'

'How great was great, Patsy, when Jonathan's hangover laid him out all the following day, and I spent the same amount of time trying to find out where my head was?' Emma delivered this in a confidential whisper, in case the three elder children heard and carried a tale of drunken grown-ups into the ears of their schoolfriends.

'Daniel likewise,' said Patsy. 'And me. Whoops, break it up, kids, the bus is coming.'

The red bus was coming down the hill quite fast towards the stop, and for a moment Emma thought the driver was going to ignore his waiting passengers and pass them by. However, he did pull up, although not without putting a strain on his tyres.

'Here we are, ladies,' called the conductor, 'all aboard, little 'uns. Nice day, eh?' He helped the kids to step up. 'Hope you're in a hurry, because me driver is,' he said to the ladies. 'I think he wants to get home to his missus. She's baking a cake.'

'How sweet,' said Emma.

'Cute,' said Patsy, shepherding the children. 'Move along, you guys.'

The conductor rang the bell and the bus, with about a score of passengers on board, moved off. It quickly gathered speed.

'Here, he's going a bit fast, what's his hurry?' complained a woman.

Patsy, Emma and their children had hardly settled into their seats before the bus entered Denmark Hill and rushed towards the next stop at the corner of Ferndene Road, where two people were waiting. It thundered past them.

'Hey, Joe!' The conductor shouted at his driver and rang the bell. The driver took no notice. He seemed to be crouched over his wheel, hugging it. 'Joe!' Again the conductor rang the bell. There was no response, and the bus continued its fast descent.

The conductor moved forward, shouting, and his obvious agitation communicated fright to the passengers. Some began to panic, especially when the heavy vehicle slewed as it rounded the bend at the bottom of the hill. It charged on, passing Ruskin Park and King's College Hospital, and headed at unchecked speed towards the junction at Camberwell Green. People crossing the road ran for their lives. The bus driver, not using his horn, was sounding no warnings. He was simply going pell-mell into the heart of Camberwell.

'Oh, my God,' gasped Emma. She had little Mark on her lap, and Jessie next to her. She clasped them both, her eyes staring as she saw the junction traffic lights coming up horrendously fast. They were red. By the grace of God there was no traffic immediately in front of the careering bus, and it shot the lights, missing only by inches a car coming out of Camberwell New Road on the left. From the pavements, transfixed people screamed at the bus driver.

Seated with her children behind Emma, Patsy gasped, 'Emma, oh, Jesus, Emma!'

Passengers were hysterical as the bus thundered along Camberwell Road, charging in the wake of a small van forty yards ahead. The conductor was banging on the window dividing the driver from the passengers, and he was almost hoarse from shouting.

'Joe! For Chrissake, man! Pull up, pull up!'

No response emanated from the hunched driver. Emma, frightened out of her life for the four children, prayed between clenched teeth. It was all too obvious now that the driver had gone off his head. He was driving straight for the back of the small van as it made a sedate progress towards Walworth Road.

The passengers, mostly shopping housewives, were clinging to whatever they could get hold of, and either shrieking or screaming. A middle-aged man came out of his seat, staggered along the reverberating floor of the aisle to join the conductor in hammering on the window and bawling at the driver.

'Stop! Stop, you crazy bugger, you'll kill us all!'

Everyone walking the pavements came to a halt as the bus, charging like a runaway, swerved with a hideous screech of tyres, and overtook the van. Now its mighty weight was on the wrong side of the road. An oncoming car spun out of the way by mounting the kerb. The bus rolled by at a suicidal speed, taking up a position in front of the van and reaching Walworth Road. Ahead were a couple of cars, and a little over half a mile further on were the traffic lights guarding the crossing from Manor Place to Browning Street. A man pushing an empty barrow heard the noisy, drumming approach of the bus. He turned his head, saw the charging monster, let go of his barrow and rushed onto the pavement. The bus hit the barrow and smashed it aside amid screams from women passengers.

Jessie was clinging to her mother, and her

mother was holding fast to her frightened daughter and her bewildered little son. And Patsy was holding onto Arabella and Andrew for dear life. Like Emma, she was praying, her body trembling from the vibrations of the thundering bus. Her eyes, mesmerized, were staring at the car immediately ahead. It seemed then as if its driver had glimpsed the raging bus in his mirror, for he overtook the second car at speed, giving quick warning toots on his hooter. And as he passed he made a hand gesture. The driver of the second car turned his head and saw the terrifying apparition of a red juggernaut almost on his tail. He put his foot down and his speed reached that of the other car. They sped away hell for leather.

In the distance, Patsy and Emma saw the traffic lights. Oh, great God, thought Emma, all kinds of images flashing into her distraught mind. The bus roared past the East Street market, which was teeming with shoppers. Everyone visible on the pavements and at the market entrance stopped moving, except for a turn of every head. Many looked dumbstruck, others yelled at the bus driver. But on he went, the middle-aged man and the conductor still thumping frantically on the window.

It seemed as if the traffic lights at Browning Street suddenly began to race towards the speeding bus. They were at red, and the red appeared to glare angrily. Jessie buried her face against her mother, her young body shaking, while Arabella gasped to Patsy, 'Mummy, Mummy.'

A parked car, fortunately empty, was hit and tossed onto the pavement like a heap of old iron. The bus passengers were white-faced and stricken as their public vehicle thundered at the traffic lights. The red turned green at the last moment, and the bus charged on in pursuit of traffic ahead. It passed shops, it passed the stately town hall, and it passed Wansey Street, where Cassie Brown lived with her family. It reached the railway bridge, rushed under it and careered towards the busy junction of the Elephant and Castle, around which were still signs of some post-war development. Not far ahead was another bus.

We're going to die, thought Patsy, all of us, Emma and me and our darling children. And Emma thought in a kind of devastating and mesmerized way that there was going to be mayhem at the Elephant and Castle. This bus is going to hit that bus ahead by the time we reach the junction, and we're all going to be crushed to death.

With unimaginable fright and hysteria prevailing on both decks, the driver suddenly slumped. His hunched shoulders collapsed, his hands came off the steering wheel, his foot off the accelerator, and with the clutch out the gears ground, the rudderless bus slewed, slowed, bumped heavily against the kerb, rolled onto the pavement and came to a stop outside shops like a red colossus devoid of all motion. Its engine stalled.

'Oh, merciful God,' gasped a woman passenger.

The conductor, expelling hoarse words of reassurance, ran down the aisle, jumped onto the pavement and rushed round to wrench open the driver's door. A crowd of stunned pedestrians had already gathered. The collapsed driver was huddled and inert, his face blue, his lips blue, and spittle issuing from his mouth.

'Gawdalmighty,' breathed the conductor, 'you near done for us all, Joe. But now I'm looking at yer, I can see you've had a bleedin' brainstorm, so I forgive yer, so help me I do. You're never going to taste your old lady's cake, not this side of Christmas, if ever.'

Chapter Twelve

A policeman on the beat had taken charge of the incident. A summoned ambulance had carried the brain-stricken driver to hospital, and a second ambulance had arrived to deal with any passengers suffering severe shock. A crowd had massed, and a second constable arrived to keep the gawping bystanders clear of the bus and the shaken, disgorged passengers.

Freddy Brown, manager of the Adams store close to the Elephant and Castle junction, emerged from the premises, saw the bus, the crowd and the ambulance, and crossed the road. Among the first people he spotted were Emma and Patsy, their children around them. He broke through the crowd. A constable checked him.

'Stay back, sir.'

'I know those two ladies and their children,' said Freddy, 'they're relatives of mine. Let me talk to them.'

'Very well, sir.'

Freddy made his way to Emma and Patsy.

'Emma? Patsy? What happened?'

'Freddy? Where did you come from?' asked Emma, pale, and with little Mark up in her arms.

'From the store. What happened, Emma?'

'The bus driver went crazy,' said Emma.

'Crazy, crazy,' said Patsy, biting her lip.

'It was awful, Uncle Freddy,' said Jessie. She, Arabella and Andrew were all shaken.

With the ambulance crew ministering to distraught women, Freddy said, 'Look, Patsy, let me get all of you out of here. There's a cafe across the road near the store where we can get hot milk drinks for the children, and some strong coffee for you and Emma.'

'What about the store?' asked Emma.

'I can leave that to my two assistants,' said Freddy, 'and there are no customers at the moment. They all left, one after the other, to join this crowd, I suppose. Let me get all of you out of it. Come on.'

He took them across the road to the cafe, Italian-owned. There, Emma and Patsy gratefully seated themselves at a table with the children, Mark on Emma's lap. Freddy went to the counter and ordered coffees and hot milk drinks.

'That bus, eh?' said Victor, the agreeable proprietor. 'On the pavement, yes? That is no place for a bus.'

'God knows exactly what happened,' said Freddy, 'I've only been told the driver went crazy.'

'The war, perhaps, eh, Mr Brown? It did many things to men.' Victor had served with Mussolini's army in the Western Desert, been captured by the British, and stayed in England after his release from a prisoner-of-war camp. 'The bus driver, yes, perhaps was a soldier left with a sick head. You think a sick head can blow up? Yes, I think too. You sit, Mr Brown, eh? I will bring the drinks.'

'Ta muchly,' said Freddy, and joined his relatives. Together, in spasms, Emma and Patsy began to give him the details of their frightening experience. Halfway through, Victor arrived with the tray of drinks. He gave a chocolate biscuit to each of the children with their hot milk.

'You like, eh?' he said to them, beaming.

'Oh, thanks,' said Jessie.

'A present from me, yes?' said Victor.

'So kind of you,' said Emma.

'We were going to have ice creams,' said Arabella.

'So?' said Victor, beaming again. 'I have ice cream. You like when you have finished your hot milk?'

'Crumbs, yes, not half,' said Jessie. 'Can we, Mummy?'

'Of course,' said Emma, and Freddy nodded at the proprietor.

'We'll all have ice creams, Victor,' he said, 'they'll cool us down.'

'Good, eh?' said Victor, and went back to his

counter. Other customers had arrived, all talking about the bus.

Over their coffee, Emma and Patsy resumed giving details to Freddy. At the end, only the presence of the children stopped him from expressing his reactions in some elementary language. All he could acceptably say was, 'Well, thank God the poor devil collapsed before he reached the junction. It's always crowded with traffic. Something very nasty could have happened.'

'I was ever so frightened,' said Arabella.

'Well, you're safe now,' said Freddy, giving her a pat on her knitted woollen hat that was topped with a bobble. 'We're all safe, and there'll be ice creams coming soon.'

'Yummy,' said Andrew.

Freddy looked at Emma, then at Patsy. They smiled, a little weakly, but their colour was back. Freddy chatted to the children, telling them that the bus driver had been showing off, that he'd get the sack for it, and so it wouldn't happen again.

'We need our buses, don't we, eh? Tell you what,' he said, 'when we've had our ice creams, I'll bring my car round, squeeze all of you into it and drive you home.'

'Freddy, that's real sweet of you, it really is,' said Patsy, 'but there's your store, and I'm sure we can raise a cab, can't we, Emma?'

'Of course,' said Emma.

'Not many taxis whizz up and down Walworth Road,' said Freddy. 'And my assistants can manage until closing time. So crowd into my car and I'll drive you.'

'Are you sure, Freddy?' asked Patsy, not too keen under the circumstances about going home on another bus. And the kids would probably take some time to regard bus rides as harmless adventures, although Freddy had been a wise guy in telling them the show-off bus driver would be fired. Actually, the poor guy was probably dead by now. 'You'll bring your auto round?'

'I insist,' said Freddy. 'You young 'uns would like to squeeze in, wouldn't you?'

'Hooray,' said Andrew, as bright as his mother and as lively as his dad. 'I'd like to.'

'Me too,' said Arabella.

'And me,' said Jessie. 'Could I squeeze in next to you, Uncle Freddy?'

'You and Arabella both,' said Freddy, 'I'm a fan of young ladies.'

Jessie giggled, the ice creams arrived, and Patsy thought how rewarding it was to be married into a family as diverse and tribal as that presided over by its matriarch, Grandma Finch. Everyone looked out for everyone else. Help and affection arrived quickly at one's door in any crisis. Polly had asked her once if she ever felt hemmed in by the manifold Adams brood. Patsy had said no, do you? My dear, said Polly, I'm one of the brood.

125

*   *   *

'Jesus Christ,' breathed Daniel, having been given details of the incident on arriving home from the office, 'is this true or are you recounting a nightmare, Patsy?'

'It's true, honey, it sure is,' said Patsy, 'and it's also a nightmare. A nightmare in broad daylight. I'm still suffering grisly shakes.'

Daniel asked how the children were, and Patsy said that fortunately, they'd been so bucked by their hot milk, chocolate biscuits and ice creams that they'd emerged from the cafe with contented tummies and happy faces. Daniel asked where they were, and Patsy said in the garden, where Arabella was teaching Andrew how to play baseball.

'Rounders?' said Daniel.

'Rounders?' said Patsy.

'Don't you know by now that that's what it's called in this country, and that it's a game for girls?'

'Well, you cutie,' said Patsy, 'it's played in America by men six feet tall and four feet wide, and it's called baseball.'

'You win,' said Daniel. 'He put his arms around her, kissed her and said, 'Love you, Patsy, and thank the Lord you and the kids weren't losers.'

'Hey,' said Patsy, overbright, 'don't you know there are no losers in the Kirk and Adams families?' Her pa was a Kirk.

'I'll hang onto that,' said Daniel.

Jonathan, on being told of the nightmare bus ride by Emma, expressed himself in the honest fashion of a country-born man, very much to the effect that the Lord Himself could bear witness to his sense of gratitude that no harm had come to anyone.

'That's a little dramatic, Jonathan,' said Emma.

'Yes, it is a bit, Daddy,' said Jessie.

'Nothing of the kind,' said Jonathan. 'I be expected to show my relief by a tiddly old grunt, like old Farmer Diprose and his pigs? More specially, like his old sow, Henrietta? That Henrietta, she were the best grunter in the country, second only to Farmer Diprose himself. And I should know, I were born not far from his pig farm. See here, young Jessie, you and your mum, and little Mark too, Providence took a hand in delivering you from calamity, and I'd be a fair old lump of wood if I didn't think so or say so. Emma, have you had a brandy?'

'No, coffee and ice cream, as I mentioned,' said Emma.

'Well, you need a shot of brandy, and so do I,' said Jonathan with all seriousness, 'and young Jessie here, she needs a cuddle. And where's Mark?'

'In bed and asleep,' said Emma.

'Daddy, could I have a cuddle and some brandy?' asked Jessie, curly-haired, fond of asking questions and sharing things with her mum and dad.

'Not brandy, no,' said Jonathan, outwardly cheerful now for the sake of reassuring his daughter, but inwardly still appalled at what might have happened if that mind-crazed bus driver hadn't collapsed. And even then, the bus could still have crashed. He looked at Emma, and opted for continued lightness. 'Gin?' he suggested.

'Gin? For Jessie? Don't you dare,' said Emma, at which point she saw through his cheerful mask. 'Jonathan, we're all right, we're at home, and we're with you. So we're very safe, love.'

Jonathan swept Jessie up into his arms, hugged her, let go with one arm and put it around his wife. He held wife and daughter tightly and closely, and they both saw that his eyes were cloudy and moist.

Jessie gulped.

'Daddy?'

'That old Henrietta,' said Jonathan, 'she were nearly as big as a bus herself.'

'Boots, you really think Coates will make an offer?' said Polly over supper.

'I think so,' said Boots.

'After they've recovered from your suggested figure of £200,000?' said Polly. 'That's if you need to drop the bombshell.'

'I think so,' said Boots.

'Some hopes, Dad,' said James. He and Gemma both knew something about the family business. Gemma, in fact, had said she'd go in for modelling the firm's fashion designs when she was old enough. All fashion designers used models to show off their clothes, she said, didn't Uncle Sammy know that? Boots said yes, but thanked her for her reminder.

'What d'you mean, some hopes?' asked Gemma of her brother.

'No-one could recover from being asked for that amount,' said James. 'It could even bring on heart failure.' James was adept at putting words together, which trait Gemma referred to as showing off.

'Oh, I think the firm of Coates is made of stern stuff,' said Polly.

'We're not selling out, in any case,' said Boots.

'Thank goodness for that,' said Gemma. 'Mind, if you did sell for thousands and thousands, Daddy, how much would I get?'

'How much?' said Boots.

'Discuss,' said Polly.

'What, now?' said James.

'No, not now,' said Polly. 'When it happens, if it ever does.'

'I don't mind it not happening,' said Gemma. 'I mean, I don't want my chance of being a fashion model to die before it's even been born.'

'You've got to be tall to be a fashion model,' said James.

'Well, I'm going to grow,' said Gemma. 'It comes naturally, growing.'

'Of course, you could be stretched,' said James.

'What, on the rack?' said Gemma.

'Well, Uncle Sammy knows a lot of useful people,' said James, 'and he could even know someone who'll sell him a rack that stretches but doesn't hurt.'

'You'll come to a dotty end one day,' said Gemma darkly.

'What happens, Boots old thing,' said Polly, 'if Coates go dotty and actually agree to your asking price?'

'We'll recommend an asylum with a sympathetic staff,' said Boots. 'No, whatever, it won't alter our decision not to sell. Now, who wants second helpings of Flossie's bread and butter pudding while it's still hot?'

'Not me,' said Gemma. 'Oh, wait a bit, though, I think I will have seconds, Daddy.'

'Tomorrow,' said James, 'I think I'll ask Flossie if her bread and butter pudding helps to stretch girls.'

And what was Gemma's response to that?

A giggle.

Gemma could take a joke.

Chapter Thirteen

Boots drove Polly to the offices the next morning. She climbed the stairs with him to say hello to Sammy and Rachel. Sammy told her about the crazed bus driver who had given Emma, Patsy and their children the fright of their lives yesterday. He'd had the story from Daniel only five minutes ago, and was about to tell Boots. Polly, aghast, looked in on Daniel, who shared an office with her stepson Tim. Daniel assured her that Patsy and the kids had recovered, but were off bus rides for the time being. Polly offered every kind of commiseration, then said she would tell Boots to phone Emma and find out how she and her children were.

'Yes, do that, Mama,' said Tim, which Polly did and then left to walk to the premises of the photographer a few doors down. Her friend, Mrs Anneliese Stevens, was picking her up there at nine thirty. They were going shopping up in town, and among their purchases would be new baby clothes for Anneliese's one-year-old infant son, Harry. At her insistence the child had been named after its father, whom she considered the kindest man ever born, in total contrast to those she knew to be unforgivably monstrous. Himmler's SS. Anneliese, once a German army nurse, had witnessed unimaginable cruelty on the Russian Front.

Polly entered the premises and admitted herself into the poky office through its open door. The photographer was absent, so she pressed the button of the bell fixed to the desk. Its ring brought the photographer out of his darkroom and into the office via an inner door. He was fortyish, had a mop of curly black hair and a very appealing smile. Polly knew him. He had once taken a portrait photograph of her for her late father, and of her father and stepmother for herself.

'Well, hello, Mrs Adams,' said Amos Anderson, 'good morning to you.'

'Good morning,' smiled Polly, 'I want to make an appointment for my son and daughter. A portrait photograph of them together. Say sometime next week, before their summer holidays come to an end, if you can fit them in?'

'Sometime next week you want?' said Amos, and opened up his appointments book. He studied it. 'Sometime next week I can do, can't I? Wednesday, at two thirty in the afternoon, how is that, Mrs Adams?'

'Fine,' said Polly, and made a note in her

pocket diary. 'I'll see you then, Mr Anderson, with my children.'

'A pleasure, won't it be?' smiled Amos.

'I hope so,' said Polly. 'Thank you, Mr Anderson. Goodbye.'

Leaving his office, she walked to the front door. The time was coming up to nine thirty. As she reached the door it was pushed open and she came face to face with a good-looking young man and a handsome young woman.

'Oh, so sorry, madam,' said the young man, his accent American, and he stepped aside to allow Polly to pass him. She took another look at him, and noted his polite smile while being conscious that the young woman's expression was stony.

'Thank you,' she said, and emerged onto the pavement. By the kerbside was a car, Anneliese at the wheel. She waved, and Polly entered the car, slipping with silky grace into the passenger seat.

'I've just arrived,' said Anneliese, 'so we are well met, Polly. And I am very free. Harry and Cindy are looking after my little one.' Cindy was her stepdaughter. 'Polly?' Boots's elegant wife, still a fashion plate, was sitting in silence.

'I think,' said Polly, 'I think I've just seen a face I know, but can't put a name to.'

'It was an unpleasant face?' said Anneliese, blonde and smiling.

'On the contrary,' said Polly. 'It was the face of a good-looking, dark young man. Well, I fancy the name will come to me eventually, so let the horses rip, Anneliese, and we'll sample the delights of the West End shops.'

'And have lunch before we return?' said Anneliese, setting the family's Austin car in motion. She and Polly were the closest of friends. She thought they each had the kind of husband most women could only dream about.

'Yes, we'll have lunch,' said Polly, settling down.

The car travelled the same route as yesterday's careering bus, but at the modest speed required by reason of the traffic. Anneliese drove through the green lights of the Camberwell Green junction, and headed for the Elephant and Castle and Westminster Bridge via Camberwell Road and Walworth Road. She loved the West End of London, now recovering well from the prolonged and austere consequences of a hugely expensive war, and she was becoming fond of her adopted country. Germany no longer had any appeal for her, although she admired the people of West Germany for the way they had rebuilt their devastated cities and their ruined economy. She little knew that Boots's stepfather, Sir Edwin Finch, was German-born, and Sir Edwin certainly had no intention of telling her.

Polly asked how Harry was. Anneliese said he had just completed his second novel, a thriller like the first. It was now in the hands of his agent, and he was waiting for her opinion. The sales of the first book had been good rather than exciting, but the advance and royalties had put enough money into his bank to make him feel reasonably happy. Further, his publishers had encouraged him to write the second thriller.

'He deserves encouragement, Polly.'

'My dear,' said Polly, 'deserving husbands cause us to wonder how deserving we are ourselves, a condition that puts us at a disadvantage. I avoid being at a disadvantage with Boots. Much better for me to always be one up on the old soldier.'

'In my case, it's my old sailor,' smiled Anneliese, travelling in the wake of a laden bus. Harry had served in the Royal Navy.

'No difference,' said Polly, as they passed the East Street market, 'they all wear trousers.'

'Heavens,' said Anneliese, whose English was perfect, if touched with a faint accent, 'don't tell me you've come to the end of your best time with Boots.'

'End? My dear woman,' said Polly, 'I've known that man of mine for thirty-six years, and if I could have my married life with him all over again, I'd start on the waking moments of our wedding day. I adore the old darling.' She laughed. 'That's disadvantage enough, in the nicest way, of course – oh, pull up, Anneliese, I'm seeing someone I know.'

'Someone whose face you can put a name to?' said Anneliese, and brought the car to a stop. Polly wound her window down and called.

'Cassie?'

Cassie Brown, waiting to cross the road to her home in Wansey Street, was carrying a shopping bag. She turned her head, saw the car a few yards away, and spotted Polly's gesturing hand. Up she came.

'Gracious goodness, hello, Polly, where you off to?'

'The West End, with Anneliese Stevens,' said Polly.

Cassie, who had met Anneliese and her husband at Boots's rousing birthday party, dipped her head, smiled at Anneliese and said hello.

'Hello too,' said Anneliese, returning the smile.

'Wasn't it a gorgeous party?' said Cassie. 'Freddy said all that champagne kept making him go pop all day Saturday in the store. Oh, he told me about Emma and Patsy having a terrible journey on a bus that finished up on the pavement by the Elephant and Castle. Are they and their children all right, Polly?'

'Apparently,' said Polly, with traffic passing by, 'but a dreadful experience for them. How are your children, Cassie?'

'Oh, fine,' said Cassie, 'except while Lewis is sort of level-headed, Maureen's kind of up in the air. She wants to be a pin-up, would you believe.'

'Must I believe?' asked Polly.

'That's what me old dad says,' smiled Cassie.

'Can anybody believe it he says. But it's a fact, Maureen's going to be photographed with hopes of seeing herself in the *Daily Mirror*.'

'Great balls of fire,' said Polly, 'don't let Grandma Finch know, or she'll want Boots to blow up the paper's printing works. Oh, well, life's still fun, Cassie, for us and the young. Happy to have seen you, love to Freddy. Bye.'

'Bye, Polly, tell Boots how much we enjoyed his party,' said Cassie. 'Bye,' she said to Anneliese, who gave her a parting smile. Cassie, watching the car move off, thought Polly was still ever so vital. And blessed if she won't be sixty herself later this month. Imagine her saying don't tell Grandma Finch about Maureen being in the *Daily Mirror*, or she'd get Boots to blow the paper up.

Laughing to herself, Cassie crossed the road and carried her shopping home.

'Now,' said Amos, 'do we like that or don't we?'

He and Leila regarded Wilhelm with mutual interest. Wilhelm was sporting a little pointed black beard and a black moustache, with pince-nez spectacles. The combined adornments gave the young man the spruce professional look of a doctor.

'What I cannot see is a representative of a fashion house,' said Leila.

'It's the glasses, they are too fussy,' said Amos. 'Fussy we don't want.'

'You supplied them,' said Leila.

'It was a thought,' said Amos. 'Let Wilhelm take them off.'

Wilhem took them off. Immediately, he looked more the part. Further, the hirsute pieces changed his normal appearance very effectively.

'Better, much better,' said Amos.

'I agree,' said Leila.

'You do?' said Wilhelm. 'Break open a bottle, Amos, the lady agrees.'

'Agreement is good,' said Amos.

'Disagreement we don't want, eh?' said Wilhelm, taking off Amos, and looked in surprise at Leila. There was actually a faint smile softening her face.

'What's causing that?' he asked.

'Sometimes idiots are amusing,' she said.

'Shall I take the photographs now?' suggested Amos. 'I have a sitter in half an hour.'

Wilhelm and Leila followed him into his studio. His camera was set up, and he did not take long to photograph them in plain passport fashion. When did they wish to collect them? Leila said she understood he always fixed them to the passports, that it was a job for professionals, not amateurs at home.

'So I'll bring the passports when I receive them from Stargazer,' said Leila. 'Wilhelm can remain under cover.'

'I hear you, Indian Moon,' said Wilhelm.

'Clown,' said Leila, but not unkindly.

'My God,' said Wilhelm, as they moved back into the office, 'what I'd give for being able to take a simple walk around the shops would make a Brooklyn down-and-out rich for the rest of his life.'

Leila pointed to Amos's soft trilby hat. As usual it was covering the phone.

'If you will lend that to Wilhelm, Mr Anderson,' she said, 'I will let him have his walk. He can wear it well turned down.'

'My hat he wants?' smiled Amos. 'It is his for as long as he wishes, isn't it? What is a hat when I have others?'

Five minutes later, with the brim of his hat pulled well down over his forehead, and the wrapped beard and moustache in Leila's handbag, Wilhelm began his walk around the shops of Camberwell Green. Leila accompanied him. He said she need not, that she could trust him to get back to the house before lunchtime. Leila reminded him she was not going to trust anyone outside of her fellow agents until he was safe in Israel. Also, she was as much in need of some exercise and fresh air as he was.

'OK, guardian, be my guest,' said Wilhelm.

'Don't strain my good nature,' said Leila.

'Strain it?' said Wilhelm, happy to be out and about among the people. 'I'm only too pleased to know you've got some – no, I shouldn't have said that. Sorry. You're doing a great job on my account, and I mean that. I guess being on the run for such a hell of a long time is finally shredding my nerves.'

'Cool down,' said Leila, 'you're doing a great job yourself. We'll get you there.'

'That,' said Wilhelm, 'is what keeps me going.'

They walked, they strolled, they stopped to look in shop windows, and when they reached a fruiterers, Wilhelm went in. Leila stayed outside, keeping watch. She did not want him to step out into the path of a patrolling policeman. In this populated area, one man was just another among crowds, unnoticeable unless he was wearing or doing something absurd. A policeman was different. No-one could be certain he did not have an image of a wanted man in his mind. She knew Wilhelm Kleibert's public execution of an Auschwitz doctor had attracted worldwide attention, and that America was still after him. The hunt might not have been so persistent if there'd been proof that the victim really had carried out inhuman experiments on children at Auschwitz. But that proof could only have been established at a trial, which Wilhelm so far had escaped. Leila had no doubt that the FBI's agents in Britain, France and other European countries were still on the lookout for him. Perhaps, she surmised, it was more to do with establishing the facts about the murdered man in court than with conducting a heavy prosecution of Wilhelm, who commanded any amount of sympathy in the

West. Nevertheless, she intended to keep risks to a minimum.

Out of the shop came Wilhelm, a brown paper bag containing a bunch of black grapes in each hand. He gave one bag to Leila.

'Grapes,' he said.

'To carry back to Mrs Wirthe?'

'No, to eat while we're walking.'

'And what do we do with the pips?'

'I'll eat mine with the grapes,' said Wilhelm. 'You can spit yours out, if you wish.'

'On the sidewalk?' said Leila. 'How disgusting.'

'Not nearly as disgusting as what was done at Auschwitz,' said Wilhelm.

'Of course, yes, you are right,' said Leila. 'Well, grapes are refreshing and I will eat mine, and the pips.' She looked at him. He was already enjoying his fruit. 'That hat suits you,' she said.

'So does yours,' said Wilhelm. She was wearing a navy blue beret with a plain but quite smart beige dress. 'I guess I mean it suits you.'

'I am not mad about fancy hats,' said Leila, as they resumed their leisurely exercise.

'Fancy hats we don't want, eh?' said Wilhelm, taking off Amos again, and once more Leila surprised him, this time by emitting a little laugh, even if it did sound like a cough with a bit of a gurgle to it.

They went along, two people among busy shoppers, each holding a bag of grapes and eating the fruit, grinding the pips to destruction with strong molars and swallowing them. Wilhelm said this part of London was hardly like New York's Broadway. Leila responded that he was far less at risk here than in any part of New York. Here, in fact, they were two thousand miles nearer Israel.

When they had gone some way along Camberwell Road, they turned back and began to retrace their steps. A uniformed policeman appeared, a solid figure of the law, deliberate in his steps as he came towards them. He eyed them. Too keenly, thought Leila. His observation of Wilhelm alarmed her. Nor did she like the way he transferred his searching gaze to the young man's bag of grapes. Did he think there was a gun in it?

Wilhelm, the idiot, spoke.

'Would you like a grape, officer?' he said, and Leila could only hope his Americanized speech would disguise the fact he'd been born a German Jew. He'd been accepted as an immigrant in 1947, along with other young concentration camp survivors.

'Well, don't mind if I do, sir,' said the constable, and Wilhelm put his hand in the bag, broke off a sprig from the bunch and handed it to the law. 'A nice day for a grape or two,' said the law. The day was warm, although the sky was full of floating white clouds. 'Where you from, sir?'

'Canada,' said Wilhelm. 'We're staying with relatives here.'

'You don't say,' said the constable, eating a couple of grapes. 'I've got relatives in Canada. An aunt and uncle in Vancouver. Emigrated in the Thirties. Would you know Vancouver?'

'Sure,' said Wilhelm, 'but we've never been there, we're from Toronto.'

'Well, have a nice time, sir,' said the constable, giving Leila a smile and a nod as he resumed his beat. He hollered at a boy who had just discarded an empty sweets bag.

'That was dangerous, opening your mouth,' said Leila.

'He'd have thought it suspicious if I'd kept it shut,' said Wilhelm.

Leila said she meant he shouldn't have started a conversation, so Wilhelm said he thought the guy was going to start asking questions. Leila mused on that, and decided this resolute survivor of Auschwitz had an inherited intelligence, except it had deserted him when he shot the SS doctor in broad daylight. He should have contrived the execution at night, and then disappeared into the darkness.

'Well, yes, I understand,' she said, 'perhaps it was more natural to say something.'

'Leila, I think you're human, after all,' said Wilhelm.

'Of all things, I dislike being patronized,' said Leila.

'Well, can I patronize you by buying you a coffee?' asked Wilhelm.

'I would not dislike that,' said Leila, 'but find a cafe where you don't have to take your hat off.'

'Sure,' said Wilhelm, 'no hat we don't want, eh?'

The little smile ghosted over Leila's face again.

Chapter Fourteen

They found a cafe in Camberwell Road, where Wilhelm kept the hat on, their conversation was murmured and minimal, and the Italian coffee good. London had proved a safe and promising haven for many one-time soldiers of Mussolini's armies with a penchant for running the kind of cafes the citizens liked, which mostly meant no spaghetti, thanks, mate.

When Leila and Wilhelm eventually left, they began to walk to the enclosed green at the junction. Almost at once, Leila slipped an arm around Wilhelm's left elbow and even lightly rested her head on his shoulder, so that they were sauntering like lovers.

'What's this for?' he asked.

'For showing we are lovers who have no worries,' whispered Leila, as an approaching old lady gave them a smile. It was the smile of old age remembering young days. 'That policeman is behind us.'

'Well, cuss it,' breathed Wilhelm, 'is he following us or there by accident?'

'Walk on,' whispered Leila, keeping lovingly close.

They walked on. They reached the inviting oasis of Camberwell Green, turned and sauntered through the open gate. The policeman kept straight on. Leila breathed with deep relief.

'I guess I like that cop,' said Wilhelm. 'Yup, and I think I've heard about the good old London bobbies.'

'We're at risk,' said Leila, 'so spare me more jokes.' Usually cool and controlled, the gradual onset of nerves these last few days was irritating her. Worrying her. But her fixed determination to get herself and Wilhelm aboard a plane for Nice was unwavering. This young man deserved the safe and protective haven of Israel, his natural home. Her natural home.

'I've a feeling,' said Wilhelm.

'What feeling?' Leila was no longer close to him.

'That luck's walking with us.'

'My God, we need it to be,' said Leila.

'Perhaps it's you,' said Wilhelm.

'What do you mean?'

'Perhaps you're Lady Luck,' said Wilhelm.

'Why do you say such silly things?' Leila was a practical woman, a first-class agent, who considered sentiment or gallantries totally irrelevant in a world in which Israel was still fighting to establish itself while almost fully ringed by hostile Arab nations. She was not asexual. She had a

146

healthy and normal body, and she also had a lover back in Tel Aviv. She allowed him to sleep with her occasionally, but she did not allow him to whisper absurdities into her ear or to think she was a marrying woman with a wish to raise a family. That was for other women. For herself, her ambition was to become Chief of Police or the top name in Mossad. 'Yes, why do you say such silly things?'

'I guess it's because I'm an idiot,' said Wilhelm.

Leila could hardly believe she wanted to laugh out loud. Life for Palestine Jews had always been far too serious for laughter, and it still was for them as citizens of Israel.

'Oh, well, perhaps you're not such an idiot as others,' she said.

It was gone twelve thirty by the time they arrived back at the home of Judith and Michal Wirthe. Judith at once asked them where they had been, since she'd begun to worry about what might have happened, that Wilhelm might have been recognized and arrested. Leila apologized, and Wilhelm explained. Judith said her nerves had taken a beating, but that she could understand their need for exercise and fresh air. However, if they intended to repeat such an outing, please to let her know beforehand.

'Yes, we'll do that, Judith, so sorry,' said Wilhelm.

'Yes, I am sorry too for worrying you,' said

Leila, realizing, as did Wilhelm, that trouble for the two of them could very well lead to consequent trouble for their hosts. She and Wilhelm were under strict orders from Mossad's chief London agent, Stargazer, to remain under cover except when vitally necessary.

'Well, it's all said and done now,' smiled Judith, 'and lunch is ready. Oh, have the photographs been taken?'

'Yes,' said Leila.

'Good,' said Judith, hoping that would mean the guests would soon be leaving.

'My son,' said Mr Greenberg to Michal, who was handing him money from a cash transaction, 'you are not a happy man.'

'Old one,' said Michal, 'I have a good wife and the prospects of being a father. I also have a good job in our new business. So I should not be happy?'

'But I've seen you arrive for your vork vith a look not happy,' said Mr Greenberg kindly. 'Is it that your friends ain't too friendly?'

'My life,' said Michal, 'would Judith have them in the house if they weren't?' The truth was, of course, that the visitors were putting a strain on himself, and on Judith in particular. The woman, Leila, had no social graces, and was interested only in her work for Mossad.

'Vell, my good son, I believe you,' said Mr Greenberg, 'but I am here and vill alvays listen if you vish to talk to me.'

148

'Who better to talk to than you, old wise man?' said Michal. He smiled and went back to his work.

Over lunch in the select atmosphere of Fortnum and Mason's restaurant, something returned to Polly's mind.

The face of the dark young man at the door of Amos Anderson's premises.

She was sure it was familiar to her. Not in an important way, or she would doubtless have immediately identified him. Perhaps she had at least met him under interesting circumstances, since that would explain why he was on her mind. Perhaps at one of her stepmother's charity functions, although they weren't always vitally interesting. One met many people on those occasions, but never saw them again. Anyway, she could still not put a name to the dark young man, or recall when it was she had met him. She supposed she had met him, sometime or other.

'Two pennies for your thoughts, Polly?' said Anneliese, her summer hat fetching enough for Ascot, never mind the West End.

'Two?' smiled Polly, her own hat delightful. Some women were beginning to dispense with any kind of hat, but that would have disqualified them from entering the Ascot enclosure, or the West End's more exclusive restaurants. Of course, London's fish and chip shops welcomed any old hat or none at all. 'Hardly worth one, my dear, let alone two. Allow me the pleasure of paying the bill.'

'No, no, it's my turn, I'm sure,' said Anneliese, whose frequent trips to the West End with Polly gave her immense pleasure. She had much in common with Boots's aristocratic wife, for she came of an aristocratic family herself. The fact that Polly could be very down-to-earth only entranced her. That trait, of course, came from Polly's time as an ambulance driver in the First World War. Polly, indeed, when provoked enough, could swear as profoundly as any bitter Tommy of the trenches. But then, so could the country's leading blue bloods. 'Yes, I will settle, Polly.'

'You are providing the buggy ride,' said Polly. 'Therefore, ducky, I'll provide the wherewithal for the lunch. Only fair, you know.'

'This is a happy argument,' smiled Anneliese.

'A discussion,' said Polly, lightly lifting a hand.

'A discussion, yes, of course,' said Anneliese. 'Very civilized, Polly.' And very English, she thought, as the head waiter arrived with the bill. Polly settled and included a handsome tip. 'I'm thinking perhaps we should each buy a jar of caviare on our way out,' said Anneliese. 'As a special treat for Harry and Boots.'

'Dear girl,' said Polly, as they came to their feet, 'Boots considers caviare highly overrated. He much prefers fresh oysters, swallowed with

Guinness, a frightful gourmet punishment to which my late papa introduced him in 1950.'

Anneliese's blue eyes sparkled.

'Ah, so?' she said. 'Is that why he looks so virile?'

'Looks can be deceptive,' said Polly, as they left the restaurant.

'But not in all cases?' said Anneliese.

'No, not in all cases,' said Polly, thinking of her years of sheer magic with Boots.

They picked up their shopping, and in the store Anneliese did stop to buy a jar of caviare for Harry. The assistant was serving a tall gentleman in a fine-tailored Savile Row suit of charcoal grey, with a black homburg. His features were clean-cut. Chiselled, the English would have said. Impressively handsome and fit, he looked to be in his early forties. Anneliese, glancing at him, glanced again, in a much more positive way. Her spine turned icy.

She knew him, and she knew she was not mistaken. She recognized him as Colonel Neumann, commander of a disintegrating group of Waffen SS troops, who, during the pell-mell and disorganized German retreat in March 1945, had used his men to shoot hundreds of Russian prisoners and scarecrow refugees on the elementary grounds that they were in the way. From a vehicle belonging to her retreating medical unit, she had seen him shoot desperate and starving refugees himself. Colonel Neumann

151

then, and Colonel Neumann now, represented to Anneliese all the horror and cruelty unleashed by Himmler, Hitler and Goering, all that had made her weep and despair for a Germany she had once loved.

She watched him now while his order was made up and packaged, and she listened as, in polished English, he instructed the assistant to debit his account.

'Sir?'

'Professor Knox.'

'Yes, of course, Professor. Thank you.'

He left, carrying his purchase, and Anneliese's spine thawed a little, but her request for a jar of the best caviare sounded slightly strained. Polly, waiting, decided to buy Boots a jar of delicious preserved ginger. She did so, and she and Anneliese left the store together. They stepped into an afternoon bright beneath large patches of blue sky and rolling white clouds.

'Anneliese,' said Polly, 'what happened at the counter?'

'My God,' breathed Anneliese, her footsteps quick and angry, 'that man.'

'Handsome enough,' said Polly.

'Yes, as handsome as the devil himself,' said Anneliese. 'I cannot believe how many have escaped the courts of justice. That one, yes, that one, I saw him murder starving refugees fleeing from the Russians. I saw him shoot them in cold blood and without a quiver, or a prayer for his soul. I know him, even though he was unshaven and had a bearded growth when I saw him. I know his name, his real name. Colonel Neumann of the Waffen SS. And now he is living here, in London, and posing as a Professor Knox. What is he a professor of? Death?'

'Anneliese, calm yourself,' said Polly.

'Because of the German Nazis, I would like to have been born English, as my grandmother was,' said Anneliese, 'but I can't be English, not today, not now. I can't be calm, I can't be calm, cool and collected, as you English say. I practised years of being that for the benefit of hideously wounded soldiers, not wishing them to know I knew they were going to die.'

'You can be calm now, and you will,' said Polly. Then, 'Oh, very well, ducky, let storm and tempest rage. Who cares that we're in the middle of the pomp and circumstance of Piccadilly? On the other hand, dear girl, I think we should talk about this in the car.'

Anneliese drew a long breath and eased her angry stride. A faint smile broke through.

'Polly, you are so typically British, and perhaps many foreigners would think you absurd and even arrogant,' she said, 'but I know you better. Yes, let's talk in the car.'

It was parked in Duke Street, and as soon as both women, and their parcels, were in the car Anneliese drove away, heading for White-hall and Westminster Bridge. Traffic was thick until she crossed the bridge, when she then spoke.

'I'm furious that that man has escaped hanging.'

Polly was well aware that this German woman was totally unforgiving of the countless Nazis who had brought her country to destruction and shame, to render it unspeakable in the eyes of the world.

'What are you going to do?' she asked.

'What should I do?'

'You could run to the police, but that would involve you in a hundred interviews and questions,' said Polly. 'You've a small child, a stepdaughter and a husband taking up your care and time. So let me speak to Boots. He has a way of solving problems.'

'Would you do that for me, Polly, speak to Boots?'

'Happily,' said Polly. 'How strange that you should see a face you recognized and could put a name to, while I saw a face this morning that I'm sure I know, but simply can't put a name to. Heigh-ho, such is life. Drive on, ducky.'

When Anneliese brought the car to a stop outside Polly's house in East Dulwich Grove, she said, 'I'm sorry I was so angry.'

'My dear, you had a right to be,' said Polly, 'although it's the first time I've seen you in a temper. Tim always insists you were the coolest

154

woman ever during the time you nursed him as a wounded prisoner of war.'

'I had to be.' Anneliese smiled. 'Otherwise, he would have cracked me wide open. Already, at that time, early in 1942, I was doubting my faith in Hitler, and I think Tim suspected it.'

'Water under the bridge, Anneliese,' said Polly, slipping out of the car.

Anneliese leaned.

'Polly,' she said, 'you are the loveliest kind of friend I could ever wish for.'

'Oh, when you see me indulging in a fit of storm and tempest myself, you'll change your mind,' said Polly. 'Pip-pip, old thing.'

Pip-pip? What did that mean? Some kind of goodbye, supposed Anneliese, not knowing only one-time flappers would have used it, and not many of them these days. Certainly not those approaching sixty. Polly was unique, still a flapper at heart in Boots's opinion.

'Goodbye, Polly.' Anneliese waved and drove away.

Chapter Fifteen

On arrival home, Boots found Polly in the living room, waiting to switch on the television set to catch the six o'clock news. Flossie was in the kitchen, preparing supper, and the twins were sitting in the garden, enjoying an unusually civilized talk about their recent holiday in Cornwall.

Boots was carrying an evening paper, which he tossed onto the settee. Polly was relaxing at one end, legs curled up under her like those of a lithe young woman. Her knees, nylon-clad, peeped like shining round caps. They might have been bony by now, but they weren't, and her legs were still shapely and slender.

'Hello, darling,' she said as he bent and kissed her. Even now, she still offered her lips to her husband, not her cheek.

'Had an economical day, shopping?' said Boots.

'Are you kidding?' said Polly. 'You throw economy out with the cat when you shop in the

West End. Otherwise, you might as well patronize Petticoat Lane. Uneconomically, I treated myself to some exquisite new lingerie. Uneconomically means fantastically expensive.'

'Age, I suppose, has nothing to do with adorning your well-preserved self in a fantastically expensive way,' said Boots.

'Absolutely not,' said Polly. 'My well-preserved self is my own work and deserves Bond Street adornment. I still have a figure, you know.'

'Have I seen it lately?' mused Boots.

'Think of my dignity,' said Polly. 'I never asked for it, it's a sign of wanting to be respected, and having bus drivers call me madam. I prefer them to call me love or dearie. But there you are, old fruit, dignity has crept up on me and I can't flaunt myself without a blush.'

'A blush?' said Boots.

'An old lady's blush,' said Polly.

'That,' said Boots, 'I can't wait to see.'

'You'll be lucky,' said Polly. 'Listen, dear man, I've something to tell you about Anneliese.'

'Fire away,' said Boots, and Polly told him of Anneliese recognizing an ex-Waffen SS officer in Fortnum and Mason's store, and how it opened up old wounds for her. What should she do that would still enable her to live her happy-ever-after life with her family?

'I'll think about it,' said Boots.

'Seriously?'

'Seriously,' said Boots.

'There's a good old sport,' said Polly. 'Sit, and we'll watch the news together.' She moved his evening paper, and as she did so she saw a photograph on the front page of Prime Minister Anthony Eden, the man who, with his Cabinet, had to decide whether or not to allow Egypt's nationalization of the Suez Canal to stand. The Prime Minister looked dark and handsome.

It came to her then, the reason why she was sure the face of the dark young man at the photographer's door was familiar to her. Of course, she had seen it in a newspaper, with a report of how the young man, a Jewish survivor of Auschwitz, had escaped custody while awaiting trial in New York for the murder of a Dr Rokovsky. Dr Rokovsky, a brilliant ophthalmic surgeon, purporting to be a Ukrainian immigrant, had been due to examine Felicity's blind eyes with a view to a possible operation. The escape of the young Jew had happened well over a year ago, since when it seemed he had disappeared from the face of the earth.

This was something else to tell Boots, and she did so while he was helping himself to his usual pre-supper whisky and mixing her a gin and tonic.

'Are you dreaming, Polly?' he asked, handing her the gin and tonic. 'It's certainly the stuff of dreams.'

'What is?'

'The suggestion that on the same day you

could have seen the executioner of a man he claimed to be an ex-SS doctor, and Anneliese could have seen a man she claims was an ex-Waffen SS officer. Well, is it possible, Polly?'

'Possible, you old doubter?' said Polly. 'It happened.'

'That's what I call the coincidence of a lifetime,' said Boots, enjoying his finger of Scotch.

'You can call it once upon a time there was an elephant with wings, if you like,' said Polly. 'I know Anneliese saw a Nazi fiend she recognized, and I know I saw Wilhelm Kleibert. Yes, that's his name.'

They heard Flossie calling Gemma and James in for supper. And they heard her next call.

'Supper's ready for the table, Mrs Adams. Coo-ee!'

'Coming, Flossie,' sang Polly.

'Polly,' said Boots, 'do we want to go after a young man who came out alive from Auschwitz, caught up with a hellish SS doctor and sent him to join Himmler and the other mad dogs?'

'You clever old Chinaman,' said Polly, coming to her feet, 'of course we don't. Aren't you a walking Solomon? Now I'll enjoy my supper. Oh, by the way, James received a picture postcard by the late post this morning. He showed it to me when I arrived home from town. It's a postcard of the Folies-Bergère. From Cathy Davidson, the saucy minx.'

Boots laughed.

'Now I'll enjoy my supper, too,' he said.

Over supper, of course, he put a question to his youthful, growing son.

'James old chap, is it true you've had a post-card from Cathy today?'

'Not half he hasn't,' said Gemma. 'It's my belief she's got a whacky crush on him. And you ought to see the picture, Daddy. It's of dancing girls showing their undies.'

'Yes, it's sort of classical,' said James.

'Some hopes,' said Gemma. 'Sexy, you mean.'

'Classically French,' said James.

'I wonder the postman was allowed to deliver it,' said Gemma.

'Might I remind you that at Dad's party your dress was mostly up in the air?' said James. 'And that you were showing your frillies?'

Gemma blushed a little, thought a little, and came up with a triumphant riposte.

'Still, I haven't been sent through the post on a card,' she said.

'You certainly haven't,' said Polly, 'and you certainly never will. Dear, dear, what was I doing in allowing your father's big day to turn into a spectacle of saucy minxes?'

'Just like the days when you and the flappers in frilly garters were doing the charleston, Mum,' said James.

'Heavens,' said Polly, 'what have I done that

my own son should let me down in such a way?'

'James,' said Boots, keeping his face straight, 'let me inform you that your mother has recently acquired dignity and should therefore be respected.'

'Eh?' said James, a forked lump of baked parsnip halting halfway to his mouth.

'Dignity?' said Gemma through chewed parsnip. 'I blessed well hope not. Old Mrs Wooderson's got dignity and it makes her blow her blouse out. Daddy, I won't know where to look if Mum's dignity does that to her blouses. I mean, what a giggle, and you can't respect a giggle.'

'I think the answer's a lemon,' said Boots.

'No, I think dignity would suit Mum,' said James, 'especially at Sunday church, Dad, or when you both come to the school on speech days. I'd expect some of the fellers would ask who that dignified lady was, and I'd be able to say she's my noble mother. Imagine that.'

'If I could imagine it,' said Gemma, 'I'd fall off my chair.'

Polly laughed. The two of them, Gemma and James. In their capacity for being comical, each was an Adams more than a Simms, although happily enough, there was some of her father's resolution about James. He was resolute when up against the odds in sport, and just as much in a crisis.

'If that's all over,' smiled Boots, 'could I hear what Cathy said on the postcard, James?'

'You won't like it, Daddy,' murmured Gemma.

'Well, Dad,' said James, 'she hoped I was in good health, and remaining faithful to her. Oh, yes, and would I like to spend Christmas in Paris with her and her mum. That was all.'

'That was enough,' said Gemma. 'It made Mum quiver all over and say shocking things. It was like – ' Gemma paused for a giggle. 'Like she'd lost her dignity.'

'I'll fight any Christmas trip to Paris,' said Polly determinedly.

'It's Cathy's soppy crush on James,' said Gemma.

'It'll be last year all over again, when her mother had a crush on your father,' said Polly. 'We had to lock him away from her, you remember. If James goes to Paris, there'll be no-one there to lock him away from Cathy. So Paris is out, James, out, and kindly understand that out out is final and absolutely definite.'

'Oh, righty-oh, Mum,' said James, 'I'll stay home and respect your dignity. It won't cost me any pain. Could I ask what's for afters?'

'One of Flossie's creamy rice puddings,' said Polly.

'Great,' said James. 'Give Gemma two helpings, Dad, and let's all watch it stretch her a bit.'

'Daddy, it's time your son got with it,' said Gemma.

'Right, James, get with it,' said Boots, 'fetch the rice pudding.'

Later that evening, Boots thought about phoning his stepfather. But Sir Edwin was close to eighty-three now, and not quite as brisk as he had been. Would he want to be involved? Boots supposed he could still effect contact with British Intelligence, with whom his reputation, built up over many years, would always mean something special. But he was living a very quiet life these days.

So Boots phoned Lizzy's son Bobby instead.

'That's you, old soldier?' said Bobby. 'I'm honoured.'

'You will be when the Foreign Office recommends your elevation to the peerage as Lord Somers of Camberwell Green,' said Boots.

'In which case, I'll get to be known as Lord Mouthful,' said Bobby, 'but thankfully and confidently I can state I'll never be in the running. Your flattering suggestion tells me you want something.'

'Just a talk,' said Boots. 'I'll drop in on you on my way to the office in the morning. Say at eight thirty.'

Bobby said that since he would be leaving for town at his usual time of eight fifteen, would it do for Boots to talk to Helene instead? Helene, he said, would undoubtedly be delighted, and probably receive her favourite English uncle in her best French two-piece. Boots said he didn't doubt that Helene in that get-up would be delightful to talk to, but it was Bobby's ears he was after, not Helene's.

'It's going to be a confidential chat?' said Bobby.

'An interesting one, I promise you,' said Boots.

Bobby said in that case he would opt for being late at the office, which wouldn't matter too much since he wasn't yet head of his department, just another cog a little higher up in the wheel. Boots said he'd been a cog in various wheels himself during his lifetime, but there were no scars.

'You're a one-off,' said Bobby. 'Fair enough, I'll expect you at half eight tomorrow morning, then.'

'Much obliged,' said Boots.

To pass the evening in an entertaining way, Michal and Judith were playing Monopoly with Wilhelm and Leila. Leila was hardly a light-hearted conversationalist, since she was always inclined to dwell in serious vein on the struggles of the Israelis in founding their State and stabilizing it in the face of Arab hostility. Michal and Judith accepted it was a serious matter to her, but too much of it dulled one's ears. And Wilhelm only sighed each time Leila began another dissertation.

So this evening, Michal had contrived for all of

them to sit around the living-room card table and seek their fortunes at Monopoly. He joked that it had its appeal to all the children of Moses. It was, however, very much a game of chance that always became a contest for possession of the Mayfair and Park Lane properties. Once they were both in one player's hands, the end was inevitable.

Leila said there was not enough skill involved, that a superior brain was no more necessary than an inferior one. Judith said that that was the fun of the game. Leila said that life in Israel was not a game, nor was it fun for many of its citizens. She said that at the moment when her throw of the dice landed her symbol on Piccadilly, owned by Judith with a complement of houses. Judith asked for rent payment.

'There, you see,' said Leila, 'it's all silly chance.'

'Yes,' said Wilhelm with a wide grin, 'that's the fun of it.'

Quite a happy moment arrived then.

Leila laughed. And she paid up.

'Now I am almost broke,' she said.

'That's serious,' said Michal.

'Oh, well, it is only a game,' said Leila. 'Who will lend me a thousand pounds?'

'A thousand?' said Judith.

'Yes,' said Leila, 'just for the fun of it.'

It could be said then that little gusts of laughter ran around the table, like titters round a court.

This encouraged Michal to call a temporary halt to the game while he uncorked a bottle of wine.

When the game was resumed, four glasses of wine gleamed redly in the light.

'Here's your thousand, Leila,' said Wilhelm, who was doing exceptionally well.

'Ah, thank you,' said Leila.

'At twenty per cent interest,' said Wilhelm.

'Twenty per cent?' said Leila. 'Twenty per cent?'

'Sure,' said Wilhelm. He smiled. 'Just for the fun of it.'

Leila actually laughed again, and for the first time since the arrival of the Mossad agent and her charge, a sociable element made its welcome entrance.

In his well-appointed ground-floor Mayfair apartment, the man calling himself Professor Knox, a practitioner of psychiatry mainly for the benefit of wealthy women with emotional problems, slept the sleep of the just.

Such a sleep was not difficult to come by for any man who had no conscience.

Not that anyone had ever pointed a finger at Professor Knox. Since his arrival from Communist East Germany in 1946, with documents recording his anti-Nazi activities during the war, and a certificate of his professional qualifications, he had quickly found his niche, in the form of consulting rooms in Mayfair Close. Adjoining these were his living quarters.

He was excellent as a psychiatrist.

Well, so thought most of his women patients.

Professor Knox also did other work quite unrelated to psychiatry.

Chapter Sixteen

The following morning, at the open door of a house in Thurlow Park Road, West Dulwich, two people met.

'Ah, how nice,' smiled Helene, splendidly French in a dark blue shirt-blouse, open at the neck, and a summery white skirt. Thirty-four, she had reached the stage of being handsome. 'Come in, come in.'

Boots stepped in.

'Apologies, Helene, for intruding at this time of the day,' he said.

Helene turned her cheek and he kissed her. She surveyed his tall, long-legged frame clad in a fine summer-weight grey suit. Conservative he might be in his choice of clothes, but then, she did not think him a man for outlandish or popular garb. He was at his best as a well-dressed and distinguished figure. She always thought of him as an English gentleman of instant masculine appeal. Had she delivered that opinion into his ear, Boots would have considered her slightly off her Gallic chump. However, as a farmer's daughter, she had never been greatly impressed by the outward charm of Parisian men, noted for the art of seduction. Husband Bobby had come into her life as a rugged, breezy and infuriatingly obstinate British soldier during the Dunkirk evacuation in 1940, and turned her existence upside down. She belaboured him with words, all of which bounced off him. So, of course, she fell in love and told herself she was mad to do so, for the man was an idiot and made terrible jokes.

'No apologies, *chéri*,' she said. 'Always, at any time, it's good to see you. Bobby will be with you any moment. But first come and say hello to the children, yes?'

'Kids are my weakness,' said Boots, and followed her into the kitchen where Bobby, on his feet, was washing his last mouthful of toast down with his last gulp of coffee, and his son and daughter were sitting at the table.

'Hi, pickles,' said Boots, adaptable enough to use the modern vernacular.

'Hi, Uncle Boots!' shouted nine-year-old Estelle and seven-year-old Robert. The boy, at Helene's wish, had been named after Boots, the girl after Helene's mother.

'Hi!' shouted Robert, as an encore.

'Who's shouting?' asked Helene.

'I am!' shouted Robert.

'He is,' said Estelle. 'He's hardly ever quiet, Uncle Boots.'

'We've all got problems,' said Boots.

'Well, Helene will look after ours,' said Bobby, 'so come on, Boots, let's talk.'

Helene shook her head. To call one's uncle by his nickname was not what happened in France. Good family manners prevailed there in that respect. But most of Boots's nieces and nephews addressed him by his nickname. So unconventional.

But rather nice, in a way.

In his downstairs study, Bobby listened as Boots outlined the story given to him by Polly.

'Familiar bells are ringing,' said Bobby.

'How familiar?' asked Boots.

'Well, old soldier,' said Bobby, 'nearly everyone in London claims to have seen a dodgy German war criminal working as a waiter or a doorman or doctor. Or whatever. But most are walking about with Mexican moustaches in Argentina or Peru, or some other place as far away from Europe as they can get.'

'That's from the horse's mouth?' said Boots.

'It's from Intelligence, and that's not a horse, it's a mine of reliable information,' said Bobby. 'Some horses are duds. Of course, it's nothing to do with the Foreign Office, but little titbits are sometimes picked up over lunch at a club, and such titbits are passed to the right quarter. However, are you sure Anneliese was positive in her identification of this professor?'

'I'm not sure myself,' said Boots, 'but Polly

is. She's convinced that Anneliese made no mistake.'

'About this bloke being responsible for murdering refugees?'

'Apparently,' said Boots.

'Of course, if I could claim diplomatic immunity I could hunt the bugger down and chop his head off myself,' said Bobby.

Boots said that that was perhaps excessive, and unlikely to meet with the approval of Grandma Finch, who was against anyone in the family using a chopper, except to chop wood. Why not simply use his position as a Foreign Office official to see that the information reached a friend in MI5?

'That seems the obvious thing to me, Bobby.'

'I thought you'd come to that,' said Bobby, 'but if Anneliese is wrong, I'll have soft-boiled egg all over my face.'

'I see your point,' said Boots, 'Anneliese could be wrong. But she could also be right. Polly and I would simply like to save her having to go to Scotland Yard, which I fancy she would do, if there was no alternative. I suggest we do our best to help her live a quiet life after all she went through during the war.'

'Fair enough, Boots old chap,' said Bobby. 'I'll have lunch with somebody.'

'Leave it to you, then,' said Boots. He returned to the kitchen, said goodbye to Helene, gave her children ten bob each for holiday pocket money, and departed for his office.

171

'What did he want?' asked Helene, as she saw Bobby to the front door.

'A favour,' said Bobby.

'What kind of favour?'

'The loan of one of my bowler hats,' said Bobby.

'Ah, very funny.'

'I'll tell you tonight,' said Bobby. 'Right now I must get off to the asylum.'

'Ah, yes?' said Helene. 'Please to remember not to send all the other inmates mad with your terrible jokes.'

But she was silently laughing as she watched him begin his short walk to West Dulwich railway station, his Foreign Office bowler hat at a jaunty angle.

Bobby did not have lunch with somebody. He made a phone call. The impersonal person at the other end became less impersonal.

'Interesting, very. Do you know the lady well?'

'Well enough.'

'And she's German herself?'

'She served as a German army nurse and one of her patients during the desert campaign was a wounded British prisoner of war, who happens to be my cousin.'

'Interesting, very.'

'You've already said that.'

'I'll see a doctor about it. The lady's reliable?'

'As reliable as my grandmother, and there's no-one more so.'

'I see. Well, I suppose we could find out if there's a file on Professor Cox – '

'Knox.'

'Knox, yes. We'll look into it.'

'I'll leave it with you, then.'

'It seems worth a look.'

'Yes,' said Bobby, 'interesting, very.'

That evening, he phoned Boots and told him that action was under way. Boots said he was much obliged. Bobby said he only hoped the investigation wouldn't put Whitehall on a false trail. Boots said if it led to a cold kipper, Polly would be very surprised, since she was sure Anneliese had uncovered a hot potato.

'Your metaphors slay me,' said Bobby.

'You're welcome,' said Boots, 'and I'm still much obliged.'

'Pleasure, old soldier,' said Bobby, who then put Helene in the picture.

Helene visibly swelled with temper.

'Kill that German swine,' she hissed.

'Steady,' said Bobby.

'Men like that! Not just murderers, but cold-blooded sadists, and every one of them should die a lingering death!' Helene's wrath was in full flow. 'Do you know they made slave labourers of thousands of Frenchmen, and sent thousands of French Jews to the gas chambers? How glad I am that Anneliese has recognized one of Himmler's butchers. When will you arrest him?'

'Personally?' said Bobby.

'Why not? I know that in this country there is such a thing as a citizen's arrest.'

'Would you mind if I left his arrest to the authorities?' said Bobby.

'To men in bowler hats?' said Helene.

'Does it matter what kind of hats they wear?' asked Bobby.

'Not if they can take action instead of filling in forms,' said Helene, firm bosom calming down a little. 'It is the same in Paris. Hundreds of government officials filling in forms all day every day, even officials of the Sûreté. I know. My father tells me so in his letters. And yes, even as a farmer, he now has to fill in forms.'

'Well, my French lily,' said Bobby, 'I'll do what I can to expedite action and cut out the paperwork. Not that I can do much. I'm a Foreign Office body of diplomatic charm, not the active head of the Home Office.'

'Ah, but you will do something, eh, *chéri*?' said Helene. 'Think of poor Anneliese, memories of terrible war crimes brought back to her, and she the one German we can all like. That man must be hanged. Slowly.'

'If he's guilty,' said Bobby, 'he'll almost certainly be sent back to West Germany for trial.'

'But the Germans will only give him a few years

in prison, as they have with other war criminals,' said Helene. 'You must arrange his assassination before he leaves this country, yes, you must.'

Bobby said he thought that was a bit out of his league. Helene said no, not at all, that he and she had been happily responsible for acts of sabotage that had blown up Nazis during their time with the French Resistance. Blow this man up, she said.

'I can't do it now,' said Bobby, 'it's time for supper.'

Helene gave him a look. A bit of a critical look. But it resulted in a smile.

'Ah, you are still a clown, Bobby,' she said, 'but a better man than a thousand professors.'

'A thousand?' said Bobby. 'You're sure that's not an exaggeration?'

'The next time we all go to France to stay with my parents,' said Helene, 'you and my father can talk to each other all day about forms.'

'Exciting,' said Bobby, 'can't wait.'

'Mummy!' Estelle called from the kitchen. 'The cooker's smoking!'

'Oh, my grilled tomatoes!' gasped Helene, and dashed.

The supper was served without grilled, peppered tomatoes. No-one ever had to eat burnt offerings in a household where the cooking was undertaken by a French mother. On the other hand, there was sometimes a little resistance to the introduction of garlic. A soupçon was all

175

right, but no more than that. More was antisocial. Estelle averred that it made schoolfriends reluctant to sit next to her in class. So usually, Helene introduced only a soupçon.

Anneliese, having been informed by Boots that action was being taken, also served a supper with no burnt offerings, and did so with relief. She was sure she wouldn't rest until the man who called himself Professor Knox had paid for his atrocious crimes. Too few of such monsters had suffered the extreme penalty, and others, who had been sentenced to long terms of imprisonment in West Germany, had been released after serving only five years, which angered Anneliese. Her husband, Harry, asked her a pertinent question. If Professor Knox was caught and extradited, would she be willing to go to West Germany and testify for the prosecution? Anneliese replied that she was willing to do that and to watch the man being hanged.

The next day, Mr Humphrey Travers of the Foreign Office called Bobby into his sedate-looking office. Sedate was the word for everything about Her Majesty's Foreign Office, especially its officials. Temperamental reactions to pressing affairs were frowned on and discouraged.

'Ah, my dear Somers,' said Mr Travers.

'Good morning,' said Bobby, sedate in his dark grey suit.

'Um – I understand someone has been talking to someone else,' said Mr Travers.

'Is that so?' said Bobby. 'What about?'

'I have no details, only a whisper,' said Mr Travers. 'However, a name was dropped.'

'That can be worrying, a dropped name,' said Bobby.

'Knox, I think,' said Mr Travers, 'a Professor Knox.'

'Well, of all things, someone dropped his name into my ear too,' said Bobby.

'Dear me,' said Mr Travers. 'Well, do keep him out of the Foreign Office, there's a good fellow.'

'He's not our problem, of course,' said Bobby.

'Quite so,' said Mr Travers. 'Mmm, does it amuse you?'

Bobby, guilty of letting a smile show, said, 'Not in the least. I was simply thinking of something my wife said to me last night.'

Mr Travers showed a small smile himself.

'Thoughts of domestic conversations are allowed,' he said.

Probably not when they take in a wife's demand for her husband to do an assassination job, reflected Bobby.

Somehow, nothing very much escaped old Humph, but Helene's demand should be an exception.

Chapter Seventeen

'What's that?' asked Cassie Brown of her daughter Maureen, when the ambitious young lady arrived home from her dull old insurance job that evening. She had a white carrier bag with her.

'It's me new dress,' said Maureen, looking as pretty as any girl next door in a thin summer sweater of a golden hue and a swirly-whirly flared skirt of royal blue patterned with yellow daisies.

'Another one?' said Cassie. 'You've already had about six new dresses this year. I don't know, the money you spend on them, and not saving a penny.'

'Mum, I don't have to start putting pennies away for me old age yet,' said Maureen, and took the new dress from the shop's carrier bag. She unfolded it and draped it over her blouse and skirt. It was a delightful turquoise blue with a fashionable flared skirt and a pinched waist. 'It's groovy, don't you think?'

'Me and your dad don't exactly know what

groovy means,' said Cassie, 'but is it for when you have your photograph taken on Saturday?'

'You bet,' said Maureen. 'Mr Anderson said the one I was wearing would do, but I couldn't resist this.'

'Well, it's lovely, I must say,' murmured Cassie, 'but is it a bit short?'

'It's not long,' said Maureen.

'There, it is a bit short,' said Cassie.

'Mum, it's inches below the knee, actually,' said Maureen. 'You can't get anything shorter than that.'

'Oh, and you'd like to, would you?' said Cassie.

'Well, I'm supposed to show me legs for the photos,' said Maureen.

'You'd better make sure you wear the right kind of stockings,' said Cassie.

'Oh, I'll wear me sheer navy blue nylons,' said Maureen. 'They're really special.'

In came Lewis.

'What's that blue stuff?' he asked.

'It's your sister's new dress that she's going to wear when she's photographed on Saturday,' said Cassie, 'so don't start being cheeky.'

'What's wrong with any of her other dresses?' asked Lewis, helping himself to an apple. Biting off a lump, he chewed and said through juicy remnants, 'She hasn't given 'em to Mrs Hobday's cat, has she? It'll eat anything, Mrs Hobday's cat, did you know that?'

'Crikey, there's hope yet,' said Maureen.

'Hope for what?' asked Cassie.

'That Mrs Hobday's cat'll make a meal of me daft brother one day,' said Maureen.

Lewis grinned and bit off another chunk of ripe apple. One a day polished up his teeth. Two a day livened up his tonsils.

'Did you buy that dress at Dad's store?' he asked.

'No, I didn't,' said Maureen.

'You'd have got a discount,' said Lewis.

'But I wouldn't have got this dress,' said Maureen.

'What's special?' asked Lewis. 'It looks like any old dress to me.'

'Lewis, didn't I tell you not to be cheeky?' said Cassie.

'Don't take any notice, Mum,' said Maureen, 'sense never comes out of boys with wooden heads. Crikey, Lewis, imagine you going all through life with a head that's only good for knocking nails in.'

'I don't fancy that,' said Lewis, making short crunching work of his apple core, pips as well.

'I shouldn't think you would, you'd end up with a head looking like a pincushion,' said Maureen, and went up to her room to try the dress on, to swirl about in front of her mirror, and to study the effect.

Then she sat on the edge of the bed and thought of the kind of poses that would make her look like the girl next door to the readers of the *Daily Mirror*.'

Downstairs, waiting for Freddy to get home before she put supper on the table, Cassie listened to Lewis saying that Maureen's chance of having her photograph printed in any newspaper was about one in five million.

Cassie asked where he got the figure of five million from. Out of his wooden head? She asked that with a laugh.

'Oh, it's me estimate of how many girls next door there are in the country,' said Lewis.

'Five million,' said Cassie.

'Well, there's Wales and Scotland as well as England,' said Lewis, as he heard the key turn in the front door to signal the arrival home of his good old dad. 'And the Isle of Wight too,' he said as a worldly afterthought.

'Well, we mustn't leave that out,' said Cassie, 'there must be at least a hundred girls living next door to people on the Isle of Wight.'

Lewis grinned. There were no flies on his mum. Nor were there on Mrs Hobday's cat. It could always track down who'd had kippers for breakfast, and get at the bones and tails before all disappeared into dustbins. Come to that, Lewis reckoned that one day it would work out how to get the lid off any kind of dustbin.

'Mrs Hobday, your cat's eating a skinned rabbit on top of your backyard wall.'

'Is it? Oh, well – 'ere, wait a bit, I bought a rabbit for me and me old man's supper tonight. Don't tell me that Pussy's eating our supper.'

'I just think you might have to make do with cheese sandwiches, Mrs Hobday.'

'Blessed if I won't drown that cat in the river one day, young Lewis.'

'You sure, Mrs Hobday? Only it wouldn't surprise me if it could swim.'

Mrs Hobday's cat was a feature of life in Wansey Street, Walworth.

You could ask anybody.

Or young Lewis Brown.

Jimmy Adams, twenty-six-year-old younger son of Susie and Sammy, left the Bethnal Green factory at the end of his day's work as personnel manager, which was some job these days. The factory not only manufactured garments, it also produced its own fabrics. The all-in staff numbered nearly three hundred. Order books were full for finished items, which included Sammy's bête noire. Jeans. Which the factory manufactured under licence, and which he considered responsible for taking skirts off girls and women, in a manner of speaking. Jeans were for sweating cowboys, skirts for feminine females. Jeans, he once said, made some women's bottoms look like pumpkins struggling to get out in time for Hallowe'en. However, he was able to put up with his bête noire (which he called his own white man's burden), on account of the fact that orders were rampant and profits ascending. Even so, the sight of family members wearing jeans made him sigh.

Jimmy began to motor home to Bow, where he lived with his young wife Clare, granddaughter of Bert and Gertie Roper, once prime factory stalwarts and now retired. Clare was not only an exciting wife, she was also a good cook and a very promising gardener. Their own vegetables were gracing the supper table these days.

'Look, all my own work, Jimmy.'

'With a little help from a friend.'

'What friend?'

'Me.'

'Oh, you're not a friend, Jimmy, you're my wedding present.'

Driving along Roman Road, Jimmy slowed for a left turn into a minor road that would take him in the direction of Victoria Park, close to his home. A large car, coming up behind him, gave him a shove that accelerated his turn and made a mess of his bumper. He hollered, stopped and turned his head. He saw the car, a gleaming black Austin Princess limousine, speed on. He took its number, RK 1234. He stopped a little way into the minor road, got out, examined his rear bumper, saw the savage dent, got back in and drove on. He stopped again, this time at the Bow Street police station, where he reported the incident to the desk sergeant.

'Your name, sir?'

'Jimmy Adams.' Jimmy also gave his address and phone number.

'The driver didn't stop, Mr Adams?'

'No, he bloody didn't,' said Jimmy, 'and it's upset my good nature.'

'Did you get his number, sir?'

'You bet I did. RK 1234.'

The sergeant's shrewd eyes showed a distinct gleam as he took note.

'RK 1234, right. Any witnesses, Mr Adams?'

'If there were, they'd all gone by the time I got out to inspect the damage. What I'm livid about is that he didn't attempt to stop or even say beg pardon, mate. I'm not in favour of bad manners. I want an apology from the cowboy and a promise to pay for repairs.'

'What was the time of the incident, sir?' The sergeant seemed extra keen about details.

'Ten minutes ago,' said Jimmy.

The sergeant checked the station clock. Five thirty-five. Jimmy had left the factory at ten past, motoring through the rush hour.

'Right, we'll say between five twenty and five twenty-five,' said the sergeant. 'Would that be right?'

'As near as you could get,' said Jimmy.

The sergeant studied his notes.

'Got him this time,' he murmured.

'What's that?' asked Jimmy.

'What? Oh, just a hope we can nail him for

leaving the scene of an accident – in fact, for causing it and failing to stop.'

'I'll leave it with you, sergeant,' said Jimmy.

'We'll be in touch, sir.'

'Good,' said Jimmy, 'I'm off now for a helping of home cooking. Thanks for your time and attention.'

'Oh, Jimmy, what a rotter, not stopping,' said Clare, twenty years old and looking fetchingly domestic in a pretty apron.

Jimmy said very unfortunately not every bloke was Christian-minded, that there were always some who were a bit heathen. However, on this occasion the coppers were bound to nail the creep, since they had the number of his car. Clare asked her legal love if he was hurt. No, said Jimmy, but our Ford bumper's had a painful time.

'Anyway, what's for supper, Clare?'

'Lamb's liver, bacon, tomatoes, mash and runner beans, Jimmy love.'

'Good-oh, that'll help me forget our groaning bumper.'

Two police constables, one a woman, called on Jimmy at eight thirty that evening. Jimmy expected to be informed that the driver of the Austin Princess had been charged.

Instead, PC Randolph said, 'About the incident, sir, can you say if there were any witnesses?'

'Look,' said Jimmy, 'I told your desk sergeant that if there were, they were gone by the time I pulled up.'

'H'm,' said Constable Randolph, looking disappointed.

'What's the problem?' asked Jimmy.

'My husband took the car number,' said Clare.

'Well, Mrs Adams,' said WPC Sarah Musgrove, 'we're up against the owner's insistence that at the time stated, his chauffeur was in charge of the car and waiting to drive him home from the Kempton Park racecourse.'

'Eh?' said Jimmy.

'Oh, yes, a likely story, I don't think,' said Clare, who hadn't been born yesterday. 'In his dreams, more like.'

PC Randolph coughed. WPC Musgrove looked sympathetic.

'What we have to tell you, Mr Adams,' said the former, 'is that Mr Rudy Karpenter – '

'Hold on,' said Jimmy, 'isn't he a dodgy club owner?'

'Yes, with his older brother Rafael,' said WPC Musgrove.

'I've heard some funny stories about that pair,' said Jimmy.

'Yes, and so's my granddad,' said Clare.

'Funny peculiar stories,' said Jimmy. 'Listen, I made no mistake about the car, a black Austin Princess, number RK 1234. He can't have witnesses to say he didn't barge my rear, because he kept driving on.'

'He's produced witnesses confirming he was at Kempton Park racecourse all afternoon and didn't leave till six o'clock,' said PC Randolph.

'Oh, that's a fact, is it?' said Jimmy. 'Well, tell me another, a really funny one this time.'

'What it comes down to, sir,' said WPC Musgrove, 'is that it's your word against his, and his is supported by witnesses. It's a shame, sir, that you don't have any.'

'I tell you what I have got,' said Jimmy, 'a rising temperature likely to boil over any minute. Stand well back. No, come on, you know the bloke's having you on. Jump him.'

'We'd like to,' said PC Randolph, 'but – '

'We can only go by the book, sir,' said WPC Musgrove, 'which means we've got to have enough evidence to charge Mr Karpenter.' Her sympathy was still showing.

'It'll be disgusting if that man gets away with all them lies,' said Clare, 'especially as my husband's as honest and upright as me dad and me grandad.'

'I'm sure,' said PC Randolph. 'We can't do any more ourselves at the moment, but you could see your solicitor, Mr Adams.'

'I'll think about that, you bet I will,' said Jimmy, and saw the constables out. They said goodbye and wished him luck. Jimmy, rejoining Clare, grimaced and said, 'Lucky we had supper before this happened, Pussycat, I wouldn't have enjoyed it like I did.'

'Oh, I feel for you, Jimmy, love,' said Clare, 'let's have a pot of tea and some of me fruit cake.'

'Spoken like a winner,' said Jimmy. 'Like Grandmother Finch, in fact, and she's been a winner all her life.'

First thing on his arrival at the factory the next morning, he spoke to his Uncle Tommy, general manager of the whole works. He told him about the incident, and that he was thinking of seeing a solicitor.

Tommy, frowning, said, 'It'll cost you, Jimmy, and that's all it'll do. Those witnesses, take it from me, will stand up in court and swear their heads off in favour of Rudy Whatsit.'

'You're saying I should leave it?' said Jimmy.

'That's it, Jimmy, leave it,' said Tommy. 'I ain't ever been in favour of backing off from trouble, but in a case like this, it's what I'm advising. And I'm pretty sure your Uncle Boots would agree.'

'Would he?' asked Jimmy.

'Try the wise old owl,' said Tommy.

'I'll phone him at the morning break,' said Jimmy.

Which he did.

Boots, having listened to the tale of an honest nephew up against a character of highly dubious references, suggested that if said character had had any sense, he'd have stopped, apologized and offered to pay for the damage, thus avoiding any police investigation. But said character, brother of the same kind, preferred to exercise muscle and influence. So Jimmy would be better off claiming on his insurance for the cost of repairing the bumper, or the fitting of a new one, rather than tangling with the Kings elect of the East End.

'Kings elect?' said Jimmy.

'Read the papers, Jimmy.'

'Well, I'll take your advice, Boots,' said Jimmy, 'but it's going to gall me.'

'Better than getting mixed up with any East End heavies, Jimmy old lad,' said Boots. 'Live a quiet life with Clare, and give her my love.'

'That'll make her day,' said Jimmy. 'I suppose you know that Clare, Patsy, Leah and Phoebe all think you've still got sex appeal?'

'Just a wild notion, Jimmy, but I'll investigate it with Polly's help.'

That left Jimmy laughing.

In the evening, Clare served up a delicious supper to console him for losing out to the East End heavies.

Chapter Eighteen

Friday, mid morning.

In her house in Poplar Walk, Boots's daughter-in-law, Felicity, felt the walls of her lounge were closing in on her. She had a thumping headache, the kind that suggested a rubber-cushioned hammer was delivering blows to her skull, particularly her forehead. She rarely had headaches, and certainly never one like this, except during the few days immediately following the bomb blast that had blinded her.

She was sick with pain now, and at the end of her tether. For the last three weeks there hadn't been a single one of those heartening intervals when sight returned for the space of a minute or so, albeit blurred. For three weeks she had been as blind as a bat, and that seemed to have led to this sickening headache. Her fortitude and resilience were draining away, and she felt she could burst into tears. That would be a weakness hard to bear.

'Mrs Adams? Mum?'

Felicity, resting along the settee, opened her closed eyes. She saw nothing, of course, but the lifting of her lids was involuntary.

'Maggie?'

Maggie Forbes, her live-in cook and house-maid, so invaluable to her, said gently, 'Isn't your head no better, mum?'

'It's bloody worse,' said Felicity in a rush of bitterness.

'Well, I've brought you a Beecham's powder mixed with water,' said Maggie, 'and you ought to drink it, it might help.'

'If there's arsenic in it, that would be all the help I want,' breathed Felicity.

'Lord, mum, don't say things like that,' said Maggie.

'Haven't I already had a Beecham's?' said Felicity, every word dragging.

'That was two hours ago, just after breakfast,' said Maggie. 'Come on, mum, drink this one.'

Felicity sat up, Maggie put the glass in her hand, and she drank the mixture, gagging on it a little. She sank back again, and Maggie took the glass from her.

'Thanks, Maggie.'

'You rest there nice and quiet, mum,' said Maggie, 'I won't be doing no noisy hoovering.' She tiptoed from the room, closing the door quietly, and feeling for her mistress's suffering. Daughter Jennifer was out with a friend, and Mr Adams was at work. Just as well, thought Maggie, it kept the house nice and quiet, and that was what Mrs Adams needed just now, quiet.

Miraculously, Felicity dropped off to sleep. It was two hours before she awoke at twelve thirty.

Relief flooded through her. The hammer had stopped its thumping, the headache gone. Completely. She moved her legs, slowly at first, just in case the hammer returned. Then she put her feet to the floor and stood up. No headache, no hammer. Wonderful. She heard voices at the front gate. The lounge overlooked the gate and the road. The voices were high and girlish, and she recognized that which belonged to Jennifer. A parting of the ways followed.

'Bye, Carol.'

'Bye, Jennifer.'

Moments later came the sound of a turning key in the front door and the advent of Maggie from the kitchen.

'Hello, Maggie, I'm back. Is Mummy's headache better?'

'Oh, we hope so, don't we? She's resting nice and quiet in the lounge, and asleep when I peeped in half an hour ago.'

'Let's peep in now.'

The door was pushed open, and Jennifer quietly entered. Eleven years old, she was dressed in a simple gingham frock of green and white check, her hair a thick, healthy dark brown, her body slender. She saw her mother standing beside the settee.

'That's you, Jennifer?'

'Yes, it's me, Mummy. Are you better?'

'Darling, I'm so much better that let's all go shopping this afternoon, shall we?'

'Oh, whizz-oh, Mums.'

Maggie appeared. She asked Felicity if she really was better, and, on receiving a definite affirmative, said it just might be all right, then, to go shopping later.

It was about four o'clock when Felicity, up in the bedroom on the return from shopping and the walk in the open air, felt light strike her eyes, the light from the sunlit window. She caught her breath, and the light opened up the little world of her immediate surroundings. There, through the window, was the clear sight of hedges, road, houses and a couple walking their dog. Felicity, eyes huge, stared. No moment had ever given her such a clear and sharp picture. Hazy or blurred visions were the usual thing.

This vision was unbelievable, this was what she had hoped for, what her specialist, Sir Charles Morgan, had said might happen. Tense with wonder, she stared almost greedily at the picture of the moving couple and their frisky dog. She stood there, mesmerized and lingering, watching as the couple moved in leisurely fashion out of her view. She heard the dog bark, and the sound was as much a part of these minutes as all she could see.

She wanted to turn and rush downstairs, to see her daughter for the very first time, but her feet seemed clamped to the floor. She made an effort. She turned, and the open door of the bedroom leapt to her sight. She heard Maggie and Jennifer talking downstairs. She activated her legs and moved.

It went then, that clear vision, it receded and died. For long seconds, she was sick with bitter disappointment. Then she remembered that Sir Charles had said any moments of clear sight might only be as temporary as the vague images. At the same time, he said, all such moments could be regarded as further steps and brighter steps on the road to complete recovery.

Felicity drew a breath, squared her shoulders in as firm a fashion as when she was a serving ATS officer, groped her way to the open door and made her way downstairs to tell Jennifer and Maggie of her long wonderful minutes of clear vision. Yes, long minutes.

'Bloody marvellous!' The exclamation mark put a dramatically emphatic finishing touch to Tim's heartfelt comment. He had just arrived home.

'Daddy, really,' said Jennifer, whose private schooling was making a young lady of her.

'Well, it is what I said,' insisted Tim, and took

Felicity into his arms. In the kitchen, in front of Jennifer and Maggie, he kissed his wife smack on her lips. 'You're a miracle, Puss.'

'Well, she will be, Mr Adams, if she gets her eyes back,' said Maggie.

'Oh, she always had her eyes, Maggie,' said Jennifer, 'it's her sight that's been missing.'

'Oh, go on, you know what I meant,' said Maggie.

Tim, hands resting lightly on Felicity's shoulders, looked into her misty if blind eyes and said, 'It's really true, Puss, you had long minutes of completely clear vision?'

'Joyful minutes,' said Felicity, emotional with hope and optimism. 'I could even make out that the couple's dog was a spaniel.'

'Maggie, where's the champagne?' asked Tim, high spirits at this moment on a par with his physical vitality, still in as good a condition as it had been during his war years as a commando. Felicity could write a commendable reference about that. In fact, male weaklings were absent from the Adams family. If one had shown up, she was sure Grandma Finch would have regarded the birth as highly suspect. 'Come on, Maggie,' said Tim again, 'where's the champagne?'

'Champagne?' said Maggie. 'Well, we bought groceries when we went shopping, but we didn't buy no champagne, Mr Adams.'

'Pity,' said Tim.

'We'll have a bottle of wine with supper,' said

Felicity. 'Or two, if you like. I'm game for a celebration.'

'Oh, help,' said Jennifer, 'it looks like someone's going to end up squiffy by bedtime.'

'I'll phone Sir Charles about this news,' said Tim, 'and if it does for him what it's doing for me, perhaps he'll tumble cross-eyed into bed himself.'

'Mr Adams,' giggled plump Maggie, 'ain't you a one?'

'Daddy's a sixer,' said Jennifer.

'Now what's a sixer, for goodness sake?' asked Maggie.

'A smash hit at cricket,' said Jennifer.

Sir Charles Morgan was delighted to hear the news, and he advised Tim to encourage Felicity to take such moments as natural and not to let her become overexcited.

But he didn't suggest he'd take steps to get himself squiffy.

The managing director of Coates, the big man himself, had been formally in touch with Sammy to say he would arrange a meeting of his board, at which he hoped Sammy and his directors would be present. Discussion on the assets of Adams Fashions could take place and a price for a full takeover agreed.

Sammy said to let him know the date, when he would then arrange for himself and the other directors, his brother Robert and Mrs Goodman, to attend. The managing director of Coates said excellent, Mr Adams, excellent.

Sammy could have said their attendence would only be a matter of courtesy, as recommended by Boots, but his good manners stopped him from chucking that banana into the arena.

He mentioned the matter to Susie during the evening. It was always a pleasure to talk business with Susie, she being a woman who had quite a bit of sense up top.

Susie said she couldn't think why a meeting with Coates was necessary, seeing any offer of theirs was going to be turned down. So Sammy, of course, referred her to the point made by Boots, that the meeting would just be a matter of courtesy.

'If I know Boots, he's laughing up his sleeve about everything,' said Susie.

'No, it's a serious point, Susie,' said Sammy, 'on account of not upsetting Coates by just saying no without a meeting, and having them stop all further contracts for supplies.'

'I bet Boots is still laughing up his sleeve,' said Susie. 'I mean, his idea of asking for £200,000, if that's not a big joke, what is?'

'He's still a wise old bloke, Susie.'

'Well, you're not far behind, Sammy love.'

'Granted, Susie, but I like you for saying so. Is that a new dress you're wearing?'

'Only something I bought from your Brixton shop six months ago,' said Susie, looking like Sammy's favourite female woman in emerald green.

'Thought it was new,' said Sammy.

'You're dreaming,' said Susie. 'By the way, Phoebe's a bit miffed that Philip hasn't been home on leave just lately.'

'I think his squadron must be doing a lot of practice flying,' said Sammy. 'I mean, they've always got to make sure they can get their planes off the ground. Still, Phoebe seemed all right at the office.' Phoebe, his adopted daughter, was nineteen and worked at the firm's offices as an assistant bookkeeper. She had a smart head for figures, and Sammy liked smart heads in the firm.

'Work stops her thinking about her disappointments,' said Susie.

'Listen, is she in love with Philip?' asked Sammy.

'Of course,' said Susie.

'She hasn't said anything to me,' said Sammy.

'And I don't suppose she's said anything to Philip, either,' said Susie. 'She's not the kind to admit her feelings unless Philip comes up with a ring.'

'Well, he's not twenty-one yet,' said Sammy.

'He's a fighter pilot,' said Susie, 'and if he's old enough for that, he's old enough to propose.'

'Perhaps he's shy,' said Sammy.

'Philip?' Susie laughed. 'Sammy, there's not a shy bone in any of you Adams men.'

'Philip's a Harrison,' said Sammy, who didn't actually believe that.

'Annabelle, his mother, is an Adams by her own mother,' said Susie.

'Our Lizzy? Well, I can't argue with that,' said Sammy. 'Tell you something, Susie.'

'What something?'

'I like your new dress,' said Sammy.

'Well, you don't say,' said Susie, who had been wearing it on and off for six months.

Later that evening, Leila and Wilhelm, in company with Judith and Michal, were watching the nine o'clock news on BBC TV. They were all interested in the coverage of the Middle East events, particularly items concerning Israel and Egypt. Egypt, at the moment, was Israel's most eloquent enemy.

As soon as the news switched to another matter, Leila, in Yiddish, made a fierce denunciation of all the Arab nations that were at Israel's throat. Michal and Judith refrained from commenting on the outburst.

Michal only said in deliberate English, 'I'd like to hear the cricket news.' The end of the bat and ball season was coming, but there were still some notable matches being played.

Leila stared at him in disgust.

'Cricket?' she said. 'Cricket?'

'Michal's a fan of cricket, and a Surrey supporter,' said Judith, while Wilhelm tried to hear what was being said about an investigation into a Soho murder. Police items always interested him.

'Cricket?' said Leila again, and in sheer disbelief. She rose abruptly to her feet and walked out, mounting the stairs to her room.

'Such a serious young woman,' murmured Judith, casting a sympathetic glance at Wilhelm.

'She feels for Israel,' he said, 'she feels it's still fighting for its life.'

'We should be unsympathetic?' said Michal. 'We aren't. In any case, Israel is already strong and well organized, and I'm frankly confident that if Egypt attacks, Israel will give Nasser a bloody nose.'

'Michal, my friend,' said Wilhelm, 'I'd like to be there when it happens, I sure would.'

'So would I, so would I,' said Michal, 'but I'm tied to the business.' He smiled, thinking of his watchful ageing stepfather, one of the old brigade of Jewish immigrants to Britain. 'Hand and foot.'

'Wilhelm, is the wait for your new papers trying your nerves to breaking point?' asked Judith. It's trying mine, she thought.

'I'll survive,' said Wilhelm.

'I'm sure you will,' said Michal, liking the young man for himself and for his valiant public execution of an ex-SS doctor. He had no doubt that Michal had known the true identity of the man.

When the report on the day's cricket began, Wilhelm went upstairs to talk to Leila. He recognized that the wait for papers and plane departures were putting a strain on the dedicated agent. He knocked on her door, opened it and put his head in.

'Leila – ' He checked. She was lying on her bed and looking as moody as hell. But her strong, firm legs were exposed, the white hem of her slip softening the dark look of her black skirt, which had ridden up. She lifted her head from the pillow.

'What the hell do you want?' She used Yiddish.

'Oh, just a friendly word or two,' said Wilhelm in English. 'I guess I'll look elsewhere.' He withdrew his head and made to close the door.

'Come back,' said Leila, reverting to English.

'Sure?' he said.

'Come back.'

Wilhelm stepped in, closed the door and said, 'We're both getting impatient.'

'I am not,' said Leila, 'I am used to waiting for the right moment, the safest moment. But those two, the Wirthe couple, how they irritate me. They are so complacent, so smug, so bourgeoise.'

'I don't agree,' said Wilhelm.

'Did you hear Michal talk of cricket? That silly English game, for God's sake.'

'I know nothing about cricket, but how do you rate baseball?'

'Baseball is just as silly and irrelevant.'

'To you, not to Americans. I quickly found that out.'

'Sit.' Leila patted the edge of the bed. 'Sit, and we can talk.'

'Cover your legs up,' said Wilhelm.

'My legs worry you?'

'Worry me? No.'

'What are you thinking about?'

'The plane that will take us to Nice.'

'Be patient. Sit.'

'No. I prefer the company of Judith and Michal. They are good people, worth more than your sulks and ingratitude.'

Leila sat up.

'My sulks? My ingratitude?'

'Yes,' said Wilhelm. 'It's no big deal, perhaps, but a little courtesy wouldn't be out of place. But don't think I don't understand. I guess it could happen to anybody, your kind of work making everything else look unimportant. You've forgotten that life can still be enjoyable. Try it sometime. Michal and Judith will help. I've been on the run for a year, but I've still had some enjoyable moments. Have a good night, Leila.'

Leila seethed as the door closed behind him.

When I land him in Israel, and the whole nation lines up to kiss him, she thought, I'll be the odd one out.

'How is she now?' asked Judith when Wilhelm reappeared.

'It's her work,' said Wilhelm, 'she can't think that anything else matters. I know she's a trial, but I'd like to ask you and Michal to be under-standing, and to thank you for your kindness in having us.'

'There's no problem, Wilhelm,' said Michal. 'Have you any idea when your contact will turn up with your new papers?'

'No idea at all,' said Wilhelm, 'and I guess Leila hasn't, either.'

'Well, let's all be patient,' said Judith.

It was the following morning when Jimmy, coming down to breakfast, took an early phone call. It was from Police Constable Randolph, who thought he would like to know that a dubious gent by the name of Rudy Karpenter, together with his brother Rafael, and members of their gang, had been caught red-handed last night while making a raid on a warehouse in the East London docks.

'Is this a fact?' asked Jimmy.

'It's a fact all right, Mr Adams. The warehouse, stacked with spirits, was half-empty when tipped-off CID men arrived, and the Karpenters' lorry half-full. We've got 'em for sure this time – apologies for phoning you this early, but thought you'd like to know, thought it might make up for you coming off worst in that car incident.'

'Not half,' said Jimmy. 'What a good bloke you are. Accept my thanks for letting me know, and best of luck to you.'

'You're welcome, sir.'

'I'm going to enjoy my breakfast cornflakes now,' said Jimmy, 'very much I am.'

And he did. So did Clare. The news, plus the fact that the insurance company had agreed to pay for their car repairs, put an intoxicating ingredient into their cereal, and when Jimmy went off to work he was rolling a bit.

Chapter Nineteen

Saturday afternoon, and Mr Amos Anderson, photographer, was showing a delighted smile.

'Blue on a summer day is good,' he said.

'D'you really like it?' asked Maureen, attired in her new creation, and sporting a stylish hair-do. She'd been at the hairdresser's during the morning.

Amos viewed her professionally. The dress was perfect, its flared skirt definitely feminine. And her make-up was excellent, favouring delicacy, not the bold. The bold was for tarty girls.

'I like it, don't I, Miss Brown?' he said.

'Maureen.'

'Well, Maureen, I'm ready to go, and so are you, don't I fancy?'

'I'm more than ready,' said Maureen, an excited young lady.

'My car's outside,' said Amos, wearing a brown and white check shirt, open-necked, and tan trousers. Maureen thought he looked just the job. 'So let's go.'

Five minutes later, on this balmy September day, they were heading south towards the Surrey countryside. Amos said he hoped to find a nice quiet spot and a farm gate, and a farmer who wouldn't sue them for trespassing.

'Oh, I'm going to pose on a gate?' said Maureen.

'Which is what we want, don't we?' said Amos. 'A girl next door out in the country on a summer day.'

'It's cloudy, though,' said Maureen.

'But the light is good and even,' said Amos, 'better than harsh sunshine and dark shadows. We'll find a spot, you bet.'

'Oh, I know a place we could use,' said Maureen. 'It's a poultry farm that belongs to someone me mum and dad have known for years. I was at a birthday party in July, for a relative of me dad's, a gorgeous bloke.' She was referring to Boots and his sixtieth. 'And I was talking to one of his daughters, the one me mum and dad know, who runs this farm with her husband. She told me where it was, the Surrey Poultry Farm in Woldingham.'

'Woldingham I know, don't I?' said Amos. 'For the gentry and their ladies, and no synagogue. Yes, I know it, Maureen, not half.'

'Oh, great,' said Maureen. 'Rosie – that's her name – told me I could come and see the farm whenever I liked. Let's go there now, I bet there'll be a field and a gate we can use.'

'She won't mind?' said Amos, deftly weaving the car through traffic heading for Croydon.

'No, course she won't,' said Maureen, 'she's a real doll.'

'Real dolls we like, eh?' smiled Amos.

'Mind, I think she's a bit over thirty,' said Maureen, which would have tickled Rosie at forty-one.

'We should worry about that?' said amiable Amos, a rakish peaked cap pulled over his barbered head of springy black hair. Amos was a likeable bloke, in appearance as well as personality. It earned him a steady flow of engagements and studio sitters. 'Real dolls a bit over thirty we still like, don't we?'

'Oh, you'll like Rosie,' said Maureen.

Rosie and husband Matthew, together with their cheerful West Indian helpers, Hortense and Joe, were in the large shed that stood on the edge of their main field, their farmhouse at their backs. Rosie was trim and elegant, even in her workaday smock, Matthew was lean and sinewy in shirt and corduroys, Hortense was buxom in apron, straining cotton shirt and long skirt, and Joe strong-shouldered and lanky, in dungarees.

They were all plucking chickens, and the floor was covered with feathers. They had a large order that had to be ready by Monday, so Rosie and Matt were giving their workers a hand. Hortense and Joe would dress the plucked fowls in the tiled scullery, a job Rosie happily delegated, and the birds would be placed in the scullery freezer until Monday morning.

The farm derived its income from the sale of dressed chickens, a multitude of fresh-laid eggs, chicks for raising as layers, and layers for households whose families wanted to keep chickens solely for the purpose of bringing their own 'home-grown' eggs to their tables. There was also an income from raising lambs for the market, since they had a flock of sheep which grazed their two large fields, and were served yearly by a hired ram.

When their intensive Saturday work was over, they would have Sunday free. Hortense and Joe, Bible-readers, would go to church. Not to their immediate local one, which was High Anglican, but to the Congregational Church in Caterham Valley. There, the atmosphere of reverence was less formal and the ornamentation simple. Matthew would drive them there and pick them up when the service was over. It was no more than a ten-minute journey.

The work of continuous plucking was hot, and lately Rosie had begun to wonder if this and other aspects of chicken farming were really what she wanted for the rest of her life. Coincidentally, a month ago, she and Matthew had received an offer for their holding from Sprowles, big in the poultry-farm industry. They had turned it down. However, she had brought the subject up again last week, and Matthew had suggested they could give the offer serious consideration, if that was what she would like. Rosie said she was at least prepared for a discussion, but asked what they would do if they sold. You could join the family firm, said Matthew, and I could run a set-up for the repair of cars. He was a top-class mechanical engineer with the highest qualifications. Rosie said well, then, they must think seriously about selling. The matter was on her mind now.

When the floor of the shed was beginning to look as if it was covered by a downy quilt, they heard a car enter the forecourt fronting the farmhouse.

'A customer?' said Matt.

'For a sackful of feathers?' said Rosie.

'Miz Chapman, ma'am, there ain't no-one gonna rid us of all these here in one sack,' said Hortense.

'The contractors will collect on Tuesday,' said Matt.

'By then, boss, us'll be standing knee-high in them,' said Joe.

A female voice reached their ears through the open door of the shed.

'Anyone home?'

'In here,' called Matt.

'Oh, goody.' The next moment Maureen appeared. 'Crikey,' she said, as she saw the multitude of feathers, a large crate containing freshly executed chickens, and a long steel-topped table

209

on which rested an extensive heap of naked fowls. 'Crikey,' she said again.

Rosie looked at the girl in the doorway, recognized her and said, 'Maureen? Well, you're a surprise. Have you come to help? Step in, then, take a seat and start plucking.'

'Me?' said Maureen.

'It's fowl work,' said Matt, his pun blatant, 'but we need an extra hand.'

'Oh, go on, Mr Chapman,' smiled Maureen. She had met Rosie's husband at Boots's special party. 'I wouldn't know where to start.' She eyed the West Indians with curiosity.

'Maureen, meet Hortense and Joe, our happy labour force,' said Rosie, wondering exactly why Cassie's daughter was here.

'Oh, hello,' said Maureen. West Indian immigrants weren't unknown to her. There were quite a few around Walworth and Camberwell. And Brixton.

'Pleasure,' beamed Hortense, fingers working rapidly on the feathers of a large, plump chicken.

'Sho' is a pleasure,' grinned Joe.

Matt, noticing how pretty Maureen looked in her blue frock and attractive hairdo, said, 'I don't think she's dressed for plucking chickens, Rosie.'

'Oh, put one of those aprons on, Maureen,' said Rosie, indicating several hanging on pegs. There was a teasing light in her blue eyes, since she was sure Maureen's reason for calling had nothing to do with helping to pluck chickens.

'Mrs Chapman,' said Maureen, not backward about coming forward, 'I hope you don't mind, but I've come to have me photograph taken.'

'Well, you look sweet enough,' said Rosie, 'but we don't do photography, we raise chickens and lambs.'

'No, I mean I've come with me photographer,' said Maureen, 'he's going to take photos of me for the *Daily Mirror*, and we thought – '

'Pardon?' said Rosie, a wayward feather lightly resting on her corn-coloured hair.

'Yes, honest,' said Maureen, 'and he wants to do them in the country, like here, and we thought you might let us go in your fields and do them there. He said getting chased off by farmers somewhere is what we don't want. He talks like that. Would you mind if we did the photos by one of your gates?'

'I wouldn't mind myself,' said Matt, 'and I'm sure Rosie wouldn't. And I don't think the sheep would object. Did you say the photos are for the *Daily Mirror*?'

'Yes, they print pin-ups,' said Maureen.

'Pin-ups?' said Rosie, and laughed.

'What might they be, Miz Chapman?' asked Hortense.

'Saucy,' said Rosie.

'Oh, my,' said Hortense.

'Mr Anderson – that's me photographer – says

211

he'll pose me as the girl next door,' smiled Maureen, not a bit self-conscious about all this.

Matt coughed, and a couple of floating feathers wavered and drifted slowly down to settle on the mass.

'The girl next door?' he said.

'Come to, Matt,' said Rosie, 'you've heard that phrase, haven't you?'

'So I have,' said Matt, 'and if I remember right, there was a girl next door to my family in my young days. There was a Dorset saying about her. Let's see, how did it go? "Down by Dorset land they tell, were a girl called Esmerelda, all round and fat she were, so her parents went and selled her."'

Maureen shrieked. Hortense giggled and Joe grinned all over. Rosie laughed.

'Matt, that's one of your worst,' she said.

'True, enough,' said Matt.

'True as the man in the moon,' said Rosie.

'Can I get Mr Anderson to meet you?' asked Maureen.

'Yes, let's have a look at the chap,' said Matt.

Maureen turned and called.

'Come on, Mr Anderson, come and meet me mum and dad's friends.'

Amos appeared. Over his right shoulder was a long leather strap, depending from which was his black leather bag containing his equipment. On his face was his friendly smile, which slightly slipped when he saw the feather-encrusted floor and four people, including two West Indians, all plucking chickens in mechanical fashion despite their interest in their visitors.

'Good afternoon,' said Amos, 'a fine day, eh? So sorry to interrupt you. I'm Amos Anderson, Camberwell Green photographer.'

'Welcome,' smiled Rosie, highly tickled.

'That's Mrs Rosie Chapman, and that's Mr Chapman,' said Maureen.

'Hello,' said Amos.

'And that's Joe and Hortense, their helpers,' said Maureen.

'Hi,' said Amos.

'Oh, and where are your son and daughter, Mrs Chapman, that I met at your dad's special birthday party?' asked Maureen.

'They disappeared into the wilds as soon as they suspected they might be dragged into this shed,' smiled Rosie.

'Kids, they know what they don't want, eh?' said Amos.

'Mr and Mrs Chapman said we can do the photos in their fields,' enthused Maureen, 'so come on, let's get started. Oh, thanks ever so much,' she said to Rosie, 'we didn't want to get to a place and have farmers' dogs chasing us off. See you all later.'

And with a saucy whisk of her flared dress, she disappeared, along with Amos.

Rosie looked at Matt.

'A pin-up for the *Daily Mirror*?' she said.

'Ought to be worth a look,' said Matt.

'Stay where you are,' said Rosie.

'That young lady, ain't she mighty pretty?' said Hortense, chicken feathers flying.

Matt, fishing one more dead fowl out of the crate, thought well, a lot prettier than this bird. Which thought made him dwell on Rosie's inclination to sell up. Well, perhaps they'd had their time as poultry farmers. His old affinity with the repair and maintenance of cars surfaced. He glanced at Rosie.

'Yes, Matt?' she said.

'There's more to life than feathers,' said Matt.

Rosie got the message, but only said, 'There are a few around today, old thing.'

It wouldn't do to discuss selling the farm in front of Hortense and Joe, their devoted and happy workers. In the event that they did decide to talk to Sprowles, they would want to make sure the prospective new owners kept the contented West Indians in their jobs.

Amos and Maureen passed the large wired enclosure protecting the commodious henhouse and a mass of fluffy yellow chicks, which were chirruping as they foraged in the earth for tiny insects. Out in the field, scores of fat Rhode Island Red fowls were darting, pecking and scratching in search of worms amid the dry summer grass.

'Well, look at all these,' said Maureen, 'there's hundreds.'

214

'Hundreds is good for your friends,' said Amos, 'one a fortnight is enough for me.'

'Well, if you ate one a day,' giggled Maureen, 'you'd grow more feathers than in that shed.'

'See, there's a gate,' said Amos.

Maureen saw it, at the far end of the long, wide field. Chickens squawked and scampered as she and Amos advanced, she with the eager step of a girl opting for a glamorous career. Perhaps she might even become a famous fashion model, like those whose photos were always in the papers, and in exclusive and glossy magazines such as *Vogue*.

Reaching the gate, they saw it opened onto a farm lane. But quiet was reigning, the lovely country quiet of the Surrey Hills. Woldingham itself was well above sea level, and much to Amos's professional satisfaction there was a natural breeze, a breeze already plucking at the skirt of Maureen's dress.

He unzipped his bag, took out his camera, already loaded, and his light meter. In the bag was a good supply of extra film. He stood back from the gate and measured the light reflected from Maureen and her dress.

'Stand there, Maureen, that's it, against the gate – no, wait, give us your handbag,' he said. 'Handbags we don't want. They're not what we call photogenic, unless you're modelling one for a manufacturer's mail-order catalogue.'

Maureen passed him her handbag, and he

placed it down at the foot of the gatepost. She put her back lightly against the gate, and fluffed at her hair a little. Amos, quite sure her make-up needed no retouching, told her to put the heel of her right shoe on the bottom bar. She did so, and with her hands resting against a bar, her pose became natural.

'Is this all right, Mr Anderson?'

'That is all right definite,' said Amos. His camera, slung around his neck by a thin strap, came up in his hands, and he opened up the viewfinder. 'My life, all right definite is good, and, well, well, so is the breeze, eh?'

It was co-operating as if under instruction, lifting Maureen's blue dress and white lacy slip. Sheer nylons gleamed in the soft light.

'Oh, me dress,' she said.

'No dress is what we don't want, though, eh?' smiled Amos, studying the picture in his view-finder. 'Skittish dress we do – my, that's very good – great – hold it now – keep that smile – great.'

Click went the camera, catching the smile of a 'girl next door', along with her breeze-blown dress and her nyloned legs.

The outdoor session had begun, the conditions perfect, especially the soft light governed by high white clouds.

Disinterested chickens clucked about, fluffy chicks hopped and twittered, and in the adjacent field sheep and lambs peacefully grazed, apart from the moments when wandering lambs went baa-ing in search of their mothers.

In the shed, feathers floated and fell, with Rosie and Matt, and Hortense and Joe, working towards the bliss of refreshing teatime.

Chapter Twenty

'Well, I'm damned,' said Major Gorringe, retired. No-one asked him what he was damned about. He was up in his roomy loft, eye to his telescope that was mounted on a tripod in front of the window. He frequently liked to let his magnified gaze sweep the countryside. It came from a habitual sweeping of enemy lines with his field glasses during his years of campaigning on the North-West Frontier throughout the Twenties and Thirties. It rarely failed to help him spot an unfriendly native blighter or two. These days, his telescope helped him to spot civilian blighters, such as itinerant gypsies heading for the open spaces around Woldingham. Not that he objected to gypsies, only to having them camp next door to him, more or less. The proximity of gypsies and their pots and kettles sent Mildred, his wife, diving for the shelter of a trench. That is, the space under the marital bed. Funny woman, Mildred, but it was his duty to protect her. Eye still glued to the telescope, he muttered, 'Can't believe my blasted eyes. Giving the place a bad name. Have to do something about it.'

Down he went, gathered up his hat and stick from the hallstand, and called to Mildred that he was going to take half an hour's walk.

'Well, no longer,' replied Mildred from the living room, 'I'll be making tea by then.'

'Right.' The major decided not to give the reason for his outing. It would shock Mildred and probably send her to the phone to call the police.

Out he went, marching briskly. He was a bluff old soldier, but a bit choleric in the way of his kind. Didn't think much of women in trousers and that tin-can rock 'n' roll music, or any music except the stirring stuff of a military band.

As he marched, legs still active, despite being over sixty, he kept a firm grip on his walking stick.

'Great – just the job – head to the left a bit – that's it – I like it, don't I?'

Click went the camera for the umpteenth time. Amos was in the lane now, Maureen perched on the outside of the gate of the adjacent field, that which was dotted with the grazing sheep and their frisky lambs. Maureen, seated sideways, had her right leg drawn up, her left leg down, but curved at the knees. Her dress and slip were the playthings of the breeze, constantly lifting and fluttering to reveal her shining stockings and the glimpse of a saucy white suspender or two.

'How we doing, Amos?' she asked happily.

'Well, I like it, didn't I say so?' said Amos, just as happy as his sitter. He was taking his time to pose her for each shot. 'What do we want, eh? The pretty girl next door, and don't we have it? Now, put your hand to your forehead, shade your eyes and look at the aeroplane.'

'What aeroplane?' asked Maureen.

'We've got imagination, haven't we?' said Amos.

'Oh, you mean pretend there's one,' said Maureen, and shaded her eyes and looked upwards. The breeze gusted, lifting her dress and slip high.

'Hey, you there! By George, damned if I saw anything more disgusting in the shadiest bazaars of Bombay.' Major Gorringe bore down on Amos, walking stick at the ready.

Maureen let out a startled squeak, and Amos backed off from the portly, red-faced figure in tweeds.

'What's up, what's wrong?' he asked.

'Wrong? Wrong?' Major Gorringe waved his stick as if signalling a charge. 'Damned if you aren't photographing this wench in her underclothes. Never saw the like in all my born days.'

'Here, d'you mind?' said Maureen, down from the gate. 'I'm fully dressed, I am.'

'Much good that's been doing you,' said the

outraged old buffer. 'Sitting on these gates, showing your drawers – '

'Here, leave off,' said Maureen, indignant but blushing rosy red, like any nice girl next door in the face of embarrassing accusations. 'Amos, give him a talking-to.'

'Kind sir,' said Amos, protecting his camera by clasping it close to his chest, 'I assure you, I'm photographing only pretty poses for the – ' He thought, he took in the tweeds and the stout walking stick. 'For *The Times*.'

'Eh? What?'

'*The Times*,' said Amos, 'a most respectable newspaper, isn't it?'

'Damned if I believe that,' growled Major Gorringe, certain the editor wouldn't accept photographs of a young wench showing her legs and unmentionables. 'I'll have you know these fields are private property, so be off with you or I'll call the police.'

'Excuse me,' said Maureen, still indignant but now unblushing, 'we've got permission to be here from the owners, and we're not in the fields, anyway.'

'Damn my ears, what a minx,' said Major Gorringe, 'I'll see about that.'

All four chicken-pluckers were now around a garden table outside the farmhouse kitchen. They were drinking welcome tea. A large, cosy-covered pot stood on the table, and so did a plate

221

containing what was left of an icing-topped lemon cake. The mild sharpness of the lemon was enough to take away the taste of chicken-feather dust. The day-long job of plucking was over, and a host of birds to be dressed now awaited Hortense and Joe.

'Hello, hello,' said Rosie, 'I think we've got another visitor.'

All heads turned. Halfway up from the gate was Major Gorringe. The old boy lived half a mile away, but had become a good neighbour and friend, if a bit eccentric at times. Striding purposefully, causing chickens to flutter in panic from his path, he eventually arrived at the table.

'Hello, Major, what brings you to our teapot?' smiled Matt.

'Afternoon, Matt, afternoon, Rosie,' said the major, and nodded, not unkindly, at Hortense and Joe, whom he regarded as well-behaved natives from the West Indies. 'Afternoon,' he said.

'Afternoon, Majah, sir,' said Joe.

'I say, look here, Rosie,' said the major, 'I'm damned if you don't have the enemy at your gates.'

'Enemy?' said Rosie.

'Some dubious photographic johnny taking pictures of a young Piccadilly tart,' growled the major. 'Seen 'em with my own eyes.'

'Did you say a Piccadilly tart?' asked Matt, hiding a grin.

'That's her,' said Major Gorringe, whisky-red face mottled. Well, it wasn't every day that Woldingham was invaded by a dose of pornography. 'Showing her legs like billy-o. And more. Mildred won't like it. Never shown any of her legs all her life. Out of respect for herself, y'know. Fine woman in her time. Won her spurs nursing the wounded in the hospital at Poona. Gone off a bit lately, but still a fine woman.'

'And still a fine figure in the saddle, I daresay,' said Matt.

'Would be, Matt, would be,' said the major, 'but we don't run to a stable and oats these days. Mildred's limbs not what they were, y'know, and she's off oats herself. Prefers a kipper. Where was I? Oh, yes, this photographic wallah and his Piccadilly hussy. Giving your place a bad name, y'know. Thought I ought to warn you what they're up to.'

'Oh, I think the photographer's quite respectable, Major, and the young lady isn't from Piccadilly,' said Rosie.

'Somewhere like that, I shouldn't wonder,' growled the major. 'The fellow had the nerve to tell me he was photographing her for *The Times*.'

'*The Times*?' said Rosie.

'Cartload of rhubarb, I fancy,' snorted the major. 'The only decent legs I've ever seen in *The Times* belonged to Lord Kitchener and his nag. Fine selection of limbs all round. I was a cadet at the time.'

'Oh, well,' said Matt, 'I get the impression one newspaper's much like another these days.'

'Not *The Times*,' said the major, firmly enough to be credited with sticking to his guns. 'Look here, Matt, the minx told me they had your permission to be here. Can't believe that.'

'It's true,' said Rosie. 'Well, the young lady's not unknown to us. Her mother's an old friend.'

'And very respectable,' said Matt.

'Well, blast my boots, could have sworn she was a bit much,' said the major.

'I'm sure the photographs won't be in the least offensive,' said Rosie.

'Skirt blowing in the wind, y'know, Rosie,' rumbled the major. 'Still, I daresay I can take your word.'

'Have a cup of tea, do,' said Rosie.

'Kind of you, Rosie,' said the major, 'but Mildred will be putting the old campaign kettle on any moment, and if I'm not back in time she'll probably phone Constable Harris and tell him to go looking for me. Gets a bit rattled if I'm not there when she's filling the pot. Must be off. Good day to you, Rosie, good day to you, Matt. Apologies for intruding, but the situation looked a bit critical to me. One can never be sure how or when the enemy will strike. And damned peculiar camouflage they use these days.' He nodded at Hortense and Joe. 'Good day.'

'Goodbye, sir,' beamed Hortense who, like Joe,

hadn't the foggiest idea of why Major Gorringe had been so purple.

Off he went, portly but fit, this time using the front gate, turning into the road to stride briskly homewards in the hope of reaching Mildred before the kettle boiled.

'Well,' said Rosie, and laughed.

'Skirt blowing in the wind,' said Matt.

'One man's eye-catcher is another man's horror story?' suggested Rosie.

'Miz Chapman,' said Hortense, 'me and Joe, we best start dressing them ole chickens.'

'Well, thank you, Hortense,' said Rosie, and the West Indian couple made their way through the kitchen to the scullery, where crates of plucked birds awaited two pairs of quick and efficient hands.

Outside, Matt said, 'Here they come.'

Amos and Maureen were entering the field, Amos closing the gate behind him. Maureen waved.

'Here we are!' she sang. 'We're finished.'

'Hope not,' murmured Matt, 'we don't want them expiring on the premises. It'll look as if the major fatally winged them, and we'll have to phone Constable Harris and let him know who's the main suspect.'

'Mildred won't like that,' said Rosie.

'No problem,' said Matt, 'I think we can count on the walking wounded to reach this pot of tea. That'll cure them.'

He and Rosie sat there, resting and waiting. Finally, Amos and Maureen arrived. Amos looked as affable as ever. Maureen looked sparkling.

'Oh, my stars,' she said, 'did a stout bloke come up and complain about us?'

'Only Major Gorringe,' said Rosie.

'Oh, that's his name, is it?' said Maureen. 'What a funny bloke, his face was all red and his eyes popping.'

'Oh, yes, regarding his eyes,' said Rosie, 'he went on about a skirt blowing in the wind.'

'Well, true, true,' said Amos, 'except dress, not skirt. And blowing in the wind we wanted.'

'Sit down,' said Rosie. She lifted the tea cosy and felt the pot. It was still hot. 'Have some tea and a slice of lemon cake. Matt?'

'Right,' said Matt, coming to his feet. He went into the kitchen to fetch two more cups and saucers, and two tea plates.

'Oh, ever so kind of you, Mrs Chapman,' said Maureen, and she and Amos seated themselves. Out came Matt with the extra china, and he reseated himself. Maureen said she and Amos had done some terrific photographs, although they'd been a bit upset by that funny old bloke, Major Gorringe, who hadn't been at all nice, and all over nothing, really. Rosie, pouring the tea, said the gentleman, actually quite kind and neighbourly, wasn't exactly on the same wavelength as younger people. In fact, said Rosie, he thought ladies' legs should remain unseen,

226

and had just declared that his wife's had been covered all her life.

'Oh, no, go on,' said Maureen, 'you're joking. Even me granddad, who was born when Queen Victoria was still alive, isn't as old-fashioned as that. He says if a girl's got good legs, who's going to complain? Crikey, fancy that funny old geezer having a funny wife. Oh, thanks ever so.' She received her cup of tea and a slice of cake with a glow of happiness. Amos received his with a delighted smile, and a few typical words.

'Tea and cake are good, eh?' he said.

'Any time,' said Matt. 'By the way, I hope you'll send us a couple of the photographs.'

Amos said that reminded him of a lamb. Rosie asked if he meant Maureen. Amos said Maureen was young and pretty, but not a lamb, and that the one he was talking about had come right up to the gate to have a good look at his camera. So, of course, he took a photograph of it. He would send a print.

'I think my husband had Maureen in mind,' smiled Rosie. 'He sees our lambs every day, but not a dress blowing in the wind.'

Amos shouted with laughter. Maureen giggled.

'Now that is funny, Mrs Chapman,' said Amos, 'and real funny we like. So, I'll send you some prints of Maureen, then, eh?'

'Or a copy of the relevant issue of the *Daily Mirror*,' said Matt.

At that point, his son and daughter, Giles and

Emily, put in an appearance. Giles was just over fourteen, Emily just under thirteen. Both were lively, Emily owning the fair hair of her mother, and Giles owning an untidy mop and a ruddy complexion that made Rosie see him as the son of his Dorset-born father.

'So there you are, scamps,' she said. 'I'm delighted you remembered this is where you live.'

'Has all the plucking been done?' asked Giles, looking ready to disappear again if the answer was delivered in the negative.

'All done,' said Matt, 'but you and Emily can help Hortense and Joe with dressing the birds, if you feel you must.'

'Ugh,' said Emily. She'd grown up on the farm and knew all about the life being down to earth, but she still nearly puked at the idea of dragging the innards from dead chickens. 'I don't want anything to do with that disgusting job.'

'Well, you can both meet our visitors,' said Rosie. 'That's Maureen, Cassie Brown's daughter, and that's Mr Anderson, a photographer.'

'What does he photograph?' asked Giles.

'Lambs,' said Matt.

'Pooh,' said Emily, and reached in between her father and Amos to grab the last piece of cake. Rosie gave her a look. Emily had been named after Boots's first wife, Rosie's adoptive mother, but lately she had developed tendencies that were uncomfortably remindful of Rosie's natural mother, a woman utterly shallow, vain and selfish, who had vanished into her own artificial world many years ago. These tendencies weren't known to Matt, but they were to Rosie. Matt, however, had had reason lately to speak to his daughter about her manners.

Maureen interceded.

'Mrs Chapman, thanks ever so much for your kindness,' she said, 'but me and Mr Anderson had best be on our way now.'

'Yes, thank you for everything,' said Amos. 'Kindness we all like, don't we?'

Rosie smiled. There was something endearing about the photographer and his way with words.

'You've both been a happy diversion,' she said.

'And an unusual event in the life of Major Gorringe,' said Matt.

Amos laughed. Then he and Maureen said goodbye and left. Emily and Giles followed them and watched them get into Amos's car.

'We've got a better car than that,' said Emily, 'and a van as well.'

'Lucky you,' said Maureen.

'You shouldn't say things like that,' said Giles to his sister. He waved as the car moved off.

Away went the photographer and the up-to-date version of the girl next door.

Chapter Twenty-One

Wilhelm and Leila were among the many people in the East Street market of Walworth. Michal and Judith were there too, shopping. Leila had actually said yes when Judith invited her and Wilhelm to join them on the excursion.

'I think it will be OK for us to go out once more,' she said to Wilhelm.

'Sure, I'd like to,' said Wilhelm.

'Wear the hat,' said Leila.

Michal said he'd drive them in the car, so that only the people in the market would see them. He didn't think either the police or any other representatives of the law would be there looking for Wilhelm. He doubted, in fact, if any serious search was now going on, except in America.

The afternoon was advancing, but the market crowds were as thick as usual. Not until about seven on a Saturday would they begin to thin. While Judith and Michal shopped, Wilhelm and Leila followed at a short distance, interesting themselves in what the cockney stallholders were offering.

'In Israel,' whispered Leila, 'the stalls would be laden with melons, oranges, lemons and other fruit.'

'I'll look forward to that,' said Wilhelm, hat pulled well down.

'Also,' whispered Leila, 'I am being pushed and having elbows jabbed into my ribs.'

'It would surprise me if you didn't find something to complain about,' said Wilhelm. 'I feel good myself at being out of the house, and mixing with all these cheerful people.'

The people did seem cheerful, the hustle and bustle good-natured and an everyday part of the atmosphere.

Unexpectedly, Leila said, 'Oh, I am sorry. You are right, it is good to be out. In the house it is always waiting, waiting.'

'I guess we both feel that,' said Wilhelm, although he remembered she had said she was used to waiting, and that it didn't worry her.

There was a sudden disturbance ahead. They saw Judith and Michal turn from a stall to watch a market bobby dealing with two men who, very much less than cheerful, had come to blows. People backed off to give the bobby room to handle the situation, which he did with commendable speed. Separating the contestants, he advised them to get lost or he'd run them in. Off the blokes went, their going a disappointment to spectators who had hoped to see a stand-up bawling and hollering fight.

The bobby came on, strolling through the crowds. Wilhelm and Leila tensed, for the uniformed policeman seemed to be casting his eyes all ways. They'd had a previous encounter with a constable, an uncomfortable one.

'He's looking for someone,' breathed Wilhelm.

'Take my arm, talk to me and walk on,' whispered Leila.

Wilhelm curled his arm around hers, talked quietly to her about American films, and made a slow way with her through the immediate crowd. The market bobby looked at them. But his glance was casual and he passed them by. Leila's arm pressed Wilhem's to signal all was well.

'It's going to be like this all the way to – ' He checked from mentioning Israel. There were always ears. 'To our home,' he said.

'We shall get there, my friend, believe me,' said Leila, pressing his arm again.

Holy Elijah, thought Wilhelm, she's softening.

The shopping over eventually, Michal drove them home, with Judith asking if they felt better for the outing.

'I sure do myself,' said Wilhelm.

'Yes, so do I,' said Leila. Then, 'Thank you.'

When they reached the house in Camberwell Grove, she immediately wondered if she had made a mistake in absenting herself. Her prime contact, Stargazer, might have phoned, since his call could come through any time.

Oh, well, if he had phoned and received no response, he would phone again later.

Half an hour later, a sound disturbed them, not of the phone ringing, but of the front door knocker being smartly used. Rap, rap.

Michal answered the summons. A slim, dark-featured man in a casual check shirt and blue jeans, and carrying a suitcase, transferred himself adroitly from the doorstep to the passage. Michal, recognizing him, closed the door.

'Shalom,' he said.

'Hello, Michal,' said Stargazer in easy English, 'how are the caged birds?'

'Flapping,' said Michal.

'Of course. Well, it's been tough for both of them, but they'll be taking wing tomorrow.'

'Tomorrow's the day?' said Michal, visibly relieved.

'I'll be picking them up at eleven thirty in the morning. Where are they?'

'In the kitchen,' said Michal. 'Enjoying a cup of tea, and another of Judith's honey cakes.'

Stargazer smiled, and his dark face became pleasant.

'You and your tea,' he said. 'I have been in London two years and have drowned in tea several times over. But I'll eat a slice of honey cake with you, and perhaps some coffee instead of tea.'

'You're welcome.' Michal led the way to the kitchen, where Judith, Leila and Wilhelm were seated at the table, keeping company with a teapot and the cake.

Leila, quick to recognize the visitor, said, 'So there you are.'

'So here I am,' said Stargazer, placing his suitcase on the floor. 'Greetings, Judith.'

'Hello,' said Judith, who did not know the man as well as Michal did. But she did know he was an agent for Mossad, and would be responsible for seeing Leila and Wilhelm safely out of the country.

He touched Leila's shoulder in a comradely gesture, and shook hands with Wilhelm. While Michal put the coffee percolator to work, the visitor apologized for the long wait, which was due, he said, to the time taken to process documentation. He was not a man who apologized very often. A Palestine-born Jew, he was as hard as steel, and, like others of his kind, had not welcomed immigrant survivors of the extermination camps with open arms. Again like others, he had actually expressed contempt for all European Jews who had allowed themselves to be herded into concentration camps without resisting, had discovered the truth of such places and still not fought for their lives. The only Jews who had fought were those of the Warsaw ghetto. They alone merited commendation, as did Wilhelm Kleibert for his deed in New York.

234

He came to the point of his visit. All documents were ready, along with plane tickets. The tickets were for a return flight, a precaution against the possibility that one-way tickets might arouse curiosity in the wrong quarter. He would, he said, be driving Leila and Wilhelm to London Airport tomorrow morning to catch their flight to Nice. They were to be ready by eleven thirty.

'I'm relieved to hear this,' said Judith. 'In fact, I'm sure Michal and I are delighted for our friends.'

'I'm frankly delighted for myself,' said Wilhelm.

'I can only say this development is not before time,' said Leila, 'but the apologies are accepted.'

'Jolly decent of you, dear girl,' said Stargazer, taking off an upper-class English type to perfection. Then, briskly, he told Leila and Wilhelm that he had the new passports, that he'd been in touch with Anderson, and would see him at six for the purpose of fixing the photographs. Leila and Wilhelm were to stay where they were and not move out of the house until he picked them up tomorrow.

'Coffee,' said Michal, interrupting on a hospitable note.

'Thanks,' said Stargazer, taking the mug. The coffee was black and strong. Michal knew the man liked it that way, but he smiled as he watched him help himself to liberal spoonfuls of sugar.

Mossad's agents, Indian Moon and Stargazer,

glanced at each other. Stargazer looked relaxed, Indian Moon looked impatient.

'There's more?' she said.

'The question of what each of you will wear.'

'So I should hope,' said Leila. 'If Wilhelm is to travel to Nice as a fashion representative, and myself as his secretary, we should not look like tourists.'

'Agreed,' said Stargazer, and advised them that Wilhelm would wear a Savile Row suit, and Leila a stylish suit with a purloined Worth label. These were in his suitcase, and could be tried on while he was with the photographer.

'Have I heard of Savile Row?' asked Wilhelm.

'Savile Row makes the finest tailored suits in the world,' said Michal.

'Will mine fit me?' said Wilhelm.

Stargazer said it would, that he had supplied the tailors with all the necessary measurements.

'Wilhelm, you'll be the smartest and best-looking young man at the airport,' said Judith.

'If that means he will attract attention, I shan't like it,' said Leila.

'Oh, only from ladies,' smiled Judith. 'Especially young impressionable ladies.'

Conversation developed, but although there was an air of relief that the waiting was now over, there was also an underlying tension. That would exist until Leila and Wilhelm were actually on the plane at take-off.

'They are two good people,' said Amos Anderson. He had stuck the photographs to the passports, one identifying the holder as Charles Philimore, fashion representative of London, the second belonging to Amy Hargreaves, secretary, also of London. He pressed the metal stamp to emboss the passports, a forged embossment. 'Wilhelm especially is a fine young man, eh?'

'He is,' said Stargazer. 'My friend, thank you for everything. If we need you again, I'll let you know.'

'Of course,' said Amos. But not too often, he hoped. Business was good, business was legal, and legal was always very good. And in a day or so he would be ready to send to the *Daily Mirror* photographs of a discovery of his, the perfect girl next door.

Stargazer departed into the twilight of the September evening, and Amos was then able to close his studio and go home to his homely and affectionate wife. It had been a busy day. In Israel, he would have had a quiet day, for there he would not have been allowed to open on the Sabbath. Orthodoxy was paramount.

A little after eight that evening, Rosie and Matthew were taking advantage of the soft air of balmy dusk to spend more time at the garden table, Matt with a glass of beer to hand, Rosie with a glass of chilled white wine. Giles and Emily were watching television, and Hortense and Joe, their long and hard day over, were having their own kind of supper in the annexe.

'Penny for your thoughts, Rosie,' said Matt.

'You're welcome,' said Rosie. 'I'm thinking we should come to a definite decision about whether or not to sell up.'

Matt said they'd been good friends to chickens and sheep for some years now, but that he personally would be happy to say goodbye to them, and to the darned old foxes and their shrieking vixens. Rosie leaned and patted his knee.

'What's that for?' he asked, a smile breaking out.

'It's for thinking as I do,' said Rosie. 'We've money in the bank, and can look forward to what the sale of this freehold farm will fetch. Matt old dear, after spending so much time today living in a shedful of feathers, I think I'd like a complete change.'

'Snap,' said Matt.

'You're really sure?' said Rosie. 'After all, you're a country boy at heart.'

'So's Jonathan,' said Matt, 'but he and Emma opted for a change from chickens, which suited Emma.' Jonathan and Emma had been their poultry-farm partners for several years. 'And this country boy never quarrelled with running a garage before the war.'

'And you'd like to do that again?' said Rosie.

'This time, mainly a car-repair set-up,' said Matt.

'I know we've already discussed being definite,' said Rosie, 'but let's make a decision before the weekend's out.'

'How about if I tell you now that I'd like us to talk to Sprowles on Monday with a view to selling before the summer's gone?' said Matt. 'We'd ask for Hortense and Joe to be considered, and for time to find a house.'

'Of all things, old sport, it would be careless to quit the farmhouse before we've a roof over our heads,' said Rosie.

'Take it from me, Rosie, we'll not make that mistake,' said Matt. 'We'll go looking, for a house first, and once we're in, I can go after finding a place in which to set up a car-repair workshop.' He smiled again. 'We won't, I fancy, look for a house down in Dorset.'

'Denmark Hill or Dulwich,' said Rosie, as the dusk turned into night and the stars came out. A fox barked and a vixen responded in her yowling fashion. 'D'you mind?'

'Foxes?'

'No, silly, moving nearer the family.'

'Where you go, Rosie, I'll never be far behind.'

'How sweet. There'll be no problems with Giles and Emily. Giles is a country boy himself, but his ideas don't run to chickens.'

'Giles is after building bridges,' said Matt. 'He'll end up as an architect and engineer.'

'He gets that from you,' said Rosie. 'As for Emily, she's already well off chickens.'

'Can't blame her,' said Matt, 'the world of the young is far more exciting for girls than in our time.'

'In my time as a teenager,' said Rosie, 'the world gave me everything I ever wanted.'

'I know,' said Matt, finishing his beer by the light coming from the kitchen window.

'Except you, Matt.'

'Except me, Rosie?'

'Happily, old dear, your arrival was only deferred.'

'My years with you, Rosie, have been the best.'

The clouds that had rolled away to uncover the stars rolled back again, but Rosie and Matt still sat there, quite content. They had made an important decision together and in complete accord, and that was something to make them feel affectionately close.

At eleven, Wilhelm slipped into bed. He doubted he would sleep. Excitement was running through his mind. He thought how much he and Leila owed to Judith and Michal, the nicest of people and the kindest of hosts.

The Savile Row suit, a charcoal grey of the finest worsted, had fitted him perfectly, just as the stylish suit of honey-brown had made Leila look uncommonly graceful.

Tomorrow, London Airport and the plane to Nice.

Wilhelm lay thinking.

The bedroom door opened quietly, and was closed almost without a sound. A pale figure moved in the darkness.

'Wilhelm?' Leila whispered his name.

'Leila?'

She was beside his bed then, and wearing nothing.

'Would you still like to find out if you're a man?'

'Holy Moses, are you offering?'

'That is why I am here.'

The whispers floated.

'My God.'

'Move over, Wilhelm.'

He shifted. She lifted sheet and blanket, and slipped in beside him. He turned to her. She kissed him and put her body close to his.

It was three in the morning when she returned to her own room, her parting comment another whisper.

'You did not need to prove you're a man. You are a man, and I'm glad for you.'

Wilhelm was sound asleep ten minutes later, mind and body content.

Chapter Twenty-Two

Sunday morning.

Breakfast time for the Brown family.

'Well,' said young Lewis, going to work on his egg and bacon, 'where's the photos, then?'

'Photos?' said Freddy, dressed in trousers, shirt and braces. He would only put a tie and jacket on if Cassie wanted them to go to church. 'Who's he talking to?'

'Me, I should think,' said Maureen, wearing a pink Sunday dress.

'Yes, come on,' said Lewis, 'where's the photos?'

'Up in the sky,' said Maureen.

'But weren't they taken yesterday?' asked Lewis.

'Yes, but you don't suppose Mr Anderson developed them on our way home in the car, do you?' said Maureen.

'If he did,' said Cassie, her looks and her summery dress knocking a few years off her age, 'he's a magician.'

'He'll do them tomorrow,' said Maureen, 'and I'm going to pop into his studio when I leave work and let him show them to me.'

'Bring 'em home,' said Lewis, 'Grandpa wants to see them.'

'I don't recollect asking,' said the Gaffer, comfortable in an old open-necked shirt and even older trousers, the latter held in place by a leather belt originating with the First World War. He never threw anything away. Cassie had to do it for him, and in her time she'd disposed of some relics which Freddy said must have dated from the Battle of Waterloo. Cassie said some of them must have been in the battle. 'Did I ask?' The Gaffer put the question to Freddy.

'No, Lewis did,' said Freddy.

'We're all interested,' said Cassie.

'What photos are they?' asked the Gaffer.

'Come on, Grandpa, they're of Maureen as a pin-up,' said Lewis. 'At least, that's what she said. Here, Mum, suppose she's been telling porkies and they're only photos of country birds?'

'Lewis lovey,' said Cassie, 'stop teasing.'

'Be a laugh, that would, if our Maureen brought home pictures of a skylark,' said Lewis. 'Well, she said they were up in the sky.'

'What a looney,' said Maureen. 'D'you think we went up in a balloon, then?'

'Maureen love, I hope you thanked Rosie properly for being so nice to you and Mr Anderson,' said Cassie.

'Mum, I told you I did when I got back yesterday,' said Maureen.

'Well, I do think some young people today don't have a lot of good manners,' said Cassie. 'Mind, you and Lewis aren't like that, thank goodness, but I just wanted to make sure.'

'Did somebody say something about a pin-up?' asked the Gaffer, coming to.

'Only about twenty times since Maureen first told us she was going to be one,' said Freddy.

'Clara Bow,' murmured the Gaffer.

'Ur?' said Lewis.

'Who's she?' asked Maureen.

'Hollywood film star,' said Freddy, 'and your grandpa's favourite pin-up.'

'Never heard of her,' said Maureen.

'Nor me,' said Lewis, 'and I don't consider meself ignorant.'

'Just big-headed, that's all,' said Maureen.

'Saucy sexpot, Clara Bow,' said the Gaffer reminiscently. 'Fine pair of limbs and all.'

'Of course, she's getting on a bit now,' said Cassie, 'she must be nearly fifty.'

'Or sixty,' said Freddy.

'Poor old thing,' said Lewis, 'no wonder I never heard of her. Mind, I have heard of Queen Victoria.'

'Choke him, someone,' said Maureen.

'Who's coming to church this morning?' asked Cassie.

'I didn't hear that,' said the Gaffer.

'I'm meeting Mary Donoghue,' said Maureen.

'I'm meeting me mates Gordon and Barry,' said Lewis.

Cassie looked at Freddy.

'I'm putting a jacket and tie on,' said Freddy.

Halfway through the morning, Tim and Felicity were in their vegetable plot at the top end of their garden. They were harvesting the fat pods of green peas, Tim by sight and quick hands, Felicity by feel and touch. Jennifer was visiting a friend and her hamster, and Maggie was in the kitchen, preparing potatoes for roasting with a joint of beef. Meat supplies were improving rapidly, and so was the economy.

Felicity was lightly singing, having reached the last lines of a nursery rhyme.

'. . . the maid was in the garden, hanging out the clothes, when down came a blackbird and pecked off her nose.'

'Dangerous,' said Tim, thinking how resilient she was, and brightly in tune with both the song and the sunny morning. Her recent moment of clear vision had really lifted her. 'Think about our own blackbirds,' he said. 'Cover your nose up.'

'Would you love me without one?' asked Felicity, snapping off a very fat pod and dropping it into her trug, her arm through the handle.

'Of course,' said Tim, 'I'd go as far in my devotion as to buy you a false one.'

Felicity laughed and straightened up. The movement – she supposed it was that – brought about one more blow from life's spiteful hand. It delivered into her head a piercing shaft of intense pain that almost felled her. She gasped and staggered. The trug slipped down her arm and dropped, spilling green pods. Tim, bending to the row of garden peas, came up and leapt at her, winding his arms around her. She gasped again, her face white, and sagged. He held her.

'Oh, my God, my head,' she moaned.

'Felicity? Puss?'

Felicity clung for long moments, then quivered, lifted her face, and rested her chin on his shoulder.

'I can't believe this,' she said, 'it's gone.'

'What has? Another vision?'

'No, a blinding head pain,' she said wonderingly. 'It came and it went. Tim, I think I need a drink.'

'A brandy,' said Tim. 'Come on, let's get you to a garden chair. I'll sit you down and fetch you the brandy.'

The brandy taken, she was herself a little later, but saying if her head was going to be frequently subjected to that kind of punishment, she'd opt for a blackbird pecking it off, ears, nose and all.

'And that's a fact, Tim,' she said.

'I'll tell you what I think,' said Tim. 'I think it's something to do with your eyes. Isn't an eye affliction responsible for headaches in some people, a good many people?'

'Such as strain caused by myopia?' said Felicity. 'Well, I haven't got myopia, Tim, far from it.'

'But you've got an affliction,' said Tim.

'Don't we both know it?' said Felicity, grimacing. 'Is the sun shining?'

'Yep,' said Tim.

'OK, then,' said Felicity, 'I'm going to sit here and wait optimistically for a sight of it, while you go and finish picking peas. I'm pretty sure Maggie will be ready to shuck them in ten minutes. Oh, let me have a bowlful out here. I can do that many myself.'

'Right,' said Tim, 'let's both be optimistic about you and the sun saying hello to each other.'

But he was sad rather than optimistic. It could be that the strain of all the damned ups and downs she'd suffered was responsible for punishing her head.

A woman like Felicity, equal to all that had been demanded of her during the rough and tumble of her time with 4 Commando in Troon, and every damn thing that blindness still demanded of her, was well overdue for a kind gesture from the presently bloody-minded gremlins.

It occurred to him on his way back to the vegetable plot that the assassin of Dr Rokovsky still hadn't been caught, not according to any news broadcasts. Although everything touching on the daylight execution in New York, including the arrest and then the escape of the suspect, was no longer a feature of the news, he was sure that recapture of the young Jewish man would make headlines again. On the other hand, if he had reached the safety of Israel, it was unlikely to be publicized by that State.

But if he wasn't there, where was he? Still hiding up somewhere in America? The United States, a huge land mass, could offer a thousand and more hideaways to any number of people on the run from the law. Until the trial of Wilhelm Kleibert took place in New York, Tim supposed for the umpteenth time that evidence showing Rokovsky to have been an SS doctor would not be made public. Certainly, no British court would allow its disclosure, on the legal grounds that it could prejudice a jury.

Tim resumed picking peas.

Felicity relaxed.

'Who the hell – ?' Michal curbed his tongue. But the knock on the front door did make him suspicious about who was calling. He and Judith weren't expecting anyone, not until half eleven, when they were sure Stargazer would arrive on the dot.

Judith glanced at him, then at Leila and Wilhelm. They were all having morning coffee in the kitchen.

'Who is at your door?' asked Leila, tensing.

248

'No idea,' said Michal, but he did know representatives of the law in the UK did knock on doors on the Christian Sabbath when critical and immediate action was necessary. 'But vanish – and Judith, get rid of their coffee cups. And Wilhelm, get your luggage out of sight.'

The knock was repeated. Speedily, Leila and Wilhelm vanished, not upstairs but in the backyard, the small garden. The took their luggage with them.

While Judith put two coffee cups out of sight, Michal took himself to the front door, braced himself, and opened it.

'Vell, vhat a fine morning, Michal, ain't it?' said his stepfather, Eli Greenberg.

'Hey, Pop,' said Michal, 'what are you doing here?'

'Calling, ain't I, and don't call me Pop. It ain't respectful.'

'I'm still asking why you're calling,' said Michal.

'Vhy, can't I come round like a caring father to see you, my son, and Judith that's vith child?' said Mr Greenberg, surprisingly impressive in a fine navy blue suit and a black homburg. Mrs Greenberg insisted on presentable attire for the synagogue on Saturdays, and out of courtesy to Gentile customs on Sundays.

Eli stepped in. Michal, perforce, stood aside. He guessed why his stepfather had come. To take a look at the visitors, and to sum up if they were hard-nosed people of a kibbutz, and accordingly troublesome. Old Eli accepted most people in a kibbutz were honest and hardworking, but suspected there were always some who became too much like the men of the Stern terrorist organization, responsible for the murder of British soldiers and civilians in the late 1940s.

'Would you like a cup of coffee, old one?' suggested Michal, leading the way to the kitchen.

Mr Greenberg said he hadn't come to stay awhile, he had only called while passing, but would be pleased to meet the visitors. Michal said they were out at the moment. Which they were. Well, out of the house, at least. But he didn't say where. Judith, seated at the kitchen table, sipping coffee, looked up at the entrance of her stepfather-in-law.

'Why, how nice, you dear man,' she said, coming to her feet, 'such a pleasant surprise. Will you have some coffee?'

'Vell, that's kind of you, ain't it?' said Mr Greenberg. 'But no. Judith, are you in good health?'

'My health is excellent, my spirits high, my expectations happy,' said Judith.

'A blessing, Judith, a blessing,' said Eli with warmth. 'But I regret not being able to meet your visitors. Michal tells me they're out.'

Judith said yes, and that she'd no idea when they would be back. Perhaps not until dinner was on the table. Eli said being out when they might have been in was a disappointment, which he would have to put up with.

'Never mind,' smiled Judith, 'here am I, and here is Michal, and we aren't a disappointment, are we?'

'Vhy, how could you be?' said Eli. 'All is fine vith these friends?'

'Old one,' said Michal, 'stop worrying.'

'I should sometimes?' said Eli. 'I should. Vell, I von't stay, no. Shalom, Judith.'

'Shalom, good Father,' said Judith, and Michal saw the old man out.

When he rejoined Judith, he said, 'He's suspicious.'

'And why is he suspicious?' asked Judith.

'He thinks our friends are of the wrong kind, and a worry to me. He thinks he can spot that worry every time I arrive at the yard.'

'The dear man is no fool,' said Judith, 'and it's as well Leila and Wilhelm made themselves scarce, for I'm sure your mother's husband has an eye sharp enough to confirm his suspicions.'

'You think he'd recognize our young man?' said Michal.

'I wouldn't bet on a blank,' said Judith.

'The point is,' said Michal, 'would he tell us to get rid of them or would he be sympathetic?'

'Sympathetic,' said Judith, 'but I think he'd still tell us we're making trouble for ourselves. My life, Michal, I'll be happy to see them go, as

251

long as it means a safe journey to Israel for Wilhelm, such a good young man.'

'Well, they'll be on their way in less than an hour,' said Michal.

'For which I'll be thankful,' said Judith. 'Our home will be our own again. That prospect fills me with bliss.'

'Bless you,' smiled Michal. 'Our friends can come back in now.'

Chapter Twenty-Three

London Airport.

Among the passengers checking in for the flight to Nice were a well-dressed man with a neat, pointed black beard, and a shapely young woman in a very fashionable suit and a soft, trilby-style hat. He had a suitcase and a briefcase. She had a suitcase and a large handbag. He appeared absorbed in himself. She appeared interested in the people shuffling slowly forward in front of her. She was, however, almost certain she could smell security men at her back. Not that she suspected they were on the lookout for a fugitive from America. No, not that. If they were in this departure hall, it would be in connection with the cold war. The cold war was hotting up, Soviet Russia and the West fanatically suspicious of each other.

All the same, eyes might focus on Wilhelm.

Reaching the check-in for BOAC international flights, Wilhelm placed the luggage on the platform and Leila handed over tickets and passports. The woman on the desk, having weighed and labelled the luggage, showed a smile as she glanced at Mr Philimore and Miss Hargreaves, and checked their passports and the tickets. She returned the passports, handed Leila the boarding cards that contained confirmation of their booked seat numbers, and wished them a good flight.

They made their way to the departure lounge, found a seat and sat down to wait for the flight to be called. Stargazer, who had been watching them from a distance, slipped away to find a viewing platform.

It was hot. At least, Wilhelm felt hot. He took off his hat and used a handkerchief to lightly dab his forehead.

'Are you nervous?' murmured Leila.

'Sure I am,' murmured Wilhelm, 'aren't you?'

'A little.'

'I guess by now I ought to be used to this kind of thing, but it still gets under my skin.'

'Go and buy a fashion magazine at the news-stand.'

'I think you should do that. By the way, is this the right time and place to tell you you have a very fine body?'

'It's something to talk about, I suppose, but it would look better if we were discussing fashion photographs in some magazine or other.'

'You'd be better at buying the right kind than I would.'

'I am not interested in fashion.'

'You should be, you look cute in that suit.'

'Cute? Cute? Wilhelm, that is like telling me I am a dressed-up china doll.'

'So sorry,' Wilhelm smiled. 'Kind of stylish, then.'

'I am not concerned with being stylish.' Leila looked around. The departure lounge was not exactly impressive. Along with the departure hall and other buildings, it was due to be replaced by a structure far more imposing. Air travel was increasing week by week. Leila could not see any obvious security men or women, but then, such people could always look innocuous.

Suddenly, their flight was called. She came alive. So did Wilhelm. Passengers rose from their seats and began to make their way to the boarding gate.

'Let's go,' said Wilhelm, dabbing lightly at his forehead again.

'Don't rush,' said Leila, and they steeled them-selves to follow other passengers.

They began their walk.

A man sped after them. He called.

'Sir? Excuse me, sir.'

Leila froze. So did Wilhelm. They turned.

'Yes?' Wilhelm, who had escaped hunters for many long months, spoke the word out of a dry throat.

'You left your hat behind.' And the man handed over Wilhelm's homburg.

'Thanks,' said Wilhelm, recovering like an old

hand at this kind of thing. 'I guess I'll leave my head behind one day.'

'We all do that kind of thing at airports,' said the stranger, and went smiling back to his seat.

Leila and Wilhelm went on, Wilhelm wearing the homburg. Both were conscious of feeling vulnerable.

'We are both idiots,' whispered Leila fiercely, 'one of us should have remembered your silly hat. And you were supposed to say very little here. Your American accent does not belong to an Englishman born in London.'

'I couldn't say nothing. Get the boarding cards ready.'

'Ah, now you are giving me orders?'

'That'll be the day,' said Wilhelm, and grinned.

Leila's firm lips twitched.

Not long after all that, Stargazer watched them traversing the tarmac along with other passengers heading for the standing plane. He watched them board, and he waited until the plane took off. Its engines powered it swiftly upwards into the canopy of blue sky and white clouds. It disappeared.

He left the viewing platform then, a slight smile on his dark face.

In the afternoon, Sammy answered the ringing phone.

'Hello?'

'Philip here, Uncle Sammy,' said pilot officer Philip Harrison. 'Is Phoebe there?'

'Hold on,' said Sammy, 'I'll call her.' He turned. 'Phoebe, phone.'

'Coming, Daddy.'

Sammy turned back to the phone and said, 'Are you locked up, Philip?'

'Not in the sin bin, simply confined to quarters, all leave stopped,' said Philip. Phoebe arrived, and Sammy passed the phone to her.

'Philip's on the line, pet,' he said.

'Well, bless me, not before time,' said Phoebe, now nineteen and attractive enough to compete with Maureen and any other girl who had ideas about decorating glamour magazines. But Phoebe's ideas didn't follow that course. Her environment was one of happy family life, especially that of her adoptive parents, and the aunts and uncles. Her mum and dad were so funny together, Uncle Boots and Aunt Polly so engaging. Then there was Aunt Lizzy taking such good care of Uncle Ned, as well as Uncle Tommy and Aunt Vi who had given a home to Aunt Vi's ageing mother. So Phoebe's ideas pointed her at a happy family life, as long as her chosen mate didn't order her about. Grandma Finch had once said out loud that husbands liked to be lords and masters, and it was up to their wives to keep them in their ordered place, which was to be protective and providing, and not to get above themselves.

'Hello, you there, Phoebe,' said Philip, cousin to her but not by blood.

'Oh, it's you,' said Phoebe, 'and not before time.'

'Might I inform you I phoned only a couple of days ago?' said Philip.

'Did you?' said Phoebe. 'Well, it seems ages to me. Where are you, at home?'

'Unfortunately, no,' said Philip, 'I'm in a phone booth and still inside the barbed wire.'

'Well, I don't think much of that,' said Phoebe. 'Anyone would think there was a war on, and you were surrounded by a Russian army with snow all over their tanks.'

The cold war atmosphere was responsible for that kind of remark.

'The squadron's still on standby,' said Philip.

'What for?' asked Phoebe.

'Don't ask me,' said Philip, 'ask our Prime Minister. Listen, I've had a rush of blood.'

'Oh, dearie me,' said Phoebe, 'is it hurting?'

'No sauce, cheeky,' said Philip. 'Phoebe, you're a lovely girl, even if you do answer me back, and I had this rush of blood on account of thinking you might run off with some fast-working Italian count.'

'Oh, flattered, I'm sure,' said Phoebe.

'So I want you to promise you won't,' said Philip.

'Give me a good reason,' said Phoebe.

'Marry me next year, say in the mad sunshine

of summer,' said Philip, heading towards twenty-one, which he considered made him eligible as a husband for a young lady six months short of twenty. He'd spent quite some time thinking this over.

'Beg your pardon?' said Phoebe, little quivers running around her spine.

'Daisy, Daisy, give me your answer, do,' said Philip.

'Philip, you want to marry me?'

'Not half.' Philip had to put another sixpence in the call-box slot before Phoebe could respond.

'Philip?'

'I'm still here.'

'Philip, I have to ask you, will you promise to love, honour and obey me?'

'Will I what?' said Philip.

'Well,' said Phoebe through mounting quivers, 'you're an RAF officer, and you've probably got ideas of lording it.'

'Listen,' said Philip, 'any bloke who could lord it over you would have to be a walking marvel, you cheeky pussycat.' That was his favourite appellation for the bright, perky star of his Aunt Susie's household.

'Crikey, what impertinence,' said Phoebe. But her quivers were overcoming her in shockingly weakening fashion. 'Would you mind telling me exactly why you want to marry me?'

'It's eternal love,' said Philip. 'At least, that's what it feels like.'

'Philip, you love me?'

'Like a lunatic.'

'Oh, I feel off my head myself,' said Phoebe, swamped by blissful vibrations. 'Yes, then.'

'Yes?'

'Yes.'

'Next June, say?'

'Lovely,' said Phoebe.

'Wear something nice,' said Philip.

'Like a wedding gown?' said Phoebe.

'Brilliant,' said Philip. 'Must ring off now, there's an impatient bloke knocking on the door. So long, darling pussycat, see you sometime, I hope, and when I do we'll go buy a ring.'

'My, all this is so sudden, but goodbye, Philip love,' said Phoebe. Putting the phone down, she danced her way into the garden, where Susie was cutting roses for the house, and Sammy, shirt-sleeved, pulling the mower from the shed. 'Mum! Dad! What d'you think?'

'That the roses are lovely this year,' said Susie.

'Oh, blow that,' said Phoebe, 'think about next June.'

'What about next June?' asked Sammy.

In breathless fashion, which was only to be expected, Phoebe let them know Philip had proposed, she'd accepted, and the wedding was going to be next June. Susie looked at Sammy, Sammy looked at Susie, and they smiled. Then Susie hugged flushed Phoebe, and Sammy said although he didn't want to lose her, it would be his highly personal pleasure and privilege to give her away in due course to Annabelle and Nick's favourite son.

'Daddy, he's their only son,' said Phoebe.

'Is he?' said Sammy. 'So he is. Well, I thought there was a reason why he's favourite. And he's a good lad.'

'Wake up, Daddy, he's a man now,' said Phoebe.

'All right, me pet,' said Sammy, 'give us a kiss to celebrate he'll be old enough next June to marry you.'

Phoebe gave him one, smack on his cheek.

'Oh, you're a lovely old dad,' she said.

'I'll make a pot of tea,' said Susie, happy for her adopted daughter, although not wanting to lose her any more than Sammy did. Phoebe was the last of their children at home. Daniel, Bess, Jimmy and Paula were all married and living their own lives. Only Phoebe, so bright and affectionate, was left. And next June would see her gone. Susie felt touched. 'Yes, let's all have some tea,' she said.

Phoebe smiled. That was how all the families reacted to news, good or bad. Let's have some tea. Would she and Philip be saying that in time to come?

Probably.

Well, even though times and attitudes were now fast-changing, she didn't think any Adams would let go of every little custom or habit that had been handed down by Grandma Finch.

The extraordinary happened. The afternoon was hot, and Felicity, who disliked feeling the least bit sticky, was about to take a refreshing shower before Maggie served Sunday tea. Entering the bathroom, she reached for the waterproof curtain that closed off the shower. She groped, found its edge and pulled. The curtain ran back on its rail, and the scales fell from her eyes. As clearly as could be, she saw the white-tiled shower, its soakaway, and the chrome tap that delivered a mixture of hot and cold water. She stared at that which until now she had only known by touch. Exultation flooded her. She turned, and the bathroom itself, walled with flower-patterned tiles lightly tinted with the palest blue, enchanted her eyes. The bath gleamed and huge white towels, fluffy, hung from chrome rails.

Felicity wanted to shout with excitement. She felt like a young girl might at seeing winged fairies emerging from a bank of daffodils. A dream come true.

She drank in the scene, then, in her birthday suit, she ran into the bedroom, to the window, and there she saw the world outside sharp and clear, as once before. The houses, the hedges, the road and the trees. The vision stayed, and she knew now, she was certain, that a blinding headache was the forerunner of sight. She was also certain the vision would fade, but this time perhaps not for quite a while. She crossed to her wardrobe, the wardrobe she could see, slid open a door and reached for her light summer dressing gown. Even a blind woman who was actually enjoying vision should not rush down to show herself naked to her husband, daughter and maid, however exultant she was.

She slipped into the dressing gown and tied the satin sash. Clear sight was staying with her, staying, but she had an instinctive feeling it was going to desert her again, and that the opening and closing was natural in the process of healing. Nevertheless, hope that vision would last long enough for her to see Jennifer encouraged her as she left the bedroom. However, when she reached the top of the stairs, and was about to descend, her instinct proved all too right. Blankness once more cut her off from her visual world. She sighed, her lips twitched in a wry smile, and she simply sat down. But eureka, the happening had lasted for long minutes again, and she was certain, utterly certain, that clear vision would repeat itself for lengthier periods until life turned about and delivered a miracle instead of a blow.

Tim, appearing in the hall, looked up to see her sitting in her dressing gown at the top of the stairs.

'Felicity?'

'Come up and sit with me, old soldier, I've something exciting to tell you,' she said.

Although blind as a bat again, she was smiling.

Chapter Twenty-Four

Monday, and Londoners trudged back to work with their umbrellas up after a sunny weekend. Soft September rain was falling over the southeast of England, but it was still as wet as any other kind of rain. Cockneys on late-season holiday in Margate put on their macs and left their boarding houses to seek shelter in arcades and gift shops.

On the second floor of a government building in Whitehall, a semi-bald gentleman who made up for the lack of hair on his head by sporting a bushy moustache, spoke to a colleague with a handsome thatch.

'So what's the answer, Toby?'

'A lemon.'

'That's no bloody help.'

'Nor is the fact that he was recognized by a German army nurse. A West German court might query any other kind of witness, but not one of its wartime nurses. That, of course, is if he's extradited.'

'Out of order, you know that. Can this German woman be bought off?'

'I feel doubtful about that, sir.'

'Well, one thing's for certain, she can't be told the facts.'

'I suppose we could consider an arrangement that would allow for her and her family to enjoy a month in the South of France, all expenses paid, in the hope that by the end of it she'll have forgotten our man.'

'Now look here, Toby,' said the senior figure, 'I had a foul weekend, and on top of that I've got a lousy Monday morning feeling, so stop making funnies. Get our man out of the country, tell him to take a holiday.'

'He'll have to give Moscow a good reason for his absence from London. He's presently passing information on developments in respect of the Suez crisis. Incorrect developments, of course.'

Which was a reminder that the man in question was a double agent. Double agents abounded on both sides of the Iron Curtain. The UK had suffered, and was still suffering, from the activities of British-born double agents, men who had become closet Communists while students at Cambridge University. Not all these men had been uncovered.

'It's his job to find good reasons whenever required to,' said bushy moustache. 'Try to get him away within a couple of weeks.'

'And what do we advise our Foreign Office

friend to tell the German woman who recognized him?'

'Nothing.'

'Nothing?'

'For the time being.' Bushy moustache paused to consider the matter. 'That is, not until our man is out of the UK and out of sight.'

'Somers will phone again if he doesn't hear from us. He has to give some answer to the lady. She is, apparently, determined to be a – um – nuisance.'

'If and when Somers does phone again, tell him Professor Knox is being investigated.'

'Somers is no unimportant clerk.'

'He's a nuisance himself.'

Anneliese, waiting for something to happen, phoned Polly to ask if Boots had made any progress in respect of the man she had identified as a war criminal. Polly, recognizing a woman utterly set on bringing the man to justice, said not to worry, since she knew Boots wasn't likely to let her down. Anneliese said she was having bad dreams about the ex-SS swine, one of Himmler's fiends out of hell. Polly told her to go to bed on a glass of hot milk and dark rum, then all her dreams would be gentle lullabies.

'That is a joke?' said Anneliese.

'No, a cure recommended by Boots for heads that lie uneasily on a pillow,' said Polly.

Anneliese said she regarded Boots as a man of

many good graces. Polly said if she told him that, he'd think Anneliese was a little feverish. Anneliese said she wasn't at all feverish, only sure that Boots would help her to put that ex-SS murderer away.

That induced Polly to phone Boots at his office.

'Now look here, old love, sorry to interrupt your busy business life and all that,' she said, 'but Anneliese has been on the line asking to know exactly what's happening about the frightful bounder calling himself Professor Knox.'

'Good question,' said Boots.

'Find out, there's a sweetie,' said Polly, 'and by the way, Anneliese thinks you a man of many good graces.'

'Well, I won't argue with such a delightful woman,' said Boots, 'I'll accept the compliment.'

'You don't think she's exaggerating?' said Polly.

'If she is,' said Boots, 'I'll give my good graces a polishing. As for Professor Knox, I'll do some prodding.'

'Good old warhorse,' said Polly.

Boots put a call through to the Foreign Office. The switchboard operator, sounding polite but starchy, wished to know if his business with Mr Somers was official. Official and urgent, said Boots, and Mr Somers will tell you so.

He was connected.

'I'm told a gentleman by the name of Mr Robert Adams wishes to speak to me,' said Bobby.

'Correct,' said Boots, 'while allowing for the fact that I query gentleman. Bobby, old lad, what's being done about putting the handcuffs on Professor Knox?'

'I'm glad you asked,' said Bobby, 'because I'd like to know myself.'

'Your contact hasn't been in touch?'

'My contact's failing me, Boots. That's to say no, I haven't heard from him. I'll phone him and pull rank. I'm nobody's office boy.'

'Leave it with you, Bobby. Will you ring me back?'

'Promise. You're nobody's office boy, either.'

Bobby made the call. Over the line, his contact in Intelligence greeted him like an old friend, much as if they'd been at Eton together, and went on to ask about the health of his children, the interests of his wife, and next year's holiday destination of himself and his family. Monte Carlo? Bobby smelled procrastination. He had not been taken on by the wartime SOE (French) for being simple-minded, or by the Foreign Office by reason of who his parents were.

So, in effect, he requested his contact to cut the cackle and let him know what was being done about this Professor Knox character.

'Ah.'

'Yes?'

'Professor Knox, you said?'

'Come clean, Toby.'

'Half a tick, old chap. Oh, yes, that fellow. Of course, yes. He's being investigated. I'll let you know how it turns out.'

'You'd better, or the lady with the information on him will probably knock on the front door of Scotland Yard. You could put a clamp on Scotland Yard, but not on the lady, believe me.'

'Now you know, old man, that – '

'No go, Toby. I know you're doing me a favour, but hurry up the investigation. Nobody wants the lady to go to Scotland Yard, or worse, to phone the *Daily Express*.'

'The *Express*? Good God, are you trying to spoil my lunch?'

'I'm just hoping you'll get a move on,' said Bobby.

'I'll do my best, naturally.'

'Good. Regards to your wife, your mother and father, and your grandparents. And have a happy Christmas.'

Thus spoke the live-wire assistant of Mr Humphrey Travers, high-up official of the Foreign Office.

Bobby made the promised return call to Boots, and told him he'd put a firework under his contact and would set light to it if nothing happened by Wednesday. Boots said he was much obliged.

'Anything for you, old soldier,' said Bobby.

269

Boots rang Anneliese that evening to inform her that something was definitely being done about the credentials of Professor Knox. Anneliese said she hoped so, very much, since the actions of Germans of that kind were particularly shameful to her, a German woman. Memories of such men and their atrocities were like staring at chapters of a revolting book.

Boots advised her not to wear a hair shirt so close and so often, since she herself had done nothing to deserve it. You've made a new life, you've a family and you have many friends, so make the most of all that and put the war behind you, he said.

'I would still like to see that man convicted and hanged,' she said.

'Keep hoping,' said Boots, who, for all his tolerance of fools and even some villains, had no quality of mercy for Himmler's SS. He had too many sickening memories of all that he had seen at the Belsen concentration camp. He remembered now his day with Polly and his stepfather at the Nuremberg trial of the leading Nazis, including Goering, a man of cunning, graft, greed and wit, a flabby creature entirely unremorseful. It had been a day of exposed infamy.

Boots's one regret was that Hitler himself had escaped having to face up to his prosecutors and a disbelieving world. He had sent millions of his own soldiers to their deaths, but a coward himself at the end, he committed suicide. Boots frankly hoped he was living in hell.

Although the war had been over for eleven years, so much of it was still fresh in the minds of many people worldwide.

The latest family news that Phoebe had become engaged to Philip had travelled all over the grapevine. It was received with the usual enthusiasm by Chinese Lady and her extensive clan, to whom every new marriage meant a natural broadening of family ties. Down in the family's old haunts of Walworth, there were one or two people who, whenever the Adamses were mentioned, would say, 'Oh, that lot breed like rabbits, yer know.'

Chinese Lady did have second thoughts, reminding Sir Edwin that Phoebe and Philip were cousins, and wasn't it against the law for cousins to marry? Sir Edwin, as soothing as ever, said not in this case, for there were no blood ties. Phoebe, he said, was an adopted member of the family. So Chinese Lady said well, if you say so, then I'm sure it'll be all right and proper, and they're such a nice young couple.

There was also Lizzy, very much like her mother in her regard for what was proper. She had the same kind of second thoughts, which Ned tried to put at rest by emulating Sir Edwin. He assured Lizzy there was nothing in the way of preventing the marriage unless Philip jilted Phoebe, or vice versa.

'Jilted? Jilted?' said Lizzy, horror-struck. 'That's never happened to anyone in the family, it's only what rich and selfish people get up to, the kind that play fast and loose with other people's feelings.'

'There you are, then, Eliza old girl,' said Ned, 'it won't happen. Phoebe wouldn't touch fast and loose with a bargepole, and nor would Philip.' Philip was their grandson, born of their eldest daughter Annabelle and son-in-law Nick.

'Well, that's a relief,' said Lizzy, giving her husband a comforting pat. He still suffered heart trouble, and she kept a constant eye on his movements, for overexertion did him no good at all.

Lizzy did not know it, but Philip's squadron had just received orders that meant an immediate departure to the Middle East. Philip just had time to scribble a hasty letter to Phoebe.

It was the last week of school holidays for the twins. Polly reminded them that on Thursday they were due to have their photographs taken.

'Did you say so before?' asked James, still tanned from his time in Cornwall.

'I did,' said Polly.

'Is it compulsory?'

'It is.'

'Let's see,' said Gemma, 'what's it for?'

'Monkeys,' said Polly, 'you both know very well it's for Grandmama Simms.'

'Oh, well in that case,' said James.

'We'll co-operate,' said Gemma. 'Did you say which day, Mum?'

'I did. Thursday, at two thirty.'

'Oh, I think I can manage that,' said Gemma.

'And I'll do my best,' said James.

'You will indeed,' said Polly.

'Especially as it's for Grandma Simms,' said James.

'How very magnanimous,' said Polly, 'we are overwhelmed.'

'We?' said Gemma.

'Speaking as queen of this castle,' said Polly, 'we are obliged to both of you for your promised co-operation. However, any backsliders will be beheaded. Is that understood?'

James and Gemma looked at each other, and Gemma addressed her elegant mother.

'Quite understood, Your Majesty. Crikey, aren't you posh?'

Chapter Twenty-Five

Maureen, leaving her work at the end of the day, hurried to the Green and to Mr Anderson's studio. He was there, in his office, having just finished photographing an old couple about to celebrate their golden wedding.

'Ah, Maureen, a good mood I'm in, such a happy old couple I photographed a little while ago,' he said, his smile almost a beam.

'Smashing,' said Maureen. She added teasingly, 'Happy old couples are good, Amos?'

'Delightful, aren't they?' said Amos. 'Now, you want to see your photographs?'

'Oh, not half,' said Maureen.

Amos had them on his desk, a number of contact sheets and several blow-ups.

'Come round,' he said, and Maureen moved to his side of the desk to inspect the black and white blow-ups with him, one at a time.

'Wow,' she said. There she was, sitting on the gate, smiling, her dress and slip breeze-lifted, nyloned legs shining, stocking-tops peeping with a glimpse of lacy suspender and thigh. She liked herself very much in the pose. It showed she did have really good legs, and that her hairdo was perfect.

'Feminine, eh?' said Amos, as they inspected others, each one just a little different, but always a playful image of what a happy breeze could do to the flared skirt of a dress. 'And feminine we want, don't we, for the girl next door?'

'Feminine?' said Maureen, thrilled at the array of blow-ups in front of her eyes.

'That's it,' said Amos, 'shy but charming.'

'Shy?' said Maureen, who had never had to struggle with that handicap.

'Sure,' said Amos. 'See how you smile in that one? That is the shy smile of the girl next door.'

'Crikey, no wonder, look at me legs,' said Maureen, although she couldn't remember any moment of shyness. 'Here, Amos, I've just realized, they're all the wrong way round. I was always sitting facing right, where the breeze was coming from. But you've got me facing left.'

Amos said that he'd done the blow-ups from reversed negatives, so that they showed her as she would see herself in a mirror, which pleased the eye of some sitters, especially pin-up girls. See, he said, if we had had a large mirror there, you would have seen yourself as you usually do in one.

'So, how do you like that, Maureen?' he said.

'Smashing,' said Maureen. 'Amos, d'you think they're really good, good enough to get published?'

'Charming, aren't they?' smiled Amos. 'With a touch of the unexpected.'

Maureen asked what the unexpected was. Amos said the playful breeze. Girls next door didn't sit on a gate with the deliberate intention of showing their legs. A breeze that lifted their skirts was most unexpected, and, of course, embarrassing. Pin-up fans will like that, he said.

'So are you going to send some to the *Daily Mirror*?' asked Maureen, eager for fame.

'That is what we want, don't we?' said Amos.

'You bet,' said Maureen, and looked at the contact sheets, five of them, and each consisting of twelve shots. 'Crikey,' she said, 'all these.'

'It's to make sure we get a selection of very good ones,' said Amos. 'In fashion, many famous photographers will take sixty shots of a model in order to get the perfect one.'

'Is that what they're famous for, taking sixty photos just to get the best one?' asked Maureen, thinking that one day a fashion photographer might take sixty of her in a Paris-designed creation.

'They're famous for producing the perfect one, which is what they want, don't they?' smiled Amos. 'See, these contact sheets show I've taken sixty of you, all but one of a lamb. So all these blow-ups are of the best, eh?'

'Oh, I do like them,' said Maureen. 'Could I have some to take home and show me family?'

'Of course,' said Amos. 'Take six, the ones you like the most, and keep them. I'll put them in an envelope for you, and I'll be in touch.'

'About what the *Daily Mirror* says?'

'Keep your fingers crossed,' said Amos, pleased with the results, pleased with himself, and pleased with his versions of a girl next door.

Maureen, of course, was just as pleased when she left with the envelope and six shots.

Cassie, Freddy and Lewis all crowded round to look at the depictions of Maureen as the shy girl next door sitting on a gate and showing her legs. Shy according to Mr Anderson, said Maureen.

'Well, my goodness,' said Cassie.

'They don't look like you, Cassie, when you were next door to someone,' said Freddy.

'I can't see anything shy,' said Lewis, 'just Maureen's legs, and I've been seeing them all me life.'

'The *Mirror* readers haven't,' said Freddy, whose experiences of hard life and jungle warfare were too broadening for him to play the heavy and disapproving father. If Maureen was set on a glamour-girl career, why not? There was more money in that than as one more insurance copy typist.

'I must say they're ever such good photos,' said

Cassie, 'but look what that breeze is doing to her dress, Freddy.'

'Legs ahoy,' grinned Freddy.

In came Cassie's good old dad, the Gaffer.

'Supper ready?' he said.

'In a minute, Dad,' said Cassie, 'we're just looking at Maureen's photos.'

'Her pin-up ones,' said Lewis, a bit tickled by his sister's ambitions.

'Eh? What?' said the Gaffer, and pushed his head in to take a look. 'Well, strike me pink, it's Clara Bow, ain't it?'

'It's your granddaughter,' said Freddy.

'Yes, me, Grandpa,' said Maureen, 'don't you think they're kind of fab.'

'Fat?' said the Gaffer.

'Fabulous,' said Lewis.

'Blow me,' said the Gaffer, 'if that's our young Maureen, someone had better pull her skirt back in place.'

'But, Grandpa, they're what's called leg shots,' said Maureen.

'That and a bit more,' said the Gaffer, 'so don't let Mrs Hobday see 'em.'

Mrs Hobday was a neighbour, a buxom body with a heart as large as her bosom. She was also a retailer of gossip and little titbits of scandal. One could say she carried them from door to door without putting a strain on her weight.

'She's a good old girl,' said Freddy.

'I don't recollect ever seeing her legs,' mused Lewis.

'Well, sit her on a gate and watch the wind blow,' said Freddy.

The Gaffer chortled, Cassie prepared to put supper on the table, and Maureen replaced her photographs in the envelope. She glanced at her dad.

Freddy gave her a good-luck wink.

It's nice having a broad-minded mum and dad, thought Maureen. If Jane Elkins, one of her friends, ever showed her legs in a magazine or a newspaper, her mum, for a start, would probably order her out of house and home, and her dad, to finish with, would probably chuck her suitcase and her favourite records after her.

That made Maureen think of all the lively young people and their parents she'd met at the sixtieth birthday party of the man they called Uncle Boots. None of the girls there were ordered out of the house for dancing like crazy to the rock 'n' roll records. It had been a riot of fun and laughter. Maureen fell a bit for one young man called Jimmy Adams, but what a let-down when she found he was married to the girl he was dancing with most of the time. A girl by the name of Clare.

Oh, well, there were lots of nice blokes all over, and some rich ones up West.

*   *   *

Phoebe received the short letter from Philip the following morning and waved it about at the breakfast table.

'Would you believe it?' she said.

'Well, I can see it, Phoebe love,' said Susie, 'but I don't know what's in it.'

'That Philip,' said Phoebe witheringly, 'one day asking me to marry him, and next day, good as, telling me he's off to see the world, like some ancient mariner.'

'He's bought a boat?' said Sammy.

'Daddy, be your age,' said Phoebe, in temporary neglect of her breakfast cereal, 'he's a fighter pilot, not a sailor.'

'Well, you said – no, never mind.' Sammy hid a grin. 'What's the problem?'

'His squadron's going abroad,' said Phoebe.

'It happens, pet,' said Sammy. 'But he'll be back.'

'Yes, but when?' Phoebe attacked her cereal half-heartedly. 'I could be a lonely maiden stuck at her spinning wheel for goodness knows how long. Mum, that's not funny.' Susie was laughing. 'And I don't know why you're grinning like a Cheshire cat, Daddy.'

'It's lonely maidens,' said Sammy.

'And spinning wheels,' said Susie.

'It's still not funny,' said Phoebe, frowning. 'I mean, just when we've got engaged, that's not a bit funny. Suppose he's not back by next June? I'll be there, waiting at the church with no bridegroom. I'll look like a leftover dummy.'

'Of course he'll be back by then, Phoebe love,' said Susie.

'RAF units often have to go overseas for exercises, but not for very long,' said Sammy. Neither he nor Susie had the Suez crisis on their minds. It was something the Prime Minister talked about in Parliament, but Susie hadn't been interested in any Prime Minster since the retirement of Winston Churchill. And Sammy only read, or paid attention to, news items about the economy and anything that related to business prospects. Or on how his favourite sporting teams were doing. 'We've still got a bit of an Empire, y'know, pet.'

Phoebe's smile was a little weak.

'Oh, well, it's something I'll have to get used to, Philip being moved about,' she said. 'And I wouldn't want him to leave the RAF until his time's up. Without being a bit goofy, I must say he looks as sexy in his uniform as Kenneth More.' Kenneth More was a rising screen and stage star who had made a name for himself in the hilarious film *Genevieve*.

Susie smiled. To the younger generation of girls, any bloke who had real man appeal was called sexy. In her day, the word had been swell for a bloke, or stunning for a girl.

'Sexy, yes,' she said. 'Sammy, were you ever called sexy when you were young and walking in the park in your best Sunday suit?'

'No, I was only addressed in regard to me generous inclination to treat a girl to tea and a bun,' said Sammy, 'which made some 'orrible holes in the trousers of me best suit, I can tell you. Anyway, glad to see you cheering up, Phoebe. Don't forget you and your mum can organize some regular shopping visits to our branches. That'll keep you perky.'

'Shopping for what?' asked Phoebe, still thinking of not being able to talk to Philip on the phone for quite a while.

'For your bottom drawer,' smiled Susie. 'I think that's what your dad meant.'

'And not forgetting you'll get a handsome family discount,' said Sammy.

Phoebe's bright spirits took over.

'OK, Mum, let's do that now and again,' she said, 'I don't think I really want to sit around with some old spinning wheel.'

Rosie took time off to go to Camberwell and have lunch with Boots at his usual pub. She'd arranged it with him over the phone.

When Boots arrived at the pub from his office, Rosie was already there, seated at what she knew was his favourite corner table. She was dressed in a cream-coloured lightweight jacket and matching skirt, with a snowy-white shirt-blouse and a loose navy blue cravat. Her little round hat, also navy blue, had an upturned brim. Apart from her healthy outdoor complexion, few people would have thought her a farmer's wife up from the country. Boots, who had never lost his special feelings for his adopted daughter, thought her delightful.

He leaned, kissed her cheek and said, 'Well met, poppet, are you early or am I late?'

'I'm early,' said Rosie. 'Oh, I've ordered an old ale for you and a glass of wine for myself. And a ham salad for both of us. How's that for a start?'

'Perfect,' said Boots, placing himself beside her on the cosy, padded bench seat. 'As usual, you look a walking wonder, and your hat's a little gem. How are you, Rosie?'

'How am I?' Rosie smiled. 'All the better for seeing you, old darling.'

'If that's the case, am I to assume there's something wrong at the farm, then?' asked Boots, hoping nothing unhappy was touching her life.

'Something wrong? No, not at all,' said Rosie, 'I made a mistake if I gave that impression. Simply, old dear, I do like seeing you.'

'I'm touched,' said Boots.

'You're welcome,' said Rosie.

Joe, the everlasting barman, brought the drinks then, together with a smile for his most regular customer.

'Thanks, Joe,' said Boots.

'Pleasure, Mr Adams, salads coming up,' said Joe, and returned to his white, marble-topped counter, as old as the pub itself, and unlikely to be replaced by something modern from a plastics factory.

'So what did you want to talk to me about, Rosie?' asked Boots.

'The future,' said Rosie, sipping white wine and taking in the old-world atmosphere of this ornamental saloon bar, which had remained unaltered for many a year.

'Whose future?' asked Boots, and took a welcome swallow of his beer.

'Mine and Matt's' said Rosie.

'What exactly does that mean?' asked Boots, always interested in the shifts and turns of Rosie's life.

Rosie waited until the salad and condiments arrived, then went into detail about the proposed sale of the farm. Alas that I have to confess Matt and I have lived with chickens long enough, she said. Boots smiled. Rosie could say 'alas' without sounding melodramatic. His French daughter Eloise could say something as humdrum as 'Oh, dear,' and sound as if the house was about to catch fire. Eloise was always excitable, Rosie usually in control of herself and events. The differences between them were entirely diverting. At least, he thought so.

'Carry on,' he said.

Rosie went on to say as long as Sprowles, the firm interested in acquiring the farm, agreed to keep Hortense and Joe on, she and Matt would negotiate the sale. Matt would like to run a car-repair workshop, and she herself felt she might be useful to a thriving business firm willing to take on an old lady of forty-one. Boots said some old ladies of forty-one didn't look their age. Some firms, in fact, would take on some old ladies for their looks alone.

'Leaving aside all the flannel,' said Rosie, enjoying her salad, 'what kind of firms do you have in mind?'

'Your kind,' said Boots.

'My kind?' said Rosie.

'That is, where would you prefer to point yourself, young lady?' said Boots.

'Young lady?' Rosie laughed. 'That's stretching it a bit, isn't it?'

'Not from a man of my age,' said Boots.

Rosie smiled.

'Tell me,' she said, 'how well is the family firm doing at the moment?'

Boots looked at her. Rosie returned his look. Eyes met eyes, smile met smile. Rosie's cards were patently on the table. Boots was not going to quarrel with that. Far from it.

'I think we've got a classic situation here,' he said. 'Two minds with but a single thought. Very classic.'

'So?' said Rosie.

'Come into the business,' said Boots.

'Is that a serious invitation, or a kind gesture?' asked Rosie.

'Charity might begin at home, poppet, but not

between you and me,' said Boots. 'I'm serious, believe me. Come into the business.'

'Well, that I'd like, very much, especially if Matt and I could find a home nicely south of Camberwell,' said Rosie, 'but I have to be serious too about your invitation. I'd need to be taken on for what I could contribute, and not because I'm family. You might like this hat I'm wearing, but I'm not going to be just a hat around the offices.'

Boots assured her that even a bowler hat wouldn't be acceptable, unless it had brains in full working order. Sammy was against paying wages to empty noddles. Further, said Boots, the firm was doing exceptionally well, and he and Rachel were so loaded with work at times that he was convinced they'd need an assistant any moment, a position that wouldn't mean merely answering the phone or sharpening pencils.

Rosie said she counted that as glad news, but in the event, could she possibly come in on a part-time basis, from nine until three, while Emily and Giles were still at school? She didn't believe, she said, that children should come home to an empty house. Boots remembered his own schooldays, and those of his sister and brothers. Chinese Lady had always been there on their arrival home, and so had a warm glowing fire in the days of winter. So had a cup of hot tea and a slice of cake. It was that kind of simple principle that built up the strength of a family.

'That won't be a problem, Rosie, we'll settle for part-time,' he said.

'Aren't you a lovely bloke?' said Rosie.

'Lovely's coming it a bit,' said Boots, 'I'll settle for obliging.'

'And I'll settle the lunch bill,' said Rosie.

'Out of order,' said Boots.

'Not on this occasion,' said Rosie. 'It was at my suggestion, and I was here first.'

'Still out of order,' said Boots. 'How's Matt, and how are Emily and Giles?'

'Matt's as fit as a gypsy's fiddle, and is going to talk to Sprowles again sometime today,' said Rosie, 'and Emily and Giles are like your two, they're growing up and having a lot to say for themselves.'

'I see.' Boots smiled. 'Much the same as all the other young people in the family. Much the same as Sammy was in his teens.' He mused. 'And as your grandma will certainly tell you, as I was.'

Rosie laughed. Other patrons looked. Older coves thought back to the days when they'd have put on their best suits and braces for so attractive a woman, and worn a carnation in one of their buttonholes.

'It's my belief, Boots,' she said, 'that when you and I are really old, South London will be populated by Grandma's descendants, and all of them making themselves heard.'

'There's already an extra family in prospect,' said Boots. 'Phoebe's marrying Philip.'

287

'So I heard,' said Rosie, 'from Annabelle. Well, Phoebe's sweet and, according to Emily, Philip is definitely very sexy.'

They said goodbye outside the pub a little later, Boots asking Rosie to keep in touch concerning events, and Rosie assuring him she would.

'So long, then, poppet.'

Rosie laughed again. Passengers on a bus beginning its climb up Denmark Hill glanced at her, and wondered, no doubt, why she was so amused.

'I think I'm the only forty-one-year-old poppet in the Western world,' she said. She kissed Boots, asked him to give her love to Polly, then left to walk to the parked family car. She turned when she reached it, and waved a gloved hand. Boots reciprocated, watched her slide into the car, and waited until she drove away. He then crossed the road to the offices, thinking that of all his nearest and dearest, Rosie was with those at the top, as she had always been.

Chapter Twenty-Six

On her way home, Rosie stopped to call in on Grandma and Grandpa Finch. Chinese Lady, opening the door to her, showed one of her rare smiles.

'Rosie love, what a nice suprise,' she said in frank pleasure. Chinese Lady had a very special affection for Rosie who, as a girl of five, neglected and abandoned by her shallow mother, had endeared herself to Boots and Emily, and to the whole family.

'I was passing and couldn't resist dropping in, Grandma,' said Rosie, kissing her. 'How are you, and how's Grandpa?'

'Oh, we're fine,' said Chinese Lady, closing the door. The spacious hall of the large, three-storeyed house on Red Post Hill was imposing with its oak-panelled walls and polished parquet flooring. The house was worth far more than it had cost Edwin when he purchased it during the Twenties. 'Edwin's in the garden, reading a book about Napoleon, but I don't know why.

Wasn't he a blessed warmonger, like that man Hitler?'

'Not quite like Hitler,' smiled Rosie, 'although they had one thing in common. They were both corporals in their younger days.'

'A pity both of them weren't done away with at the time,' said Chinese Lady in one of her moments of death-to-the-ungodly. 'Well, come and say hello to Edwin, Rosie, and if you've got time, I'll put the kettle on.'

'Sweet of you, Grandma, but I've only just finished having lunch with Boots,' said Rosie, 'and that included two glasses of wine. But I've time to sit in the garden with you and Grandpa for a while, then I must get home.'

They went through to the garden. Sir Edwin, relaxing comfortably in a deckchair on the patio, looked up as the ladies emerged from the kitchen. He put his book down and came to his feet, and Rosie thought that even at eighty-three he was still a distinguished man. A little thinner, perhaps, a little more lined, but his silvery hair was suffering no loss, and his colour was really quite good. If any man knew how to grow old gracefully, Sir Edwin did. Such a wonderful couple, he and Grandma, and so devoted. Each was of the old school. But then, so are Boots, Lizzy, Tommy and Sammy. And so am I.

'Rosie, such a pleasure to see you,' said Sir Edwin, wearing an old-fashioned striped blazer, white shirt, blue tie, and dark blue trousers. The blazer was inimitably English. Perhaps it represented its wearer's affection for England and English customs and traditions. Boots was still the only member of the family to know his stepfather had been born a German. 'My dear Rosie,' smiled Sir Edwin, 'you look quite delightful.' He kissed her.

'Thank you, Grandpa,' said Rosie, 'and you look wonderful. You both do.'

'My, how kind,' said Chinese Lady. 'Mind, I suppose I'll feel my age one day, but I don't feel it yet. Sit down, Rosie love, and you can give us all your family's news.'

They all seated themselves, the day warm and bright, although rain was forecast for tomorrow. Rosie spoke of the decision she and Matthew had made in respect of selling their farm. Chinese Lady said she was never more suprised, but of course Rosie and Matthew would know what they were doing. Mind, she said, Rosie and Matthew were the only ones she knew who had gone in for bringing up chickens. She'd had a tame rabbit herself when she was young, which she kept in a hutch in the backyard, and when it died her dad lifted up one of the paving stones so's they could dig a grave for it and give it a proper burial, which they did. She used a kitchen skewer to scratch 'RIP' on the paving stone.

'Very touching, Maisie,' smiled Sir Edwin.

'But of course, a rabbit's not the same as chickens,' said Chinese Lady.

'Nor does it have feathers,' said Rosie.

'Rosie, my dear, when you sell up,' said Sir Edwin, 'what comes next for you and Matthew?'

'Matt wants to go back to poking about in cars, to running a repairing workshop,' said Rosie, 'and I'm going to take on a part-time job for the family firm. It has to be part-time while Emily and Giles are still at school.'

'You're going to work for Boots and Sammy?' said Chinese Lady.

'Boots assured me I had talents that Sammy would welcome,' said Rosie. 'I'm happy to believe him. So there you are, as soon as the farm has been sold, and we've found a new home, I'll be ready to enter the firm. I'm delighted.'

'You're going to do some house-hunting?' said Sir Edwin.

'We must,' said Rosie.

'Where?' asked Chinese Lady, who always interested herself in the location of family members. She had a quaint idea that related families ought to be within walking distance of each other, or at least only a bus ride away. It was almost a grief to her that Bess, Sammy's eldest daughter, had settled down in Kent with her American husband, Jeremy Passmore, and that Alice, Tommy's daughter, was living in Bristol with husband Fergus MacAllister. To Chinese Lady, these places were almost like foreign parts. To many other families, the farther away they were from certain relatives, the better they liked it. Australia was a good place for some. But Chinese Lady, of course, was Victorian in her clanish outlook. 'Where, Rosie?'

'Somewhere around here,' said Rosie.

Chinese Lady looked happily at Edwin.

'Rosie,' he said, 'it's not for us to help you decide, that's for you and Matthew alone. But it so happens there's a rather handsome house some way up from us. We know the owners, the Clayburns. They're moving to Guildford in late October, and will be putting their house up for sale any moment now.'

'Really?' said Rosie, quick to give it thought. The location was splendid, the hill and the immediate area exclusively residential, roads and avenues tree-lined. The prospect of an early acquisition might save her and Matt from weeks of looking for something suitable and well located. 'It's a fine family house, Grandpa?'

'If you have time right now, Rosie,' said Sir Edwin, 'why not take a little walk there with me? I always think the exterior of a house is the first thing a purchaser should find pleasing. Certainly pleasing enough to invite a full inspection of the interior. If you like the look of the place, Rosie, I'll speak to Mr Clayburn this evening, and ask him if he'll show you over before he puts it up for sale.'

'I've time to take a look,' said Rosie, not in the least averse to the prospect of living near her grandparents. 'And I'd like to, very much.'

'Let's all do the little walk,' said Chinese Lady.

Which they did, once she had put her hat on. Never, from the time when she first began to wear hats, had she been seen out of doors without one. It simply wasn't proper.

It was a measured, seven-minute walk up the hill for Chinese Lady and Sir Edwin, and from the gate Rosie took a long look at the frontage of the house, built of warm, russet-coloured brick and red tiles, the tiles mossy. There were two storeys and a loft, or attic, with an attractive eyebrow window. A porch led to the oak door, which was central, and the windows of the ground and first floors were latticed, giving the house an old-world charm. It was fully detached, and a garage had been built to the right of the property.

'Grandpa, I'm impressed,' said Rosie. 'I like it enough to want to look it over with Matthew.'

'You're really interested, Rosie?' said Sir Edwin.

'Seriously so,' said Rosie. 'I'll talk to Matthew.'

'Then I'll have a word with Mr Clayburn,' said Sir Edwin. 'He may be delighted with the prospect of finding a buyer before putting the sale in the hands of an estate agent.'

'Well, won't that be nice for everyone?' said Chinese Lady, more than happy at the possibility of having Rosie and her family close by.

'We'll see how things work out, Grandma,' said Rosie. 'Now, I really must get home.'

Chinese Lady and Sir Edwin walked back with her to their own house, Rosie noting that her grandmother was still upright, her grandfather still quite able. She said goodbye to them at their gate, then entered her car and drove away, a gloved hand gesturing in farewell out of the open window.

'Such a nice girl,' murmured Chinese Lady.

'Girl, Maisie?'

'Well, you know what I mean, Edwin.'

'I know,' said Sir Edwin. It meant that the matriarch of the Adams clan never allowed herself to accept that certain members of the family had grown up.

'It's as well you never knew her wretched mother, a woman that never gave her own child any love, and thought only about herself,' said Chinese Lady, still standing at their front gate with her husband. 'I couldn't hardly believe it when Boots told me she'd gone off and left Rosie, and the child only five. Even Boots – well, you know how airy-fairy he is about people and their faults – even Boots hated her for that.'

'I think, Maisie, that when Rosie's mother abandoned her, it was perhaps the best thing that could have happened,' said Sir Edwin. 'It gave Boots and Emily the chance to adopt her and care for her.'

'Well, I'm glad to hear you say so, Edwin,' said Chinese Lady. 'Let's go in now, and I'll make us a pot of tea. You'd like a nice cup of tea, wouldn't you?'

'Maisie, you are the most civilized woman on earth,' said Sir Edwin.

At that moment, a dizzy spell took hold of him, and suddenly his legs seemed about to lose control. He faltered a little as he followed Chinese Lady into the house. Saying he had a letter to write, he managed to slip into his study off the hall. Chinese Lady, going straight through to the kitchen and her kettle, said she'd call him when she was ready to pour the tea.

In the study, Sir Edwin sank gratefully into his desk chair. He was dizzy indeed, and his legs felt as if they did not belong to him. With his body slumped, he asked himself a question. The uphill walk, although taken slowly, was that responsible? Yes, probably, that and my age, he thought, amid the giddy sensations afflicting mind and limbs.

He sat there, applying himself sensibly to a complete relaxing of his body and faculties. His elbows on his desk, his face resting in his hands, thoughts intruded. If his time was up, he could not complain. His life had been long and adventurous. He had known Imperial Germany at the height of its glittering martial pomp, Berlin alive with colour, uniforms and military bands, its Kaiser a figure of self-important majesty. His years in espionage for the German Secret Service, more especially the years spent as an agent in England, had had a profound effect on him. Eventually the time had come when, disillusioned with the Kaiser and his warlike generals, and their conduct of the First World War, he had defected to England to serve the country he had come to admire and care for.

Since then, he had known the happiness of his marriage to Maisie and his acquisition of a ready-made family, a family entirely remarkable. He admired no man more than Boots, a cherished friend who had kept his every secret.

No, he could not complain.

His mind, clearer, acknowledged that fact.

'Edwin?' Maisie was calling. 'I'm just going to pour tea.'

He straightened his body. Magically, it was no longer threatening to fail him. The dizzy spell had gone from head and limbs. In quite exultant relief, he came to his feet, and all morbid thoughts and maudlin reflections made their exit. He smiled. Perhaps he had a little more time left, after all.

'Coming, Maisie.'

Old Mrs Blake of Walworth had been a friend and neighbour to Chinese Lady for years before and after the First World War. She was over eighty now, and so was her husband, who had once driven one of London's horse-drawn coal carts.

Mr Blake was having a little nap in an armchair

at this moment, while his old lady entertained an unexpected visitor, a woman in her sixties who had dressed herself up in an attempt to look younger.

'Well, me memory ain't what it was,' said Mrs Blake, after ten minutes of chatting with the visitor, 'and I don't have much recollection of you, but I'm beginning to get a sort of vague idea you did live close to Mrs Adams and her family.'

'Oh, I was a real friend to them, dearie,' said the visitor, 'but I ain't seen much of them since I had to go away due to me circumstances at the time. You sure you don't know where I can find some of them?'

'I could ask around,' said Mrs Blake, whose memory really was failing her. Otherwise, she'd have remembered a lot more about her visitor. 'Yes, I could do that for you. There's still some neighbours that might know.'

'Well, ain't you kind?' said the dressed-up woman. 'Um, I suppose you couldn't give me a bed for a couple of nights, could yer, ducky? Only I'm right down on me luck, me old man having passed on a year ago.'

Mrs Blake, born like many Walworth people to be neighbourly and hospitable, especially to those suffering a hard time, said, 'Oh, we can find you a bed all right, just for a couple of nights, except I hope you won't ask me to make up the bed for you in the mornings.'

'Well, I might be down on me luck, dearie, but I know me natural obligations.'

'Well, you're welcome, then, and while you're here, I can do me asking around,' said old Mrs Blake.

'I must say that's real kind of you, and I won't be no trouble.' The visitor emitted a little laugh. It sounded a bit cracked. 'I'm past me high-kicking days. Well, I was on the stage for a bit, yer know.'

'My, you must tell me about it,' said Mrs Blake, scenting some interesting titbits of a saucy nature. She might be over eighty, but her hearing, unlike her memory, wasn't failing, and she was still game for taking in a fund of such titbits.

She listened to some while her old man napped on.

Bobby received word from his contact in Intelligence that Professor Knox had slipped them. Bobby expressed his disgust forcefully, and the telephone line, shocked at having to transmit such undiplomatic language, almost fell apart. Certainly, for a brief moment, it blurred a word or two. However, British Intelligence, represented by Toby, took in Bobby's earful, and responded by suggesting that that kind of language was a bit off, old man. Bobby said the Foreign Office would send a note of protest to the Home Office at such unbelievable incompetence.

'Look, do we want a hornets' nest flying about, old chap?' said Toby.

'Find the bugger,' said Bobby.

'I say, what's happening to the Foreign Office? Oasis of calm, usually. None of us can touch you fellows for good manners. Usually.'

Bobby said his good manners were taking a holiday, and wouldn't get back until Professor Knox was limited in his movements by an old-fashioned ball and chain.

'Find him.'

'Look here, old fellow, I must point out – '

'That you don't take orders from the Foreign Office? I know all that, so don't bother. Who let go of Knox's collar?'

'Ah, yes. Well, as I understand it, he was in urgent need of his bathroom, and while we were letting him relieve himself, he climbed out of the window and disappeared.'

Bobby couldn't believe he was being given a chestnut as old and as hoary as that. Something was going on, something that didn't add up.

'I've a feeling you're giving me fairy stories,' he said, 'and I stopped listening to those on the day I found out Daddy Christmas didn't come down our chimney.'

'Oh, my dear old mater put me wise to that not long after I was out of my cradle. Very practical woman, you know, and no-nonsense stuff. Sorry about naughty Knox, but we'll do what we can to find him.'

'I'll be sending a uniformed messenger round between now and tomorrow morning,' said Bobby. 'With a shotgun.'

'I like your sense of humour, old chap.'

'You won't like it when the German lady arrives on the doorstep of the *Express*,' said Bobby, and hung up.

Curse it, he thought. The Foreign Office, of course, was officially supposed to stay in its own backyard. But it could still exert influence. In a case like this, however, only with the approval of the Foreign Minister himself. And that important bloke was presently locked in daily with the Prime Minister while they discussed the Suez crisis. The possible uncovering of a German war criminal was of minor importance, anyway. Thousands had been uncovered since the end of the war, and one more would be of no great interest.

So what should Boots tell Anneliese now?

Chapter Twenty-Seven

Rosie, arriving back home, was greeted by the news from Matt that he'd had a long phone conversation with Sprowles, and that agreement had been reached, including the company's willingness to retain the present workers, namely Hortense and Joe. Sprowles would be writing to confirm everything, including the purchase price of £7,500, two thousand more than Matt and Rosie had originally paid for the freehold of land and farmhouse. Matt had told the kids, who hadn't been in the least upset. Both seemed to feel that chickens and sheep didn't rate as much as the teenage world that was going on outside a chicken run. They were into this rock 'n' roll gig.

'Gig?' said Rosie.

'That was the word Emily used,' said Matt.

'I think teenagers are inventing a new language,' said Rosie. 'Matt, what about Hortense and Joe, did you tell them?'

Matt said yes. The prospect of working for new employers had laid them back on their heels for a moment, he said, but they liked it here, they liked the work and their only regret would be in having to say goodbye.

Rosie said she would hate it if the idea had made them miserable. We must, she said, give them a large handshake, say fifty pounds each. Matt agreed. His mind was pleasantly fixed on his new venture, a car-repairs workshop, which would do away with those nights when lambing time brought him out of bed at two in the morning to deal with foxes prowling in search of the helpless new-born. Sprowles would sell off the sheep and increase the chicken yield.

'How did your lunch with Boots go, Rosie?'

'Happily,' said Rosie, and told him that the lovely old warrior had offered her a job with the family firm on a part-time basis. Matt asked if she was really keen to commit herself to a job outside the home. Rosie said yes, she couldn't stomach the idea of having nothing to do after years of so much mental and physical activity on the farm. Housework would only take up a small part of her time. Then she informed Matt she'd called on Grandma and Grandpa Finch on her way home, and described the house they had looked at on Red Post Hill.

'A whizz,' said Matt.

'Whizz?' said Rosie.

'Meaning great, according to what Emily and Giles will probably say,' said Matt.

Rosie laughed.

'Well, I suppose we ought to learn their language,' she said, 'or we'll get left behind in this new world.'

'If Grandpa Finch can help us not to get left behind in the house-hunting race,' said Matt, 'that'll be something to celebrate.'

'Is there an old Dorset saying for that?' smiled Rosie.

'There be an old Dorset saying for everything,' said Matt. 'In this case, "Down by Dorset land a man needs much more than strawberry jam, for his family housing calls for a roof and four good walls." Durn my shirt tails, Rosie, how about that?'

'Corny, but acceptable,' said Rosie, 'and hang onto your shirt tails.'

Boots was talking to Sammy, and Sammy was listening with both ears.

'It's definite, Rosie and Matt are selling up?' he said, interest sparking.

'Definite,' said Boots, 'and as soon as they're settled elsewhere, Rosie will be joining the firm as assistant to Rachel and myself, and Matt will be after a place he can convert into a car-repair workshop. So now, Sammy, what does the property company own in the way of an undeveloped site?'

'For sale to Matt? Hold on.' Sammy phoned through to the property office. 'That you, Daniel? Good, come and see me, will you, you and Tim?'

The joint managers of the property company presented themselves to Sammy and Boots, and were asked about undeveloped sites. Was there one that could be sold to Matt and turned into a garage and workshop? Tim said there was, in Peckham High Street, and accordingly well worth considering. But Matt was still bringing up lambs and chickens, wasn't he?

'Not for much longer,' said Boots, and explained in detail.

'Well, shoot my hat off,' said Daniel, 'our Rosie joining the firm, and Matt going back to pulling cars to bits? I'm chuffed.'

With an eye to business, Tim said the company would like a quick decision, since various contractors were interested in the Peckham site, and he and Daniel had been playing one off against the other in order to get the best offer.

'What's your best offer so far?' asked Boots.

'Good question,' said Sammy.

'Five thousand,' said Tim.

'And what did we pay for it?' asked Boots.

'Two thou, two hundred, two years ago,' said Daniel.

'Congratulations,' said Boots, dry humour uppermost. He looked at Sammy. Sammy nodded. 'Offer it to Matt for three, Tim.'

'Seriously?' said Tim.

'Matt's family,' said Sammy.

Daniel said, 'Might I remind you elderly gents that Tim and I are entitled by terms of our contract to receive twenty per cent of all profits on all site sales? Ten per cent each?'

'Ignoring your saucy reference to elderly gents, which your grandma wouldn't like,' said Sammy, 'Matt's still family.' He looked at Boots, and it was Boots's turn to nod. 'Keep fifty per cent of the profit, which, if me mental equipment is still working, means two hundred quid apiece.'

'That's welcome talk,' said Tim.

'Well, you're family too, you and Daniel,' said Sammy.

Matt received a phone call later from Tim, who asked if it was true he was after a site for a garage and workshop. Matt said yes. So Tim told him a site in Peckham High Street was available. Would he like to come and look at it? The property company could offer it to him for three thousand.

'Damn me,' said Matt, 'three thousand? I thought I'd have to fork out far more than that for the right kind of site. It's not a postage stamp, is it?'

'We only buy postage stamps for sticking on envelopes,' said Tim. 'Call here as soon as you can, and I'll take you to see the site.'

'Tomorrow morning, say about ten?' suggested Matt.

'You're on,' said Tim.

'Who's responsible for this offer?' asked Matt.

'The family,' said Tim.

*   *   *

Boots, having been advised by Bobby that Intelligence had lost Professor Knox, phoned Anneliese during the evening. It was her husband Harry who answered the call.

'Hello there, Boots,' he said in amiable greeting. Harry was so easy-going that he was a pushover for his precocious daughter, Cindy. 'Let me guess, are you going to tell me something satisfying about the Professor Knox character? Anneliese is bathing Harry junior at the moment, as you can probably hear?' Their infant son was thirteen months old and lusty-lunged.

'Give mother and junior my regards,' said Boots. 'As far as Professor Knox is concerned, however, the blighter's slipped the investigation, apparently.'

'That'll please Anneliese, I don't think,' said Harry, and they talked about his German wife's certainty that Professor Knox was an SS war criminal who had escaped the Allies.

There was a young German Jew, thought Boots, just as certain, it seemed, that the ophthalmic surgeon he had shot dead in New York had been a fiendish SS doctor at Auschwitz. Wilhelm Kleibert had also slipped away. From American police custody. Incredible that Polly was sure she had seen him at the photographer's studio.

'Tell Anneliese that I don't intend to leave it at that, Harry,' said Boots, which meant that Bobby was going to continue worrying his contact, since he thought something fishy was going on in the murky bowels of a certain government building.

'I'll tell her,' said Harry. 'Thanks for calling. Regards to Polly and the twins. So long now.'

'Before you hang up,' said Boots, 'how's your new thriller coming along?'

'Painfully,' said Harry.

'I've heard that some authors go through fire and water with every novel they write,' said Boots.

'Oh, they're the soul-searching kind, I imagine,' said Harry.

'And what does that mean?' asked Boots.

'That they suffer agony if they find they've split an infinitive,' said Harry. 'I split several on every page, and hope no-one will notice.'

'They passed me by in your first thriller,' said Boots.

'What a pal,' said Harry.

Subsequently, when passing Boots's message to Anneliese, Harry rather expected her to lose her cool. She could remain cool under all kinds of circumstances, but never when reminded of what Hitler, Himmler and their infamous SS battalions had done to Germany. On this occasion, however, her calmness prevailed.

'He won't escape,' she said.

'Knox won't?' said Harry.

'The man who calls himself that,' said Anneliese.

'Why are you so sure?' asked Harry.

'Instinct,' said Anneliese.

'Hold onto that, then,' said Harry, 'I think it's called feminine intuition, and I'm told it's highly reliable.'

Wednesday.

Mr Humphrey Travers of the Foreign Office regarded his chief assistant thoughtfully. Bobby was used to that look. Old Humph was never lost for thought.

'Ah, Somers my dear fellow.'

'I'm in the soup?' said Bobby.

'Good heavens, perish the idea. I merely wanted to point out that that extraordinary young man – um, Wilhelm Kleibert – need no longer worry us or the Home Secretary, if the latest rumour is true.'

'What rumour, sir?'

'That Kleibert is now in Israel.'

'He's made it?' said Bobby.

'It's only a rumour, of course,' said old Humph.

'There's been nothing in the press,' said Bobby.

'It's possible that *The Times* will ask questions, but I'm sure the Israeli government will deny the rumour.'

'Which could mean it's true,' said Bobby.

'We shall accept the denial,' said Mr Travers.

'Best thing,' said Bobby.

'Quite, quite.'

*   *   *

In Tel Aviv, Wilhelm was being fussed, congratulated and honoured, all on the quiet. There were promises of a new identity and a well-paid position with an organization devoted to the uncovering and hunting down of Nazi war criminals.

In her apartment, Leila was in confrontation with Zeke Freyer, her lover.

'You're telling me it's over between us?' he said.

'I'm telling you exactly that,' said Leila.

He protested vigorously and argued heatedly. The crunch came when he asked her if there was someone else.

'Come on, is there?'

'Of course. Someone who wishes to marry me.'

'But you're not the marrying kind.'

'True. But it's what he wishes, and I've said yes.'

'The hell you have. Who is it?'

'Wilhelm.'

'Wilhelm? Wilhelm who?'

'Kleibert. Goodbye, Zeke.'

Chapter Twenty-Eight

The following day, in the time-honoured fashion, Rosie and Matt killed two birds with one stone. Together, in company with Tim, they viewed the Peckham site, found its potential excellent and its location, in the heart of busy, bustling Peckham, all that Matt could have hoped for. He clinched the deal with Tim, and at the offices he and Rosie left a dozen freshly-dressed chickens for the family.

In the afternoon they looked over the house on Red Post Hill, its owner, Mr Clayburn, giving them a guided tour. The place was in perfect order, apart from some rear window frames that needed replacing, and the garden was large and well kept. Rosie and Matt accepted Mr Clayburn's asking price, thus avoiding any time-wasting, which suited Mr Clayburn very well.

'Once a week,' said Mrs Hilary Shoesmith, 'my depression lifts delightfully.'

'And what would you say was the reason?'

asked Professor Knox, fluent, well-spoken, soothingly professional, and sheltered under the umbrella of MI5. Any suggestion that he had slipped some kind of investigation was someone's porkie. But porkies did fly about when it was necessary to protect a useful double agent.

'The reason? Why, you must know it's my weekly consultation with you,' said Mrs Shoesmith, a lady in her mid-thirties. She was extremely attractive, but also neurotic, and in Professor Knox she had found a psychiatrist very much to her liking, so sympathetic, so understanding, so uplifting. And so handsome. He never suggested at any time that her troubles were of her own making, as her previous consultant had. 'Doctor, I so look forward to my appointments with you.'

'I'm here, dear lady, to do all I can for every patient,' said Professor Knox, regarding her with a soothing smile. The couch he provided for his patients was a sofa with red plush upholstery and restful head cushions. Mrs Shoesmith lay there, expression dreamy, body relaxed inside a silk dressing gown. She always insisted on undressing down to her lingerie, since the removal of her outer garments, she said, removed her troublesome inhibitions and freed her mind. Professor Knox, careful of his ethics, insisted in turn that she wear a dressing gown. Which she did. On this occasion, the gown had parted to reveal a glimpse of her nyloned legs.

'You do wonders for me,' she murmured.

'It's satisfying to know these consultations lift your depression,' he said. 'Does it return as soon as you get back to your home? You have said it does. Does it still?'

'Unfortunately, yes,' she said. 'Every room in my home resembles four walls that always seem to be closing in on me.'

'As a child, did your parents ever put you into a dark cupboard as a punishment for being naughty, perhaps?' His voice was a vibrant baritone untouched by any accent, although he had been born in Bavaria. He was a natural linguist. He spoke Russian, Hungarian, and French, as well as English and his own tongue.

'My parents adored me and gave me everything I ever wanted as a child.' The patient's voice was murmurous and silky, rather like that of a woman imagining herself in the arms of a lover. 'So I never had cause to be naughty.'

'You suffered nothing in your childhood or at college that caused fits of angry resentment or deep depression?'

'Nothing, dear doctor.'

He passed the unwanted endearment by. As for his doctorate qualifications, these were represented by a splendid forgery. His practice of psychiatry was an amusement to him, as well as a cover.

'You've told me that your periods of depression began two years ago,' he said. 'And that this condition became permanent six months ago, when it began to affect your marriage. Is that still the case?'

'It's hardly a marriage any longer,' she murmured.

'Why?' What a silly woman she was, deluding herself into believing she was suffering depression when her state was only boredom.

'I no longer enjoy making love,' she said. A pause, a turn of the head, and an inviting smile. 'Except I know I would with you.'

'Madam, you must know I don't want to hear that kind of response.'

'But I'm sure it would help me.'

'It would destroy my practice,' he said, 'and you know that too.' He looked at his watch. 'The hour is up, and this is the right moment to end it, I feel.'

He stood up. Mrs Shoesmith's smile was still inviting.

'The same time next week?' she said. Her consultations were always from three to four in the afternoon, and the last of the day for Professor Knox. His hours were from ten to four, with an hour's break for lunch. He had other work to perform, the kind that had nothing to do with analysing the minds of confused men and bored women.

'Unfortunately, I can make no appointments for a little while,' he said, 'I'm taking a holiday.'

She made a face.

Outside, a well-dressed, broad-shouldered man was speaking to the receptionist.

'Is my wife, Mrs Shoesmith, with Professor Knox at the moment?'

'Yes, sir,' said the receptionist, an entirely innocent party.

'Right.'

'No, sir, wait, you can't go in.'

But Mr Shoesmith wrenched at the handle of the door to the consulting room. He flung the door open, and burst in. He saw his wife on the sofa, her right leg slipping from her dressing gown, foot on the floor, her hand extended in a gesture. Professor Knox, leaning, was about to take her hand and help her to her feet, as far as he would go in physical contact with any patient.

'Bitch!' Mr Shoesmith shouted the word at his startled wife. 'So this is your lousy love nest, is it?' Then he shouted at Professor Knox in the traditional way of cuckolded husbands. 'You filthy swine!' He hurled himself at the pyschiatrist, and struck him a violent blow in the chest. Professor Knox fell backwards, and his head made crushing contact with the white-painted metal radiator. The central heating system was off, the radiator cool, but still as hard and rigid as steel could be. The violent contact of the back of Professor Knox's head with the radiator smashed his skull, and red blood spattered the white paint. The victim slumped and lay lifeless.

The man had not been killed because of being a war criminal or a double agent working for Communist East Germany and Britain, but for what Mr Shoesmith thought him to be, his wife's lover. Which he was not. And death, though violent, had been accidental, for Mr Shoesmith had only sought to beat him up.

Mrs Shoesmith screamed and fainted.

Mr Shoesmith stared down at the body, at the seeping blood, his eyes transfixed, his face white.

There was another scream. This time from the receptionist, who then rushed to the phone on her desk and called the police.

Only High Omnipotence knew what the gods of mercy thought, but perhaps they considered the death, albeit by accident, of ex-Colonel Tomas Neumann of the Waffen SS, alias Professor Knox of Mayfair, not entirely undeserved.

From the West End police station, a sergeant and a constable were on the spot in quick time. Mr and Mrs Shoesmith and the lady receptionist were in paralysed shock, Professor Knox indisputably a corpse. The police constable phoned for an ambulance, and he also contacted the dead man's doctor, while the sergeant asked necessary questions. The receptionist answered stammeringly, Mrs Shoesmith answered faintly, and Mr Shoesmith answered like a man standing stricken at the gates of hell.

Mrs Shoesmith and the receptionist were able to confirm death had been caused by the victim's head smashing against the radiator, and its blood-spattered paint was further evidence of this. Nevertheless, the police sergeant said he would have to report the matter to the CID.

When the doctor arrived, the ambulance crew were examining the dead man. The doctor took over. Mrs Shoesmith, fully dressed by now, was huddled on the couch in a distraught condition. Mr Shoesmith was still on his feet, but looked only a ghost of his usual self. The police sergeant and constable were waiting for the arrival of CID colleagues.

A man, casually attired in an open-necked brown shirt and camel-coloured slacks, entered the house and walked into reception. The receptionist was there, seated, elbows on her desk, face in her hands.

'Excuse me,' he said.

She looked up, her eyes bleary with lingering shock and tiredness.

With an effort, she said, 'The consulting room is closed.'

'Well, yes, it usually is at this time of the day, I know,' said the caller, 'but is Professor Knox available? I need to see him.'

The receptionist struggled to overcome emotion.

'I'm afraid – I'm afraid that isn't possible. Are you a friend or – '

'An acquaintance.' The man saw the open door to the consulting room, and his ears picked up the sound of voices. 'Is Professor Knox entertaining?'

'Oh, God, I wish he was,' said the receptionist, and broke down. The man, kind and persuasive, elicited stumbling information from her. His manner, matching his clothes, changed. The receptionist's head sank eventually, and she buried her face in her hands again.

The police constable, coming out of the consulting room, found her sobbing. No-one else was there. She was quite alone.

The time at that stage was close to five thirty. Government departments in Whitehall were disgorging Civil servants. However, some people were still at their desks.

The following morning, when Bobby picked his daily paper off the mat, his eye was caught by a short report at the bottom of the front page. It concerned the death of a well-known London psychiatrist, one Professor Knox. He had been attacked in his consultancy by the husband of one of his women patients, had fallen heavily and suffered a fatal skull fracture. The police were investigating the tragic incident.

'Jesus,' breathed Bobby.

'Breakfast, Daddy, breakfast,' sang Estelle from the kitchen.

Well, thought stunned Bobby, one bloke who

won't be enjoying cornflakes and toast is Professor Knox.

He kept quiet about this dramatic news over breakfast. It wasn't something to be talked about in front of his children. When Helene saw him to the door on his way out to the station, he spoke a few words to her.

'Look at the front page of our *Telegraph*.'

'Why?' asked Helene.

'That bloke, Professor Knox, has had a nasty accident. He's dead.'

'Dead?'

'He is, according to that report.'

'Well, I'm not going to weep for him,' said Helene. 'I shall tell Anneliese, and I'm sure she won't weep, either.'

Bobby grimaced, kissed her, and departed.

'So we've lost him,' said the senior man, the one with the bushy moustache.

'By an unfortunate accident,' said his deputy, the man called Toby.

'If you'd managed to get him out of the country, that accident would have been avoided.'

'He was making arrangements to go. He'd cancelled all his appointments for a month.'

'It's a stinker, Toby, a stinker. You've spoken to Scotland Yard?'

Toby said yes, he had, last evening. He was still at his desk when in came the man who had spoken to a shocked receptionist. From him he had received the news of Knox's unfortunate demise. Scotland Yard had said it looked like death by accident, but there'd be complications if the coroner's inquest returned a verdict of manslaughter. Bushy moustache said bloody hell, a criminal court case could leave all kinds of dirty washing hanging on the line. The press would start ferreting. The last thing the department wanted to be made public was even a hint that a German war criminal had been turned into a double agent by the UK for the benefit of the UK.

'The Home Office would slap a restriction order on the press, sir,' said Toby.

'But, possibly, not until some damned rag printed an opener. For God's sake, Toby, do something to ensure the accident to our man is played down by the Yard.'

'I also perform miracles in my spare time,' said Toby, 'and we'll need one if the inquest does return a verdict of manslaughter.'

'You're going to turn my fishing weekend into one in which the fish won't bite,' said bushy moustache. 'What about the nuisance from the Foreign Office?'

'He's nothing to worry about now, nor has the German lady. If they've read their morning papers, they'll know Knox is dead.'

'Pity. Very useful agent. However, his death gets the Foreign Office chap off our back.'

* * *

All the same, Toby received a phone call from Bobby half an hour later. Bobby wanted to know if the press report was definitely true, or a put-up job manufactured for some reason entirely dubious.

Toby assured him that dubious really was out of order, old chap, and that it could be arranged for him to inspect the body, in company with the German lady, if that was what she would like. The body was in the freezer, and would remain there until the inquest was over. And the police were satisfied that death was accidental, that the husband of the woman patient only intended to give Knox a bloody nose.

'So you see, my dear fellow, everything straightforward and above board, although very unfortunate for Professor Knox.'

'Tell me,' said Bobby, 'how did he come to be at his practice?'

'Mmm?'

'You informed me he'd slipped your investigation and was probably out of the country.'

'Ah. Yes. Yes. It seems he slipped back under our noses for some reason or another. We'd called off our bloodhounds at the time.'

'Now tell me the one about Goldilocks and the Three Bears,' said Bobby.

'Of course, even though he's now a stiff, we'll probably continue our investigations into his background. By the way, my dear chap, heard from your old pal Guy Burgess lately?'

Bobby ground his teeth. Burgess, now in Moscow, had worked for the Foreign Office. He had favoured Communist Russia since his time as a student at Cambridge University. During his years at the Foreign Office, he had supplied Moscow with a feast of valuable information. When he realized British Intelligence was beginning to investigate him, he fled to Moscow with another of his ilk, another Cambridge man, Donald Maclean.

Cambridge was still blushing, and so was the Foreign Office.

Bobby, irked but unblushing, said, 'Next time we have lunch together, you old bugger, I'll think of something painful to shove up your waistcoat.'

'Yes, let's have fun, mmm? Oh, give my regards to the German lady. She's a splendid woman, I'm sure.'

Chapter Twenty-Nine

Boots had called on Anneliese on his way to work.

'You've seen your morning paper?' he said.

'Harry saw it first,' said Anneliese. 'It astonished him, and yes, myself too. But, Boots, our very good friend, I'm sure that to please me you didn't actually hire the patient's husband as a hit man, did you? That is right, a hit man? Harry says so.'

Boots, standing with her in the hall, laughed. She liked the sound. Men such as Harry and Boots had an infectious baritone vibration to their spontaneous laughter.

'A hit man? I think not, Anneliese.' Boots sobered. 'That poor devil seems to have been the victim of unhappy circumstances. I doubt if he meant to kill Knox. The police are investigating it as accidental death.'

'Well, dear Boots,' said Anneliese, 'I wish him well, and I wish the dead man a long stay in hell with Himmler. In any case, somehow or other, I feel you waved a magic wand.'

'I also dance with fairies,' said Boots. 'Whatever, you can now put Knox right out of your mind, and live your life with your family. Oh, by the way, you're all invited to my mother's eightieth birthday knees-up next Saturday week. Sunday is the actual day, but the family's organizing the event to begin at six on Saturday evening, and we'll toast her the moment her old Westminster chimes mantlepiece clock strikes the last note of midnight.'

'Boots, how lovely, we'll all be delighted to be there.' Anneliese sparkled with pleasure. 'But a knees-up? What is a knees-up?'

'You'll find out,' said Boots, and departed smiling.

Rosie, invited by Mr and Mrs Clayburn to inspect the house again, did so. She wanted to take note of exactly what kind of new furniture was necessary, and what items of her existing furniture would fit in.

On her return to Woldingham in the late afternoon, Matt emerged from the farmhouse kitchen as soon as she alighted from the car.

'Matt, I've a list of – '

'I think you'll have to keep it for later,' said Matt. He grimaced. 'There's a woman here who says she's your mother.'

'What?'

'I hope to God she's not,' said Matt. He knew all about Rosie's life, from her lonely and desolate childhood through her years of happiness as the adopted daughter of Boots and his first wife, Emily. In the farmhouse now, gulping tea, was a woman old, painted and raddled, a creature who had said that, as Rosie's natural mother, she'd come to live with her. He gave Rosie an outline.

Rosie might have come out with something totally at odds with her civilized self. Instead, she spoke quite calmly, if firmly.

'She's not my mother. My mother, Mrs Emily Adams, is dead.'

That denial of her natural mother was not the first. She had made it before, on other occasions. Right from the day when Boots and Emily took her in and later adopted her, she had seen them alone as her true parents. She had loved them from the beginning, particularly Boots, to whom she genuinely felt she belonged as if born of him. Although she eventually discovered her natural father, Charles Armitage, was an entirely likeable man, he remained secondary to Boots. His indiscreet dalliance with a flighty young woman called Milly Pearce had occurred in the heady atmosphere of August 1914. It resulted in Rosie's birth, unknown to the father at the time.

Charles Armitage was eventually killed during the Western Desert Campaign of the Second World War, and Rosie, who had come to care for him, was genuinely saddened by his loss, and emotionally touched to find he had left her the sum of twenty-five thousand pounds to ensure she never wanted.

The woman of her childhood, Milly Pearce, she had put out of her mind years and years ago.

Heavens, was she really here, in the farmhouse?

'Who's that, who's there? Is it you, Rosie?' The questions came from the kitchen, the voice both whining and ingratiating, and its owner appeared at the open kitchen door.

Rosie could not believe her eyes.

The woman wore a bright pink dress, a dress fashioned for the young, not the old. And old she was, her face rouged and powdered, her mouth a lipsticked slash, her hair bleached to a brittle blonde. If ever old mutton had been dressed up in the hope of looking like lamb, this was an example of hope impossible.

Peering curious eyes took in the picture of Rosie, neither painted nor bleached. Her complexion was nature's handiwork, her hair a natural corn-coloured gold.

Matt, repelled by the visitor, said, 'I asked you to wait in the living room.'

'Now don't be like that,' said the old hag. 'I need a bit of comforting now I'm down on me luck, don't I?' The eyes peered again at Rosie. 'Here, who's that? She ain't me daughter, is she? Come on, where's me little girl, where's me Rosie?'

Hortense was feeding meal to the chickens, Joe

transferring the sheep from one field to the other. Both had seen the strange woman, and both were keeping their distance. Giles and Emily were out with friends, making the most of their last holiday week before returning to school.

The visitor was staring, staring at the well-dressed woman standing by the car. Rosie hadn't moved. But she spoke then.

'I'm Rosie, Mrs Rosie Chapman. Who are you?'

'Well, my, ain't you fancy, Rosie, and all grown-up? You look like you've done well for yourself. I'm your mother, come to pay you a visit.'

'You are not my mother.' Rosie was still quite calm. 'I've just reminded my husband that my mother, sadly, is dead.'

'No, I ain't Rosie love, I'm standing right here.' Mutton hopelessly dressed up as lamb essayed a wheedling smile. It parted the red slash. 'I know I'm not as young as I was, but I'm your mum all right, so come and give us a kiss.'

Rosie felt utter distaste. She was very much like Boots in her ability to ride life's unpleasanter moments, and to tolerate misfits, but there was nothing about this particular misfit she could accept. There was no love, no affection, no caring.

'I'm sorry, but I recognize only one woman as my mother, and that isn't you,' she said.

'My, Rosie, ain't you proud and haughty?' The pink dress shimmered on the thin body. 'Mind, it does me eyes good to see how well me daughter's done for herself. It's always hurt me that I wasn't able to bring you up meself, owing to me hard-up circumstances, and it near broke me heart when I had to give you up to be adopted, didn't it? But I told meself it was best for you, didn't I?'

Matt's grimace had become permanent. He felt too helpless to intervene. This confrontation had to be decided by Rosie.

Rosie had only a dim recollection of what her mother had looked like. Her memory recalled a vague figure of oppression, a woman forever finding fault, a woman who obviously wished her child had never been born. She regarded her now as an apparition both repellent and totally unwelcome. She asked a question, quietly but witheringly.

'Tell me,' she said, 'how much were you paid for your sacrifice?'

Boots and Emily had handed over several hundred pounds before this woman would agree to sign the adoption papers. Rosie had found that out from Grandma Finch.

'Now don't be hurtful, Rosie,' the crone whined. Matt looked on in disgust. He knew what this must be doing to Rosie, and his one instinct was to bundle the old bitch off the premises with money to pay her fare back to where she had come from. Rosie owed her nothing, nothing at all, but the cost of the fare would be willingly forthcoming. What was the woman saying now?

Again that she was down on her luck, that she only had her widow's pension. Yes, her husband had passed on last year. Rosie remembered him, didn't she, Mr Rainbould, Mr Clarence Rainbould?

Rosie said she had no recollection whatever of the gentleman. Boots could have told her that Clarence Rainbould had been a second-rate conjuror and magician, but Rosie had never asked questions about either her natural mother or the man she married in the hope of going on the stage herself.

'No, I don't recollect him in any way.'

'My, don't you talk nice and educated, Rosie? I can see that letting you be adopted was best for you, even if it did grieve me something painful. You can give your old mum board and lodging for a while, can't you? And a bit of money for odds and ends, can't you, dearie?'

'Absolutely not.' Rosie was still in control of herself. 'You must understand that I mean it when I say I don't regard you as my mother, which is entirely your own fault. How did you find my address?'

'Rosie love, I wish you wouldn't keep saying I ain't your mum. As to finding where you lived, well, old Mrs Blake and some neighbours down the street helped me. My, she's gone to seed a bit. Me, I've always tried to keep meself looking smart, specially when I was doing stage work with me husband. I've had a hard life, Rosie. It was

329

always a struggle for me and Mr Rainbould, but I always kept hoping that one day we'd be comfortably off so's I could bring you back and give you the kind of life I always wanted to but couldn't afford.'

'I'm sure,' said Rosie, gently sarcastic. She sighed. What was she supposed to do? Strangely, as the voice of self-pity whined on, she felt the onset of pity herself. Perhaps this woman had had a hard life, perhaps her attempt to make herself look younger than she was pointed to a struggle for self-preservation. All the same, what could be done about such a wreck?

Matt did intervene at that point, thinking correctly that Rosie would like to talk to him. He addressed the tarted-up woman.

'Would you like a drink?'

That hit the jackpot. An eager smile opened up the red slash and cut the rouged face in half. False teeth gleamed.

'Well, I would, mister, I ain't touched a drop for a week and more. Mind, I'm not one of your soaks, I just like a small glass now and again. Would you have some gin handy?'

'Come inside,' said Matt. He glanced at Rosie, indicating she was to stay where she was. Then he took the painted widow through to the living room. He reappeared a few minutes later. 'She's settled with a glass and the bottle, Rosie. So now, what's on your mind?'

'What to do for her,' said Rosie, 'and I think

I'd like to phone Boots. He knows far more about her than I do or you do, believe me. Would you mind if I spoke to him?'

Matt knew she was asking him to accept that her adoptive father was the best one to consult.

'Go ahead, Rosie darling, use the extension phone in the shed.'

'Thank you, Matt.'

Not long after that, Boots took a phone call in his office.

'Rosie, that's you?'

'Yes, Daddy darling.' That was Rosie as a girl, as a woman. 'Can you spare a few minutes?'

'I can always spare unlimited time for you, poppet.'

'I badly need your advice,' said Rosie, and went on to tell him her natural mother had turned up, looking for board and lodging at the farmhouse. Boots, stunned for a moment, came to.

'God Almighty,' he said.

'You'd say a lot more than that if you could see her,' said Rosie. 'She's well past her best, if there ever was a best, but, dear man, how can I simply send her away? On the other hand, how can I let her stay? I shudder at the effect it would have on Giles and Emily.'

'Give me a moment to think,' said Boots.

'Take all the time you want,' said Rosie, 'but this really is a cry for help.'

There was an interval of silence at the other end of the line before Boots spoke again.

Then he said, 'There's one thing that counts in her favour, Rosie, the fact that she gave birth to you. Whatever she was herself, she gave birth to a child of sweetness and light, for which I personally will be forever grateful.'

Rosie, gulping like a child, said huskily, 'Are you trying to make me cry?'

'No, poppet, only suggesting you and I, and Matt, owe her something, after all.'

'Don't tell me you think Matt and I should give her a home with us.'

'Perish that hideous thought,' said Boots. He suggested there was one way out, to give her twenty pounds now and to begin with, and then make arrangements with her bank to pay her thirty pounds a month on her assurance that she would find herself lodgings and stay there. The arrangement would stop the moment she attempted to foist herself on Matt and Rosie. That might sound hard, but it was no more than reasonable, and if he was any judge of her character, the thought of an allowance of thirty pounds a month would make her jump through hoops to get at it.

'Oh, you lovely man,' breathed Rosie, 'she would get that on top of her widow's pension. Thank you, darling, for being what you are.'

'And what am I?' asked Boots, his smile in his voice.

'My dear and caring father. Don't you know even now that you were born for me, and I was born for you?'

There was another little silence before Boots said, 'I only know I love you, poppet, that I always have and always will. What more could I ask of life? Rosie, you and Matt have heavy expenses to meet in the immediate future, and if it would help for me to take on the payments to – '

'Nothing doing, old sport,' said Rosie, still a little husky, 'the interest I get from the property company for my investment will easily take care of that.'

'Quite sure?'

'Yes, you old darling, and what would you like for a Christmas present?'

'Well, since you ask, a Christmas card and a bottle of fine old malt whisky. By the way, if Matt has a bottle of gin to spare, tell him to give that to the old lady, along with the twenty pounds, and I'll guarantee she'll toddle off as happy as a Billingsgate fish porter heading for a pub.'

'Aren't you a clever old soldier?'

'That's your imagination, poppet. Phone me again if you need to. Regards to Matt, love to the kids.'

'Goodbye, Daddy love, and a thousand thanks.'

Chapter Thirty

Parental advice had been taken, with Matt's approval, and the deed was done.

Mrs Milly Rainbould, carrying a suitcase containing her worldly goods and a wrapped bottle of gin, and with twenty pounds stuffed eagerly into her handbag, boarded a train at Woldingham railway station, a train that would take her to London Bridge, and drop her close to the pubs and lodgings of Southwark.

Matt, who had driven her to the station, stood on the platform, determined to see the train depart, and her with it.

The train began to move, its old but still gleaming engine puffing smoke. The compartment window jerked down. A face appeared, and in the fading afternoon light its paintwork looked as if it needed repairing. The red slash opened.

'Here, dearie, tell me darling Rosie I'll be all right now, and give her a kiss for me.'

'Look after that gin,' said Matt.

The face moved back a little as the train pulled out, but there were still more words to come.

'Oh, I will, ducky, it's me consolation. Ta-ta.'

The face disappeared. The train gathered speed. Matt watched until it was out of sight, then he walked back to his car and drove himself home. Giles and Emily had just returned from their outing, and Rosie was asking Emily to mind her manners. The girl was grabbing at fruit buns made by Hortense.

Matt little knew Rosie's suspicions of her daughter's tendency to take after the raddled old bag had suddenly hardened.

'Everything fine, Matt?' she asked, thankful that her good-tempered husband had hastened the departure of the woman before the boy and girl returned.

'Fine, Rosie, fine,' said Matt. He saw her relief. 'So's this piece of old Dorset doggerel. "Down by Dorset land they say, old folks come and often stay, best then to do more'n pray, by sending such folks on their way."'

'Passable,' smiled Rosie.

'But what's it mean, Dad?' asked Giles.

'Nothing much,' said Matt.

'Why'd you say it, then?' asked Emily.

'Because I'm a Dorset man,' said Matt. 'Here come Hortense and Joe, so let's put the kettle on for a cup of tea, shall we?'

'I'll do it, Dad,' said Giles.

*   *   *

Later, when he and Rosie were comfortably alone, Matt said he'd seen the old biddy off for certain, since he didn't think she'd jump off the train in case it damaged the bottle of gin.

'I still feel upset that she turned up,' said Rosie.

'I'm not surprised,' said Matt. 'I tell you, Rosie, it beats me all ends up that a woman like her ever managed to give birth to you. I'm giving thanks to Boots for adopting you, and for working out how to deal with the woman.' He couldn't bring himself to call her Rosie's mother, any more than Rosie had ever been able to regard her as such. 'First-class solution, burn my braces.'

'You really didn't mind my talking to him?' said Rosie.

Matt came up from his armchair, moved close, bent and kissed her.

'I've never minded anything you've ever done, Rosie, and you know, don't you, how much you've always meant to me? There's no other Dorset man ever been as lucky as I've been.'

Rosie smiled.

'Is there an old Dorset saying for that too?'

'Surely,' said Matt. '"Down among the Dorset men, there's women sweet and tall, but for him, the luckiest, there's one the best of all."'

'You're forgetting something,' said Rosie.

'Am I?'

'Yes. You're forgetting I'm the luckiest. I'm

336

closely related to the two best men ever born. My husband and my adoptive father.'

Matt kissed her again. Like Boots, and like Rosie herself, he saw how marriage could develop into cherished companionship.

It was that which Chinese Lady was enjoying with Sir Edwin in the twilight of their lives.

The photographs of the twins had been taken by Amos Anderson without his studio having trembled and tumbled by reason of their un-bounded energy. Indeed, neither he nor Polly had found it necessary to curb them. They were astonishingly co-operative. Well, the fact of the matter was the chosen portrait was for Grandma Simms, a lady of charm and generosity. The twins could always rely on super birthday and Christmas presents, together with postal orders of munificent value. It was not the gifts alone, however, it was the affection they had for their maternal grandmother that made them behave perfectly during the sitting.

Polly, having chosen the shot she and her stepmother liked best, called on Amos to collect the finished item. He had fixed it into the frame she had also chosen. The whole thing was frightfully expensive, although not as far as Polly was concerned. She liked it far too much even to think about the cost. There they were, the twins, seated back to back, heads turned to face the camera. Gemma was dreamy-eyed,

James showing the lightest of smiles, these expressions induced by Amos during the sitting, the head and shoulders portrait perfect.

'Lovely, Mr Anderson, lovely,' said Polly, 'but can these two angels really be the imps I encounter at home?'

'Imps we like, Mrs Adams, don't we?' said Amos. 'And, Mrs Adams, will you accept from me two whole plate prints of the one I took of you with your twins?'

He had persuaded Polly to pose with Gemma and James for the last shot on the roll of film. Polly did resist persuasion initially, for she was no longer enamoured of herself as a subject for anyone's camera. She was sure she would come out looking her age and, horrors, even worse. Polly was not growing old gracefully, but very reluctantly. Perhaps there were times when she thought Boots's eyes might wander to a younger woman, although she rarely doubted his fidelity. He was, and always had been, his Victorian mother's son.

However, she gave in to persuasion, which came not only from Mr Anderson, but from Gemma and James too. So just the one shot was taken, and there it was of herself and the twins. She had thought their youth would emphasize her decline, but wonder of wonders, there was no frightful comparison, no crow's feet, no lines and no neck wrinkles. Not that she yet had any of the latter, although she was sure they would arrive one day. No, everything was so smooth and complimentary that she looked years younger than she was.

'Mr Anderson, how did you get such an effect?' she asked, delighted not only by her own image, but by those of the twins too.

'Mrs Adams, by reason of my sitters, didn't I?' said Amos, keeping to himself, of course, that he had delicately touched up both prints by deft and artistic use of an airbrush. Such a fine woman, a true lady, deserved a little help. 'You would accept them as a gift from me?'

'I'd be delighted,' said Polly, 'but will pay for you to frame them, as you have with the twins' portrait.'

'Well, well, then we shall both be delighted, won't we?' said Amos. 'If you have time to spare, I'll frame them now.'

'Thank you,' said Polly, 'one for my husband and one for my mother.'

'A moment, then, while I get the frames,' said Amos, and disappeared.

Polly, seated at his desk, which was heaped with all kinds of photographic paraphernalia, noticed a photograph beside his hat, under which was his phone. It took her attention, and she could not resist turning it.

A picture of a girl sitting on a gate, her dress fluttering, her nyloned legs showing, came to her eyes. Deliciously saucy, and yes, she actually knew the girl. Cassie and Freddy Brown's daughter

Maureen. Polly, no prude, smiled to herself. She turned the photograph back round.

Amos reappeared, with the frames. He sat down, dismantled the frames and inserted the photographs. He showed the finished results to Polly.

'Perfect,' she said. 'Thank you so much, Mr Anderson. Now, how much do I owe you altogether?'

Amos quoted the cost, informing her there was a discount of twenty per cent on the two frames she had just ordered. The amount was still high, but Polly said she considered he had more than earned his charges and wrote him a cheque there and then.

'Sometimes, Mrs Adams,' he smiled, 'sometimes my work, which is always a pleasure, is more so, isn't it?'

'And sometimes a customer is more than satisfied,' said Polly. 'Mr Anderson, do forgive me, but I couldn't help noticing that photograph of a girl on a gate. You see, I know her. She's the daughter of old friends of my husband.'

Amos positively beamed.

'Maureen Brown? Well, well, a small world, isn't it?' he said. 'I photographed her for the *Daily Mirror* or other newspapers or magazines as a girl next door – '

'Excuse me?' said Polly.

'Yes, don't you see?' Amos showed her the print. 'Shy, but appealing, isn't she?'

'Shy?' Polly laughed. 'Young Maureen?'

'I'm hoping she'll come to represent the country's girl next door, which we both would like,' said Amos, his smile containing a twinkle.

'I'm fascinated,' said Polly.

'Happily,' said Amos, 'I've just received a letter from *Weekend*, a Saturday paper, to which I sent shots similar to this one. I've just heard from them to say one will be published next Saturday. I must now let Maureen know.'

'Will you do me a favour?' asked Polly. 'Will you let me tell her first? Then I'll ask her to phone you.'

'You'd like to do that, Mrs Adams?'

'Mr Anderson, it would tickle me.'

'Ah, being tickled we all like, don't we?' beamed Amos. 'Yes, tell her, I don't mind in the least, and ask her to come and see me tomorrow morning, will you?'

'Promise,' said Polly.

Amos wrapped up the three framed photographs, gave them to her and saw her out.

'Goodbye, Mrs Adams, and perhaps I'll have the pleasure of seeing you again sometime, eh?'

'I'm sure,' smiled Polly, and left.

There are people and people in this world, thought Amos, there are people like the SS savages, and people like Wilhelm Kleibert and Mrs Adams, for whom we should be grateful to God.

*   *   *

'Polly?' Boots, home from the office, was looking at a framed portrait photograph of his wife and children, a quite enchanting work of art. He had already seen the portrait of the twins, and expressed unreserved approval. 'Polly, it's a delightful portrait of you and the kids. It's for me?'

'For you alone, ducky, for your study,' said Polly. 'I want you to have it on your desk to give you a daily reminder not to forget.'

'Not to forget what?'

'Why, you old sweetie, that we belong to you, what else?'

'Are you all going away, then, say to darkest Africa?'

'I've been to Africa. I went there before the war. To get you out of my system. God, I can still remember I was no sooner there than I was desperate to get back. No, old love, I give you that photograph in the hope you like it, very much.'

'Love it,' said Boots, 'it's a beaut, especially of you.'

'Yes, don't I look good?' said Polly triumphantly. 'Mr Anderson has worked a miracle, of course. Could he, I wonder, feed five thousand starving Chinese with five fishes?'

'He could, if he could also walk on water,' said Boots.

'Listen, dear man, I've something that will tickle you.'

'Is it something I've been on close terms with during our marriage?'

'Whatever do you mean?' said Polly.

'Is it something else, then?' asked Boots.

'Very much something else,' said Polly.

Boot spent the next several minutes being tickled, Polly insisting on telling him about the saucy photograph of Freddy and Cassie's daughter Maureen, how Amos Anderson intended to promote her as the UK's girl next door and had received word from *Weekend* that it would publish one of the shots next Saturday.

'Freddy's family,' said Boots, 'which means this is the end of all that Chinese Lady holds dear. Someone will have to tell Edwin to keep that paper out of her way. Do we take it?'

'No, but we could order it,' said Polly.

'Do that,' said Boots. He laughed, Polly laughed. At which point the twins showed up. Invariably, when one appeared, the other was never far behind.

'What's funny?' asked Gemma.

'Jokes, usually,' said Boots.

'Darlings,' said Polly, 'here's your framed portrait all ready to be given to Grandma.'

'Oh, let's see,' said Gemma, and she and James studied the finished work of photographic art. 'Crikey, is this us?'

She and James exchanged ribald comments, but decided the portrait was just about good enough for their maternal grandmother.

Flossie called.

'Supper's ready, Mrs Adams.'

This meant it wasn't until later that Boots was able to talk to Polly about his phone conversation with Rosie.

Polly listened with intense interest. She knew how Rosie had come to be adopted, but had never known the natural mother, never met her, and had never heard Rosie speak about her. Boots's solution to the problem of how to get rid of the woman struck her as expensive but salutary.

'I'm proud of you, old fruit,' she said. 'Rosie and Matt have more than enough to do in selling up, moving home and beginning new lives. You've saved them taking on a cross as heavy as Mrs Thingamajig.'

'Mrs Milly Rainbould,' said Boots.

'That's as much of a thingamajig as anything else I can think of,' said Polly. 'Would you like a shot of Scotch, old warrior?'

'Haven't I had one?'

'Not yet. Allow me.'

'Polly?'

'Well, lover?'

'You're a poppet.'

Chapter Thirty-One

'Hello?' said young Lewis Brown.

'To whom do I have the pleasure of speaking?'

'Me,' said Lewis.

'Billy Butlin?' Billy Butlin was the originator of imaginative holiday camps.

'Crikey, me Billy Butlin? No, I'm Lewis Brown.'

'Good evening, Lewis, I'm Mrs Polly Adams.'

'Oh, Aunt Polly? I'm honoured.'

'I'm sure. Is your sister at home?'

'She will be when I tell her it's you – hold on a tick. Maureen! Aunt Polly on the phone!'

Maureen arrived at the phone.

'Aunt Polly?'

'Hello there, Maureen. I've news for you.'

'No, really? What news?'

Polly told the girl about Mr Anderson and *Weekend*, the light-hearted Saturday paper. Maureen went over the top, and a little shriek of delight pinged into Polly's ear.

'Crikey, that's great! He really said that? I'm really going to be in *Weekend* next Saturday?'

'So Mr Anderson said. As the nation's shy girl next door.'

'Shy? Isn't he funny? He asked me if I could blush a bit, and I said how could he photograph a blush, and he said he could make me look as if I was. Crikey, am I excited, it could be the start of me life in glamour.'

'I wish you luck,' said Polly. 'Oh, Mr Anderson would like you to call on him tomorrow morning.'

'Oh, I'll go and see him in me lunch hour. Thanks ever so much, Aunt Polly, for letting me know.'

'Not at all,' said Polly, 'I'm tickled.'

'Well, blowed if that ain't a reg'lar knockout,' said the Gaffer.

'Our Maureen in that weekly paper,' said Cassie.

'Clara Bow and all,' mused the Gaffer, comfortable with a half-pint of his favourite wallop. 'Saucy minx, she was, tent pegs up to her bum.'

'Now, Dad,' said Cassie.

'How much will the paper be paying you, Maureen?' asked Freddy.

'Oh, they pay Mr Anderson, and he gives me twenty per cent,' said Maureen, still flushed with excitement.

'Well, that ain't right, is it?' said Lewis. 'I mean, it's not his legs, is it? And who'd want to see his, anyway?'

'But he's the photographer, they're his copyright on account of him being professional and posing me to me best advantage,' said Maureen. 'And I've already had three pounds.'

'Anyway, how much will he get?' asked Freddy.

'I don't know yet, do I?' said Maureen. 'I expect he'll tell me when I see him tomorrow lunchtime.'

'I ain't seen a picture of Clara Bow since I don't know how long,' said the Gaffer, raising his glass and wetting his whistle. 'Nor her legs.'

'Just as well, Gaffer,' said Freddy, 'she might have varicose veins by now.'

'Reg'lar sexpot, she was,' said the Gaffer.

'Dad,' said Maureen, 'on the day *Weekend* comes out with me photo in it, can you order lots of copies to be delivered?'

'If your dad doesn't, I will,' said Cassie.

'I'll take one to school,' said Lewis, his summer holiday now at an end.

'Dad, stop him doing that,' said Maureen, 'I don't want any pimply kids goggling at me photo.'

'Lewis,' said Cassie, 'you're not to let any of them boys do any goggling, d'you hear?'

'What about the ones like me that don't have pimples,' said Lewis, 'is it all right for them to goggle?'

'Dad, hit him,' said Maureen.

'I've done a bit of goggling in my time,' said the Gaffer, 'at pictures of Clara Bow. Called the

347

"It" girl, she was. Reg'lar tease. Now what've we got? I asks yer.'

'Girl next door, that's what we've got,' grinned Freddy.

'I've just thought,' said Cassie.

'Let's hear it, Mum,' said Lewis.

'I just hope all this won't make us notorious,' said Cassie.

'Clara Bow,' mused the Gaffer, 'I tell yer, tent pegs all the way up to her bum.'

Maureen saw Amos during her lunch hour the following day. Having phoned *Weekend*, he was able to confirm next Saturday was the big day, that the paper would pay twenty guineas, and would be sending a reporter to interview her this evening.

'Crikey,' breathed the glowing girl next door, 'fame and fortune all at one go.'

'A fortune we'd like, eh?' said Amos. 'Well, you'll get four guineas out of the fee. And we'll take some more pin-ups before the weather gets cold, won't we?'

'Not half,' said Maureen.

The meeting of the directors of Adams Fashions with the senior directors of Coates took place on Monday afternoon, at Coates's head office in Kensington.

Accompanying Rachel, Sammy and Boots was their chief auditor, Isaiah Binney. Isaiah, friend as well as auditor, was fifty-six and a widower. He was one of several eligible gentlemen who had hopes of marrying Rachel, but Rachel had no thoughts of marrying again. She was too content with her life as it was, added to which she looked after her benign and revered father, now over eighty and a widower himself for many years.

Isaiah was frankly flabbergasted that his respected clients, prompted by Boots, intended, if necessary, to quote two hundred thousand as their asking price.

'My friends – '

'No buts, Izzy,' said Sammy.

'Boots – '

'No buts, Izzy,' said Boots.

'Rachel, I implore you – '

'No buts, Isaiah,' said Rachel. 'In us, you see the three musketeers, and you shall be our d'Artagnan.'

'Heaven preserve me,' groaned Isaiah, 'I could never ride a horse.'

However, he figuratively mounted a fine charger when presenting the accounts to Coates, whose managing director chaired the meeting. All three senior directors were commendably friendly and forthcoming, and their hospitality included a tea tray laden with cakes and biscuits, teapot, coffee pot, cream and milk. Sammy willingly accepted a generous slice of fruit cake, while Isaiah rode into the fray with a formidable array of balance sheets going back to 1950. Reaching the end of his presentation, he paused and waited for a response. The chairman looked at Boots.

'And your estimated turnover for the current year, Mr Adams?' he said.

Boots addressed Isaiah.

'Mr Binney?'

'Double the year '54–'55,' declared Isaiah with professional confidence.

'Is that a guess or a certainty?' asked the chairman of the meeting.

'A promise,' said Isaiah, 'I have the balance sheet for the first six months of the current year.' He issued copies to everyone present. The Coates directors devoured the figures and compared them with last year's.

They whispered among themselves.

'Well, Mrs Goodman and gentlemen,' said the chairman, 'we know a great deal about Adams Fashions, gained over our years of trading with you, and we feel we know something about your future potential. For lock, stock and barrel, we are willing to offer £50,000.' So saying, he sat back in happy anticipation of a delighted response. Or at least a welcome one.

'Ah,' said Isaiah, alias d'Artagnan, feeling his steed beginning to collapse under him.

'It's with you, Mr Adams,' said the chairman.

'Ah, yes,' said Boots, 'generous but conservative.'

'How conservative?' said the slightly surprised chairman, looking at Sammy this time.

'Well,' said Sammy, 'not liberal, if you get me.'

'Not quite,' said the chairman. 'Do you have a figure?' This was asked of Isaiah, who had a figure but felt it was too heavy for his weakening horse. 'Mr Binney?'

'My clients,' said d'Artagnan, 'do have something in mind that doesn't –um – quite agree with yours.'

Rachel spoke up.

'We thought we would begin the financial negotiations at a hundred thousand,' she said.

'A hundred thousand?' Backs stiffened.

'To see how favourably you regarded it.'

'Favourably? Is a hundred thousand the figure your auditor has in mind?'

D'Artagnan fell off his charger. That is, he sighed, slumped and looked appealingly at Boots.

'What I think we'd like to do at this stage,' said Boots, 'is to go away, give ourselves time to consider your offer and whether a compromise can be reached. Then we'll come back to you. As it is, we've enjoyed this meeting, and your hospitality, never forgetting how much we've appreciated all these years of trading with Coates. Thank you, gentlemen.'

D'Artagnan sighed again, this time with relief, and everyone shook hands.

Isaiah departed in his own car, and Boots drove Rachel and Sammy back to Camberwell.

'Well, what do we all think?' asked Rachel.

'It's going well,' said Sammy, 'we've laid the ground on which we can pull out gracious and no hard feelings.'

'I think they'll meet our figure of a hundred thousand,' said Boots.

'That's when we come up with two hundred thousand?' said Rachel.

'No need,' said Boots. 'That's when we quote a refusal to sell by our shareholders.'

'So what was two hundred thousand all about?' asked Sammy.

'To see how we ourselves regarded a figure as high as that,' said Boots, weaving into the busy stream of traffic leading to Waterloo Bridge. Eleven years from the end of the war meant an increasing number of cars on the roads and streets of London and elsewhere. 'And we agreed no amount of money would persuade us to let go of your own particular baby, Sammy old lad.'

'I'm appreciative of that reminder, Boots old cock,' said Sammy. 'Which reminds me of something else.'

'What, Sammy?' asked Rachel.

'I hardly touched my slice of fruit cake,' said Sammy, 'but forget about going back for it, Boots.'

The Riley car quivered with laughter as the three musketeers entered the north side of

Waterloo Bridge. Which was another reminder, that of Wellington giving Napoleon his last run-around

That evening, by arrangement, a lady reporter from *Weekend* called on Maureen to interview her, to find out what kind of personality she had, what her interests, recreations and ambitions were, and what her background was like. The inferences drawn in that order were bright, varied, typically teenage, unlimited (as long as they put her into a glamour world), and cheerfully cockney.

The interview, conducted in private and in the nicest possible way, made Maureen feel she was famous already.

Afterwards, Freddy treated the lady to a gin and tonic, which she downed in a flash. Cassie accepted a sherry, Lewis a Coca-Cola, Maureen a daring port and lemon, the Gaffer half of old ale. Oh, and the lady reporter had another gin and tonic, and went home feeling her job that evening had been well done.

On Saturday morning the paperboy delivered a shipping order of ten copies of *Weekend* to the house in Wansey Street, and at breakfast in the cosy kitchen, everyone had a copy. Cereals were neglected, and pages rustled about as they were opened up.

'Crikey!' gasped Lewis.

'I can't believe it,' said Cassie.

'I can, it's in black and white,' said Tommy.

''Swelp me,' said the Gaffer, 'is that our Maureen?'

'Yes, it's me, Grandad, don't I look famous?' said Maureen, delighted.

Famous was in the form of a fluttering dress and lace-hemmed slip, nyloned legs and an inch or so of bare thigh.

And a headline, 'WALWORTH'S GIRL NEXT DOOR', followed by a write-up, which ended with an implication that the readers would see more of her.

'Hold up,' growled the Gaffer, 'what's more of her if this ain't enough? Freddy, you ain't going to let her show more of herself, are yer?'

'Don't worry, Gaffer,' said Freddy, crunching toast, rereading the write-up and gulping hot tea, 'we'll put her in trousers.'

'Here, Dad, give over,' said Maureen, 'I'm not going to do glamour poses wearing trousers.'

'Just a sweater and knickers, I suppose,' said Lewis.

'Hit him, someone,' said Maureen.

'Now, Lewis love,' said Cassie, 'you shouldn't be teasing Maureen on her big day.'

'But, Mum' said Lewis, 'if Dad puts her in trousers, and she takes them off –'

'Suit of armour, more like,' said the Gaffer, 'she won't get that off in a hurry.'

'Talking of a hurry, I'd better go and open up the store,' said Freddy.

354

'And I'd better get off to meet a mate,' said Lewis.

'I don't think I'll bother to go to work on Monday,' said Maureen.

'Yes, you will,' said Freddy.

'But, Dad, now I'm into fame and fortune, I don't need any boring job,' protested Maureen.

'Don't count your chickens,' said Freddy, 'go to your work on Monday, me girl.'

'Yes, you'd best go, Maureen love,' said Cassie.

'Here,' said the Gaffer, rustling through his copy of *Weekend*, 'ain't there any pictures of Clara Bow?'

Polly had ordered a copy of the paper. She and Boots discovered the published photograph of Maureen before the twins came down to breakfast. Polly was tickled all over again, Boots vastly amused.

'Saucy,' he said.

'Sexy,' said Polly, 'in a sweet kind of way. What d'you think of the blurb?'

'Promising,' said Boots.

'That it'll invite enquiries from model agencies?'

'What's a model agency?'

'That question doesn't fool me,' said Polly, 'you're not quite an old Victorian yet. And why are you looking at me like that?'

'I'm wondering,' said Boots, 'if next time Mr Anderson photographs Maureen, you shouldn't join her as the Dulwich girl next door. You're

355

still the proud owner of a fine pair of legs and some flashy nylons.'

When the twins came down to the dining room only seconds later, they found their newly dignified mother belabouring their distinguished dad with a ringed table napkin. They gawped.

Flossie put a stop to it with her singing voice.

'Breakfast coming up, Mrs Adams.'

A letter addressed to the managing director arrived at Coates's head office during the third week in September. It was couched in the most tactful terms, regretfully advising him that at a shareholders' meeting, the board had accepted a vote to retain full ownership of Adams Fashions Ltd. It was hoped that this would not affect the trading relationship that Adams Fashions had enjoyed with Coates over many years.

Chapter Thirty-Two

On the evening of the third Saturday in September, Chinese Lady was chief guest of honour at the party given to celebrate her eightieth birthday at the handsome home of Boots and Polly. Earlier in the week, she had phoned Boots to implore him not to have any loud music. She wouldn't mind, she said, if Lizzy played some nice tunes on the piano. Lizzy could play quite nice, she said. So Boots told her he'd ask Lizzy to play the kind of songs he knew she liked. Yes, like 'Roses of Picardy', said Chinese Lady. All right, old lady, will do, said Boots. Don't call me old lady, said his mother, and what's 'will do' mean? It means I'll ask Lizzy to play that song and others like it, said Boots. Well, you ought to say so, said Chinese Lady. Still, you've grown up quite respectable, she added, so I'm not actually complaining.

Polly had also done some imploring of her husband as long as a month ago.

'Listen, old sport, make the celebrations joint,'

she said. 'I honestly don't want my age to be the sole reason for any ragtime high jinks. I know I'll be sixty, but I want to avoid it being made too obvious. Combine your mother's eightieth with my sixtieth. After all, my birthday arrives only a few days after hers. Naturally, she must be the bright star of the evening, and I'll be happy to glow dimly in something dowdy.'

'Dowdy?' said Boots, raising the proverbial eyebrow.

'Well, not too dowdy,' said Polly. 'Arrange a combined celebration, will you, dear man?'

Boot said he understood, and would arrange it just as she wished. He'd let the family know.

'However,' he added, 'on the actual day of your sixtieth, you and I, just the two of us, will go up to town and have evening dinner at the Ritz. Would you like that, Polly?'

Polly said he was an utter darling, that she couldn't think of anything she would like better.

Everyone belonging to Chinese Lady's extensive family, except Philip, now in the Middle East with his squadron, turned up for her eightieth, and Polly's sixtieth, birthday carousal. The turn-out included family members whom Chinese Lady thought of as living in foreign parts: namely, Alice and Fergus from Bristol, Bess and Jeremy from their farm down in Kent, and David and Kate from their Westerham farm. Together with old friends and some new ones, the guests totalled a most appropriate number. Seventy, which was midway between eighty and sixty. Boots, with the support of Lizzy, Tommy and Sammy, had arranged that very neatly, and no-one of any significance had been left out. Some of Polly's old friends of the '14–'18 war were present, as was Lady Simms, of course, as well as old Eli Greenberg and Mrs Greenberg, and Rachel Goodman.

On arrival, each guest was greeted by Chinese Lady, welcomed by Sir Edwin and presented to Polly, who implored all of them to take absolutely no notice of her, but to concentrate on the marvel of Boots's enduring mother, who looked all of upright. She wore a new dress which, out of family loyalty, she had bought at Sammy's Brixton shop, Lizzy accompanying her and helping her to choose an oyster-coloured creation with a well-fitting bodice that showed her bosom still seemed firm and proud, although not in the least buxom. She had never been that. Her dark brown hair, now tinted with grey, was dressed high in an Edwardian-style upswept crown that suited her perfectly.

Rosie, on arrival with Matt and their children, was greeted with warmth and affection by both Chinese Lady and Sir Edwin, and then by Polly.

And Polly, of course, said, 'Aren't they a darling couple, Rosie? I beg you to take absolutely no notice of myself, even if it is my sixtieth, curse it. I want nothing taken away from Boots's mother, nothing.'

'In that case,' said Rosie, 'why are you wearing such a stunning dress?'

'Darling, this dowdy old thing?' said Polly, shimmering in a Paris-inspired sheathline Tricel creation of turquoise green, mid-calf length.

'In that old thing,' said Rosie, 'you can't fail to be noticed.'

'Rosie darling, I assure you, I merely wanted not to look like something the cat left over for the mice,' said Polly. 'Out of respect for Boots and in honour of – oh, hello, Matt, how well you look on lamb and chicken. As I was just saying to Rosie . . .'

By six-twenty, all guests had arrived, and from then on they circulated, chatted, gossiped, talked of Grandma and Grandpa Finch and how marvellous they were for their age, and wasn't Polly at sixty simply ravishing, stunning, terrific or whizzo, according to who was paying the compliment. Drink also circulated, keeping pace with general intake, and a team of caterers ran a buffet of unlimited food of first-class quality. Lizzy, Tommy and Sammy were all contributing to the costs, along with Boots.

Young people gradually became a congregated clump of vitality, and Phoebe asked when the jiving would start.

'Oh, I'm afraid we're not having that,' said

Gemma, originator of the wild session at her dad's sixtieth.

'No, not this time,' said James.

'No rock 'n' roll?' said Linda, sister of Philip, the one absentee.

'Or jiving?' said Anneliese's stepdaughter Cindy, who frequently regarded James as someone who could make himself useful to her by carrying her shopping bag. She was fond of shopping, mostly for teenage items. Anneliese, her well-off mother, and Harry, her generous dad, kept her purse well stocked.

'Isn't it going to be a proper party, then?' asked Clare, wife of Sammy's younger son, Jimmy.

'Of course it's a proper party,' said James, 'it's in honour first of all of Grandma Finch – '

'And there's no-one more proper than Grandma Finch,' said Gemma.

' – and secondly in honour of our dignified mother,' said James.

'Mrs Polly Adams,' said Gemma.

'Dignified, did James say dignified?' asked Linda, almost spluttering white wine.

'It's a newly won condition,' said James amid the buzz of conversation going on in the lounge, the living room, the dining room and the spacious hall. 'And much to be respected.'

'Gemma, I've got to ask,' said Maureen, recently Walworth's girl next door, 'is your brother real? I mean really real?'

'Well, no, not really real,' said Gemma. 'Our dad says he's what you call a one-off, but it's not my fault. I'm just lumbered with him.'

'Oh, I sort of like him,' said Cindy, 'even if he's not much good going round shops with me.'

'Nor's Jimmy with me,' said Clare.

'I admit I've got some faults,' said Jimmy, enjoying a second half-pint of old ale. The caterers had mounted a cask of it on a stand, and it had been well tapped already.

The atmosphere was warming up.

'Is it serious there's going to be no rock 'n' roll?' asked Maureen, dying for someone to ask to see her *Weekend* splash. She had a cutting in her handbag.

'Oh, there'll be music,' said James, 'my Aunt Lizzy's going to play the piano sometime during the evening.'

'Play the piano?' said Linda, looking numbed. 'Play the piano?' She had a feeling it would be one of those concertos that went on for ever.

'Oh,' said Maureen, who had a different feeling, a hopeful one, 'does she play boogie-woogie like Louis Armstrong and Fats Waller?'

'Well, no,' said James, 'she's going to play tunes like "Irish Eyes Are Smiling" and "My Bonnie Lies over the Ocean".'

Collapse of the best part of the young people.

Some of the older generation were on a different level.

'Got to admit it,' said Sammy, 'the old lady's fit

to go on for ever. Look at her, giving old Eli Greenberg a bit of a talking-to. Probably telling him it's time he put his horse and cart out to grass.'

'Wouldn't do the cart much good,' said Tommy, 'carts don't eat grass.'

'Now you know what I mean,' said Sammy. 'Vi, you've got an empty glass, let me get you a refill.'

'Later, Sammy, thanks,' said Vi, 'but I wouldn't mind another slice of that lovely salmon.'

'Here, young 'un,' said Sammy, grabbing the arm of a passing lad, who happened to be Giles, son of Rosie and Matt, 'do your Aunt Vi a favour, eh? Bring her a helping of salmon.'

'Give us your plate, Aunt Vi,' said Giles. He took it from her and darted to the buffet set up along the wall of the large dining room.

'Where are all the children?' asked Tim, eye on Felicity, who was talking by the door with Rosie and Lizzy. He could guess this was one more frustrating occasion for her, hearing everything but seeing nothing and nobody. No moments of further hope had happened during the last week or so, no headaches and no vision. She was at the stage of actually wishing for a headache, since she was sure it would lead to a marvellous if brief interval of clarity. 'Yes, where are all the young kids?'

'They're upstairs, in the twins' old playroom, taking turns to ride the rocking horse,' said

Susie. She was referring to the four- to nine-year-olds, all of whom considered a rocking horse much more fun than being crowded in among chattering grown-ups. All children under four were at their respective homes being looked after by obliging neighbours or babysitters. 'Boots thought it a good idea for them to ride the rocking horse, he said it would avoid them being trodden on down here. Polly's Flossie and your Maggie are keeping an eye on them, Tim.'

'My old man can still have brainwaves,' said Tim.

Giles returned. He handed Vi's plate back to her. It was piled high with goodies, including two slices of the salmon.

'Goodness,' said Vi, 'I didn't ask for all that, Giles.'

'Do you good, Aunt Vi,' said Giles, and went to join some of his contemporaries.

'I can't eat all this,' said Vi, 'I've already had plenty.'

'No problem, Vi,' said Sammy, and he, Tommy, Freddy and Jeremy raided the plate, leaving Vi with just one slice of salmon.

'Great, this Scotch salmon flavour,' said Jeremy, Bess's American husband. 'Do you guys come here often for your eats?'

'Of course,' said Susie, 'every time Grandma Finch has an eightieth birthday.'

'Bless us,' said Cassie, 'I can't wait for the next one.'

'Lend me your ear, Sammy,' said Jeremy. 'I know you import American denim for the manufacture of jeans. Try importing New England lobsters – they're great too.'

'What for?' asked Sammy. 'Manufacturing shell-armoured bras for shy ladies?'

'No go, Sammy,' said Susie, 'shy ones went out when Hitler's bombs blew skirts off.'

The celebrations went on, Chinese Lady circulating to make sure she had a chat with everyone, while Boots, carrying bottles of red and white wine, saw to it that glasses requiring refills were serviced. Other drinks were being served by the caterers.

Nine o'clock came up all too soon, and he then rang a bell. It caught everyone's attention.

'Friends, family, relatives, time for some music,' he said.

'Oh, hurray!' exclaimed a young feminine voice.

'My talented sister Lizzy will oblige with some piano melodies,' said Boots, looking easy and casual in shirt, tie and trousers. All the men had been invited to shed their jackets, for the September evening was warm. 'So shift to the lounge or as near to it as you can get.'

'What's he mean, the lounge?' asked Chinese Lady of Sir Edwin. 'Doesn't he mean the parlour?'

'Correction,' said Boots, 'I meant the parlour. Where's Lizzy?'

'Here,' called Lizzy, emerging from a ruck and looking splendidly buxom in a dress which, with its long, slightly flared skirt and defining bodice was remindful both of the New Look and the modern look. Lizzy didn't believe in being frumpish, even if she was fifty-eight.

'The piano's waiting,' said Boots.

'Oh, I'd like some nice piano tunes,' said Chinese Lady.

'Go on, Aunt Lizzy, swing it!' called Rosie's daughter Emily, which made Chinese Lady look mystified.

Lizzy reached the lounge piano, seated herself, touched the pedals, struck a few notes and, amid encouraging voices, began a musical repertoire.

She commenced with what she knew was a great favourite of Chinese Lady, 'Soldiers of the Queen'.

Young people looked blank, older people hummed the tune, which Lizzy played with the verve of a natural. She followed that with 'Roses of Picardy'. Young people looked at each other, older people began to sing the refrain.

Then came 'Shine on, Harvest Moon' and 'Drink to Me Only with Thine Eyes'. Young people began to think the party was in a state of disintegration, but older people sang rousingly when the next tune, 'I've Got a Lovely Bunch of Coconuts', arrived from under Lizzy's rhythmic fingers.

Feet began to tap when 'Down at the Old Bull

and Bush' came forth from the ivories. Mature voices belted out the lyric. Chinese Lady looked quite misty-eyed. Every song reminded her of her young days, and of the time when she was being courted by the man who became her first husband, Corporal Daniel Adams of the Royal West Kent regiment, the long-gone father of her children.

'There's No Place Like Home' followed, at which stage one or two inwardly groaning young people thought they might as well go home. Old Aunt Victoria, sitting with Ned, said songs like these made a party. Ned said some of the young people probably thought them a bit old-fashioned. Old Aunt Victoria said they didn't have a right to.

Lizzy, quite enjoying herself at the keyboard, was smiling. She'd had two glasses of port and lemon, and there was a twinkle in her eye. Suddenly, she found different chords, and what happened then? A rousing piano rendition of 'Roll out the barrel'.

Young people perked up. Young legs began to jig. And Chinese Lady said, 'Boots, that's a catchy tune, what is it?'

'Oh, something about a beer barrel,' said Boots.

'Well, fancy that,' said Chinese Lady, 'Lizzy's doing my birthday celebrations proud, bless her.'

It was the young people who were singing now, and they were also swinging it. Lizzy, her twinkle brighter, went into another popular number, 'Ragtime Cowboy Joe'. She followed that with her own rendition of 'Singing the Blues'. And then, of all things, 'Rock around the Clock'.

The young people were well away now, and Chinese Lady was thinking what nice catchy new tunes Lizzy was playing. Of course, the rippling notes of a piano were delightful to her ear compared to the sound of Gemma's record player blasting forth at full pitch from the loudspeakers.

'Dig it, Linda.'

'Move, Maureen, move.'

'Crikey. Gemma, your Aunt Lizzy is hep, nearly as good as Fats Waller.'

And so on.

Revelry was the order of the moment.

Chinese Lady only knew the tunes from the piano were really quite catchy, but she had no idea why the young people were doing all that funny dancing. She asked Boots if he could get them to do foxtrotting and waltzing.

'Well, I could, old lady,' he said, 'but I think you'd find them falling over their feet.'

'Don't none of them go to dance classes?'

'Some do,' said Boots, 'but not, I fancy, for waltzing and foxtrotting. Have a little more port.'

'Well, perhaps I will have just another little drop, Boots.'

Chapter Thirty-Three

Lizzy took a rest. Boots thought it a good time for the birthday cake to be made public and for the caterers to uncork the champagne. The cake, wheeled into the hall on a trolley, was hailed with enthusiasm, its white icing top decorated with the pink figures 80 and 60 entwined with green ivy leaves, chosen for ivy's longevity. There were two slim candles, one eight inches high, the other six. The champagne fizzed, glasses were filled, and it was Lizzy who proposed the combined birthday toast.

'Oh, hello, everyone,' she began.

'Hello, Lizzy!' responded a wag.

'It's me that Boots said – '

'Hello, Boots!' responded a host of wags.

'Because I'm her only daughter, Boots said it was me that ought to make this speech to my mum and – '

'Hello, Mum!'

Chinese Lady, having had a couple of neat ports, and a little drop more, nodded graciously.

'To my mum and Polly – '

'Hello, Polly!'

'Stop interrupting,' said Lizzy. 'Look, it's a kind of honour – '

'Hello, Honor!'

'What kind is she?'

'If some of you don't shut up,' said Lizzy, 'I'll get my big brother to – '

'Hello, big brother!'

'I mean the one with the big shoulders.' Lizzy was persevering, and she still had a twinkle, no doubt brought about by a glass of white wine that had been topped up several times. 'Yes, Tommy, I mean – '

'Hello, Tommy!'

The wags included Tommy himself. He'd had two pints of old ale.

'If I might be allowed to finish?' said Lizzy.

'Carry on, Lizzy,' said Boots, his smile permanent.

'Well,' said Lizzy, 'it's my pleasure to ask you all to let our mum and Polly know how much we admire them for being eighty and sixty respective – '.

'Hello, respective!'

'And to ask them to step forward and cut their birthday cake together.'

'Hello, birthday cake!'

Shrieks of laughter ran around the hall.

Chinese Lady advanced purposefully on the cake, Polly approached in gliding fashion.

Anneliese, watching both of them, saw one as a magnificient matriarch, the other as surely every foreigner's idea of sublime English poise.

Boots struck a match and applied the flame to one candle, then the other.

'Carry on, Lizzy,' he said.

'Come on, Mum, come on, Polly, blow the candles out together,' said Lizzy.

'Hello, blow!' shouted almost everyone.

'Boots,' said Chinese Lady, 'I don't know why you let hooligans in.'

'Blow,' smiled Boots.

Chinese Lady bent forward, Polly dipped, and they looked into each other's eyes.

'Together, then, dear lady?' murmured Polly, and together they blew. Out went both candles.

There was a farrago of rousing cheers.

Boots raised his glass of champagne.

'Friends, family, relatives, here's long health to our birthday girls, and may they always be as close in your affections as they are in mine. I give you Maisie and Polly.'

'Hello, Maisie and Polly, long health and long luck!' called Ned, getting through the evening without any problems.

The rest of the guests echoed his words, and champagne glasses glittered with light as they were tilted to lips.

After which, Maisie and Polly cut the cake together.

If Lizzy's speech had been short and Boots

had said only a few words, that was what Chinese Lady had wanted, while Polly had asked for as little mention as possible. All through her many years, Chinese Lady had discouraged being fussed, while Polly had always preferred good company to windy speeches.

Jeremy, a dab hand himself at inducing a piano to bring forth melody, took over the ivories and jazzed them up. Delight grabbed the young people as they accepted the invitation to swing it. Chinese Lady, now seated in company with Sir Edwin, old Aunt Victoria and Ned, looked on with a feeling it had all happened before, at Boots's sixtieth. Except the sound of the piano was a lot nicer than Gemma's records. But all those girls, well, what had happened to modesty she couldn't think, and said so to her husband. Sir Edwin said he couldn't think, either, and perhaps it was all due to the changes brought about by the war. Chinese Lady said that that was something else to blame Hitler for, that he ought to have been drowned at birth.

'I never knew anyone more horrid,' said old Aunt Victoria.

'I never knew him myself,' said Ned, 'but I'm willing to believe Satan was either his brother or his dad. Well, he's long been a heap of ashes, so don't let him spoil the celebrations.'

Old Aunt Victoria closed her eyes, not because she was tired but to blank out what some of the girls were showing as their skirts or dresses swirled high.

The jiving, the rock 'n' roll and the champagne went on until a few minutes before midnight, when Boots established a little order and asked for quiet.

'What for quiet, Uncle Boots?' asked Phoebe.

'So that we can hear Grandma Finch's mantelpiece clock strike twelve o'clock,' said Boots.

'But we won't hear it from here,' said Lulu, Socialist wife of Paul, younger son of Tommy and Vi.

'Take a look,' said Boots, and took a covering off the old Westminster chimes clock, now reposing on the trolley in the hall, where most guests were gathered.

The wags responded.

'Hello, clock!'

It showed a minute to midnight. Everyone took the cue and waited, while Boots brought Chinese Lady to her feet. She was a little flushed on port and champagne, but not in the least cross-eyed.

The clock struck, and the chimes spelled out the musical passing of time.

Midnight became morning.

A rousing welcome.

'Happy birthday, Grandma, happy birthday!'

'And long may it last,' said Boots, and kissed his mother. Up came Sir Edwin, Lizzy, Ned,

Tommy, Vi, Sammy, Susie and Polly, all of whom kissed the birthday lady in turn.

Boots looked at Lizzy, whose twinkle had taken on the sparkle of champagne. She nodded, entered the lounge and sat down at the piano again.

Delighted shouts accompanied the first chords of 'Knees up, Mother Brown'. Action followed immediately, and Anneliese experienced her first viewing of a knees-up, into which she was dragged by Harry and Cindy.

Floors, walls and ceilings vibrated, hitched skirts whisked, and old Aunt Victoria shut her eyes again. Respectability had always meant more to her than even to Chinese Lady.

'Mummy darling, come on, you can do this,' begged Jennifer of her blind mother. Felicity was on her feet. Every light in the house was on, and the light was hurting her eyes. And her eyes were wide open, staring at her precious daughter. This time she moved without effort, she flung her arms around the girl she was seeing for the first time in her life.

'Jennifer!'

'Mummy?' said Jennifer amid the noise of stamping feet, singing voices and general revelry.

'I can see you! Darling, where's Daddy?'

Jennifer, overwhelmed, hugged her mother for long seconds before turning her head. She spotted her father in his white shirt and blue trousers, doing the knees-up with Aunt Susie.

'Daddy! Daddy!'

Tim, hearing her, and seeing her with Felicity's arms around her, knew immediately what had happened. He rushed over. Felicity lifted her head, and as he arrived beside her, the wonderfully clear vision faded. Her daughter and husband blanked out, but what did it matter? It was happening, the process of recovery, she knew it was, and she had seen how lovely Jennifer was.

'Happy birthday, Tim' she said, groping to touch his cheek.

'It's not mine,' said Tim, understanding the touch.

'Yes, it is, old thing, it's yours and mine and Jennifer's.'

The knees-up went on, a rousing, rumbustious and traditional gesture in this joyous celebration of Grandma Finch's eightieth birthday.

Felicity, Tim and Jennifer danced it together.

Tuesday. Midnight again. Out of the Ritz Hotel came two people, one a tall, long-legged man in a dinner jacket, the other a slender woman in a gown. Around her head was a colourful bandeau with a long glossy feather tucked into it, and anyone who had known the years of the Wild Twenties would have recognized that the bandeau and feather were the emblems of the flappers.

The night was rainy. The uniformed doorman sheltered them under his umbrella as they walked to their chauffeur-driven hired limousine. He opened the passenger door for them. Polly slipped in, Boots following. He tipped the door-man a pound.

'Well, thank you, m'lord, thank you, and good luck.'

'I've had that all my life,' said Boots, and put himself beside Polly.

The limousine purred away into London by night, the wet streets shining under the street lamps, the windows of clubs glowing, the caped bobbies keeping an eye out for drunks. Polly, head resting on Boots's shoulder, was dreamy with well-being and deep affection.

'Boots?'

'Well, Polly?'

'Lovely.'

'The dinner?'

'Everything. If I could have my years with you all over again, I'd ask for nothing more.'

'I'm touched, and I'd like to ask for something myself.'

'Ask, old darling, and you shall receive.'

'Could you do something about your feather? It's getting up my nose.'

THE END

Ups and
Downs

THE ADAMS FAMILY

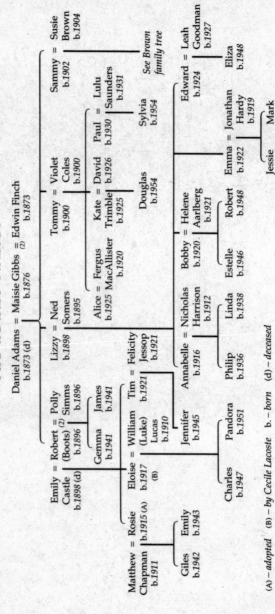

Daniel Adams = Maisie Gibbs (2) = Edwin Finch
b.1873 (d)   b.1876   b.1873

Sammy = Susie Brown
b.1902   b.1904

See Brown family tree

Tommy = Violet Coles
b.1900   b.1900

Lizzy = Ned Somers
b.1898   b.1895

Emily = Robert (Boots) (2) = Polly Simms
b.1898 (d) b.1896   b.1896

Gemma b.1941   James b.1941

Matthew = Rosie Chapman
b.1911   b.1915 (A)

Giles b.1942   Emily b.1943

Eloise = William (Luke) Lucas
b.1917 (B) b.1910

Charles b.1947   Pandora b.1951

Jennifer b.1945

Tim = Felicity Jessop
b.1921   b.1921

Annabelle = Nicholas Harrison
b.1916   b.1912

Philip b.1936   Linda b.1938

Alice = Fergus MacAllister
b.1925   b.1920

Kate = David Trimble
b.1925   b.1926

Paul = Lulu Saunders
b.1930   b.1931

Sylvia b.1954

Douglas b.1954

Bobby = Helene Aarlberg
b.1920   b.1921

Estelle b.1946   Robert b.1948

Emma = Jonathan Hardy
b.1922   b.1919

Jessie b.1946   Mark b.1954

Edward = Leah Goodman
b.1924   b.1927

Eliza b.1948

(A) – *adopted* (B) – *by Cecile Lacoste* b. – *born* (d) – *deceased*

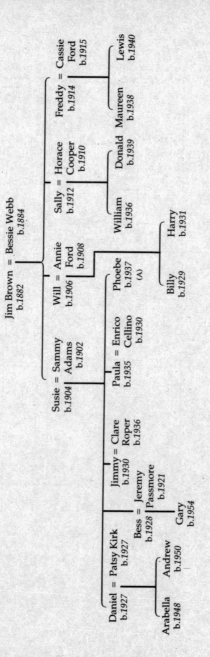

THE BROWN FAMILY

Jim Brown = Bessie Webb
b.1882   b.1884

Susie = Sammy Adams
b.1904   b.1902

Will = Annie Ford
b.1906   b.1908

Sally = Horace Cooper
b.1912   b.1910

Freddy = Cassie Ford
b.1914   b.1915

Daniel = Patsy Kirk
b.1927   b.1927

Jimmy = Clare Roper
b.1930   b.1936

Bess = Jeremy Passmore
b.1928   b.1921

Paula = Enrico Cellino
b.1935   b.1930

Phoebe
b.1937
(A)

Billy
b.1929

Harry
b.1931

William
b.1936

Donald
b.1939

Maureen
b.1938

Lewis
b.1940

Arabella
b.1948

Andrew
b.1950

Gary
b.1954

Chapter One

December, 1956.

Mrs Patsy Adams, American wife of Daniel, elder son of Sammy and Susie Adams, was upset, and to such an extent that she was storming around her house in Kestrel Avenue, close by Denmark Hill in south-east London.

She and Daniel had had their first real quarrel, all over their son, six-year-old Andrew. The boy hadn't wanted to go to school that morning, saying he didn't feel well. Daniel said he'd tried that before. Patsy said no, if he didn't feel well he should stay home. Daniel said there was nothing wrong with the lad except liking his own way, and he packed him off to school with his sister, eight-year-old Arabella. Then he told Patsy she was spoiling the boy. That did it. They quarrelled, and were still throwing wounding words at each other when Daniel left for his work at the Adams offices in Camberwell Green.

Patsy fumed. High-spirited and as mettlesome as any modern American woman of twenty-nine, she threw things about. Cushions from the lounge furniture went sailing through the air to pummel the walls. She couldn't believe that Daniel, her fun guy, could have been ratty enough to accuse her of spoiling their son. Her temper wasn't improved by knowing she did give in to the boy sometimes, but after all, he was only six.

The advance of the morning didn't cure her of her upset and resentment. At eleven o'clock she came down from tidying up the bedrooms. Reaching the open door of the kitchen, she stiffened. There was a face at the window, a grubby bearded face under an old floppy hat. The face of a tramp. He didn't see her, his eyes were travelling around the kitchen. He moved, he disappeared, and she heard the slight sound of the back door handle being turned.

Patsy was in too much of a temper to be frightened, and when she heard the sound of the back door opening, she rushed, picked up a saucepan, rushed again and came face to face with the intruder. He was clad in a tatty old overcoat, and she caught the smell of unwashed clothes and body. He stared at the sudden apparition of a flushed, seething housewife with a saucepan in her hand.

384

Patsy struck, and the saucepan bounced on his floppy hat. His head rang muffledly from the metallic blow. Patsy struck again. The tramp staggered, flung up his mittened hands to ward off another hurtful whack, turned and ran out through the open back door. Patsy chased after him in the cold of the damp morning. Around the side of the house he went, down the drive and out through the gate, Patsy on his heels and close enough to hit him again. He gasped and pelted down the avenue as fast as his legs could carry him, his head suffering. Patsy, breathing hard, pulled up and waited until he disappeared, along with his bruised and aching head. She felt a bit better then.

At which moment a small white van appeared, bearing the sign BEADLES THE FLORISTS. It pulled up outside the house, and the driver, a woman in white overalls, stepped down. She was carrying a wrapped bouquet of huge bronze chrysanthemums. She met Patsy at the gate.

'Mrs Adams?'

'Yes?'

'Our pleasure, Mrs Adams.' Smiling, the woman handed the bouquet to Patsy, who gathered it to her, along with the saucepan.

'You're sure these are for me?' she asked, flush receding.

'Quite sure, Mrs Adams,' said the woman,

checking the house number. 'Good morning.' She returned to her van, while Patsy carried the bouquet and the saucepan into the house by way of the still-open back door. She dropped the saucepan into the sink, where it rang with the satisfaction of a job well done. Then she looked for a card. She found one. It bore just a few words.

'I still love you. Daniel.'

At which Patsy, of course, sat down and cried.

Five minutes later, Daniel took a private phone call in his office.

'Daniel?'

'Patsy?'

'Don't ever make me so miserable again.'

'Hearing you, Patsy, but haven't you received my gesture of apology, some flowers?'

'Yes, and they made me cry. Daniel, I'm so sorry we quarrelled like that. Don't let it happen again.'

'You held your own, you know.'

'It was awful. Let's be forgiving. The flowers are lovely.'

'So are you, Patsy.'

'We'll talk to Andrew this evening.'

'Good idea.'

'Daniel, thank you.'

'See you, Patsy.'

'See you, Daniel.'

They talked to Andrew that evening and discovered what the real trouble was. He didn't get on with one of the teachers.

So the following morning, Patsy went to the school herself, spoke to the teacher in question, pointed out that Andrew was only six and persuaded her to be more tolerant of his little bouts of childish obstinacy. He did have such moments. Patsy had her own way of getting on the right side of people, including harassed teachers, and as a result Andrew received kinder words in class, and made no more fuss about going to school.

Patsy's arrangement of the chrysanthemums glowed in its vase.

The year had seen more than the occasional tiffs among lovers. It had seen, for instance, the ever-growing popularity of Elvis Presley, a former truck driver from America's deep South. Now undisputed king of rock 'n' roll, he had a voice like melting velvet. It was a voice that sent American teenage girls dotty, stopped the traffic and actually overtook the crooning tones of Frank Sinatra in the charts, and induced rapture in vast numbers of young females in the British Isles. Further, at live American concerts his rhythmic body language brought him extra renown as 'Elvis the Pelvis'. That really got to susceptible girls. Some fainted and keeled over. Others had fits of bliss. In Britain, young girls like Emily Chapman, thirteen-year-old daughter of Rosie and Matthew Chapman, worshipped Elvis from afar, and sent their parents potty by playing his records over and over again.

Generally, however, the United Kingdom's young stars, such as Tommy Steele and Terry Dene, had created their own following of teenagers, leading them into undreamed-of realms of jive and swing. It looked as if young people in the West were beginning to enjoy a world of their own.

It was a pity, accordingly, to note that in Eastern Europe things were uncomfortably different. Indeed, in Hungary an uprising by the people against the oppressive rule of Communism had been crushed by Soviet tanks. But then, the Kremlin discouraged musical self-expression, full stop, and if an Elvis Presley or a Tommy Steele had emerged in Moscow or Budapest, either would have disappeared overnight as a corrupter of Communist culture.

Chapter Two

Two months ago, in October, France, Britain and Israel had all declared war on Egypt. Its President, Colonel Nasser, had taken over the Suez Canal, thus claiming control of this vitally important waterway, which suited France and Britain not at all.

However, the war proved only a half-hearted attempt to seize it back. For a start, President Eisenhower wasn't in favour. He considered his wartime allies well out of order. Further, no great enthusiasm for the conflict was shown by the people of France and Britain.

A few bombs were dropped, a few ground sorties took place, but it was plucky Egypt that grabbed the headlines. And the opposition of America, now the world's supreme power, quickly induced the French and British governments to withdraw their forces. Britain's Prime Minister, Sir Anthony Eden, found himself decidedly unpopular. He was a nice enough bloke, with high principles, and he dressed impeccably. But he was no Churchill, and he resigned without a fight in January 1957, whereupon he was replaced as Prime Minister by Harold Macmillan.

This somewhat upset a certain Lady Maisie Finch of Red Post Hill, south-east London. Born a cockney in Walworth in 1876, she had travelled through life from a hard-up beginning and years of striving widowhood to become the wife of a man of distinction, Edwin Finch. His services to the Crown had earned him a knighthood several years ago, and that made Mrs Maisie Finch no less than Lady Finch, much to her embarrassment at the time. She had learned to live with it, but was always telling someone or other in her family that it wasn't what she was born for. It was different with people like Lady Eden, she said, she was born a lady.

'And why a nice gentleman like her husband had to resign, I'm sure I don't know,' she said, when his name came up over breakfast one morning.

'Unfortunately, Maisie, even the nicest people occasionally make a mistake,' said her husband, Sir Edwin, slim and silver-haired at eighty-three. Actually, he was too slim for her liking. Sometimes alarm bells rang on his account, although their doctor assured her Sir

Edwin was as fit as a man ten years younger. However, Maisie, still known to her sons and daughter as Chinese Lady, a nickname that went back to her days in Walworth, did worry about him. She herself expected to go on for ever, almost, and she wanted Edwin to be with her. She listened as he went on to say that Sir Anthony Eden's mistake in going to war with Egypt had been a rather foolish one.

'Oh, that,' said Chinese Lady, 'I don't call that much of a mistake. We didn't get any air raids or sirens, nor soldiers coming home all bandaged up, like that first war. I can still remember wounded men with crutches and only one leg.'

Sir Edwin smiled. Her memory was taking her back, as it often did, to the Great War of 1914–18, the Kaiser's war, when casualties of a single day's battle ran into many thousands. And one could indeed see crippled soldiers in hospital blues taking the air in the grounds of military convalescent homes.

'Well, Maisie,' he said, 'despite the mistake of trying to win back control of the Suez Canal, our casualties were so light they were hardly noticeable. And the family has the consolation of knowing that Phoebe's fiancé, Philip, will soon be returning home, or so I imagine.'

He was referring to Phoebe, adopted daughter

of Sammy and Susie Adams, and Philip Harrison, one of Chinese Lady's great-grandsons. Philip, a pilot officer in the RAF, had been out in the Middle East with his squadron since the days leading up to the abortive war with Egypt.

'Well,' said Chinese Lady, 'I just don't know that Philip ought to be flying one of those war aeroplanes, especially when he's so young and such a long way from home with no-one to keep an eye on him.'

Sir Edwin coughed, then said, 'Maisie, I must point out he's nearly twenty-one.'

'Yes, didn't I just mention he's too young?' said Chinese Lady, and this time Sir Edwin let it go. One couldn't always find the right answer to some of his wife's inimitable observations.

In their solid old Victorian terraced house in Bow, East London, Jimmy Adams, younger son of Sammy and Susie Adams, was listening to his wife, Clare. They'd been married three years, and were still lovey-dovey. Clare was twenty-one and bubbly, Jimmy twenty-six and elastic. That is, he could give and take, and, like his dad, stretch his principles a bit if obstinacy didn't pay. He worked for his dad as personnel manager at the family firm's factory in the East End, which meant looking after the interests of over two hundred employees for the mutual benefit of both the workers and the firm. Jimmy, along with his elder brother, Daniel, had inherited a fair slice of Sammy's business acumen. All three knew that watching the interests of the workers induced them to accept the fact that bosses liked to make a profit. Such a policy helped to keep yearly balance sheets looking pretty.

'So what do you think?' asked Clare finally.

'Let's see now,' mused Jimmy, 'what was it you were talking about?'

'You can ask that?' said Clare. Her dark hair, touched with auburn, and her dark eyes, framed by thick lashes, were very much in the approved mould of an Adams wife. 'If you can, then you haven't been listening.'

'Was it something about a family?' suggested Jimmy.

'Well, it would be nice to start one of our own,' said Clare. They had spent three years enjoying married life and each other, having agreed in the first place that that was what they'd like to do before becoming parents.

'Now I know what you were talking about,' said Jimmy, 'yes, I get you now.'

'You'll get something else in a minute,' said Clare, 'a poke in the eye.'

'Never mind knocking me about, let's be

serious,' said Jimmy. 'Let's start proceedings now by having an early night.'

'That's not being serious, that's being a comic,' said Clare. 'In any case, it's only eight o'clock and I want to watch Jimmy Edwards in *Whack-O!*'

'Good idea,' said Jimmy, 'let's have a laugh before we do get serious.' The weekly television show in question was a laugh all the way, Jimmy Edwards being a natural comedian capable of sly winks and saucy innuendoes.

So they watched the programme of mirth and jollity, then they had a cup of tea and a ham sandwich each, then they tidied up and went to bed.

There they engaged in the serious matter of procreation, except that seriousness floated away up the bedroom chimney and they had fun together. Well, it wasn't just a one-off event. It repeated itself. Clare had a healthy body, Jimmy a vigorous one, and well did the twain meet. There was an interval, of course, during which Jimmy went downstairs and brought up three bananas, two for himself and one for Clare, which they scoffed happily. They both believed in the efficacy of bananas as an energizing fruit. Even so, not long after, Jimmy quit the field on the grounds that he'd run out of engine power.

'Never mind,' he said, 'let's eat a large breakfast tomorrow and do it again.'

'Crikey, tomorrow after Sunday breakfast?' breathed Clare.

'Tomorrow night,' said Jimmy. 'It's definitely a serious business, starting a family and making sure of it.'

'What a man,' murmured Clare, and sank into sleep.

They had bacon, eggs and tomatoes for breakfast. Oh, and a banana each to start with. Imported fruit had become plentiful after many years of austerity.

Chapter Three

March, 1957.

Phoebe, daughter of Sammy and Susie Adams, received a letter from her fiancé, Philip Harrison.

'Dear Phoebe,

'I'm still missing you. The squadron's still stuck here, and here is somewhere in the Middle East.' His squadron had taken up that station some months ago in the expectation of action in the war against Egypt. Although that had fizzled out, the squadron remained under orders in the event of an emergency, since another conflict, a real one, was violently disturbing the peace. Egypt and Syria were at war with Israel in an attempt to smash that independent young nation. 'Lord knows what we're doing here, not very much, believe me, and I could be doing a lot more if I were home and swinging it with you.'

I know what I mean by swinging it, thought

Phoebe, but what does he mean? They're a wild lot, these fighter pilots. Still, I wouldn't want my one to be a tame wallflower.

'In one of your recent letters, you said you enjoyed a lively Christmas with your family. There are some WAAF personnel here who might have helped to make our Christmas a bit lively too, but they're all very correct and you can't get that type to wear paper hats or step under the mistletoe unless they're a bit tiddly, which our lot weren't.

'Life here in winter sunshine is all right up to a point, but at the moment I'd rather be making snowballs with you back home and chucking them at saucy kids or our dads, seeing yours and mine are both sporty. There's one bloke here, Chippy, whose dad is a university professor and so absent-minded he sometimes forgets he's got a wife and two sons. Last time Chippy saw him he asked if they'd met before. Imagine your dad asking that of you. Anyway, so long for the present, keep looking fabulous and let's hope I'll be home by June. Lots of love and kisses. Long live Elvis and his pelvis. Philip.'

Phoebe wrote back at once, telling him he'd better be home by June or else, because the third Saturday in that month was their appointed wedding day. (Liking 'appointed', she underlined it and used it again.) Appointed wedding days were supposed to be sacred, she said, and not even the RAF should be allowed to mess them about. And as for your trying to get WAAFs tiddly so you can drag them under the mistletoe, you've got a nerve even mentioning it to your forthcoming wife. (She crossed out 'forthcoming' and substituted 'future'.) If I showed your letter to my dad, she went on, he'd think twice about allowing me to marry you, so just watch it, my lad.

'Still,' she wrote, 'I just have to put my trust in you as an officer and gentleman. When I told Mum the other day about me marrying an officer and gentleman, she said I couldn't marry him as well, it would be bigamy. Just make do with Philip, she said, he's quite nice and we all like him. You'd never think my mother only had an elementary education, because she's really smart in lots of ways, especially when putting Dad in his place. Dad's a born loser when it comes to getting the better of Mum but he keeps trying because he doesn't know it, and even if he did he wouldn't believe it.

'Oh, that reminds me,' she continued, 'Dad says to tell you to remember who's supposed to wear the trousers in marriage. What's he mean by that? Do you know? I think I do, ha ha.'

Phoebe ended by asking her officer and

gentleman to come home soon as it was a bit dreary without him, and they were missing all the latest excitements of rock 'n' roll concerts, and new bands that were all inspired by Bill Haley and his Comets.

'With love from your one and only Phoebe.'

When Philip received this epistle, Phoebe's own gem, he laughed over it, read it three times and then put it with other prize billets-doux she'd written.

Mrs Rosie Chapman and her husband Matthew had sold their farm and were now living with their children, Giles and Emily, in a lovely family house on Red Post Hill, close to Grandma and Grandpa Finch. It also put them closer to more of the Adams clan, for most lived in that area of south-east London. Family ties with that part of London went back to the days when Chinese Lady's sons and daughter were successively in their cradles. Matthew soon found that Sunday teas with various of his Adams relatives happened quite frequently. Not that he minded, not a bit, for he was a family man himself, and was all in favour of old-fashioned customs, like Sunday tea in a parlour. Regrettably, young Emily confided to her new schoolfriends that Sunday teas with relatives were boring. Now if Tommy Steele or Terry

Dene were invited, she said, she'd feel she was living. Some hopes, said her new schoolfriends. A girl can always dream, said Emily, already on close terms with precociousness. But then, so were other young girls in an era when teenagers were beginning to instinctively oppose the idea that children should be seen and not heard.

Rosie, on giving up chicken farming, had joined the family firm on a part-time basis, as assistant to her adoptive father, known simply as Boots, and to Mrs Rachel Goodman in the offices at Camberwell Green. They soon found her invaluable. Rosie had graduated with honours from university years ago, and was accordingly no slouch in the matter of intelligence.

Her uncle Sammy, founder of the whole outfit, called her in one day. She entered his office in a smartly styled dress of royal blue, her hairdo a golden crown. Well, thought Sammy, here's a wife who's the mother of teenage kids, and what do I see? Female managerial material, which Chinese Lady might think wasn't what God ordered. Chinese Lady didn't believe in female managers, only female wives and mothers, as per the Lord's wise design.

'You wish to see me, sir?' said Rosie.

Sammy grinned.

'How did I get to be sir?' he asked.

'Well, you're my chief,' said Rosie. 'You're everyone's chief.'

'The first time I get to be your dad's chief,' said Sammy, 'will be the day when the man in the moon takes a donkey ride to Southend. Have you ever been to Southend, Rosie?'

'And had a plate of cockles and mussels?' said Rosie. 'So far, no.'

'Well, if Tim and Daniel, on behalf of our property company, can bring off purchase of a shop there, we'll be opening up a Southend dress emporium,' said Sammy. Tim, Boots's son, and Daniel, his own son, were joint managers of the property company, and running it well.

'A dress shop in Southend, the holiday favourite of London's workers?' said Rosie.

'Where they spend their money like they were rolling in it,' said Sammy.

'But only during the holiday season,' said Rosie.

'Clever girl,' said Sammy.

'So you mean a shop that opens only during the summer months,' said Rosie.

'It's a prospect' said Sammy, 'and you can always get shop assistants just for the holiday season in Southend. So one day later on, I'll take you and Rachel there, and you'll see for yourself the kind of summer wear we'll be stocking. Popular designs at popular prices.'

'I'll enjoy a day trip to Southend,' said Rosie.

'I'll throw in a fish and chips lunch,' said Sammy. 'Now, about our shop down below.' The offices were above his original shop. 'It's all right up to a point, but not a great money-spinner these days on account of the build-up of heavy competition and being on the wrong side of the Green's post-war development. Take a pew, Rosie.'

'Thank you, Uncle Sammy,' said Rosie, seating herself, 'how kind.'

'Don't mention it,' said Sammy, and went on to refer to the fact that the firm had applied more than once for change of usage as far as the shop was concerned. So far, the council's response had been negative. But the office staff had expanded considerably.

'Waistlines are a problem?' said Rosie, tongue in cheek.

'Numbers,' said Sammy, and pointed out that they needed to turn the shop and its storeroom into something that accorded with modern staff requirements. 'There's nearly thirty of us, Rosie, and you might have been told by your dear old dad that we're thinking of a staff canteen.'

'My dear old dad, bless him, has told me that, yes,' said Rosie, 'but what can I do about it?'

'Well, seeing you and Rachel have got what me and your dad haven't, female sex appeal,' said Sammy, 'we thought we'd follow up our last application to the council by getting you and Rachel to corner the planning committee chairman in his office, and pin him to the wall. His name is Cox, he's new to the job and has said he's willing to listen to a detailed outline of the firm's new application.'

'Sammy, how charming of you to mention our sex appeal,' smiled Rosie, 'but pinning a council officer to his wall is out of order.'

'Well, you know what I mean,' said Sammy. 'Arrange an appointment with the bloke, take yourselves along and spin the kind of stuff he won't be able to say no to. No gent could fail to appreciate a heartbreaking fairy story from two female charmers like you and Rachel. Ask after his family and his old mother, something like that.'

'Exactly who suggested this?' asked Rosie.

'Your dear old dad,' said Sammy.

'My dear old dad deserves a poke in the eye,' said Rosie, 'but I'm game, if Rachel is.'

'She is,' said Sammy. 'I'd like to point out, by the way, that the storeroom alone would give us enough space for a canteen.'

'Shall we call it a workers' cafeteria?' suggested Rosie. 'The council might favour that.'

'Good point, Rosie, it's a Labour-controlled outfit,' said Sammy.

Rosie said it might also favour the possibility that change of usage to a canteen and extra office space might mean an increase in the rates. Could the firm cope with that? Sammy said Rosie's mental equipment was working right under his nose. The firm could cope easily enough with a rates increase, and selfsame increase might make Mr Cox lick his lips.

'I'm tickled, Rosie, to know you've got your full share of mental facilities.'

'Faculties?' said Rosie.

'Same thing,' said Sammy.

'Your compliments, Sammy, are welcome,' said Rosie, and looked at her watch. The time was coming up to three, her leaving moment. She was always home before Giles and Emily came in from school. 'I must go now.'

'Regards to Matt,' said Sammy. Her husband, Matthew, was busy developing a site in Peckham for the repair of cars and vans, as well as for the sale of petrol. He had bought the site from the firm's property company at a very reasonable price. Well, he was one of the family, and Sammy was against excess profit at the expense of any member of the clan. In fact, when Matt was open for business, Sammy fondly expected the family as a whole to give him their custom in respect of any car repairs.

Charity, in Sammy's opinion, began at home.

Sometime later, Rosie had cause to fall out with daughter Emily. Like Giles, her brother, the girl usually arrived home from school by not later than four thirty. Today it was nearly five fifteen before she turned up. Rosie, fretting and worrying, had phoned the school to find out if Emily had been kept behind for some reason or another. She was assured this was not the case, that Emily left when classes ended. So when the girl belatedly appeared, Rosie wanted to know why she was so late. Emily said she'd been at the house of a schoolfriend, Marion Mortimer. Marion, she said, had invited her in to listen to some new records. There was nothing wrong with that, was there?

'Why didn't you phone me to let me know where you were?' Rosie was cross.

'I couldn't,' said Emily, 'their phone wasn't working. I had a laugh about it, I said to Marion it was because her dad hadn't paid the bill. Anyway, it wasn't as if—'

'I wasn't laughing here,' said Rosie, 'I was worryng about where you were, and what might have happened to you. Didn't you think about that?'

'Mum, of course I thought about it,' said Emily, 'I would have rung you if the phone hadn't been out of order, wouldn't I? Anyway,

Marion's home is only in the next street, so I was as good as only next door. You didn't need to worry.'

'Don't be so silly,' said Rosie. 'I'm not telepathic, I had no way of knowing where you were. You're not under any circumstances to do this kind of thing again – Emily, are you listening?'

'Yes, Mum,' said Emily. 'Is Giles having tea and cake? I'd like some too, I wasn't offered anything at Marion's.'

'How would you like bread and water?' asked Rosie.

'Oh, all right, I'm sorry about not letting you know,' said Emily, 'so is there some tea in the pot?'

Rosie shook her head, not to indicate the teapot was empty, but to suggest talking seriously to her daughter was like pouring water on a duck's back.

It didn't affect the inevitable outcome. The duck sat down to a cup of tea and a slice of cake a minute later.

Chapter Four

It was a week later when Mr Gerald Cox, chairman of the council's planning committee, received two representatives from Adams Enterprises Ltd in his office. A man of pleasing looks and amiable disposition, he was also highly principled and unlikely to crumple under any two-pronged attack, except by elephants. Nevertheless, he blinked a little when the representatives turned out to be two ladies, one a handsome, full-bodied woman of lush brunette looks, the other an entirely lovely blonde. It has to be said, however, that neither looked expensively attired, for although the day was wintry, both had chosen not to wear furs, just plain and simple coats. Boots had suggested that a Labour council official would hardly look kindly on two ladies whose apparel implied they were rolling in lolly, and might accordingly be part and parcel of a business profiteering at the expense of downtrodden workers.

The time was nine fifteen, and Rachel and Rosie had come directly from their respective homes.

'Hello, am I expecting ladies?' Mr Cox, recovering from his initial shock, asked the question of the elderly clerk who had shown them in.

'Yes, Mr Cox. From Adams Enterprises. And by appointment.'

'I didn't know I was going to mee—' Too late. The clerk was already gone. 'Well, good morning, ladies. Might I have the pleasure of knowing exactly why you're here?'

'It's to do with our application for a change of usage for the shop,' said Rachel. 'You've been kind enough to let us know you'd be willing to listen to a detailed outline of exactly what we have in mind.'

'Is that so?' Mr Cox looked amiable but doubtful. 'I think there's some mistake. I don't discuss planning committee matters on a personal level. However, do sit down while I call my clerk.' He raised his voice. 'Mr Grimling?'

The door, ajar, opened up and the elderly clerk reappeared.

'Mr Cox?' he said.

'Mr Grimling, who arranged this appointment?'

'There was a phone enquiry, which I took,

and which, on reference to you, resulted in an arrangement to see two representatives from Adams Enterprises.'

'Ah, yes, now I remember.' Mr Cox smiled at the ladies. 'But was it necessary?'

'At the time, it was a matter of courtesy,' said the efficient Mr Grimling. The dialogue was taking place over the heads of Rachel and Rosie.

'Oh, yes, Adams Enterprises, of course,' said Mr Cox. 'So sorry to be vague, ladies, but the pressure of work, with a continuing stream of applications arriving every week – well, yes, I'm sure you understand you should be dealing with Mr Grimling.'

'Do we assume that no decision has yet been made in respect of our long-standing application?' said Rachel.

Mr Cox fingered an eyebrow.

'I recall something relevant,' he said. 'Isn't there a letter somewhere, Mr Grimling?'

'There will be when it's been typed,' said Mr Grimling.

'Good, perhaps you'll get it typed now and then hand it to these ladies,' said Mr Cox. 'Good morning, Miss Um – good morning, Miss Er – thank you for calling. Do excuse me now.' He ushered them out into the care of Mr Grimling.

Neither Rachel nor Rosie knew quite what to

say, not when the moment was almost comical. However, Rachel, coming to, addressed the clerk.

'What's in this letter, Mr Grimling?'

'Oh, merely the committee's decision on your application,' said Mr Grimling, thereby implying the decision was all one to him, whatever it was. 'Of course, I'm not allowed to divulge the contents here and now, it's against the rules. As to your appointment with Mr Cox, I think he forgot to cancel it once the decision had been made. So sorry, but he's such a busy man. Perhaps you'd like to wait in reception while I get the letter typed? I shan't be long.'

When Rachel and Rosie left twenty minutes later, Rachel was carrying the letter, but had no idea what was in it. Nor had Rosie. Mr Grimling had emphasized the rules wouldn't allow him to speak on a personal level, any more than Mr Cox could. Which Rosie thought a lot of well-cooked rhubarb.

'Curiosity is killing me,' she said, 'so if it's all right with you, Rachel, I suggest we have morning coffee now, and over it we'll unseal the envelope and see for ourselves what dark secrets lie within.'

'My life, what an excellent idea,' said Rachel, 'and after all, we don't have to go along with council rules. Also, we're on closer terms with

Mr S. Adams, Managing Director, than anyone on the planning committee.'

Rosie said it was against her better judgement to carry the letter back to Sammy without knowing what was in it. To do so would reduce her and Rachel to the status of mere messenger boys.

'No go,' she said.

'No go,' agreed Rachel, and they took themselves off to a Lyons teashop. There, while they waited for their coffee, Rachel was able to carefully lift the flap of the envelope by rolling a silver pencil under it. Newly sealed, it came free without spoliation. Rosie said if Rachel ever resigned from Adams Enterprises, she could get a job with MI5. Rachel said she wasn't cut out to be a Mata Hari, especially if it meant the risk of being shot at dawn by a KGB firing squad.

The coffee arrived just as she drew the letter from the envelope. She devoured its contents, then passed it to Rosie. Rosie read it, looked up, returned Rachel's smile and put the letter back in its envelope. She carefully resealed it. Then she had a murmured heart-to-heart with Rachel. They agreed that Boots and Sammy were a couple of crafty old darlings who had sent them into the lions' den to do what, for once, they hadn't been able to do themselves, win a face-to-face discussion with council

411

officials. They had tried more than once, without success, and Boots, unused to such failure, bore scars. So did Sammy.

'So sending us was a last desperate throw of the dice?' said Rosie.

'My life, what a throw,' said Rachel, 'it was a hope that your sex appeal would do the trick.'

'Mine?' said Rosie modestly.

'Yours, my dear, is far younger than mine,' murmured Rachel. She was fifty-four, Rosie forty-two. 'Mine, in fact, is only a figment of someone's imagination.'

Rosie smiled. There weren't many members of the family who didn't know that Sammy had always had a soft spot for Rachel, although it had never led him into any acts of major indiscretion, the kind that would have badly interfered with his marriage.

'Well, someone's figment needn't be considered way off the mark, Rachel.'

'I should be hopeful of catching the eye of an eighty-year-old millionaire?' said Rachel, laughing softly. 'I can live without one, thank you. I now propose we let Sammy and Boots have this letter, and allow them to infer we were responsible for the decision being made in the firm's favour.'

'Not half,' said Rosie, 'why not? And by inference, as you suggest. No porkies.'

'Perish the thought,' said Rachel.

'We deserve some credit,' said Rosie.

'How much?' asked Rachel. 'I mean, what did we actually do?'

'We caught Mr Cox off guard,' said Rosie, 'which was as good as pinning him to the wall. Which was recommended by Sammy as a starter.'

'One has to admire his way of making himself understood,' said Rachel.

They finished their coffee, and left the tea-shop to make their way to the firm's offices at Camberwell Green.

'Well?' said Sammy on the arrival in his office of his long-established personal assistant, Rachel, and his niece, Rosie.

Rachel said yes, they had kept their appointment with Mr Cox of the planning committee. Rosie said he had proved a likeable gentleman. Rachel said they seemed to have caught him at a vague moment, but he really had been very charming.

'Very,' said Rosie.

'I'll say this much,' observed Sammy, 'charming council gents are a bit rare, but as I'm up to my ears at the moment, I don't have too much time to listen to Mr Cox's man appeal. So could you just give me the nuts and bolts?'

'It took us a little time,' said Rosie ambiguously.

'Putting our case?' said Sammy.

'My life, Sammy, you must know one can't rush council officials,' said Rachel. 'They're all subject to rules and regulations.'

'Do I know that?' said Sammy. 'You can bet your life insurance I do. The point is, who won?'

'Neither Mr Cox nor his assistant gave us the answer on the spot,' said Rosie, 'but they did hand us a letter.'

'Do I like the sound of that?' asked Sammy.

'Here it is,' said Rachel. She extracted the letter from her handbag and placed it on Sammy's desk. He eyed it suspiciously.

'Be of good cheer, Uncle Sammy,' said Rosie. 'Mr Cox's assistant was nicely helpful at the last moment, getting the letter typed on the spot, and we happen to know that a change of usage has been granted. I think you'll find the letter says so.'

'Eh?' said Sammy.

'Yes, permission granted, Sammy,' said Rachel.

Sammy opened the letter, read it, then rang through to Boots and asked him to come in. Boots entered seconds later.

'So you're back,' he said to the ladies.

'And before your very eyes,' said Rosie, taking off Arthur Askey, the short-legged comedian of radio and television.

'And with highly welcome news,' said Sammy, looking proud of the part he had played in persuading the ladies to go get the chairman of the planning committee, while he himself stayed back at the ranch.

'How high is highly?' asked Boots, regarding Rosie with the affection of a father never able to fault his adopted daughter.

'Change of usage granted,' said Sammy, 'so how about that for a piece of expert negotiation by Rachel and Rosie?'

'I'm impressed,' said Boots, 'considerably.' Rachel and Rosie smiled sweetly but modestly. He smiled himself. There was more to these two charmers than met the eye on some occasions. 'Well done. Incidentally, how was it done?'

'Oh, in about twenty minutes or so,' said Rosie, staying with ambiguity. 'Mr Cox lent a very receptive ear, especially to Rachel.'

'Oh, just as much to Rosie,' said Rachel.

'I'm delighted,' said Boots, not in the least taken in, but quite happy, under the circumstances, to go along with whatever details the ladies came up with. 'And I'm doubly impressed.'

'Oh, no problem, ducky, so don't mention it,' said Rosie.

'Any conditions?' asked Boots.

'I believe the committee wants to see and approve our architects' plans covering the conversion,' said Rachel. 'I think it's all in the letter.'

'There's a letter?' said Boots.

Sammy waved it about like the flag of St George.

'It's here, Boots,' he said. 'Rachel and Rosie charmed old Cox and his committee. What a pair of turtle doves.'

'Coo-ee,' cooed Rosie.

It was one up to the ladies.

Maureen Brown, eighteen-year-old daughter of Cassie and Freddy Brown of Walworth, was living on cloud nine these days. With the help of Amos Anderson, photographer of Camberwell Green, she had become London's girl next door in the eyes of the readers of popular dailies and men's magazines. Generally, her poses were representative of a shy young lady 'accidentally' showing her good-looking, nylon-clad legs. Such shots promoted the girl-next-door image, and since this was the age when some periodicals were venturing into the realms of saucy sex appeal, especially if it looked accidental, Amos was not short of editors willing to buy. He paid Maureen twenty-five per cent of all fees received, which had prompted her into giving up her job as a copy typist to aim for the heights as a top glamour model and cover girl. She was hoping that Amos would come up any moment with a really super assignment for her.

Amos, affable but shrewd, knew his stuff and the wisdom of having started Maureen off as a girl-next-door type. Copy typists were nobodies. Shy but leggy girls were much in demand. Copy typists were paid a few quid a week. Photogenic girls doing pin-up poses could earn two guineas an hour when sitting for a photographer.

At this moment, in his studio, Amos was after a new angle. Well, new as far as Maureen was concerned. London's girl next door was wearing a defining yellow sweater and a blue flared skirt over a snowy petticoat. And she was riding a bike against a painted rural backdrop, creating an impression of how to bring sex appeal into the countryside. In blue nylons, her round knees sparkled and shone.

'Is this all right, Amos?' she asked.

'It's OK, better than all right,' said Amos, fortyish and cheerful, and always able to achieve rapport with his sitters, whether kids,

417

newly-weds or grandmothers. Or cockney girls wanting to be pin-ups. There were always some. Most, however, lacked personality. Personality of the right kind was something that imbued a photograph with a bit of magic. Maureen had that kind.

'I think it's ever such a good idea, getting me on a bike in a skirt,' she said, feet obediently working the pedals.

'You're in a skirt, not the bike,' said Amos, eyes concentrating on his subject.

'Pardon?' said Maureen.

'No worries,' said Amos.

'Is my outfit nice?' asked Maureen.

'Just right for a bike ride in the country,' said Amos. 'Sailors like legs, soldiers like sweaters, and airmen like flying high, isn't that so? And they all like oomph. Don't they?'

'My oomph?' said Maureen. She was riding the bike with her hands on her hips so that her back was straight, her sweater tightly pouting.

'Both of them,' said Amos, clicking away from various angles.

'Amos, you cheeky thing,' said Maureen, but with a giggle.

'So sorry,' said Amos, his professional ethics always governing his attitude to pin-up sitters, which meant not to be foolish by being familiar. He was one of Camberwell's busy Jewish people.

Like Rachel Goodman, however, he was of the unorthodox kind, which enabled him to work on a Saturday without offending himself. 'Ah, that's good, Maureen, very good – we love it, riding a bike, don't we?' The pressed plunger of his Rolleiflex camera created an instant and brief flood of light that bounced off the ceiling and captured the appeal of London's girl next door.

'Yes, and look, no hands,' said Maureen. They were still clasping her hips. Her feet were pedalling, knees going up and down, her frilly white petticoat shyly peeping, legs, nylons and bosom to the fore.

'No hands on the bars is good, isn't it?' smiled Amos, curly hair dark and springy. 'It gives you an air of careless rapture, keeps your back straight and your – er – chest out.'

'Crikey,' said Maureen, legs taking a rest, 'I don't want to look like one of those female sergeant majors that's in the WAAFs.'

'You won't, and you can take my word for it, not half,' said Amos. 'We shall see you again in one of the dailies and in men's magazines as the girl next door on a bike, won't we? You bet.'

Maureen resumed posing, her back straight, her skirt and white frills riding up, her dazzling sweater outlining her figure.

Talk about oomph.

Not that Chinese Lady would have approved. Bosoms should be proud but not forward, that was her fixed belief.

Maureen, however, had never heard Chinese Lady expressing herself on the subject of bosoms. Come to that, nor had even the closest members of her family. The subject was sacred, and accordingly not for discussion. The nearest she had come to airing her opinion was when, one day some years ago, she and Boots had passed a thin woman with hardly any bosom to speak of.

'Poor woman,' Chinese Lady had said.

Boots didn't ask what she meant. He knew.

Chapter Five

Late March.

Phoebe was in an excited state, having been the thrilled recipient of a letter from Philip to say that his squadron would soon be back at their home station. Would Phoebe put the kettle on and wear something eyecatching as he'd seen all the Arabian burnouses he ever wanted to, thanks very much. He's daft but sweet, thought Phoebe, happiness surging.

'Mum, Dad, Philip's coming home,' she said, exhibiting the letter over the breakfast table. 'Isn't that great? He'll be knocking on our door soon.'

'Lovely,' said Susie.

'Where's his plane landing?' asked Sammy. 'On our front lawn?'

'What a thought,' said Phoebe. 'Mum, we can definitely order my wedding dress for June now.' She had held back on that, thinking superstitiously that if the gown was in her wardrobe before

June, the bridegroom would fail to be home at the right time.

'So we can,' said Susie, 'and the bridesmaids' dresses too.'

'Let's see,' said Sammy, 'how many bridesmaids will there be?'

'Four,' said Phoebe. 'Cousins Linda, Jennifer, Gemma and Emily.'

'That's a platoon,' said Sammy, enjoying a welcome Saturday morning breakfast of eggs and bacon, which could be eaten at leisure. 'So who's forking out?'

'You are, Sammy love,' said Susie, 'as well as for a new outfit for me.'

'Don't say things like that out loud,' said Sammy, 'or my wallet will faint.'

'Tell your wallet that forking out is the privilege of the bride's father,' said Susie.

'Well, seeing it's going to make our Phoebe happy,' said Sammy, 'I'll try to make it a pleasure as well.'

'Good old Pa,' said Phoebe, a girl presently in love with life.

Naturally, she spent most of the morning composing a rapturous reply to Philip's letter.

On a Sunday afternoon later that month Chinese Lady was at her kitchen sink, washing up the dinner dishes. Sir Edwin was doing the drying, the tea towel flapping about. The day was cold, and they were both looking forward to two hours beside the fire in their living room before visitors arrived for tea. Sir Edwin, glancing at Chinese Lady's rubber-gloved hands dipping plates in and out of the hot water, frothy with suds, wondered how many thousands of times she had done this particular chore.

'Maisie,' he said, 'I know you've turned down the suggestion before, but I'm now going to insist that we take on a housemaid at least for weekdays. It's time, my dear, that you did have a daily help, and I hope you won't say no.'

Chinese Lady, who had long cherished being independent of any kind of daily help, was touched. Accordingly, her response was a happy surprise to her husband.

'Well, Edwin, perhaps it would be nice to have some work taken off my hands,' she said.

'So you'll let me advertise for a daily?' said Sir Edwin.

'It's very kind and thoughtful of you, Edwin.' She was thinking of him as much as herself. He had always helped her with some chores, such as the washing-up, and she felt he ought not to have to worry about it any more on weekdays. As for Sundays, well, it would always be nice to have the house to themselves on the Sabbath.

'Of course, neither of us is very old, but we're not as young as we were.' Which was a gentle piece of wishful thinking now that they were both in their eighties. 'We'll see if advertising will bring someone nice and respectable to our door.'

'I'll do something about that tomorrow,' said Sir Edwin, delighted at her willingness. He knew she would come to appreciate a daily help. True, she was far from frail, but age was slowing her down just a little, and their home was far too large for her to continue the housework unassisted. 'Meanwhile, who are we expecting to tea today?'

He knew something else, that Sundays for Maisie were never quite what they should be unless someone came to tea. And she was still a good cook, still able to produce a fine oven-baked cake or a medley of fruit buns and jam tarts.

'Oh, yes, Lizzy and Ned,' she said. Daughter Lizzy and son-in-law Ned were frequent visitors to Sunday tea. She and Lizzy enjoyed a good gossip, while Ned and Sir Edwin talked about world affairs, anathema to Chinese Lady. To her, world affairs only ever meant some politicians somewhere were making life difficult for some people elsewhere. That man Hitler had made life difficult for just about everybody everywhere. 'Boots and Polly are coming too, and they're bringing Lizzy and Ned in Boots's car.' That was a reference to the fact that Ned, because of his acute heart condition, no longer drove. And Lizzy wasn't keen on taking his place. She'd had two lessons, and two were enough to convince her she'd never be able to make a car do what it ought. She was convinced it was much more likely to run away with her.

'Are Boots and Polly bringing the twins?' asked Sir Edwin hopefully. He enjoyed the company of the youngsters.

'Not this time,' said Chinese Lady, 'they're going to a friend's tea party today.'

'Oh, well, some other time,' said Sir Edwin, always philosophical about ups and down, little or not so little.

Boots and Polly were at the home of Lizzy and Ned at three forty. Lizzy opened the door to Boots and received an affectionate, brotherly kiss.

'Ready, Lizzy?'

'Yes, we're ready, Boots, I'll just get Ned away from his Sunday paper,' said Lizzy, and crossed the hall to the living room, where Ned sat in front of the fire with his Sunday read. The paper was on the floor, however, and he looked as if he'd nodded off. His head was forward. Lizzy touched his shoulder. 'Wake up, love, Boots and Polly are here.' There was no answer, no stirring. 'Ned, come on.' She lightly shook his shoulder. No response, none at all, except that his head lolled. Sudden alarm took hold of her. She stooped and lifted his chin. His eyes were open, and lifeless. Her heart seemed to stop. 'Ned, oh, my dear, no!'

But she knew he was gone, she knew it. His faulty valve had at last given up. All the years, all of them since their marriage in 1916, all gone now, and life would never be the same for her. Such a good man, such a caring husband and father. Gone during the few seconds she had taken to answer Boots's knock. Was it right for a man to be snatched so quickly from life and family? Was it a kindness that he had probably suffered only a fleeting moment of pain? Her heart froze at her sudden loss.

'Lizzy?' Boots was at the open door of the living room, hat in his hand, his eyes expressive of concern, for his sister's face was stricken.

She swallowed and spoke, huskily.

'He's gone, Boots, Ned's gone.'

Boots moved swiftly to stand beside her. He leaned, put a hand under Ned's chin and lifted the lolling head. He looked at the waxen face and the sightless eyes, and there he saw the

426

death of his oldest friend who, years ago, at the age of only seventeen, had met and fallen in love with Lizzy, then a mere fourteen.

'Jesus Christ.' Boots was stunned. He and Lizzy looked at each other, Lizzy white and tragic.

'Boots, are we . . . are we sure?'

'Your GP, it's Dr Mason?'

'Yes.'

'Stay here, Lizzy, while I phone him.'

Using the phone in the hall, Boots rang the doctor. Although not on duty, he said he would come at once. Boots thanked him, put the phone down and stood in silence, wondering how to do the impossible, console his sister.

A shadow fell across the open front door.

'Boots, why the delay?' It was Polly.

Boots crossed the hall, drew her in and closed the door.

'Polly,' he said, 'I think Ned's heart has just given out.'

'What?' Polly's fur-clad body quivered, then stiffened. 'Boots, no.'

Very quietly, Boots said, 'I think we've just lost one of our own, one of the old brigade.'

That was it, one of the old brigade, one of the men who had served in the war of the trenches. In that war, Ned had lost a leg, Boots had been blinded, and Polly had spent four long years driving an ambulance. The three of them were old comrades.

Polly was as stunned as Boots. No-one in the family had ever quarrelled with Ned, or about Ned, a peace-loving man if ever there was one.

'Boots, are you telling me it's just happened?'

Boots, thinking of Lizzy, sighed.

'It seems, Polly, that he went in between Lizzy answering the door to me and going to tell him you and I were here.'

'Oh, my God, poor Lizzy,' breathed Polly. 'Where is she?'

'In the living room with Ned. Go and talk to her, Polly. I've phoned Dr Mason and he's on his way. I'll wait at the door for him.'

Polly took a deep breath, then went into the living room. Dr Mason arrived in his car only a minute later. Boots was at the front gate when the doctor alighted, bag in his hand, his expression full of concern. Lizzy and Ned were his friends as well as his patients.

'Mr Adams?' he said. He knew Boots.

'Glad to see you, doctor,' said Boots, 'but shattered by what I'm sure has just happened.'

'Let me see.'

Lizzy, Polly and Boots were all present as Dr Mason carried out the necessary examination, unbuttoning Ned's jacket, waistcoat and shirt to test his heart. He took time to reach a conclusion, sighing as he freed the stethoscope from Ned's lifeless body.

'Doctor?' whispered Lizzy.

'Mrs Somers . . . my dear lady . . . I'm terribly sorry.'

'He's really gone?' said Lizzy, catching her breath.

'I'm afraid so. Heart failure. I can issue a certificate to that effect.'

Lizzy slumped into an armchair and covered her face with her hands. A sob racked her. Boots crossed to the cabinet. He knew where Ned kept his brandy, a fine old cognac. Ned had been a connoisseur of wines and spirits, having ended up a long career in the trade as a director of the company for which he had worked since 1912.

Glancing at Dr Mason and showing him the relevant bottle, Boots received a nod of approval. He poured a little of the cognac into a glass and took it to Lizzy. She lifted her head, showed wet and cloudy eyes, and took the glass.

'You need it, Lizzy,' said Boots.

'May I have a little?' asked Polly, voice strained.

'Shall we all have one?' suggested Boots. 'As a farewell toast to Ned?'

Lizzy might have considered that entirely out of order, but she didn't. She understood it as an antidote to collective shock, and as a human gesture. So did Dr Mason.

'I think I'd like to join you,' he said. 'I think I'm as shattered as all of you. Just give me a moment, Mr Adams, while I phone for an ambulance.'

There were no words over the cognac. Each made a silent farewell to Ned after Dr Mason had finished his phone call. The spirit mitigated the shock felt by Boots and Polly, and put a little colour back into Lizzy's cheeks, although it didn't take the stark grief from her brown eyes.

Chinese Lady was beginning to worry about what could have happened to her expected guests, and Sir Edwin was just about to enquire by phone, when the front door knocker sounded. Answering the summons, Sir Edwin found Boots on the doorstep, and he knew at once from his expression that something was very wrong.

'Boots?'

'I need to talk to you,' said Boots.

'Come in, Boots, come in,' said his step-father.

Chinese Lady stayed in shock all day at the news of Ned's death. She regarded every related person as her own, from her sons and daughter all the way down to her great-grandchildren. For some she had a special affection, and Ned had been one of those. He had given Lizzy all she had ever wanted, a house with a bathroom and a garden, he himself as a husband, and, in time, children. Together, they had built a family home, and Ned had never failed as a husband and father. Nor had he ever looked at anyone else from the time he first met Lizzy. And he'd been an army officer when he married her in 1916, she of humble background but always clean, respectable and remarkably pretty.

It was cruel to have him depart this life when he was only sixty-one. To Chinese Lady, and others of her kind, that was far too young for any nice man to die. Her day of grief for Lizzy was bearable only because of the comforting presence of Edwin, although he himself was as shocked as she was. He had been the family's lodger in Walworth during Lizzy's growing years, and had come to feel a deep affection for her. Indeed, it was this affection for Lizzy, and a special regard for the family as a whole, that influenced him so much in his eventual decision to break with the aggressive militarism of his native Germany. It was a decision he had never regretted.

Now, with Chinese Lady, he grieved for Lizzy.

By the end of the day the various Adams families knew they had lost Ned. They included those who lived well away from south-east London. Down on their Kentish farm, Bess and her American husband, Jeremy Passmore, had been informed. So had Alice and her Scottish husband, Fergus MacAllister, at their home in Bristol, and so had David and Kate Adams at their Westerham dairy farm.

Ned's daughters, Annabelle and Emma, and his sons, Bobby and Edward, were shaken to their core. All had known a caring and understanding father, one who had never laid down the law. Bobby and Edward took charge of the funeral arrangements in concert with Shakespeare and Sons, undertakers of Camberwell Green. Boots asked if he could help.

'Yes,' said Bobby, 'be chief escort to my mother, while Edward and I look after our wives.' His own wife, Helene, had wept copious tears at the death of a man who, with Lizzy, had been so kind and welcoming on her arrival from German-occupied France in 1940.

'Polly and I will both take care of Lizzy,' said Boots.

Chapter Six

The funeral took place at the Denmark Hill church on Friday, five days after Ned's death. The undertakers had never known so many floral tributes, so many cards of remembrance, although the coffin was crowned with just one solitary and colourful wreath, that from Lizzy herself. However, the graveyard reception area was carpeted with every kind of floral arrangement.

The day was kind, for it was mild and clear. All members of the Adams families were there, except for Philip, still abroad. Also present were many friends, as well as old colleagues of the wine trade. The service was simple but moving, the hymns chosen by Lizzy. 'Now the Day Is Over', and 'O, Valiant Heart'. That was how she would always remember Ned, valiant all through his existence, as a striving young man, as a soldier of the trenches, as an old soldier with an artificial leg, and as a husband and father who worked to give his family all he could, no matter what.

Arm in arm with Boots, she said her final goodbye to her husband at the graveside, spilling tears along with a handful of earth. The tears she could not help, much though she strove to control her emotions.

Beside her, Polly dropped something else on the coffin in addition to a handful of earth. It was a wreath of red poppies, secured through the good offices of the British Legion's local branch. There was a card with the wreath, bearing the words 'To Ned. Never forgotten, old comrade. Love from Polly and Boots'. The poppies had been Polly's idea, the words her own.

Brittle though she still was sometimes, Polly could not deny herself such a gesture. Rosie, watching from close by, loved her for it.

Lizzy's own wreath, of flame-coloured lilies, Ned's favourite flowers, bore its card. Its message was typical of her kind, the kind who always believed in God and the hereafter.

'Goodbye, darling Ned, we'll meet again one day. All my love, Eliza'.

He had always called her by her baptismal name.

The funeral breakfast was at Lizzy's home, and put together by her daughters, Annabelle and Emma, with help from her daughters-in-law, Helene and Leah.

The house was full of mourning black, and echoing to voices that having been fairly hushed all through the funeral, now began to let words flow freely, if soberly. Older members converged until they formed a group consisting of Boots, Polly, Tommy, Vi, Sammy, Susie and Rachel.

'I'm so sad,' said Rachel, 'such a kind and civilized man, wasn't he? My poor Leah is heartbroken at losing so good a father-in-law.'

'We've lost one of us,' said Sammy. 'You realize that, Boots? One of us.'

'I realize it, Sammy,' said Boots, who, along with Polly, had known it from the shattering moment of truth five days ago.

'It's still a shock to me, I tell you,' said Tommy. 'I mean, he wasn't old, not much more than any of us. It'll take Lizzy ages to get over it.'

'Tommy love, don't make me feel worse than I already am,' said Vi.

'Have any of us any idea of what Lizzy is going to do?' asked Susie.

'You mean will she go and live with Bobby and Helene?' said Vi.

'Annabelle says she can't live on her own, especially not for the first few months,' said Susie.

'Annabelle's a nice girl,' said Sammy, 'but I don't know if she's right about her mum.'

'What do you think, Boots?' asked Tommy.

A faint smile touched Polly's face. It would always come down to that in a crisis. It would always come down to asking for Boots's opinion and letting that govern the collective decision, if a decision was necessary.

Boots said, 'If some of you will join me, I think I'll opt for a stiff drink.' Away he went, then stopped, turned and said, 'Tommy, I think we all know Lizzy will never leave this house, not until her own time comes and she's carried out feet first.' And he made for the table on which bottles and glasses had been laid out.

'He's right all right,' said Sammy, 'but I wish on a day like this he hadn't mentioned feet first. Come on, let's have a drink, we all need one.'

They all gravitated in the right direction, all, that is, except Polly. She waited, staying apart for the moment from the general throng. She felt, as she had on the death of her father, that with Ned's going, the country had lost one more of its old and distinguished warriors of Flanders fields. She needed something to lighten her sadness, and she wondered exactly what Lizzy needed, aside from a miraculous resurrection of Ned.

'Polly?' Boots was back, with a Scotch for himself and a gin and tonic for her.

'Thank you, darling,' she said quietly.

'You're welcome,' said Boots.

'To Ned?' she said.

'To Ned,' he said, and they touched glasses before drinking. It was one final gesture.

'Where are the twins?' asked Polly.

'In the parlour, with their grandparents, talking with Lizzy,' said Boots.

'The young and the old, consoling Lizzy together?' said Polly. 'I like that. Let's join them.'

Rosie and Matt came up, and all four entered the parlour, where they found not only Gemma and James, but also Rosie's own two, Emily and Giles, along with Tim and Felicity's daughter, Jennifer. Also present were Phoebe, Chinese Lady and Sir Edwin. Everyone had something appropriately touching to say to Lizzy. The family regarded funerals with ingrained, old-fashioned respect, inherited, as so much else was, from the behavioural patterns of the matriarch, Chinese Lady.

The house was crammed with relatives, friends and close neighbours, and as usual at any large gathering, everyone in the family seemed to be talking to everyone else. Someone had to knock twice on the front door before it was answered. Sammy did the necessary. On the step stood a young and lanky RAF officer, recognized immediately as Philip, son of Annabelle and Nick, and presently due to keep an important appointment with Phoebe.

'Hello, Uncle Sammy.' Philip spoke soberly.

'Hello yourself, Philip,' said Sammy. 'You're home, then, and you know, do you?'

Philip, stepping in, said his squadron was back a day earlier than expected, and that a neighbour had told him why no-one was at home.

'I can't tell you how sorry I am, Uncle Sammy. Grandpa Ned was a fine man, and I expect the whole family's cut up. I thought I'd come round and see Grandma Lizzy, and everyone else.'

'I think Phoebe would like to talk to you first,' said Sammy. 'Stay put for a tick and I'll let her know you're here.'

Philip stayed in the hall, conscious that the sound of many voices was a subdued but constant flow. From the parlour, a girl in a black costume emerged, her hat a little grey pillbox. But the black and grey were offset by the glow on her face. She swooped.

'Philip!' She was unable to deny gladness, the kind that sat involuntarily on sorrow. 'Oh, it's good to see you.'

438

Philip took her into his arms, and with her face buried in his shoulder, the happiness of reunion struggled with the sadness she felt for Aunt Lizzy. That turned her eyes wet.

'Go ahead, Phoebe, I understand,' said Philip.

'Oh, it's so sad, Philip . . . Aunt Lizzy's being so brave . . . but we all know she's grieving . . . we all are.' Phoebe spoke in muffled spasms.

'So am I, Phoebe, now that I know,' said Philip. 'How's my mother taking it?'

The question was very relevant, since his mother was Grandma Lizzy's elder daughter.

'She's badly shaken.' Phoebe thought of her Aunt Annabelle's tears at the graveside. 'Well, you know how much she and Emma loved their dad. Philip, look, shall I fetch her and your dad so they can talk to you here?'

Annabelle and her husband Nick appeared then, along with Philip's sister Linda. Sammy had told them of Philip's arrival. Annabelle, so like her mother in her brunette looks, was growing a little plump at forty. Nick, forty-four, still looked fit and healthy. Linda at eighteen was over the years of being thin, and had developed belatedly but happily. She was a sweet-natured girl, and ready to meet a kind young man, who didn't have to be the equivalent of Prince Charming. Simply, someone quite nice would do, even if most modern girls, when dreaming, were apt to conjure up images of Elvis Presley.

Linda and Phoebe, together with Annabelle and Nick, formed a talkative quartet around Philip, and mourning was put aside for the moment. Bronzed from his time in the Middle East, the young pilot officer looked vital and alive, and far removed from the dead and the dying of this world. He was, to Phoebe, her definite idea of the man she most wanted to spend the rest of her life with.

Talking came easily enough. They spoke, of course, of Grandpa Ned's sudden death and of how difficult it was going to be for Grandma Lizzy to cope without him. But they also spoke of the excitement of the forthcoming wedding, and at some length, until Philip said he really ought to go and pay his respects to his grandma. Lizzy received him with a brave hug, a kiss of welcome, and delight at knowing he was home again.

Philip wanted her to know that if she ever needed the kind of help that he could give, he'd be only too pleased to give it. Lizzy assured him that her sons and daughters intended to keep an eye on her, and that this probably meant there'd be a lot of unnecessary fussing. She was quite all right, she said, even if the occasion was a sad one. Naturally, she was missing Ned and would do so for a long time to come, but no-one was to worry, she'd see the day through. Philip gave way then to other relatives who wanted to pay their respects to his endearing grandma.

The day was a strain for her. There were all Ned's friends as well as so many relatives pressing around her in their wish to do what they could to console her. However, Lizzy had reserves of strength and spirit that would indeed help her to see the day through.

For Phoebe, things were a little better, while Jimmy, Sammy's younger son, and his wife Clare thought it tactful to say nothing of the fact that, on this day of mourning for a relative gone, a new life was on its way. Clare had just been informed she was pregnant. That news was for the family's ears on a happier day.

Vi's mother, known to the families these days as old Aunt Victoria, wasn't present. Almost seventy-nine, she was in failing health and keeping mainly to the room she occupied in Vi and Tommy's house. Staying away from the funeral, however, did not mean Ned's death hadn't upset her. In her eyes, Ned had always had the makings of a gentleman, and Aunt Victoria favoured that kind. Which meant she turned her nose up a bit at cockneys, while going out of her way to look admiringly at Boots, who, although born in cockney Walworth, was in her opinion a gentleman by nature.

On the return home of Vi and Tommy from the funeral, she wanted to know all about everything, particularly what the funeral service had been like. Had it paid proper respect to Ned, who'd always been so well behaved and respectable? Vi assured her it had, and described the burial itself for her mother's interest. The old lady nodded in approval.

'Well, if he had to go, poor man,' she said, 'he went quick and without suffering. I'm glad his funeral was fitting, like he deserved. Did you give my condolences to Lizzy?'

'We did,' said Tommy, 'and she sent you her thanks and good wishes.'

'I hope her family won't leave her to herself tonight,' said Aunt Victoria.

'In that respect,' said Tommy, 'Bobby will make the right decisions. He's the one with most up here.' Tommy tapped his forehead. 'Annabelle, well, being the eldest, she'll have her say, you bet, like she always does, but Bobby's the one that'll work things out for Lizzy's best interests tonight, tomorrow and the future.'

'Tommy, you just made a nice speech,' said Vi.

'Could someone make me a hot chocolate for my bedtime?' asked old Aunt Victoria.

As it happened, Bobby and Helene stayed with Lizzy all day and overnight. On Saturday they were rejoined by Annabelle and Nick, Emma and Jonathan, and Edward and Leah. Annabelle, first in seniority, opened the discussion by insisting that this family conference about her mother's future was necessary, which meant they were to decide where she was to live and with whom. In that respect, she said, Nick and herself had first claim.

Helene may have been only a daughter-in-law and not a daughter, but she spoke her piece immediately.

'Naturally, Annabelle, if Mama is to live with any of us, it will be with Bobby and me.'

'Why naturally?' asked Edward, at thirty-two not disposed to see himself disadvantaged as the younger son.

'It is not a question you need to ask,' said Helene, a firm-bodied and firm-minded Frenchwoman who had become as much an Adams as any of the in-laws. She meant that Edward, as the younger son, did indeed have to give way to Bobby in the event that a choice was necessary. Further, as far as it concerned Annabelle, Bobby was wiser and more sensible than his elder sister.

'Jonathan and I can always find room for Mum,' said Emma.

443

'True,' said Jonathan, Sussex-born. 'Emma and me, we be ready and willing now and any time.'

Bobby said nothing. He knew that if the question was going to be resolved, then his mother would resolve it herself.

In fact, before any of her well-meaning family could persuade the others to believe she was a helpless old lady, Lizzy cut the conference short. She had no intention of going to live with any of them, she said, and had every intention of staying where she was until her time was up, thus echoing the comment made yesterday by Boots. She knew what was in their father's will, she said, something for all of them and the remainder to herself, including the house.

'With my—' She stilled a momentary quiver of her lips. 'With my widow's pension and what your dad is leaving me, I shan't be in want.'

'Full marks to Dad's foresight,' said Bobby quietly.

Annabelle fidgeted, then said she honestly didn't like the idea of her mum living alone.

'Well, Annabelle lovey,' said Lizzy, pale but in control for the most part, 'I'm sure you're all concerned, and I won't say it won't be a bit hard for a while, but I'll manage. You've all got your own lives, busy lives, what with your children and everything, and that's a good state to be in. You're all young too, and don't need any help from me, bless me, no. I'll be all right here in my own home.' What she meant, of course, was that living anywhere else would be like leaving Ned. She was sure his spirit was still around, and she could take comfort from that. 'You don't have to worry about me, any of you.'

Full marks to you too, Mum, thought Bobby. She was being entirely sensible, in his book. But Annabelle, as the eldest, spoke up again, saying she still didn't like the idea of their mum being alone. Lizzy said she wouldn't really be alone, that their dad would always be present in spirit, and in any case, she'd be busy around the house. There'd always be something to do, and chores to catch up with. She wouldn't, she insisted, do any sitting around and moping. Emma came up with the declaration that, like Grandma Finch, their mum had always been independent, and accordingly wouldn't want to rely on others until she was in a wheelchair. Then she'd really need help and someone close by.

'My life,' said Leah, 'should we speak of wheelchairs?' Twenty-nine, she was a dark-eyed brunette with looks that her husband Edward thought were like those of Elizabeth Taylor, the film star, and only the very critical would have said he was biased.

'I was just making a point,' said Emma.

'You could have been more tactful,' said Annabelle.

'No, I know what Emma meant,' said Lizzy, 'and of course, I'm not going to be backward in asking for help with the garden.'

'Mama, Bobby and I will do that,' said Helene. She and Bobby had regularly helped Ned with his garden. 'Nothing could keep us away.'

'Any time you and Bobby can't make it,' said Emma, 'I'll send Jonathan along.'

'Kind of you, Emma,' said Jonathan, with the lightest of smiles. He was mightily fond of his Emma, not thirty-five but still with a great sense of fun. Her sister Annabelle was nice enough, but had developed a streak of bossiness.

'No-one gardens quite like Jonathan,' said Emma, 'and my kitchen floor proves it.'

That produced a light moment. Everyone knew Jonathan could not break himself of the habit of coming in from the garden still wearing his gumboots.

'Well, in my time,' said Lizzy, 'I did have cause to tell Ned off a few times about that kind of thing.' She ended with a catch in her voice, but at once brought herself back under control. 'I'll be after Jonathan with my broom if he walks into my kitchen in his gumboots,' she said.

'Now we'll all have a nice cup of morning coffee.'

And that was that. Nothing was going to make Lizzy live anywhere except in the home she had shared with Ned for forty years.

That night, in their bedroom, Polly watched from the bed as Boots came in from the bathroom. He was, as usual, wearing only his pyjama trousers. He always went through his last ablutions of the day in that way. It did not diminish him, for he still had a fine, firm body. One might have said he went through life almost casually for the most part, thus avoiding the strains and stresses that afflicted other men.

As he slipped into his pyjama jacket, Polly said, 'Are you over it a little now?'

'Over the funeral?' Boots mused. 'I've wondered what Ned thought of it. I've a recollection that he once mentioned he favoured cremation.'

'If he ever mentioned it to Lizzy,' said Polly, 'I'm sure she'd have talked him out of the idea.'

Boots leaned over the bed and looked down into her eyes, glimmering in the glow of the bedside lamp.

'I agree, Polly. What kind of goodbye is there for a tin container of ashes?'

Polly's arms reached and encircled his neck.

'Do me a favour, old sport,' she murmured.

'Such as?'

'Stop the clock.'

Boots smiled.

'For you and me?' he said.

'Yes, for you and me,' sighed Polly, as if she and Boots alone were destined to grow old and feeble.

Boots smiled again and lightly kissed her.

Out went the lamp and he slipped into bed beside her. She turned and they snuggled up, much as if Ned's passing had brought them to a new awareness of how much they meant to each other.

Chapter Seven

June arrived and with it a lessening of Lizzy's grief. She kept herself busy and there were always some members of the family rallying round in support.

The summer days were alternately bright and not so bright. However, it was lovely on the fifth day of the month when Sammy Adams called on his old friend, Eli Greenberg, at his Camberwell yard, a place stacked with second-hand furniture under a new roof. Sammy knew what the new roof meant. Business was profitable, something he and Mr Greenberg had both favoured all their lives.

'You there, Eli old cock?'

Mr Greenberg at once appeared at the door of his office. His office was an old green shed. He himself at seventy-seven was a prime example of how not to let age turn a man decrepit. His frame was still sturdy, and if his hair and beard were flecked with white, they were still bushy, and his face showed no deep wrinkles. His round rusty black hat never left his head in favour of a trilby except on his Sabbath, and, as a courteous gesture to his Gentile homeland, on Sundays.

Seeing Sammy, he beamed. If he loved any family more than his own, it was the Adams clan.

'Vhy, Sammy, vhat a pleasure, ain't it?' He had given that greeting many times to Sammy during their long years of doing business together.

'Same here, Eli,' said Sammy, a figure of wholesome masculinity in his light summer suit of fine grey worsted, hat in his hand, his dark brown hair well brushed. At fifty-five, he was as mentally energetic as ever, blue eyes quick and electric. Women were beginning to eye him invitingly. Some women, that is. Widows and the lonely, and minxes who favoured mature men. There were frequent undercurrents at the Camberwell offices, all to do with the man appeal not only of Sammy, but of Boots as well. Both, despite maturity of age, were still personable enough to cause a bosom to flutter, or even to heave a bit. It all passed Boots and Sammy by. In any case, neither had ever fallen for a heaving bosom outside of marriage. Along with brother Tommy, they'd been brought up by Chinese Lady to behave in strictly proper fashion, which meant hands off what didn't legally belong to them.

'What brings you to my yard, Sammy?' asked Mr Greenberg, still beaming.

'Your pony and cart,' said Sammy.

'Vhich I don't keep here, Sammy, but in a stable down New Camberwell Road, ain't it?'

'Which is convenient,' said Sammy, 'seeing there's a family wedding taking place next Saturday fortnight.'

'Sammy, you giving me advance notice that you vant me to do the usual honours?' Mr Greenberg's beam glowed.

'Family custom, Eli old mate,' said Sammy. It went back a long way, the custom of Mr Greenberg driving an Adams bride to the church in his pony and cart. In fact, it went back to 1916, when Lizzy married Ned. 'Phoebe's going to make a happy bloke of Philip. The ceremony's taking place at twelve at the Denmark Hill church. Can we rely on you, Eli, to be at my front door by quarter to twelve?'

'Sammy, von't it be vun more pleasure, and ain't I honoured?' said Mr Greenberg effusively. 'Young Phoebe, is it? Vell, there von't be a prettier bride, and I'll vear a suit and a top hat, von't I?'

'Be my guest,' said Sammy. 'And about expenses—'

'There von't be any expenses, Sammy, not a penny. Vould I charge for the privilege after all these years? No, no, Sammy, not a penny.'

'Much obliged, Eli, and consider yourself and your missus invited to the reception,' said Sammy.

'I'm touched, Sammy, touched,' said Mr Greenberg and blew his nose on his large red handkerchief, one of several as old as his rusty hat. He was always comfortable with the old and familiar.

'Mutual,' said Sammy. 'Have to push off now, I'm up to my ears back at the office.'

'Vhen veren't you, Sammy, eh?'

'Well, it won't do to let the overheads suffer on account of not being where I should be,' said Sammy. 'So long, Eli.' He shook hands with his old friend and left. He did have work to do, work involving reorganization of the offices. The shop and the rest of the ground floor were being pulled apart and knocked about for the purpose of providing extra office space and a staff canteen. The two shop assistants had been transferred to other branches of the Adams retail business. Now Sammy had to consider employing a cook and a serving assistant. Lunches would be provided at a nominal cost of one shilling and sixpence, tea and coffee free, cakes or biscuits a few pence.

Together, Sammy and Rachel had worked out that prices would cover cost of ingredients, after which the firm would stand the outlay, including wages for cook and assistant. If that dented profits a bit, well, as Rachel pointed out, some sacrifice could be made without causing any real pain, and the goodwill between employer and employees would increase twofold. Sammy said he supposed twofold meant twice as much. Rachel said yes. So Sammy said she was right, that there'd be no real pain.

He had a word with her when he got back from seeing Mr Greenberg.

'Rachel, I've been thinking. What I know about cooking and making up a menu is nobody's guess. At home, I just eat what Susie serves up, and as I haven't been disappointed yet, I've got faith in what women know about menus. So as soon as the canteen is beginning to take shape, I'll leave you to interview applicants for cook and assistant.'

'Very well, Sammy, and thank you for the compliment,' said Rachel. 'By the way, do you realize one of our lady bookkeepers has a bit of a crush on you?'

'No, I don't know,' said Sammy, 'so don't tell me. It'll make me nervous. I once had a funny female assistant who kept brushing up against my suit. Fortunately, she migrated somewhere. To the Isle of Cats and Dogs, or some place like that. Which makes me ask you, Rachel old friend, what's up with some females?'

'Men like you and Boots, Sammy.'

'Well,' observed Sammy, 'I can understand about Boots, him being educated and a wartime general—'

'Colonel, Sammy.'

'Same thing to a dotty female. But he's getting on a bit, so if anyone in these here business offices does have a crush on him, tell him to wear his Crimean war medals and to talk to her like a grandfather. Incidentally, what's all that hammering down below?'

'It's the building contractors, Sammy, doing the conversion job.'

'Someone tell 'em to mind my head.'

Rachel was smiling on her way back to her office. Sammy, the love, couldn't cope with feminine adulation. It simply embarrassesd him. Boots treated it like a head cold. Head colds had a short life and a definite finishing date.

The lady bookkeeper in question, the one who fancied Sammy, was actually a married woman of thirty-three, Mrs Lily Chambers. She and her husband had no children, and as he was only a postman, with only a postman's wages, being free to earn a wage herself meant they had been able to afford the small luxuries that would otherwise have been denied them, as well as paying off the mortgage on their little house in Bavent Road, near Coldharbour Lane. Her own small luxuries were new clothes bought at sale times. A blond woman of round countenance and rounded figure, her machine-knitted jumpers paid their tribute to her figure, and her lipstick gave a touch of 'kiss-me-quick' to her looks. A bit of a flirt, she nevertheless had a serious side, and it was this that had pointed her at bookkeeping during her last year at school. She liked the look of books devoted to the entry of numerals that related to the excitement of pounds, shillings and pence.

She had been working for Adams Enterprises for just over a year, having left her previous employment with a firm of heating engineers after responding to an advertisement in the *South London Press*. The subsequent interview told her she would earn twelve shillings and sixpence more with Adams Enterprises. She enjoyed the job from the start, because there was a kind of up-and-coming atmosphere present, even if the senior bookkeeper was a bit of an old goat. After all, she wasn't actually working for him, but for the bosses, the two

Adams brothers. And one of them, Mr Sammy, was a man after her own heart. He too loved to see a book that recorded entries of pounds, shillings and pence, especially if it was obvious that the figures relating to income were keeping a healthy lead over those relating to expenditure. A man like Mr Sammy could take that in at a glance. It was always a pleasure to have him occasionally inspect the books she kept concerning the income and expenditure figures of the firm's retail shops. Numerals invigorated him, just as they invigorated her. What an interesting man he was, to be sure. He often made her wish he would take as much notice of her figure as some of those entered in her books.

One evening at home, when her husband Joe was down at the local pub, playing for the darts team, she was entertaining her sister. She took the opportunity to make a confession.

'Listen, Ivy, I've got something to say to you. I think I'm probably going to have an affair.'

'You're what?' said Ivy, a single woman of thirty-five who worked at Woolworth's in Peckham High Street, and lived in a flat over a shop. 'You're what?'

'I think I'm probably going to have an affair,' repeated Lily.

'Either you're out of your mind or I'm not

hearing straight,' said Ivy, almost put off the cup of tea and slice of cake Lily had set before her. 'Did you actually say you're going to have an affair?'

'Probably,' said Lily.

Ivy came to a little and took in a mouthful of cake.

'Of course, you're not serious,' she said.

'Well, I am, actually,' said Lily, 'I've got a fancy for a very sexy man.'

'Oh, no, not another one,' sighed Ivy. 'You're always getting fancies for some bloke or other, you silly moo. Might I remind you that even on your wedding day you had a fancy for Archie Cope, Joe's best man?'

'Oh, that wasn't serious,' said Lily.

'Nor were any of the others,' said Ivy, drinking hot tea to fortify herself for argument. Lily had always had a roving eye for a good-looking pair of trousers, but it had never amounted to much more than some flirtatious winks and coy gestures. If, during her married years, any bloke she made up to started to respond in earnest, she as good as ran a mile. She had never been serious, although sometimes Joe reckoned he had good reason to come close to smacking her bottom. Joe was easy-going, up to a point. He wasn't going to like the fact that for the first time Lily was actually talking about having an affair. 'Come on, this one's not really a serious fancy, is he?'

'He's special,' said Lily.

'So have all the others been,' said Ivy, 'but nothing's ever happened, lucky for you. Isn't it about time you stopped behaving like a soppy schoolgirl having crushes?'

'I'm not having a crush now,' said Lily, 'I'm having this feeling about starting an affair. I don't get much out of Joe these days, not now we've been married for fourteen years.'

'You don't have to let him down by going in for adultery, do you?' said Ivy.

Lily said she'd be obliged if her sister didn't use nasty words like that. She wouldn't be surprised, she said, if Joe was living it up with some woman on the evenings when he was supposed to be playing darts. Some husbands do that sort of thing, she said. Ivy said she didn't think Joe was that kind of husband, and that Lily on the whole was fortunate to be his wife. She reminded Lily that she herself had been robbed by the war of the chance to marry her fiancé of the time, because he was killed in the desert fighting. The poor man was driving a tank, and all he did was to pop his head out for just a tick to get a bit of air, and in that time it was blown off, which was horrible for him and tragic bad luck for her.

'Yes, I remember that,' said Lily, 'and we all sorrowed for you and his family, but it's got nothing to do with me and me present fancy.'

'Yes, it has,' said Ivy, 'because it should tell you you're lucky and that you ought to be grateful. Who is this bloke you're soppy about?'

'I'm not telling you,' said Lily. 'If I do, you'll tell Joe and Joe will go round to see my fancy and do something silly.'

'Something silly? A bit violent more like,' said Ivy, 'and who'd blame him? I ask meself who would and I answer I wouldn't, for a start.'

'I don't want any trouble,' said Lily, 'just a chance to enjoy a bit of romance.'

'A bit of adultery, you mean,' said Ivy.

'Didn't I ask you not to use nasty words like that?' said Lily rather querulously. 'Look, I wanted to talk to someone about me feelings, and I thought me own sister would be the right one.'

'Well, I am the right one,' said Ivy, 'because I'm telling you you're talking like a daft parrot. Anyway, I don't believe you really are serious, I think it's just another of your silly crushes that only last a fortnight.'

'I'm in love,' pronounced Lily.

'Oh, me aching foot,' said Ivy, 'you'll make me suffer heart failure in a minute.'

'Course you won't,' said Lily, 'you're not the kind.'

'I can only stand so much of all this bunkum,' said Ivy.

'Listen,' said Lily, 'don't you realize I've met a man I really admire?'

'All I realize is that you're off your silly head,' said Ivy. 'That was a nice piece of cake, by the way. Is there any more?'

'There you are, help yourself,' said Lily, and lifted the deep lid of the china dish to disclose what was left of a home-baked madeira cake.

'Oh, ta,' said Ivy, and cut herself a slice. She also helped herself to another cup of tea. Discussion and argument fuelled one's appetite for cups of tea and home-baked cake. 'Lily, you wouldn't really do Joe down, would you?'

'I couldn't answer for what me passion might make me do,' confessed Lily, which nearly made Ivy choke on cake. 'It comes on very urgent sometimes, especially when he's close to me.'

'Don't say any more,' begged Ivy, 'I'm having a fit. If you could only hear yourself, you'd have one too.'

'One what?' asked Lily, mentally calculating the answer to three pounds, twelve shillings and sixpence multiplied by fifty-three. Fifty-three was the number of weeks she'd been working for Adams Enterprises.

'One what? A fit, of course,' said Ivy.

'Bless me, who'd have believed it?' murmured Lily, having reached the sum of a hundred and ninety-two pounds, two shillings and six-pence as an answer. Some people did crossword puzzles. She did mental arithmetic. 'All that much?'

'Now what you talking about?' asked Ivy.

'I think I've said enough.' Lily was firm about that. 'You'll have to leave me to decide my own fate.'

Ivy said that whatever that might be, watch out for what Joe might do if he finds out.

Chapter Eight

Chinese Lady was living a new kind of existence, due to the fact that Sir Edwin had managed to hire someone very willing and efficient to help her with the housework, a forty-two-year-old widow, Mrs Harriet Plumstead. With her two daughters off her hands, and living in a small flat in Herne Hill, Mrs Plumstead was only too pleased to do a daily job from nine to two thirty, including Saturdays, at two shillings an hour, which amounted to three pounds and six shillings a week. This was pretty good money for a char, and entirely due to Sir Edwin's recognition of a deserving cause. He had instinctively felt the lady would be deserving. Those earnings, added to her widow's pension, would, she said, help her to live like a queen.

A bony, strong-looking woman, Mrs Plumstead was of the perpetually cheerful kind. Not at all awed at working for what she told her daughters were a lord and lady, she addressed Chinese Lady in cockney fashion as 'ducks' or 'dearie' or 'mum'. Chinese Lady found this a mite more acceptable than something like 'Your Ladyship'. As she informed Sir Edwin, she had never been born a ladyship, just one of the people. Sir Edwin assured her they were both of the people.

Conversations between Mrs Plumstead and Chinese Lady were generally of the following kind.

'I've done the bedroom, dearie, I'll start downstairs now, if it pleases you.'

'Yes, do that, Mrs Plumstead.'

'Oh, like I've said, you don't have to be formal. Call me Harriet, like me friends do. How's yer hubby this morning? What a nice gent he is, to be sure. Me own old man, Johnny, he was nice too, and it was 'ardly fair him being taken when he was still young.' Mr Plumstead had been a bus driver for years until pneumonia took him off at the age of forty-four, which Mrs Plumstead considered unfair indeed, considering some men with no manners and no graces were still getting on people's nerves at sixty.

Mrs Plumstead liked work, liked being busy. She washed up the breakfast things when she arrived, then began the housework, made coffee at ten thirty, did more housework, and cooked lunch for one o'clock. Chinese Lady insisted she had her own share of the meal, and she did, enjoying it in the kitchen. After that, she washed up, tidied up, made sure that nothing that should have been done was left undone, and then departed. Incidentally, on Tuesdays she ironed what was necessary from the Monday washing. Chinese Lady was particularly grateful for that, since ironing had begun to give her a backache.

The paragon was paid daily by Sir Edwin, which pleased her no end. It meant, she confided, that she always had a bit of money in her purse, which she hadn't had before.

To Chinese Lady, the important factor was that the hired help relieved her of the major part of her domestic chores, which gave Sir Edwin a deal of satisfaction on her behalf, and pleased her more than she would admit. At the same time, however, she declared she didn't want her hands to get idle. Sir Edwin encouraged her to take up knitting again, and in a busy way, so she was now turning out woollies for her great-grandchildren, of which there were more than a few. Sir Edwin, hearing her humming old-fashioned songs, felt convinced that hiring a competent daily help was the best thing he had done for his wife in years.

Mrs Plumstead addressed him as 'Sir' in acknowledgement of his distinguished look and his good manners, not his title. She considered him a genuine gent, both in appearance and graciousness.

'Sir, I've done your study right through this morning. My, all them books you leave about, I've tidied them up again.'

Sir Edwin refrained from telling her he didn't want them tidied up. He felt she'd insist, anyway. She was a great believer in tidiness. It caused him to consult Chinese Lady at times.

'Maisie, have you seen my morning paper?'

'Oh, it's been tidied up, Edwin.'

'And where has it been tidied up?'

'In the rack for papers and magazines, Edwin, and it's nicely folded.'

One could accept an excess of zeal from such a worthy asset, but all the same, Sir Edwin made what he thought was a relevant point.

'I beg you, Maisie, to assure our invaluable help that should the thought occur to her, there's no need to iron my *Telegraph*.'

'Edwin, what a silly idea, no-one irons a newspaper.'

'Some butlers do, I believe, and I've a feeling that one day, Mrs Plumstead might begin to iron mine.'

So, at an opportune moment, Chinese Lady spoke to her hired help. It was when the agreeable lady was 'tidying up' Edwin's newspaper.

'Mrs Plumstead, you're not thinking of ironing that, are you?'

'Beg pardon, mum?' said Mrs Plumstead.

'My husband says there's no need to.'

'To iron his newspaper?' Mrs Plumstead looked bemused for a moment. Then, 'Oh, d'you mean he'd like me to? I never heard of any gent before that wanted his newspaper ironed, but if that's what your hubby would like, I'd be pleasured to oblige.'

'Oh, I only meant that if you were thinking of doing so, you needn't worry.'

'Well, I won't, dearie, I won't put an iron to any bit of your hubby's newspaper.'

'I'll tell him that.'

'Tell him it's a promise, mum.'

Chinese Lady told Sir Edwin. The telling so diverted him that he laughed out loud, so Chinese Lady, of course, wanted to know what was funny about it.

'I confess, Maisie, that I never thought you'd take me literally,' said Sir Edwin.

'What's that mean?' asked Chinese Lady. 'I just thought you wanted me to make sure Mrs Plumstead didn't run a hot iron over your paper.'

'Well, that was very nice of you, Maisie, and I'm greatly obliged for your intercession.'

'I don't know what intercession means,' said Chinese Lady, 'I just know you won't have to worry about your paper being ironed.'

'Thank you, Maisie. What a good woman you are.'

On a day during the second week in June, Rachel took on the responsibility of interviewing two applicants for the job of canteen cook.

The ground-floor conversion was progressing well, and the question of hiring a cook and assistant for the canteen needed to be attended to. The first applicant for cook was a large, rosy-faced lady whose blouse buttons were straining at the leash. She was expansive of mood as well as figure, beaming happily as she detailed her credentials. She was a married lady of fifty, but used to doing a weekly job. A job such as was being offered, a canteen cook, was just up her street, seeing the kind of experience she'd had.

'What experience is that?' asked Rachel, looking like the firm's most comely executive.

'Why, the kind that you want, I'm sure,' beamed the lady. 'Didn't I spend years doing the customers proud in the Walworth Road fish and chip shop?'

'You mean your experience was in the frying of fish and chips?' said Rachel.

'Wasn't I doing that for a good seven years and never getting one complaint?' The applicant beamed again in happy self-satisfaction.

'I'm not sure we have lunches of fried fish and chips in mind,' said Rachel. 'I think we favour a choicer menu.' She referred to her notes. 'I see that when you phoned for an interview, you did say you had wide experience as a cook.'

'Yes, that's right, madam, I did say that, and I said right, because before I did me seven years at the fish and chip shop, I worked ten years at the pie and mash shop in the East Street market, where the menu was very choice. Customers could have just pie and mash, or pie, mash and baked beans, or pie, mash and green peas.' The large lady beamed yet again. 'Then there was me hot gravy, which customers got very fond of.'

Rachel, with an effort, kept her face straight.

'So your experience as a cook has been mainly confined to hot pies and mashed potatoes, and fried fish and chips?' she said.

The happy, self-confident applicant said not to forget all the cooking she'd done for her husband as well, and right through thirty years of marriage, and never once had her old man

468

suffered a stomach ache on account of what she served up daily, although during the war when he did a lot of ARP duties and needed a bit of good food, her cooking at home was affected by rationing. Her old man liked a hot stew, for instance, especially in winter, but you couldn't get the proper ingredients while the war was on. Of course, now and again she was able to take home some pie and mash for both of them.

'With a jug of me gravy as well,' she added. 'Of course, I warmed it all up in the oven when I got home. That's if there wasn't no air raid on. If there was, we had to wait till it was over.'

'Frightful days and nights,' said Rachel.

'Yes, wasn't they?' said the expansive lady. 'When would you like me to start the job? I'm not working at the moment, so any time will suit me, and what would be the hours?'

As tactfully as she could Rachel explained that she had other applicants to interview, and that she wouldn't come to a decision until she'd seen them all.

'Then we'll write to you,' she said.

'Oh, all right, but you haven't said what the hours would be.'

'We're thinking of from ten in the morning until four thirty in the afternoon, since the provision of afternoon tea will come into the reckoning,' said Rachel. 'The lunch hour will

469

be from twelve thirty to one thirty, the tea break from three thirty to three forty-five.'

'Well, all that'll suit me fine,' said the large lady, and departed still beaming. With her going, Rachel detected that something went with her. The faint aroma of fried fish and chips.

The second applicant was much more encouraging, being a young woman who had excelled in domestic science at school, particularly in all that appertained to the skills of a chef. Just married, she needed a part-time job, she said, and preferred a local one rather than having to travel up and down to somewhere in town. As a newly married woman, she wanted to make sure she had time to cope with the housework, as well as with the preparation of the evening meal.

Rachel, at this early point, recognized the picture of the happy and eager young newlywed who, after spelling out her qualifications, sensibly asked what were the hours of work, and what was the pay. Rachel quoted the hours, and said the pay would be four pounds, ten shillings a week. The young woman, Mrs Mary Tindall, expressed sastisfaction with that, and the interview continued. Rachel pointed out that all staff would use the canteen, and that included directors and managers. Mary Tindall, with a smile, said she would welcome the challenge of preparing menus to tempt the high as well as the low.

'I think you might suit us very well,' said Rachel, 'but I must be frank. Do you and your husband propose to start a family?'

What had Sammy said? Try not to take on any married female whose husband might be thinking of putting her in the club. We don't want her leaving just when she's well into the job. Someone about forty would be best.

Young Mrs Tindall was nowhere about forty, or even thirty. Accordingly, Rachel had to ask the necessary question.

Mary Tindall answered promptly.

'Well, I'm only twenty, and my husband's only twenty-two, and we both come of large families, which means we've both got all the relatives we need right now. We're not going to start our own family for at least two years. That's so we can enjoy Saturday night dances, rock and roll concerts, and be active members of the Elvis Presley fan club.'

'Mrs Tindall,' said Rachel, 'I'll speak to our managing director, and if he accepts my recommendation, that will mean the job is yours. I'll write you accordingly, and let you know the starting date. Will that do for now?'

Mary Tindall said thanks very much, and that

she hoped to hear she really had got the job. When she had left, Rachel popped into Sammy's office and let him know how she had got on with both applicants. Sammy fell about when told of the large, expansive woman who thought fried fish and chips or pie and mash alone should form the canteen menu. He liked the sound of Mrs Mary Tindall, however, and when assured by Rachel that the young lady and her husband were far more interested in Elvis Presley than babies, he expressed himself willing for her to be taken on.

'But might I ask incidental who this bloke Elvis Presley is? I sometimes get a feeling he's the Invisible Man following me about.'

'He's the world's top pop star,' said Rachel, 'and you could well call him the Invincible Man as much as the Invisible. My daughter Leah informs me he's unbeatable, and has left even Frank Sinatra far behind. My life, Sammy, Leah is thirty this year, and here she is with the same taste for pop music as teenagers.'

'Not to worry, it won't last,' said Sammy. 'It'll be on the way out in a year of so, and we'll get Bing Crosby back as the number one crooner.'

'Sammy,' said Rachel, 'should I argue with that? I should. Crooners in another year or so will be as dead as the dodo.'

'Pity,' said Sammy. 'Anyway, back to work, so ask Mrs Whatsername to let me see the February and March bank statements for our Clapham and Brixton shops, will you?'

'I think you mean Mrs Chambers,' said Rachel, hiding a smile. Mrs Chambers was the woman who had a thing about Sammy. Sammy, the dear man, had no idea his favours were coveted by the lady.

Chapter Nine

When told she was wanted by Mr Sammy, and why, Lily showed a slight flush. It signified an undercurrent of pleasure, sweet excitement and an erratic pulse. Carrying the required statements, she went down to Sammy's office.

'Come in,' called Sammy in response to her knock, and in Lily went, round face tinted with light, attractive make-up. Her ivory, pearl-buttoned blouse and long brown skirt seemed, as far as style went, halfway between a 1920 fashion and the New Look era. Neverthless, the outfit suited her.

'Oh, good afternoon, Mr Sammy,' she said, trying not to gush, 'I've brought the Brixton and Clapham bank statements that Mrs Goodman told me you wanted to see.'

'Yes, I do want to see the entries for February and March,' said Sammy. Although every Adams shop now had its own bank account, all statements were sent to the head office. Lily placed the relevant documents on Sammy's desk, in front of him. A little sighing breath escaped her. Mr Sammy Adams, what a man. He had gorgeous blue eyes full of life and energy. He made younger men look really dull. As he took hold of the top statement, she leaned over the desk, and her sighing breath turned into a murmur.

'Mr Sammy?'

'Yes?' Sammy was already into figures and not, therefore, looking into her dewy eyes.

'Would you—'

His desk phone rang. He picked it up.

'Hello?'

'Mr Tommy from the factory wants to talk to you, Mr Sammy,' said the switchboard operator. 'I'll put him through.'

'Right,' said Sammy, unaware that love and hope were hovering. 'Hello, Tommy, what's up?'

'Who's fed up, you mean,' said Tommy, general manager of the factory, 'and if you want to ask I'll tell you it's me. I've got the union on my back again. Like I've mentioned before, I never was in favour of having the workforce unionated.'

'Unionated?' said Sammy, with Lily gazing down at the top of his head and admiring the healthy look of his dark brown hair. 'Is that an operation or something to do with a prostate?'

'Unionated or unionized,' said Tommy, 'what's the difference? It all amounts to the union thinking it's their factory, not ours. I've just had the shop stewards in my office asking for a seven and a half per cent pay rise across the board.'

'Eh?' Sammy couldn't believe his ears. Seven and a half per cent across the board? For two hundred workers? 'Eh?' he said again.

'I think you heard,' said Tommy,

Sammy had heard all right, and was as good as speechless for the moment. Lily, still leaning, drew a breath and prepared to put a question to him while the brief silence lasted.

'Would you like to go to bed with me, Mr Sammy?'

Well, that was what was on the tip of her tongue, but at the precise point when she was about to release it, Sammy came to. He looked up from the phone into the soulful eyes of the lady bookkeeper and said, 'Never mind now, leave these statements with me and I'll let you have them back later.' Then he spoke to Tommy again. 'Listen, did you rate the shop stewards as serious? I mean, is it possible they were trying it on?'

'Oh, they were trying it on all right,' said Tommy, 'and doing it seriously.'

'Well, sod that,' said Sammy, 'they're taking

their orders from Barney Burridge, of course.'
Barney Burridge was the local union big
shot, and an old bowler-hatted opponent of the
Adams brothers. 'He's having a barmy day-
dream if he thinks the garment-manufacturing
industry will wear that kind of pay rise for the
workers.'

Tommy said that that was exactly what he
had told the shop stewards, and he went on at
length about their thick heads and aggravating
arguments. During this discourse Lily departed
from Sammy's office to make her way back
to the bookkeeping department on the second
floor. She climbed the stairs with a sigh, but not
without telling herself that when Mr Sammy
was ready to hand back the bank statements,
she would have a second opportunity to let him
know they could find bliss together. She had a
vague image of Sammy driving her out into the
countryside one day, say as far as Reigate,
where they would make love in some romantic
spot golden with buttercups, and get back to the
office by teatime.

Sammy, totally ignorant of what lay in wait
for him, interrupted Tommy.

'Listen, Tommy old cock, talk to the shop
stewards and tell 'em to tell Barney Burridge to
go fry his bedsocks. Let 'em know that other
factory owners won't wear the demand, and

that I'm objecting personally. Meanwhile, I'll have a word with Boots.'

'Do that, Sammy,' said Tommy, and hung up.

Sammy took himself into Boots's office. His elder brother was in the process of handing to Rosie correspondence she could attend to first thing tomorrow, and thus save him some work he could do without.

'I need to talk to you, Boots,' said Sammy.

'I'm just going, Uncle Sammy,' said Rosie, and Sammy thought what a treat she was to the eye. She always had been, right from her years as a girl, and still was, even though she'd passed forty. Come to that, Susie was still a bit of a looker, even at fifty-two. As for Polly, she was a corblimey miracle at sixty. The family could be proud of its females and their looks. Nobody could have said any of them were like the six-foot circus woman with a beard.

'Don't let me rush you, Rosie.'

'No, I really am just going, it's nearly three o'clock,' smiled Rosie, and left the brothers to each other. Sammy lost no time in acquainting Boots with the garment union's demand for a seven and a half per cent rise across the board. Barney Burridge and his brother bowler hats were trying it on, he said.

Boots gave the matter some thought before

responding. Then he said, 'Sammy, any rise from five to seven and a half per cent has to mean more than one thing for our workforce, never mind what it might mean at other factories.'

'I know it means an injurious leap in overheads for us,' said Sammy, 'and it means cherries on an iced cake for the workforce.'

'Not quite,' said Boots. 'It'll mean they can't even have the cake. That is, in order to offset the cost of increased wages, we'll have to cancel their twice-yearly bonuses and double wage packet at Christmas.'

Sammy smacked his forehead.

'Now why didn't I think of that?' he said. 'Blind O'Reilly, where else could any factory workers get an earnings deal as good as we give 'em? Two bonuses a year, and a Christmas box every December?'

'Sammy,' said Boots, 'tell Tommy to tell Barney Burridge that irrespective of other factories, the case for our workers is that they're being greedy. Not good union publicity, that Sammy, not good at all. Further, get Tommy to point out that the Government's not going to like any rise that increases the price of export goods. The garments industry exports in quantity.'

'One day,' said Sammy, 'I'll get Susie to

479

congratulate me in public for having an educated brother. Believe me, Boots, I often wish I'd been educated meself.'

'Oh, you're educated, Sammy,' smiled Boots, 'and to a degree that has seen off many a pain in the elbow like Barney Burridge.'

When Tommy heard from Sammy that Boots had come up with a blinder, he asked what it was, and Sammy told him.

'Blimey, I'm getting old,' he said. 'I should have thought about the bonuses when the shop stewards were trying to fry my brains. I'll lay ten to one that none of our workers will want to give up what they get extra twice a year and Christmas as well.'

'And I'll lay the same odds that none of the other factory owners will wear any demands for any kind of a rise right across the board,' said Sammy. 'Skilled workers will always want more than the unskilled, and that includes percentages.'

'I'll talk to the shop stewards, and they can talk to Burridge,' said Tommy.

'Good idea,' said Sammy, 'let them have the privilege of spoiling Burridge's afternoon cuppa.'

'Don't let's laugh yet,' said Tommy soberly. 'The special case for our workers won't stop the big noises like Burridge from calling the workers

480

out. That'll mean ours along with everybody else's. Also, I've just thought. Burridge will tell the shop stewards to stand their ground over the bonuses, and the union won't care a burnt banger about what the Government thinks.'

He was right, because when Barney Burridge heard from the shop stewards that the workers at the Adams factory were against pressing for a rise, and that the Government wouldn't like any rise to increase export prices, he simply said the workers would do as their union instructed them and the Government could cry its eyes out from now until Christmas as far as the TUC was concerned. It was every union's job to win fair do's for its members, so go tell Tommy Adams that.

Tommy, receiving the message, saw trouble ahead. These days, he said, the unions frighten the Government more than the Government frightens the unions. If the crunch came, he didn't think the factory's workforce would disobey an order from the union to down tools and walk out. No worker wanted to be labelled a blackleg, not unless he could take the next boat to Australia and join a gold rush.

Boots, when advised of Burridge's reactions, suggested they should all sit on the problem, and let the union argue the case with the big industrialists of the garments trade. The federation will fight any demand for a rise, he predicted, certainly anything over two and a half per cent. The Government will have to oppose the granting of any rise that affects exports, and they'll hope for public backing.

'Of course,' he added, 'the public would support the Government stance if they thought the union was being influenced by its Communist elements. If the press got hold of a rumour that that was the case, they'd headline it. Since our factory workers mostly live in Bethnal Green or thereabouts, some probably rub shoulders with the local red revolutionaries. What does this country dislike most, Sammy?'

'Red revolutionaries,' said Sammy, which gave Boots the cue to remind him that Chinese Lady and her like still felt Bolsheviks were bewhiskered bomb-throwers who could give children nightmares. 'I think you're hoping that someone in Bethnal Green will slip a rumour to the local paper,' said Sammy.

'That would be a start,' said Boots.

'Good thinking,' said Sammy.

Lily had no chance to talk to Sammy again that afternoon, for when the working day ended he was still busy on matters other than the bank statements. She would have to wait until tomorrow. Not that she felt disappointed or thwarted. She wasn't the type to be in a hurry. In fact, time fostered anticipation. You could think up all kinds of things for when the happening came, like, in this instance, would Sammy Adams turn out to be as exciting as he looked? She could imagine him being firm and masterful, because that was how he was as a boss. If they did make love in a country field, she hoped being firm and masterful wouldn't get in the way of him taking his shoes and socks off. She admitted she was a bit fussy about that sort of thing.

Once, in the early days of her marriage to Joe, they had made love in a nice quiet spot near Abbey Wood, but Joe had spoiled it a bit by keeping his boots on. Afterwards, when she was remonstrating with him, he said he didn't see how a bloke at that stage of the proceedings could be expected to even unlace his boots, let alone take them off. The trouble with Joe was that he could be a bit common at times. Also, he wasn't exciting, and nor did he bother with romance any more. Darts, they were his real love. He could spend hours fussing over his sets, while he hardly fussed over her at all.

Anyway, tomorrow at the office, when Mr Sammy gave her back the bank statements, she'd definitely ask him if he'd like to make love to her. He might easily be rapturous about the offer, since she supposed his wife, being middle-aged, as he was himself, didn't encourage him to do much else in bed except sleep.

At home that evening, Joe asked her if she had something on her mind. At first she said no, then corrected herself and said well, yes, she did. Could he get a new lid for the dustbin because the present one was so cracked it let smells escape in their back yard, and their neighbours might complain any moment. Joe said she shouldn't let a dustbin lid play on her mind, and not to worry, he'd get a new one from the hardware shop tomorrow. Lily thought well, imagine if tomorrow turns out to mean a dustbin lid for Joe and a romance for me, what a day.

'When's your next darts match?' she asked.

'Tomorrow night,' said Joe, and she thought there, that's it, out most nights at the pub and leaving me all alone Joe just doesn't deserve me. He'd be just as happy with a parrot as with me.

At home with Susie, Sammy was asked by his one and only better half if there really was a danger of a strike at the factory.

'Unfortunately,' said Sammy, 'the answer's in the altogether.'

'Does that mean yes?' asked Susie, who was waiting for the radio music programme to come across with one more rendering of Harry Belafonte's international hit, 'Island in the Sun'.

'Afraid so,' said Sammy. 'We can fight a local dispute whenever Barney Burridge gets a bit stroppy, and we've done that more than once. But as an individual factory we can't fight a national dispute, apart from putting in our pennyworth of protest. What I don't like is the prospect of a long shutdown. That could cost us pound notes and customers. Losing pound notes is hurtful, Susie. Losing customers is worse.'

'Oh, dear,' said Susie. 'Never mind, love, the firm will still have earnings from our shops and our property company.'

'I don't like saying so,' said Sammy, 'but there won't be too many earnings from the shops. Most of what they sell is supplied by the factory.'

'Oh, well,' said Susie philosophically, 'no strike lasts for ever, so I don't suppose we'll actually finish up on the dole.'

'We might come close to having to sell the piano,' said Sammy.

'Sammy, we haven't had a piano for years,' said Susie.

'That's done it,' said Sammy, 'we're worse off than I thought.'

Susie didn't comment on that. She was listening to Harry Belafonte.

Elsewhere, in the house on Red Post Hill, in fact, Chinese Lady was listening to the same music programme while busily knitting. And Sir Edwin was taking in a special report in his newspaper concerning the European Common Market, set up in March by France, West Germany, Holland, Belgium, Italy and Luxembourg. It was an exponent of free trade and harmonization of industry and agriculture. Elements within the British Conservative party thought it might be a good idea for Britain to join. Sir Edwin thought the Market might prove very advantageous to its members, but he wasn't sure if France and West Germany hadn't fashioned the whole thing for their greater good. Time, he thought, would tell. In any event, it was a very interesting development.

While open-minded about it, he was sure Chinese Lady would totally disapprove of any move into Europe by Britain. In his wife's views, Europe was full of foreigners, and Germany was the birthplace of Kaiser Wilhelm and Adolf Hitler. It was no good telling her that Hitler had actually been born in Austria. Chinese Lady had long ago placed him alongside Kaiser Wilhelm

486

as a German warmonger who ought never to have been born, or to have been drowned as soon as he first saw the light of day. His silly moustache, she once said, ought to have told the doctor he was going to be a nuisance to everyone.

Sir Edwin pointed out that at birth Hitler would have had no moustache. Chinese Lady said she was convinced that at birth he had his moustache and all his wicked intentions as well. She said it was like when the Devil was born and God's angels saw that he already had horns. That was why he was cast out. And look what happened, he'd been a wicked nuisance ever since. Lord knows what would happen if the Devil and Hitler were both alive together. Blow the world up, I should think, she said.

One could not dispute with Chinese Lady on this particular subject. One accepted it was one of her favourite hobby horses, and that she rode it frequently and at length.

Chapter Ten

'Right, here we are, Deirdre,' said Sammy at twenty past ten the following morning.

'It's Lily, Mr Sammy,' said the lovelorn lady from the bookkeeping department. 'Deirdre's one of the invoice clerks.'

'So she is,' said Sammy. 'Silly me. Got a lot on my mind, that's the trouble. Anyway, you can have these bank statements back for your files now. I've seen all I want to.'

Mrs Lily Chambers leaned over his desk and reached for the statements. Sammy looked up into her eyes, and she looked down into his. His were blue and very clear, hers were hazel and kind of misty again. She drew a needful breath. She was quite confident about her looks and her sex appeal, but all the same, asking Mr Sammy if he'd like to romance with her in a field of cowslips or whatever, well, it wasn't the easiest thing in the world.

'Mr Sammy—'

'You all right, Lily?' said Sammy. 'Only you look a bit fuzzy.'

'Oh, I'm all right in meself,' said Lily, 'it's me emotions that are getting the better of me.' She sighed, leaned further over and whispered, 'Mr Sammy, if I asked you if you'd like to—'

A knock on Sammy's office door interrupted her, and in came one of the general office girls. She was carrying Sammy's morning coffee and biscuit. Oh, blow, thought Lily, I didn't think about it being as bothersome as this to get Mr Sammy to myself for a few minutes. But I might have remembered how busy these offices always are, especially where Mr Adams and Mr Sammy are concerned. By Mr Adams, she meant Boots. As the eldest of the three brothers, that was how he was addressed.

'Coffee, Mr Sammy,' cooed the girl, glancing at Lily as she placed the refreshments on the desk. Lily smiled kind of vaguely.

'Thanks, Jane, just the job,' said Sammy. He looked up at Lily.

'There we are, then, take the statements and go and enjoy your own coffee.'

'Oh, right,' said Lily, and was accompanied out by the general office girl. I'm being persecuted in a way, she thought. Well, that's what it feels like. But I won't let it stand in my way, I've got to let Mr Sammy know I'm in love with him. I wonder if he'd feel flattered? After all, he's middle-aged, so he might feel flattered at having a young woman in love with him. I'm hardly much over thirty. Well, thirty-three is still young compared to middle age. Not that Mr Sammy looks middle-aged. More like just how a real man should look. Joe doesn't look much except in his best suit, and then not a lot.

I wonder if Mr Sammy will want to meet me regular outside the office, say in a hotel—

'Wake up, Lily, you'll fall over in a minute.'

The sound of a colleague's voice brought her out of her dreams. She realized she was back in the bookkeepers' office and was simply standing there, in front of her desk, the bank statements in her hand.

'Oh, silly me,' she said, 'I was thinking about going to see that film, *Bridge on the River Kwai*. They say it's ever so good.'

The senior bookkeeper reminded her she could think about that in her own time, not the firm's, so would she kindly get on with her work. What an old goat, thought Lily, he'd never understand any woman's emotions.

At the end of the day, Lily made her way down to the first floor. Passing Mr Sammy's office, she stopped, turned back and knocked on his door.

'Come in.'

Lily opened the door and put her head in. Mr Sammy was alone at his desk.

'Oh, I just wanted to say goodnight, Mr Sammy,' she said.

Sammy was poring over a report on the present position of the property company, a report prepared by the company's joint managing directors; namely, his elder son Daniel, and Boots's son Tim. If the garments factory was under threat of a possible strike, well, the progress of the property company at least made for a happy moment.

Looking up to see who it was at his door, he said, 'Yes, goodnight, Lily.'

Lily drew one of her emotional breaths, stepped in, closed the door and advanced with the swiftness of a bird in flight. Arriving at Sammy's desk, she leaned over it and whispered.

'Mr Sammy?'

Sammy came to.

'Lily?'

'Yes, it's me,' breathed Lily, looking down once more into his clear blue eyes. 'I want to ask you something.'

'Something?' said Sammy, ready to leave as soon as he had finished his reading of the report.

'Yes, something very intimate,' whispered Lily, feeling a bit giddy and a bit breathless.

'Come again?' said Sammy, startled.

'Would you like to come and see where I live?'

'Eh?'

'Mr Sammy—'

The door opened and Mrs Rachel Goodman, invaluable asset to the firm, called, 'Goodnight, Sammy – oh, and goodnight, Lily.'

'Wait a tick,' said Sammy, a trifle hoarse.

'I'm in no hurry,' said Rachel, stepping in and holding the door open for Lily.

Lily, thwarted once more, had no option but to step out, doing so with a slightly bitter glance at Rachel. She went down the stairs to the ground floor and out into the street, thinking there had to be a way of locking herself in with Mr Sammy. There had to be some way of preventing any interruptions.

In his office, Sammy spoke to Rachel.

'I think I'll have to talk to Lily sometime.'

'Oh?' said Rachel. 'Sammy, are you looking a little bothered?'

Sammy said he'd just had a narrow escape from a fainting fit, brought about by Mrs Lily Chambers asking him something very intimate. She needed help, he said, and he might have needed some himself if Rachel hadn't appeared at the right moment.

'Why, what happened?' asked Rachel.

Sammy said he hardly knew how to explain. Rachel urged him to try.

'You won't believe it,' said Sammy, still off balance, 'and I don't know I believe it meself.'

'Try me,' said Rachel.

Sammy, mentally wandering about in the land of the unbelievable, said Lily had asked him if he'd like to come and see where she lived, and he knew what that meant. He was just about to have the aforementioned fainting fit, he said, when Rachel came to his rescue by appearing at his door. Talk about a lifeboat for a drowning man.

'Might I enquire why you're laughing, Rachel?' he asked.

'I should be crying?' said Rachel. 'Poor Sammy. I told you the lady fancied you.'

'Well, someone had better tell her it's out of order, especially in working hours,' said Sammy. 'She's a married female, ain't she?'

'True, Sammy, she is.'

'Then someone's going to have to tell her to fancy her old man, which is legal and proper,' said Sammy. 'I don't want her to give me another fainting fit.'

'I think everyone here would leave you to do the talking, Sammy,' said Rachel.

'It's just occurred to me that it ought to be woman to woman,' said Sammy.

'Oh, I think man to woman in this case,' said Rachel, quite sure she preferred to stand aside, and that Lily Chambers would accept a talking-to from no-one except Sammy himself.

'Well, I suppose it's got to be me,' said Sammy, 'although I don't know I'm cut out for telling a married female bookkeeper to stick to her ledgers and forget about adultery.'

'You'll find a way, Sammy,' said Rachel, smiling. It had its funny side. Sammy in the sights of a fanciful female was not so much an energetic and fearless business boss as a confused man looking for a way out.

'Be firm, be fatherly.'

'That's something else I don't want to be,' said Sammy.

'And what's that?' asked Rachel.

'Her daddy,' said Sammy. 'Incidentally, Susie's against illegal goings-on.'

'I know,' said Rachel, who, during the course of many long years, had never attempted in the slightest way to come between the twain, even though she had always preferred Sammy to any other man. 'But my life, Lily Chambers isn't? There's a surprise for the innocent. Yes, talk to her, Sammy.'

'I'll have to,' said Sammy, figuratively wiping the sweat from his brow.

*   *   *

'You wanted to see me, Mr Sammy?' said Lily the following morning, Friday. She was at the open door of his office, having received a summons.

'Yes, come in, Lily,' said Sammy, bracing himself. Lily entered in a spirit of hope. She'd had a worrying time at home last night. Well, perhaps not worrying. More like puzzling. Getting to be alone with Mr Sammy, even if only for a few minutes, did seem a bit of a puzzle. Joe had asked her again if she'd got something on her mind, which she had, but which she couldn't tell him. And he didn't give her time to, anyway, because he was off to his Thursday darts match almost as soon as he'd asked the question. This morning, however, the summons to come down and see Mr Sammy had raised her hopes. 'Close the door,' he said.

Lily closed the door and Sammy found himself alone with this female bookkeeper who apparently fancied him. Didn't she know he was a happily married man looking forward to the wedding of his youngest daughter? They were a funny lot, women. They didn't coincide with men, so a bloke could never be certain what any of them were thinking. He'd asked Boots once what could be done about the way some women carried on. Boots

495

had said find a magician who can rearrange them.

'Mr Sammy?' said Lily hopefully, her mind on what she had said to him last evening.

'Oh, yes, it's you, Lily,' said Sammy, who was trying to convince himself she hadn't said anything except goodnight. 'Sit down.' Lily seated herself. She looked very nice in a light grey suit and a white shirt-blouse. 'Now,' said Sammy.

'Yes, Mr Sammy?' said Lily, who couldn't think that an hour in the buttercups with him could actually be counted as sinful. Her gaze was soulful.

'How are you finding your job these days?' asked Sammy, doing his best to avoid falling into this barmy female's starry eyes. Long ago, he'd fallen into Susie's optics, and had never been the same since.

Lily, hoping for something more than questions about her job, said she was enjoying her work as much now as when she first started. She liked bookkeeping, she said, much more than typing or operating a switchboard or just being a general office clerk.

'I hope, Mr Sammy, you haven't found me wanting, like,' she said. 'I mean, I hope no-one's had cause to complain about me work.'

'No, no-one,' said Sammy. 'It just occurred

to me that you might be finding it a bit nerve-racking.'

'D'you mean is the work getting on me nerves?' said Lily. 'No, nothing's getting on me nerves except my husband's darts. He's darts mad. But it's not that that's affecting me emotions, it's something else and it's sort of taking me over.' She plunged on. 'It's what made me speak very intimately to you last evening, I just couldn't help meself, and if—'

'I'm trying to forget that.' Sammy's interruption was hasty. 'In fact, I'm trying to tell myself it never happened.'

'Oh, it happened, Mr Sammy—'

'Frankly, it's all a blur to me.'

'Mr Sammy, you fancy me a bit, don't you?'

'Listen, Lily, my favourite female woman is still my wife.'

'Well, I honour you for that, but it needn't mean you can't enjoy a bit of romance with me now and again.'

'It means exactly that.'

'Mr Sammy, don't you want to make love to me?'

'Eh? In my office in working time?' Sammy was totally confused.

'Lor', no, not in here, Mr Sammy, more like in a country hotel or somewhere nice and quiet.'

Sammy nearly fell off his chair. It took a little time to gather himself and talk turkey to her. He told her then that she was halfway round the bend, that she had a husband, he had a wife and that if she didn't get back to her work by the time he counted ten, he'd call in a doctor and have her examined. He also told her it was against the rules to think illegal things in office hours, and that she'd be better off if she took up darts with her old man.

Lily tried the protest of a woman who'd only had their mutual interests at heart. It didn't work. Sammy left her with no option but to return to her desk. She did so unhappily, but after ten minutes or so was convincing herself he was probably already feeling he'd been unkind to her, and also a bit barmy to have turned her down.

Opening up ledgers, she thought again of love in a meadow, and she didn't worry that she was thinking about it in office hours. She was ever the optimist, and often the airy-fairy. As for Sammy, he let Rachel know that he'd talked to Lily and told her to be like her old man and go in for darts. Rachel, of course, thought that very amusing.

On Monday, the daily papers carried reports of a threatened strike in the garments industry.

The union concerned spoke of underpaid workers, and of the necessity of obtaining a reasonable wage rise for both skilled and unskilled operatives. What was reasonable? Not less than seven and a half per cent. Seeing that in black and white almost spoiled breakfast not only for Sammy, but Tommy as well.

The reports included comments from representatives of the employers' federation, mainly to the effect that a seven and a half per cent rise across the board was not only far from being reasonable, it was non-negotiable. The union, accordingly, must think again. Sammy concurred, while at the same time sweating, along with Tommy, over what a strike would do to the firm and its retail shops.

On Tuesday, the press reported that the employers' federation had countered union threats with a threat of their own, that of closing down their factories indefinitely. Sammy thought about offering up a prayer, but common sense told him the Almighty would hardly concern Himself with an East End garments factory when there were earthquakes happening in the wider world. Later in the day came reports that the employers had made an offer, a rise of two and a half per cent. If that was not accepted, then the federation would order the shutdown of all factories. The union at once declared their workers had been insulted, and demanded not less than five per cent. Failure to agree would compel the union to order all workers out. Sammy and Tommy spoke to Boots, and Boots said they only had one option. What was that? Wait for the next move, said Boots.

On Wednesday, when Sammy was beginning to feel ill, and Tommy's loyal factory workers were reluctantly preparing to down tools, the employers' federation upped their offer to three per cent. The union leaders discussed this at lunchtime over a glass of beer and a pork pie. By four thirty that afternoon, a compromise figure of three and a half per cent across the board had been agreed. This cured Sammy's feverish brow, since he knew the firm could absorb the cost of that increase without making the balance sheet look unhappy. On his way home from the office, he bought a bottle of champagne. Over supper, he, Susie and Phoebe celebrated the outcome of the negotiations. Phoebe said that what she liked about champagne was that it made you feel expensively squiffy. Susie said that what she liked about it was that it didn't make her feel squiffy at all, just happy. And Sammy said that what he liked about it was the reason for buying it.

Yes, what with the outcome of the strike negotiations and the fact that Lily Chambers had accepted a fatherly talking-to, Sammy considered the reason for buying the bubbly was as good as it could be.

He little knew Lily was lying in wait, as it were.

Chapter Eleven

On the third Saturday in June, the day was bright and clear, with not a cloud in sight. Miss Phoebe Adams, in shimmering white, with a delicate veil and a headdress of imitation orange blossom, arrived at the Denmark Hill church well on time. That is, only five minutes late, which was pretty good going considering how long it had taken her mum and her bridesmaids to get her ready to their and her own total satisfaction. It had been worth every minute. Pretty, dark-haired Phoebe, twenty, looked positively the bride of the year. Well, that was what Sammy thought. And so did Susie.

She arrived in state, Sammy beside her in Mr Greenberg's polished-up cart, pulled by a pony also polished up. Sammy wore a morning suit and a grey topper. Mr Greenberg wore his Sunday suit and a black topper. The pony wore some gleaming brass.

Sammy, descending, helped the bride to

alight, in a rustle of silk and lace. Silver-stockinged ankles peeped above silvery slippers. Phoebe considered that every young lady should look perfect from head to foot on one day in her life, her wedding day.

'Proud of you, pet, proud of you,' smiled Sammy.

'I love you, Daddy, you've been so good to me,' whispered his emotional adopted daughter. She knew the whole tragic history of how she came to belong to Sammy and Susie. The murder of her parents by a madman had left her, a small child, alone and bereft, and subsequently found by Sammy in a Walworth street near the Elephant and Castle. If the story, once it was made known to her, had haunted her, never had she failed in her love for her adoptive parents. Her life was paralleled by that of Rosie, who had been adopted by Boots and his first wife, Emily.

Phoebe straightened the flowing skirt of her gown while Mr Greenberg, having put a nosebag on his pony, did the right thing by preceding bride and father into the church, where he joined Mrs Greenberg. Then, on Sammy's arm, Phoebe advanced to be met by the smiling vicar, with the pink-clad brides-maids standing to one side, all enchanted at Phoebe's arrival in full array.

Inside the church, the organist heralded the entrance of the bride, and the congregation came to its feet. Heads turned. Following the vicar, Phoebe and Sammy slowly walked forward, the bridesmaids behind them, amid murmurs of delight at the colourful appearance of the ritual procession.

Since most of the assembled people were related to both the bride and the groom, there were equal numbers on either side of the aisle. By the chancel steps stood the groom and the best man. Philip was in his RAF uniform, his best man being cousin Jimmy. He watched the advance of his bride with a warm glow in his eyes.

'Jimmy, is that my Phoebe?' he whispered.

'Can't hear a word you're saying,' murmured Jimmy. The organ music was at its mightiest.

Arriving at the chancel steps, Sammy relinquished his daughter to Philip and stepped back. From under her veil, Phoebe regarded her bridegroom. A smile glimmered. Philip returned it.

'Phoebe, you angel,' he whispered.

The vicar took charge then, and the service began. Various members of the Adams families dreamed their dreams of their own times at an altar.

Chinese Lady and Sir Edwin sat on the left

with Susie, Chinese Lady thinking there was simply no end to weddings and births in her extensive family. She knew, as everyone did now, that Jimmy and Clare were going to be parents in October. And before her very eyes, here was young Philip being married to Phoebe. She glanced at her husband, and was pleased to note he was quite alert, following the service with a little smile on his face, as if he was remembering all the other family weddings he and she had attended. He was happy about the fact that she had found a real blessing in Mrs Plumstead. He had said an invaluable maid of all work was her due. Well, not in all her born years had she ever thought anything like that would be her due, especially as she'd been a maid of all work herself in her single days. Dear goodness, how strange life was, and how good the Lord had been to her since her striving days in Walworth following the death of her first husband, Daniel, on the North-West Frontier. If her reflections then took her back into the past, her subconscious kept her in tune with the marriage service.

On the right of the aisle sat Philip's parents, Annabelle and Nick Harrison, with Philip's grandmother Lizzy. Annabelle looked a little misty-eyed. She was remembering her own wedding, more than twenty years ago. She touched her husband's hand. Nick glanced. She smiled. He pressed her fingers. She might be getting a little bossy, but she was still his Annabelle.

Lizzy, of course, was thinking emotionally of her wartime wedding to Ned at St John's Church, Walworth, in 1916. She thought of her ride to the church in Mr Greenberg's pony and cart, and then the ride with Ned to the reception at the old family house in Walworth. It was long, long ago, but today it seemed like only yesterday. Today, Ned was with her in spirit, she was sure. Well, he was most days.

Tommy and Vi sat with Vi's mum, old Aunt Victoria. The aged lady had managed to attend, the warm weather and the special aspect of the occasion drawing her out of doors and into the church. She was mumbling softly to herself, as if repeating the words of the service. Or she might have been inaudibly taking Philip to task for being far too young to shoulder the responsibilities of marriage. Old Aunt Victoria could still spill a grumble or two, mellowed though she was.

Polly and Boots sat with James, Tim and Felicity. Felicity had blurred views of the spectacle, alternating with brief spells of clarity.

Which she rated as miraculous.

It meant that her blinded eyes really were

being cured by a long-term process of natural healing. At least, that was what she and Tim believed, and what her specialist encouraged them to believe. She was living in a world that, after many years of being blank to her, had been gradually opening up over a period of a year and more. At this particular moment, Phoebe was a blur of misty white. Seconds later she emerged from cloudiness to become clear and shimmering. The bridesmaids, including Felicity's own darling daughter Jennifer, came through in similar fashion, a blurred conglomerate of pink one moment, and four clear figures of enchantment the next.

Life's punishing hand was easing its grip, positively so.

'How are things looking, Puss?' whispered Tim.

'Lovely.'

The service ended.

'I now pronounce you man and wife.' So said the benign vicar.

Phoebe lifted her veil, showed her happy face to Philip, and received her first kiss as his wife.

There, one more wedding, said Chinese Lady to herself, and who's next, I wonder?

Well, there were several who, by reason of their age, wouldn't be long before they were courting. (Chinese Lady took no notice of the fact that the word 'courting' was now regarded as outmoded as the bustle.) The twins, Gemma and James, and Rosie's two, Giles and Emily, were all in their teens. Lord, she thought, I just hope that some of this fast modern living that I see on television doesn't rub off on any of our young people. I'm sure it isn't what the Lord ordered. I heard Boots say only a little while ago that these days some young people don't recognize the Lord, only Elvis Presley, but he didn't say who Elvis Presley was. I must remember to ask him, though I don't suppose I'll get a sensible answer.

The reception was held in the church hall, the wedding breakfast the responsibility of caterers, the place packed with relatives and friends. Cindy Stevens, fifteen-year-old daughter of Harry and Anneliese Stevens, friends of Polly and Boots, collared James and treated him to an exposition on how she was managing her social life and how she was getting on at her Camberwell grammar school. James, fifteen himself and looking progressively more like his father as he grew up, said he didn't really want to discuss education as he was living with it most days and liked to get away from it at weekends and family weddings.

'Still,' he said kindly, 'you look nice in your

508

new frock, and I daresay Bruce and Clive will like it.' Bruce and Clive were a regular part of Cindy's social life in Camberwell. Even at only fifteen, she liked more than one string to her bow. In addition, she liked boys who didn't mind being ordered about. In this respect, James played his own tune.

'I'm dressed special for the wedding,' she said. Her lemon-coloured creation was delightfully pretty. 'You sure you like it?'

'Great,' said James.

'D'you want to kiss me, then?' asked Cindy.

'Not just now,' said James. 'I'm eating bits and pieces at the moment.' The wedding breakfast was buffet style, and James, like most people present, had a plate of food in his hand.

'Later, then, when I leave,' said Cindy. 'Oh, I'm going dancing with friends this evening at Brixton. D'you want to come with us?'

'I'll ask my parents,' said James.

'Crikey, you don't actually have to ask them, do you?' said Cindy. 'Don't you just say you're going?'

'No, I ask,' said James, 'that's the way it is in my family. I suppose I could have fought it when it first started, but I didn't, and so I'll have to stick to the rules till I'm older. It's force of habit.'

'Well, your parents are awfully nice, so that

makes up a bit for those rules,' said Cindy, who for years as a very young girl had virtually ordered the life of her widower dad, Harry. He was now married to Anneliese, a German woman, so Cindy had passed her responsibilities to her stepmother, which left her free to enjoy the exciting social life of a modern teenager. 'Oh, there's Giles,' she said, 'I must say hello to him.' And away she went to give James's cousin Giles the benefit of her company and a close-up view of her frock.

'Wow,' said Giles, fifteen and pretty cool, 'is that you, Cindy?'

'None other,' said Cindy. She was coming to see Giles as a bit special, and Giles sometimes thought about having her as a regular girlfriend. But his mother thought regular girlfriends were the privilege of boys of seventeen or more, and his dad said no point in committing yourself at fifteen, sonny, it'll give you a headache. Well, it was all something to think about in a couple of years or so.

'Cindy, you're looking great,' he said.

'Come on, let's eat together,' said Cindy, and they made their way to the buffet and to an afternoon of lively companionship.

Meanwhile, the bride and groom were going the rounds and giving everyone a chance to wish them well. That took time, because every friend and relative had plenty to say. Certainly, plenty to say was endemic with most Adamses, and friends were always encouraged to speak their piece. Eventually, however, the speeches were made and the toasts drunk amid laughter and revelry. Subsequently, while the afternoon was still young, the happy couple were showered with confetti as they were driven away by Mr Greenberg to Phoebe's home. There they would change and Sammy would drive them to the station on the first leg of their journey to their honeymoon destination at Salcombe in Devon.

'Good luck, Phoebe!'

'Good luck, Philip! Happy landing!'

'Yup, watch your undercarriage!'

That brought shrieks of laughter, which somewhat puzzled Chinese Lady. She enquired of Boots what Tommy meant by shouting at Philip to watch his undercarriage. Boots thought about an answer, then said that Philip was an airman and that every plane had an undercarriage, including his own, that it held the wheels and that Tommy was merely reminding Philip not to let them fall off. All of which was as good as double Dutch to Chinese Lady, but typical of her only oldest son's habit of confusing her more than answering her.

Down Denmark Hill the newly-weds travelled,

Mr Greenberg keeping his equipage at a slow walk for the benefit of delighted passers-by and people watching from their windows. The pace also gave the young couple time to enjoy the moment, to which Mr Greenberg thought them entitled.

'Vell, vhat a happy vedding, eh, Mr and Mrs?' he chuckled.

'Lovely,' said Phoebe, eyes bright, and face a little flushed.

'Wizard,' said Philip in RAF lingo. 'Who caught your bouquet? I didn't notice.'

'Jennifer,' said Phoebe.

'Not a bad piece of fielding for a girl only twelve,' said Philip.

True, young Jennifer did have the bouquet. It was resting in her arms as she and the other bridesmaids, colourful in the sunshine, watched the pony and cart on its journey down the hill. She was giggling over her armful.

'See, you're next,' said Gemma, fifteen, and much like Polly, her mother, because of the piquant look of her features.

'Well, I don't suppose it'll be next week exactly,' said Jennifer.

'Or next year even,' said Emily, two months short of fourteen, but with all the self-assurance of an older girl. Her hair, like that of Rosie, her mother, was the colour of golden corn.

512

'Well, I'm not in a hurry,' said Jennifer, and waved as the pony and cart progressed further down the hill. Then she glanced at Linda. Linda, she knew, would be nineteen next month. 'Go on, Linda, you have this,' she said, and pressed the bouquet into her arms.

'I don't think it counts unless you catch it,' smiled Linda, noted for her undemanding nature. Grandmother Lizzy thought her a sweet girl.

With some guests ready to move from the pavement back into the hall, a young man in a cream-coloured sports shirt and blue slacks approached at a smart pace. He slowed, however, when he saw Linda and the bridal bouquet. He stopped to smile at her.

'A wedding?' he said. He looked to be in his mid-twenties, with a widow's peak to his black hair.

Startled by his directness, Linda turned faintly pink.

'Beg pardon?' she said.

'Have I bumped into a wedding and the bride herself?' asked the young man blithely.

'Me?' Linda went pinker. Jennifer, Gemma and Emily giggled.

'That's your bridal bouquet?' said the young man, looking at it.

Linda made a recovery.

'The bride's in white,' she said, 'and you've just missed her.'

'I get it now,' said the young man, not a bit bashful as he took note that all four girls were clad in delicate pink. 'You're the bridesmaids.'

'Brilliant,' said Emily.

'And you caught the bride's bouquet,' said the young man, addressing Linda again. 'That means you're going to be next. Who's the lucky chap?'

'And who's not backward in coming forward?' said Gemma aside.

Linda addressed the young man.

'Excuse me, but do you know me? I don't think I know you.'

'No, I don't know you,' said the young man, 'but I've been overcome by a feeling that I'd like to.'

'Crikey, listen to him,' said Gemma, a teenager with style, and all four girls became involved with the interloper while the rest of the guests lingered to watch the pony and cart turn into the drive of Sammy's house far down the hill. It was a day for lingering in the sunshine, and for the intrigued bridesmaids to take stock of a young man not suffering from shyness or inhibitions.

'So what's your name?' He asked the question of Linda.

'Blessed impertinence,' said Gemma.

The young man said he was guessing that this was the wedding of Phoebe Adams, daughter of Mr Sammy Adams, well-known South London businessman.

'We're not telling,' said Jennifer.

'It's Linda,' said Emily, always inclined to make up her own mind, whether or not it was against the majority.

'What a pretty name,' said the young man, his smile exclusively for her. 'Well, I'm very pleased to meet you.'

'Come along, you girls,' called Annabelle. All the guests, except the bridesmaids, were moving back into the hall.

'I think you'd better go away before my father wants to know what you're up to,' said Linda to her admirer.

'You're right, I'm butting in,' he said. 'Still, how about if I call on you and introduce myself to your parents?'

'I can't believe I'm hearing this,' said Linda.

'Nor me,' said Gemma, fascinated by this prime example of how a bloke went about picking up a girl.

'You'd better buzz off before you get a black eye,' said Emily, 'and, anyway, we're all going back into the hall now.'

'Yes, goodbye,' said Linda, and she and

the other bridesmaids followed the rest of the guests into the hall. But she looked over her shoulder to see the young man going on his way. He was whistling.

'Crikey, Linda, you made a hit,' said Jennifer.

'But talk about his nerve,' said Gemma.

'Still, he was a bit of a looker,' said Emily.

Linda kept quiet. She preferred not to be the centre of attention.

Chapter Twelve

At her parents' home, Phoebe said goodbye and thanks to Mr Greenberg, telling him the ride had been terrific. Philip added his own thanks. Mr Greenberg wished them long life and happiness, and as he drove back to the hall to pick up his wife, even his beard wore a smile.

In the house, Phoebe ascended the stairs in billowing style, while Philip followed on. On the landing he kissed her, lovingly and with feeling. Phoebe said to mind her gown. Philip said he'd be happy to put it in an old oak chest and mind it for ever. It would always remind him of the day he acquired a bride, a lover and a cook. Phoebe told him he'd mentioned that in his speech, and it was no funnier now than then. Philip said he couldn't remember one word of his speech, because although the occasion had been really wizard, it had also left him a bit dizzy.

'When's your dad coming to motor us to the station?' he asked.

'In forty minutes,' said Phoebe.

'We'd better get changed, then,' said Philip.

'Yes, you there,' said Phoebe, pointing to what had been her brother Jimmy's bedroom, 'and me here.' She opened the door of her own room.

'Wait a bit,' said Philip, 'we're married now.'

'Yes, but I'm not used to it yet,' said Phoebe, 'so you don't think I'm going to undress in front of you, do you?'

'I could turn out to be a great help, and I could learn something about you,' said Philip. 'Something memorable.'

'Goodness me, I couldn't allow that,' said Phoebe, 'I've still got my full quota of modesty. Ask me again in a month or so. Go on, change in Jimmy's room.'

'Funny girl,' smiled Philip, but did as she wanted. One had to acknowledge that a bride could be shy, even if she did now own all his worldly goods and was due to share the honeymoon bed with him.

That took place late at night, in their room at a Salcombe hotel. Despite her declared modesty, Phoebe was a natural in her responsiveness, being healthy of mind and body. And Philip was already a worldly young man by reason of his time in the RAF, which had included some bomber raids on Port Said during the brief war against Egypt. Not that his advances towards his bride were aggressive. He certainly didn't drop bombs on her. His flight was accurate but loving, his landing definite but gentle.

The evening's recreation capped the wedding celebrations for some of the young people. Giles, Emily, Gemma, James and Cindy all went to a dance in Brixton on the promise of being home by ten thirty. Although the band was only a local one, it wasn't half bad. The youngsters, together with two boyfriends of Cindy, swung and jived to the beat, and Emily was picked up by a Teddy boy whose prowess impressed her. He had a quiff to his hair like that sported by Tony Curtis, rising young Hollywood star. If Emily was impressed by his sinuous movements, he was even more impressed by her teenage allure and vivacity.

'Man, oh, man, you're something, baby,' he said in reckless abandon.

'You're not bad yourself,' she said, conscious that brother Giles was watching her. She took no notice of what might be bothering him. Her life was her own.

'What's your name?'

'None of your biz.'

'I'm Brad.'

'Brad?'

'Short for Bradley.'

'Is that a name or a town?'

'It's my baptismal.' His baptismal was actually Albert. Albert Thompson. But he called himself Bradley because he liked its American sound. Impressively, he executed a bit of a jig, perfectly in harmony with the beat, his drainpipe trousers clinging to his legs and a slight dent in his carefully moulded brilliantined quiff. 'So what's yours, Queenie?'

'It's not Queenie, I'll tell you that much.'

This friendly fencing went on for a few more minutes, by the end of which Emily had surrendered her name and Bradley had reset his quiff. The time was now coming up to ten o'clock, and some youngsters were beginning to leave in order to be home no later than the hour set by their parents. Somewhere out in the world was a youth movement advocating that young people should be free to set their own time. Everyone was a free individual, wasn't that so? Not yet, and not according to parents who believed they were still in charge of their children's comings and goings. But there was a movement, all the same, or the beginning of one.

★   ★   ★

At her home on Red Post Hill, Rosie glanced again at the lounge clock. Five minutes to eleven.

'Matt, what's happened to them?' she asked of her husband.

'I'm asking myself that,' said Matt, unwinding his sinewy frame from his deep armchair and coming to his feet. Four years older than Rosie, he was now forty-six, and the couple had reached their prime in a spirit of undemanding content. Any real worries they had concerned the future of Giles and Emily, for they were both aware of changing attitudes, and of the tendency of many young people to adopt a completely new way of life. And that new way did not appeal overmuch to either Rosie or Matt, for it seemed to be based on a lack of responsibility. It was a time when much was being made of the importance of young people's feelings, interests and expectations, and this was encouraging the young to feel important.

'Eleven o'clock is too late for a thirteen-year-old girl to be out,' said Rosie, never one to ask the unreasonable of her children.

'Well, at least we know Giles is with her,' said Matt. He waited several more minutes, then said, 'I think I'll phone Boots and find out if James and Gemma are back, and if they know what's happened to our two.'

To Rosie's relief, the missing pair arrived home then. Matt went to speak to them. She heard them in the hall. She heard Giles say something.

'I tell you, Dad, she's been a load of trouble.'

'No, I haven't, I just forgot the time.' That was Emily. 'Anyway, it isn't late.' It was ten past eleven. 'Not really late.'

'It's well over your time,' said Matt, and he returned to the lounge with the boy and girl following. 'Here they are, Rosie.'

Rosie was on her feet. She noted the apologetic look of Giles and a suspicion of defiance in Emily.

'What happened?' she asked.

'Nothing,' said Emily, 'we're home, Mum, aren't we?'

'Forty minutes late,' said Rosie, 'and that's not playing the game. What happened, Giles?'

'I blundered,' said Giles, a dark-haired, sinewy boy not unlike his rangy father. 'I let her disappear. Well, she was there one minute and gone the next, with a Ted who looked like Tony Curtis. And it was ten then, time for us to leave, along with James and Gemma. They stayed to help me find her.'

'I don't like the sound of Teddy boys who look like Tony Curtis,' said Matt.

'He was all right,' said Emily, 'and I didn't

disappear with him. We just went with the swing. Then I forgot about the time. Anyway, as I said, it's not really late. There were a lot of other young people on our bus.'

'Not as young as thirteen, I hope,' said Rosie.

'Well, I don't know what any of them thought of the way Giles went on at me, like an old fusspot,' said Emily.

'Giles had the responsibility of finding you and getting you home,' said Matt. 'Don't let it happen again. I expect your Aunt Polly worried about Gemma and James being late.'

'Crikey, Dad, I hope you're not going to be a fusspot too,' said Emily.

'Watch out for me being a tough one myself if it does happen again,' said Rosie.

'Do I always have to have Giles with me?' asked Emily.

'Yes, you do,' said Rosie.

'To my sorrow,' said Giles, who considered that being responsible for a sister as awkward as Emily was a bit of a burden for a brother. But there it was, while she was still so young he had to keep an eye on her, and to make sure she didn't get involved with the wrong kind of person. It was a parental dictum. Giles understood that. Emily, however, thought it had something to do with Queen Victoria and covered-up table legs.

Chapter Thirteen

Sunday morning.

Susie and Sammy, at breakfast, were fully aware that their home was going to be quieter now that all their children had lives of their own. Quietness was much valued by some people, but not necessarily by parents who had enjoyed the sounds of buoyant offspring growing up, never mind the moments when the sounds and the buoyancy were a bit primitive.

'I'm feeling – I don't know what I'm feeling,' murmured Sammy.

'Flat?' Susie was sympathetic.

'Something like that,' said Sammy.

'Never mind, Sammy, it was a lovely wedding,' said Susie.

'Except it's made today feel a bit half-baked,' said Sammy. 'They've all left us now, Susie. Daniel, Bess, Paula, Jimmy and Phoebe. We're going to miss Phoebe like we've missed the others.'

'I know that, Sammy love,' said Susie, 'but we've still got each other.' She smiled. 'And the business.'

Sammy perked up.

'That's a point,' he said. 'Better than just sitting around, you doing knitting and me twiddling me thumbs. I've got to be thankful for that. Listen, d'you think Phoebe will make it with Philip?'

'Make what, Sammy?'

'Happy ever after.'

'Of course she will.' Susie was definite. 'Those two were made for each other.' She smiled again. 'Sammy, you may be a tough businessman, but you're still an old softie.'

'Hope they'll get some decent married quarters,' said Sammy.

'I'm sure they will, they're getting officers' quarters, aren't they?' said Susie. Phoebe was going to travel up to Philip's station two days after they returned from Salcombe. 'Which reminds me, we'll have them with us for the weekend when they get back.'

'So we will, at the end of the honeymoon,' said Sammy. A little grin flitted. 'Newly-weds being a bit quick off the mark, Susie, I wonder how soon we'll be talking about more grandchildren?'

'It's not something you need worry about,' said Susie.

'Except that more grandchildren really will make me feel old,' said Sammy.

'Oh, you'll cope with that as long as you can still keep your eye on the business overheads,' said Susie, 'and in any case, you've still got a few unwrinkled years in front of you.'

'I'm obliged to hear you say so, Susie.'

'Don't mention it, Sammy.'

At ten fifteen Annabelle answered a knock on her front door. A smiling young man in a sweater and slacks greeted her.

'Good morning, am I addressing Mrs Harrison?'

'I'm Mrs Harrison.'

'Hello, Mrs Harrison, I'm Nigel Killiner, how d'you do?'

'I'm very well, thank you,' said Annabelle, 'but what brings you to my door, might I ask? I'm sure we don't know each other.'

'I had the pleasure of meeting your daughter yesterday,' said the young gent called Nigel, 'and I wondered if she—'

'Excuse me, but my daughter was at a wedding yesterday,' said Annabelle, 'the wedding of my son. So I don't think you could have met her.'

'Oh, it was like this,' said Nigel, and explained in winning fashion exactly how he had met Linda, one of four bridesmaids, pointing

526

out she had been in possession of the bridal bouquet at the time. Annabelle, studying the caller with suspicion, said she didn't consider that a proper meeting, much more like a piece of cheek.

'I see your point,' said Nigel, 'but I couldn't help myself. It's strange how a chap can plan his day in very conventional fashion, and then have it all changed by something that can rise up out of nowhere. I don't want to be pushy, but is there any chance of seeing your daughter this morning?'

'Not as far as I'm concerned,' said Annabelle, 'and you're definitely being pushy.'

'I don't mean to be,' said Nigel, not in the least put down, 'I'm simply hoping to get to know your daughter, and wondered if I could do that in a walk round the park with her this afternoon. Or does she happen to be involved in a serious relationship?'

Well, thought Annabelle, I don't know if I trust this specimen and his barefaced cheek.

'Who's that, Mum?' Linda herself appeared in the hall. Spotting the young man on the doorstep, she blinked and said, 'I don't believe it.'

'Good morning, Linda,' said Nigel, noting how summery she looked in a dress of apricot, 'I've called to see if you'd like to come for a walk round the park with me this afternoon.'

'Beg pardon?' Linda fell a victim to astonishment.

'That's if you're not otherwise engaged,' said Nigel.

'Oh, really?' said Linda.

'Let me introduce myself. I'm Nigel Killiner—'

'Thrilled, I don't think,' said Linda, defending her sense of what was right and proper. 'Kindly don't bother me.'

Annabelle hid a smile. Her daughter, caught off guard at first, was now on her mettle as a well-brought-up girl not given to falling for a smoothie.

'Linda, I think I can leave you to deal with this young man,' she said. 'If he persists, call your father.'

'Believe me, I don't bite,' said Nigel.

'My father does, and so do I,' said Linda.

Annabelle, moving aside, then did her stuff as a wise mother, particularly as she quite liked the look of the young man. True, his impertinence was outrageous, but some girls responded more to that kind of approach than to a conventional one.

'Yes, I'll leave you to deal with him, Linda,' she said, and went back to her kitchen.

'How d'you feel now about a walk round the park this afternoon?' asked Nigel of the young lady who had apparently taken his fancy more than somewhat.

'The same as I did when you first mentioned it,' said Linda, 'that I can hardly believe I heard right. And nor can I hardly believe you've got the nerve to actually come knocking.'

'I felt I had to,' said Nigel, who seemed likely to remain on her doorstep unless a typhoon carried him off. He happened to be the kind of bloke who, once he'd made up his mind about something, didn't easily give up. 'You sure you wouldn't like to take that walk with me?'

'I feel amazed that you think I would,' said Linda, not prepared to conjure up a typhoon herself. Well, she didn't often have this kind of intriguing cut and thrust with someone on the family doorstep, especially on a Sunday morning. A girl had to see it through before going off to church with friends of her own sex.

'You can trust me, you know,' said Nigel, who had no complaints about being kept where he was. It could turn out to be a kind of starting point to the parlour and to other things, and she really was worth the effort involved in taking his time. 'I'm entirely respectable.'

'Oh, really,' said Linda. 'How do I know you're not some kind of lunatic?'

'Well, I can tell you I'm not certified,' said Nigel. 'I'm twenty-six and a schoolteacher.'

'You're what?' Linda goggled.

'A schoolteacher. At a local—'

'Never mind.' If there was one thing Linda was certain of, it was the conviction that she wasn't made to be any teacher's girlfriend. Teachers were all right in their way and very useful to the community, but, from what she could remember of them during her schooldays, too much like their profession. They sort of talked at you. Which was just what this one had been doing to her. He might be a personable young man, but she could easily imagine that a walk round the park with him might be like a history lesson. 'Good morning, thank you for calling, Mr Kilner.'

'Killiner.'

'Good morning, Mr Killiner,' said Linda, and that was her cue to close the door on him. But it didn't happen. Hesitation raised its head, which gave Nigel the opportunity to ask her if she'd like him to call some other time. 'Certainly not,' she said. 'Oh, well,' she added weakly, 'what time this afternoon did you have in mind?'

'For walking you round the park?' said Nigel, looking surprised and pleased all at once. 'I could call for you at three, say.'

'I think you'd better come in and meet my dad,' said Linda.

'Pleasure,' said Nigel, and finally vacated the doorstep as Linda took him through the house to the garden, where Nick was doing something to the mower. Linda introduced her visitor. He was on easy terms with her dad inside a couple of minutes. Nick, like Annabelle, thought him an agreeable bloke, even if he had been a bit barefaced in his approach to Linda.

'So what's the proposition?' Nick asked the question of his daughter.

'Oh, a walk in the park this afternoon,' said Linda.

'Well, if that means the two of you want to get to know each other, go ahead,' said Nick, who thought that a boy-meets-girl event didn't always have to be in strictly approved circumstances. As for Annabelle, when told that the walk round the park was on, she raised no objections. She had decided that the agreeable side of Mr Nigel Killiner more than made up for his cheek. She was, however, surprised to know he was a schoolteacher.

'I don't think many schoolteachers have come knocking uninvited on our door,' she said to Linda after he had gone. 'It seems you made quite an impression on him yesterday.'

'D'you think so?' said Linda, not at all displeased. 'I'm just hoping that my time in the park this afternoon won't be like a history lesson, or how to find the square root of sixty-six.'

That raised a smile in Annabelle.

'Go and tell your father he can come in from the garden, that his coffee's ready,' she said.

'Yes, all right, then I'm off to church,' said Linda, thinking that her mother was inclined these days to give orders instead of making requests. Her dad usually made light of it, saying that slightly bossy mums compared very favourably with the occasional housewife who ran off with the milkman.

'Well, old sport,' said Polly to her husband in the balmy air of the afternoon, 'what d'you think of these?'

They were both in their large garden, James and Gemma being out. Polly, wearing a smock over her dress, was inspecting her runner-bean seedlings. Boots, in an old shirt and old slacks, was hoeing around a long bed of early green peas.

'What do I think of your runners?' Boots smiled. From the early days of their marriage, Polly had taken to gardening, although this was confined mainly to vegetable plots. She thoroughly revelled in the rewards of her labours, and always talked of the harvests in the possessive way of a lady who had personally nursed them from seeds through to fruition. 'Your runners, as usual, Polly, look as if they mean to grow ten feet high. And your early peas will be ready to pick any moment, if not sooner.'

'Well, keep hoeing, old scout, and you shall be served the first mouthful,' said Polly, carrying her years commendably well. The sunshine was kind to her. At her age, the bright light might have shown up natural defects. But Polly had the kind of application and approach to her physical self that ensured a happy degree of preservation. A few crow's feet around her eyes she could put up with. The lines that defaced many sixty-year-old women were still struggling to surface on Polly. This eased certain worries. As Boots's wife, she had a dread of hearing herself referred to as the old lady in his life.

On the other hand, Boots himself had said she was growing old gracefully, and that he hoped he was too. If not, the reverse might come about, and he might be referred to as the old man in her life. He laughed now as those thoughts came back to him.

'What's funny?' asked Polly, noting with a frown that one bean seedling had been under night attack from slugs.

'A politician in charge of a grocer's shop,' said Boots.

'A comedy of errors? We could all laugh at that,' said Polly. 'By the way, what did you think of Gemma's account of how Giles lost young Emily for half an hour last night?'

'I thought it a much longer account than the one James gave us,' said Boots, turning weeds so that their roots were unmercifully exposed to the sun. 'It was Gemma who told us that Emily insisted she wasn't lost, she was with a new friend.'

'A Teddy boy,' said Polly. 'Was that a happy revelation, d'you think, or a gruesome one?'

'I couldn't say unless I knew the chap,' said Boots, 'but I understand Teddy boys on the whole are quite harmless, that they're society's peacocks.'

'In which case, perhaps Emily was a little dazzled by the feathers,' said Polly. 'I say, old love, look at this seedling – the abominable slugs have made war on it.'

'Well, slip out after dark tonight with a torch and a slug-crusher,' said Boots. 'That's the best time to catch them, after dark.'

'I know,' said Polly, 'I know from bitter experience that they wait until night falls before they emerge from hiding. That way they escape being noticed. Flossie recommends buying a pet tortoise.' Flossie Cuthbert was their daily help. 'Tortoises, apparently, are natural destroyers of the abominable. Slugs are not only a curse, they're also repulsive.'

'Created on one of nature's bad days,' said Boots.

'By the way,' said Polly, 'if Emily did get dazzled by the peacock and his feathers, Rosie could have early problems as a caring mother.'

'Rosie will cope,' said Boots, 'so will Matt. Have we had a pot of tea yet?'

'Not yet,' said Polly.

'Well, I'll go and do the necessary,' said Boots. 'You stay here writing love letters to your beans.'

'Kind of you since I need all this fresh air,' said Polly, now hoeing the bed. 'I can't take wedding revelry as well as I used to. How did I manage to escape a hangover?'

'No problem to any woman who was a Bright Young Thing in the Wild Twenties and patronized forbidden nightclubs,' said Boots. 'That's not to say I don't feel for your slight frailty today.'

'Thank you, dear man,' said Polly.

'But I don't suppose the happy pair will be worrying too much about it,' said Boots. 'They're probably still riding white clouds through blue skies.'

'Very imaginative,' murmured Polly.

'However,' said Boots, 'if one of them should phone to ask, I'll tell them you and I are enjoying a garden party.'

And off he went to make a pot of tea, leaving Polly thinking that while it was absurd to claim that any marriage was made in heaven, there were some that were worth a celestial mention. Her own, for instance.

In Salcombe, the newly-weds, strolling hand in hand by the sun-dappled ocean, looked happy. And no, they weren't worrying about the folks or frailties back home. They were telling each other that they were very much in favour of the wedded state. Philip qualified the declaration by saying that for his part, it meant with Phoebe alone, of course. Phoebe said she was happy about that, and definitely in favour of current events.

'The wedding laws should be changed,' she added, 'so that happily married couples could do it more often.'

'It?' said Philip. 'Is there a law, then, about only doing it once a week? If so, that's news to me.'

'I meant, smarty, that happily married couples ought to be able to have a repeat wedding every anniversary,' said Phoebe, so taken with her present state that she was in earnest recommendation of the idea.

'Well, we're a happily married couple now,' said Philip, 'and providing the vicar can't think up any real opposition, there's nothing to stop us celebrating our wedding by doing it again every year and twice every leap year. We won't need an Act of Parliament.'

'Man, you're brilliant,' said Phoebe.

'Glad you think so, blossom. How about a Devonshire cream tea in that place over there?'

'Lead me to it, Sir Lancelot.'

'This way, then, missus.'

Chapter Fourteen

Boots was placing the sugar bowl on the tray when into the kitchen by the back door came Gemma, young, skittish and, in a dress of light yellow, looking like the spirit of summer, even if rain had been forecast for tomorrow morning.

'Oh, hello, Daddy, are you making tea?' she asked, tossing her handbag onto the dresser. Gemma rarely had much to do with acts of slow deliberation.

'I'm making a mid-afternoon pot for the workers,' said Boots. The time was twenty to four. Full tea, Sunday tea, would be at five thirty. 'You're home early, aren't you, poppet?'

'Well, my girlfriend Sarah found a new heart-throb in the park, and James is doing hammer-and-tongs tennis stuff with three other guys,' said Gemma. 'So I've come home to take my record player into the garden and put on some of my Bill Haley numbers.'

'Bill Haley?' said Boots, pouring boiling

water into the teapot. 'Is that the man who rocks around the clock?'

'Yes, isn't he great?' said Gemma.

'Not in the garden on a Sunday afternoon,' said Boots. 'Doesn't he know about English Sundays?'

'I don't think he knows about them being sacred to Grandma Finch,' said Gemma, taking a look at a tin of biscuits.

'And to me and your mother, and most of the neighbours,' said Boots. 'Would you mind sparing us Bill Haley?'

'Is that a desperate request, Daddy?' asked Gemma, selecting a biscuit and biting into it.

'Absolutely,' said Boots, picking up the laden tray.

'Oh, all right, then,' said Gemma, 'I'll come out and share the pot of tea with you and Mum.'

'Bring another cup and saucer, then,' said Boots, 'and that tin of biscuits.'

Over the pot of tea around the garden table, Gemma said she was afraid Sarah Maggs, a schoolfriend, was going down the path of no return.

'Oh, dear,' said Polly, sipping tea with all the gratitude of a woman enjoying a perfect summer Sunday. Long gone were the days when restlessness afflicted her. 'Is it already fatal, Gemma?'

'She can't stop running after every boy she sees, poor thing,' said Gemma. 'I keep telling her to wait for the right one. We all ought to do that. It's my belief that if you go looking, you end up with the wrong one. Whenever I do any looking myself, say at dances, I almost always end up with some kind of freak. You know, the kind of freak we all feel sorry for – Daddy, have you picked up a chest cold?'

'Not that I know of,' said Boots.

'Well, something made you cough,' said Gemma, a girl with a happy belief in herself. 'Anyway, I don't feel any great need to have a boyfriend yet. My most genuine feeling is that boys are too young to be really interesting, whereas I'm sure adult males can appeal to a girl's intellect. That's important, our intellect.'

'It's important to me to know you have some,' said Boots.

Gemma smiled kindly at him.

'Did you mention adult males?' said Polly, fascinated by her daughter's social philosophy.

'Yes, young men who've spent their time sensibly growing up instead of playing about,' said Gemma. She glanced at Boots and made a thoughtful aside. 'Like Daddy did, I'm sure.' Boots coughed again. 'I expect he was very interesting to girls as an adult male.'

'Girls?' Polly laughed. 'Don't you know

540

that before he was twenty-one, he became the father of your half-sister Eloise by a French war widow?'

'Oh, yes, I know all about that,' said Gemma. 'It just shows the difference in male appeal between blokes who never grow up and those who do. I think I'll wait for the time when I can expect one or two really grown-up fellers to cross my path instead of looking for them now. At fifteen, a girl can afford to wait. Mummy, are you trying to say something?'

'Nothing that can't be left unspoken on a peaceful Sunday afternoon,' said Polly. 'But I wonder, do girls find James too young to be interesting?'

'Oh, some get soppy about him,' said Gemma, 'like Cathy Davidson and Cindy Stevens. You remember Cathy, don't you, who lives in Paris now with her mother?'

'I remember her mother all too well,' said Polly. 'We had to put a twenty-four-hour guard around your father to keep her from getting her hands on him.'

'Well, Cathy hasn't written to James for ages,' said Gemma, 'and Cindy's devotion only lasted about a month or so. Cindy just likes lots of strings to her bow.'

'Quality with quantity, or just as they come?' asked Boots.

'I couldn't say,' said Gemma. 'It all amounts to what I've been talking about, that at fifteen we're simply not old enough to form serious relationships.'

'So you've decided to wait a few years before committing yourself to someone tall, dark and – um – mature?' said Boots.

'I'm sure that's sensible,' said Gemma. 'Where are you going, Mummy?'

'Well, darling, fascinating as your dreams are,' said Polly, on her feet, 'I think I'll come down to earth by getting back to my onion bed.'

Linda's walk in the park with Nigel Killiner was not, after all, turning out to be like a history lesson. Nigel was proving to be far from a bossy teacher. The outing was actually fun, for he was full of the kind of light-hearted banter to which a young lady was readily responsive. She especially liked his anecdotes about certain schoolkids, the kind destined, he said, to be a danger to civilization if they weren't that already. What could be done, he asked, about boys who turned classroom wastepaper baskets into obstacles intended to trip him up and disable him? Linda suggested they should be reported to the headmaster or to their dads. Dads, she said, could always deal properly with misbehaving sons. Her own dad, she said, had always known how to make her brother Philip behave, which had helped him to accept discipline when he joined the RAF.

The park was a sunny retreat for people on this Sunday afternoon. Social mores might be changing, and radically, but Ruskin Park on a summer Sunday still drew the young as well as the old. Nigel and Linda, sauntering in close company along the paths, looked as if they had been friends for ages. Certainly Linda felt very much at ease with Nigel now, and listened absorbed as he told her he was delighted to know her brother was in the RAF. The RAF, he said, was a service he had always admired, and might have entered himself if he hadn't preferred to make his contribution to society by becoming a teacher. Mind you, he added, that preference had taken its course before he realized some schoolkids spent their time thinking up ways and means to inflict teachers with permanent injury.

'I think you must have more than your fair share of those at your school,' said Linda, smiling.

'Believe me, every school has always had more than its fair share,' said Nigel, and went on to say that in his opinion this was how the Empire was made, by unruly Britons overcoming uncivilized natives. Which was as far as any kind of dreaded history lesson made its appearance, for Nigel seemed to be fully aware that a young lady should be entertained, not treated as if she needed to be educated. He asked Linda what kind of a job she had, and when she told him she was a copy typist with a firm by Camberwell Green, he said he thought her more suitable for work as a window dresser for clothes shops. Linda, of course, immediately asked him why he thought that.

'Well, it's a matter of being visibly decorative,' he said.

'Visibly what?' asked Linda.

'Decorative,' said Nigel. 'And in a shop window, so that passers-by could have the pleasure of confirming first impressions.'

'First impressions of what?'

'That you're a very attractive girl,' said Nigel, 'and I hope I'm not offending you by saying so.'

'No, thanks for your compliments,' said Linda, 'but I don't think I'd want to put myself in a shop window for people to look at. I'd feel like a dummy.'

Nigel laughed. They kept to their leisurely walk, along with other people. The peace and calm of the park invariably induced users to relax, to enjoy a Sunday stroll in place of a weekday hustle and bustle. Nigel said really attractive girls

544

shouldn't appear in shop windows for everyone to gawp at, and that if he ever had the good fortune to be attached to one, he'd like to think the last kind of job she'd want would be as a window dresser. Linda pointed out he'd just suggested that was where she should be, in a shop window and visibly decorative to the public. That was what he had said, visibly decorative. Nigel assured her he'd spoken without thinking, that girls as attractive and charming as she was didn't belong to the public, like Marilyn Monroe and other Hollywood female stars. Linda said she couldn't bracket herself with Marilyn Monroe, not in a month of Sundays. She supposed he simply meant she was entitled to her own private life, as everybody was.

They carried on in this way for some time until Linda said she was going to get embarrassed if they didn't talk about anything except herself. Nigel said the subject wasn't embarrassing to him, that from the moment yesterday when he first saw her, she had made her mark on him, and so had her nice personality. Did she mind him saying so?

No, she didn't mind too much, she said, except that considering this was the first time she'd been out with him, it really was a bit embarrassing to have him talk about her looks so much. Nigel said he must apologize for that, and hoped she'd forgive him. Linda said she didn't think it was serious enough for him to ask to be forgiven, only that she'd like it if he would spare her blushes.

'Oh, right,' said Nigel with a touch of briskness, as if that was now the key to their relationship. 'I fully understand, I suppose I was jumping the gun a bit, and being too personal. But to me it doesn't feel as if we've only just met, it feels as if I've known you for ages. I'll have to take care that I don't make myself as indigestible as some precocious schoolkid. I've met more than a few of that ilk in the short time I've been teaching.' That led him into more droll anecdotes.

In the sunshine of the park, Linda allowed herself to be entertained. If his interest in her was rather pronounced, well, it wasn't actually so embarrassing as to make her run for home, and at least he wasn't like some fellers whose only interest was in themselves. Also, she liked his way of speaking. It made him sound nicely educated, which one would expect of a teacher. But he wasn't a posh person. Which reminded her that the Adams family didn't encourage posh persons to enter their ranks, although Aunt Polly, very posh, had been allowed in, and Uncle Boots was known to have been referred to as Lord Muck in his young days. But, of course, Uncle Boots could get away with anything.

She asked Nigel about his family. His parents, he told her, lived in Hampstead, his father a City stockbroker, his mother a star turn in creating stunning floral arrangements for the glorification of the local church. His sister was at Durham University. He himself lived in lodgings in Bessemer Road, close to his school. His landlady was a good sort, but didn't encourage visitors. He hoped, he said, that none of that put Linda off him, and wondered if they might meet again next Sunday afternoon.

'Oh, if you'd like that, yes,' she said, 'and when we go back to my home in a few minutes, would you like to stay for tea with me and my parents?'

Nigel expressed positive delight, and when he took her home she had no trouble in persuading her parents to let him stay for tea. In fact, Annabelle and Nick were happy enough to accept the company of this engaging young man who had obviously made a hit with Linda. And the fact that he was a schoolteacher did away with any thoughts that his background might be suspect. Although Annabelle and Nick both had cockney antecedents, they'd become middle class in their outlook and way of living, and as parents they liked to be sure that a newcomer was suitable enough to begin a relationship with their daughter, whether serious or casual.

Over tea, they found Nigel all of suitable in his conversation and behaviour. He entertained them much as he had entertained Linda, with anecdotes about uncivilized schoolkids, and he readily offered information about himself and his family in an amusing way. They didn't fail to notice that he had impressed Linda with his personality. Well, it was time she found a steady young man.

When he finally left to go home to his lodgings, he had fixed up to call again for Linda next Sunday. Nick then spoke to her.

'I think you might be at the beginning of a heavy relationship,' he said with a bit of a teasing grin.

'Not heavy, I hope, Dad,' said Linda, 'I couldn't cope with anything like chain mail.'

'Chain mail?' said Annabelle.

'Yes, that's heavy,' said Linda, who felt she'd enjoyed an unusually entertaining day, and was already looking forward to next Sunday.

'Hello, yes?' Rosie, answering the phone on Monday evening, found herself communicating with a young baritone voice.

'You're not Emily, are you?' it said.

'No, I'm not Emily, I'm her mother.'

'Howd'youdo, lady. Could I speak to Em? Tell her it's Brad calling. Bradley Thompson.'

'Are you the young man she met at the dance hall on Saturday evening?'

'None other, lady. What a shindig. We merged.'

'Merged?'

'You've heard about soulmates?'

'I have.' This was Rosie's first social encounter with a Teddy boy, a phenomenon of the Fifties, and she was feeling her way, although not without a sense of amusement. 'But at a mere thirteen, Emily is nobody's soulmate, nor is she ready to merge, not even with Elvis Presley, every girl's dream, I believe.'

'Elvis we all dig, don't we? And I'd still like to talk to Em.'

'Very well, Mr Thompson, I'll—'

'It's Brad, lady. Mr Thompson, that's my old public bar.'

'Pardon?'

'My pa, lady. Could you get Em on this piece of equipment?'

'Hold on.' Rosie placed the receiver down and climbed the stairs in search of Emily. The girl was up in her room, doing her homework while listening to a pop record. 'Emily, a new

549

acquaintance of yours is on the phone. Bradley Thompson. He wants to speak to you.'

'Bradley Thompson?' said Emily, frowning over a mathematical question. She was never on friendly terms with mathematics. In her opinion, mathematics represented something totally gruesome in the life of any schoolgirl. She would have been quite happy for the subject to be exclusive to boys, never mind that up-and-coming female undergraduates would have considered that unacceptable. 'Who's Bradley Thompson?'

'You met him, I believe, on Saturday evening,' said Rosie.

'Oh, him,' said Emily, apparently not impressed.

'I also believe he was the chief reason for your late arrival home, an event that's not to be repeated,' said Rosie.

'Oh, he's all right,' said Emily. 'For about an hour. Still, I'll go down and talk to him.' When she arrived at the phone, she picked it up and said, 'This is Emily Chapman. Who's that?'

'Brad.'

'The Brad who talks like the Lone Ranger?'

'Sure is, man.'

'Well, don't ring me, Ranger, I'm too busy doing homework in the evenings to take phone calls. If you want to see me, see me at the dance hall on Saturday. I'll be with my brother.'

'Brother? Em, that's tough on any doll.'

'I keep telling my mother that. It makes no difference. Goodbye.'

'Man alive, Em, I thought we had something going.'

'Yes, I'm going,' said Emily, 'back to my homework. See you Saturday evening, perhaps.'

'Hold on, Em—'

But this time Emily hung up. Her interest in Brad seemed to have been very short-lived. Actually, she felt he could be a stepping stone to more exciting heights. Teddy boys had a kind of relationship with up-and-coming bands.

Her mum and dad, however, happily assumed that some precocious Teddy boy was not their daughter's idea of teenage romance.

Chapter Fifteen

Mr Sidney Witchet, a retired clock and watch repairer, lived in an avenue off Denmark Hill. His wife having died five years ago, he had sold his business, with the shop and the goodwill, for a very tidy sum. That, added to the savings which he and his late better half had made, provided him with sufficient interest to enable him to live comfortably.

Some men are notably handy around the house. Some are hopeless. Mr Sidney Witchet was among the former, and he soon taught himself to cope with cooking, washing, ironing and other domestic chores. He was accordingly much admired by a number of neighbouring housewives, and pointed out to their husbands as an example of just how useful a man could be. Such husbands naturally came to look on Sidney Witchet as a pain in the elbow, although their wives said some lonely widow might be lucky enough to catch his eye. Not if she's a

Winnie, said one husband. Who wants to be known as Winnie Witchet?

It was true that Mr Witchet, born in Peckham of cockney parents, had known the trials of kids making fun of his surname during his schooldays. 'Oi there, watch it, Witchet.' Or, 'Was yer granddad a widget, Witchet?' Or, on the football field, 'Come on, kick it, Witchet.' Lots of that kind of stuff went on, so later in life, when he had improved himself and was doing well in his trade, with his own shop, he and his wife moved out of rumbustious Peckham to sample the more peaceful surroundings of the Denmark Hill area. He left behind kids who were as saucy about his name as those of his schooldays. ''Ere, Mr Witchet, me ma's got the fidgets. Can yer mend her?'

In the lower-middle-class area, Mr Witchet blossomed, along with his wife Amy. It was a sad day for him when she died, but he came out of mourning to apply himself to his life as a widower, overcoming each little problem in sterling fashion. He was essentially a man of positive qualities, with a great deal of self-belief. Uncharitable acquaintances sometimes referred to him in terms that implied he'd turned into a pompous old parrot.

He had just passed the age of sixty when, on this morning in June, he left his house at precisely ten thirty to call on a near neighbour. He was carrying a bunch of multicoloured sweet peas, cut from the early-flowering plants in his garden. Arriving at the neighbour's door, he knocked.

The lady of the house, Mrs Lizzy Somers, answered the summons and found the portly but healthy-looking gentleman on her doorstep.

'Good morning, Mrs Somers,' he said, lifting his trilby hat, 'might I be so bold as to suggest you could accept these flowers from my garden? I'm sure you must still be a grieving woman, but feeling just a mite better now, I hope, which might help you to enjoy these sweet peas.'

'Well, it's very kind of you, I'm sure,' said Lizzy, 'and I don't know I could have turned down such a nice present at any time. I can smell the scent from here.'

'Do me the honour of accepting them,' said Mr Witchet, and pressed the bunch into her hand. 'You might have noticed that although I attended Mr Somers's funeral, I've refrained from calling on you until now. I pride meself on knowing when to leave a sad neighbour to her grief, and when to offer her a consoling hand. Might I suggest that your feelings as a newly widowed woman have taken a turn for the better? I don't mean, of course, that you're over your loss. That can't be. Knowing Mr Somers

554

as a good neighbour and an upright man, as I did, I'm sure it'll be a long time before you manage to get over your grief. As I daresay you know, it took me more than a while to get over all the grief when my dear wife passed on. However, in taking it on meself to call today—'

'Yes, it's really very kind of you.' Lizzy, thinking it was time to interrupt her talkative neighbour before he overwhelmed her, broke in gently but firmly. 'But I'll never come to terms with losing Ned.'

'Ah,' said Mr Witchet, and his homely features took on a very visible expression of sympathy. 'Might I say I can understand that, seeing I still miss the late Mrs Witchet?'

'I'm sure,' said Lizzy, wondering how to get rid of the man. He and his wife had been near neighbours for many years, and although she and Ned had never had much in common with them, neither had they found any real fault in either. Mind, Ned had once said it was a matter of guesswork as to who turned into an old woman first, Sidney Witchet or Amy Witchet. Well, both liked to be heard.

On the other hand, both were useful people, Mrs Witchet being adept at sewing and embroidery, and Mr Witchet being a very good gardener. Since losing his wife, his gardening had become his major recreation, and he was well known for offering surplus vegetables to his immediate neighbours. They naturally spoke highly of him, thereby exacerbating the unkind feelings of those husbands who had to listen to their wives singing his praises.

'Well, it really is kind of you to think of me and to give me these lovely sweet peas,' said Lizzy in an effort to close the conversation, 'and I do appreciate it.'

Mr Witchet's plump but firm-bodied frame seemed to expand in pleasure.

'Might I be so bold as to offer my services whenever you need any kind of help around the house?' he said. 'If I do say so meself, I can handle most problems – mind, I'm sure Mr Somers always could, knowing him as I did, but now you're alone – well, as I say, if you do need any help in the house or in the garden—' Mr Witchet paused to let a new thought take root, but Lizzy cut in before he could elaborate.

'Well, thank you, Mr Witchet,' she said, 'but my family look after any little problems I have about the house, and my eldest son and his wife look after all the heavy work in the garden.'

'Mrs Somers, I couldn't be more pleased for you,' said Mr Witchet. 'It's comforting for me as a neighbour to know your family take a helpful interest in your life as it is at present, but any time there's a kind of emergency I'd be pleased to come along double quick and offer my services. You need only ask.'

'Well, thank you, Mr Witchet,' said Lizzy again. 'I'll remember that.' Which meant she'd remember not to ask, for however well meaning he was, he wasn't her first choice for help with her boiler or her electric toaster. 'Good morning to you, and thank you again for calling and for these sweet peas. I'd best find a vase for them right away.'

For some reason, Mr Witchet consulted his watch.

'Ah, yes, it's coming up to elevenses time, I see,' he said.

'Oh, is it?' said Lizzy, suspecting he was angling for an invitation to coffee. He was on barren ground there. She still wasn't up to entertaining neighbours, close or otherwise. Ned's death continued to give her painful moments, and only members of her family were of any comfort to her. In the matter of elevenses, she had a sure feeling that if she did invite Mr Witchet to join her, it might take all day to get rid of him. 'Time does fly, doesn't it?' she said busily. 'I'd best finish tidying my living room. Good morning, Mr Witchet.'

'Good morning, Mrs Somers,' said Mr Witchet, and offered a friendly smile. A woman passing by saw the sturdy man of sixty in company at the open door with a comely woman. Lizzy at the near age of fifty-nine was still attractive, and the passing woman no doubt thought the man was aware of it. He looked as if he was. The woman smiled and went on. Mr Witchet said, 'Might I take meself off in the hope of being allowed to call again?'

'If you don't mind, I'm not up to regular visitors yet,' said Lizzy. She said a firm goodbye and closed the door.

Sidney Witchet, thinking that the newly widowed Mrs Somers was standing up bravely to her loss, departed like a man whose morning had been very enjoyable, even if he hadn't been invited in for coffee. On reaching home, he inspected his garden and wondered if the lady would like a selection of his vegetables from time to time. Neighbourly gestures were part of the pleasant side of life, and would probably be very much so to a still grieving widow, especially when coming from a widower who had known his own sorrows.

Lizzy, having found a vase for the sweet peas, made a colourful arrangement of them. Aware of the fragrance of their scent, she told herself Mr Witchet really had been very kind. Then she forgot all about him.

★　　★　　★

That evening, on his way home from the office, Boots dropped in on Lizzy. He'd been doing that regularly since the death of Ned. He had an abiding affection for his sister. During their growing years, especially the years when they were aware that life was a struggle for Chinese Lady, their ever-enduring mother, their relationship had been close and confiding. It still was.

'Well, Lizzy?' he said, when she opened her door to him.

'Oh, I'm all right, Boots, and it's nice to see you,' she said. 'Come on in, I've been watching Wimbledon.'

It was the first week of the All-England Lawn Tennis Championships, and as usual, the BBC television service was covering the event. Lizzy didn't know much about tennis, or who was who in the game, but she did like watching it on the television and hearing the commentator make his occasional reference to the Wimbledon speciality of strawberry and cream teas.

'What's on at the moment?' asked Boots, following her into the living room.

'It's a men's singles match,' said Lizzy.

Boots looked at the flickering images of two players battling it out on the famous Centre Court, which was bathed in hot sunshine. Despite previous forecasts of rain, the weather had become tropically hot and dry, and although the television set could only transmit its pictures in black and white, some of the atmosphere of the Centre Court on a sunny day came through.

'That's Lew Hoad,' said Boots, referring to the player about to serve. Lew Hoad was a young Australian tennis star and favourite for the Wimbledon title.

'Oh, yes, I know some of the names,' said Lizzy. 'Isn't Mr Hoad a handsome young man?'

'I haven't taken much note of his looks,' smiled Boots. 'My Wimbledon fancy was for the young American lady, Gussie Moran, who turned up a few years ago wearing specially designed Centre Court panties. The press at once labelled her Gorgeous Gussie, but the Wimbledon committee fainted to a man. I think she only wanted to show there was more to tennis than racquets.'

'And strawberries and cream?' said Lizzy, as she and Boots stood watching the screen.

'I wonder if Chinese Lady was right when she recently complained to me that very soon nothing in this country will be sacred,' said Boots. He and his sister and brothers still used the long-standing nickname for their mother. 'If so, then we'll be seeing strawberries and cream sailing to and fro over the net instead of tennis balls.'

'That'll be the day,' said Lizzy. 'Boots, would you like a drink?'

'Thanks, Lizzy, but no, I'll wait until I get home,' said Boots. His sister always made the offer whenever he dropped in and he always made the same response. His homecoming drink was one he ritually enjoyed with Polly. His was a whisky, hers a gin and tonic. Lizzy understood that.

'What made Mum complain about nothing being sacred?' she asked.

Boots waited until huge applause from the Centre Court crowd for a spectacular rally had stopped echoing around the room. Then he said that Chinese Lady found it difficult to accept the behaviour of modern young people, particularly their tendency to consider themselves outside the conventions practised by their elders. That wasn't exactly how she put it, of course, he said. Lizzy said no, that she'd bet what Chinese Lady did say was more like the young people will all end up in purgatory if they go on as they are doing.

'True, that was more like it,' smiled Boots, sitting down.

'Well, I must admit some of them do go a bit wild,' said Lizzy, switching off the television. It seemed somewhat antisocial to have it on while she and Boots were chatting. 'Especially

561

at these concerts when they all climb over one another to get close to singers like that young man Lonnie Donegan who plays a washboard of all things.'

'I don't think Chinese Lady regards Tommy Steele as a singer,' said Boots. 'I think her idea of a singer would be Paul Robeson or Peter Dawson.'

Lizzy said she was pretty sure that that would make her grandchildren suggest their grandmother was a bit ancient. Boots said it was quite possible they'd suggest he was too, since he shared Chinese Lady's opinion on who could be called a singer and who couldn't. Lizzy said that what bothered her was the feeling that many young people sort of looked at anybody over forty as if they didn't belong, or were too old to matter. Boots said he had no objection to being left alone by young people of the helter-skelter kind, as long as the other kind didn't disappear when they saw him coming. He said he thought present trends only marked the beginning of social change, and there was always the hope and possibility that this beginning represented a false alarm.

'Oh, that's what you hope, do you?' said Lizzy.

'I simply hope young people looking for new excitements don't mistake quantity for quality,' said Boots. Then he asked where the scent was coming from.

'From those sweet peas,' said Lizzy, indicating the vase of flowers that stood on a table inside the bay window. 'Aren't they lovely?'

'Delightful,' said Boots. 'Are you growing them this year?'

'No, these were given to me this morning by a neighbour,' said Lizzy. 'Mr Witchet.'

'Witchet?' said Boots.

'Yes, Sidney Witchet,' said Lizzy.

'I think I've heard of him,' said Boots, 'I think Ned mentioned him once or twice as a neighbour.'

'Yes, he and his wife moved here about fifteen years ago,' said Lizzy. 'Ned and me never got round to entertaining them, though. They were just neighbours, and we just said hello to each other whenever we passed by. Mrs Witchet died a few years back, and Mr Witchet's looked after himself ever since. Everyone says he's very capable. He called this morning to ask if I needed any help, which I don't, seeing my family, especially Bobby and Helene, are all very helpful. Still, it was kind of him to offer, and I was pleased to have the sweet peas.'

'I'm sure.' Boots mused. He might have suggested the offer of help and the gift of sweet peas pointed to something more than a wish to be a good neighbour, but he knew Lizzy wouldn't go along with that idea, particularly as she would consider Ned wasn't yet cold in his grave. Lizzy had the same kind of conventional attitudes as Chinese Lady. She would probably wear some kind of mourning black for years, just as their mother had following the death of their soldier father in 1908.

Not under any circumstances would Boots have attempted to change his sister's outlook, but he had a feeling Mr Witchet might have that in mind himself. When a widower bearing gifts calls on a widow suffering loneliness, one should sit up and take notice, but refrain from interfering. Boots stood up. 'Well, I'll shoot off home now, Lizzy. Everyone's pleased to know you're managing, and I'm delighted that Bobby and Helene are such a help to you. If they're not around any time you especially need them, give me a buzz.'

'I will,' said Lizzy, and saw him out. As she watched him walk through the open front gate to his parked car, she thought, as she often did, how well his years sat on him. His tall figure was as fine as ever, his gait long-legged and easy. He turned before he entered the car, and made a hand gesture of goodbye.

'So long, sis,' he called.

'Bye,' called Lizzy. She did not close the door until she had seen him drive away.

The house seemed lonely and quiet then, and not for the first time during these recent months, she experienced the pain of loss as if it had happened only yesterday.

Chapter Sixteen

'There you are, Polly.' Boots handed his life-loving wife a gin and tonic, iced.

'Thank you, darling,' murmured Polly. This was something that had become very enjoyable over the years, the custom of marking Boots's arrival home from the office with a glass of what-you-fancy for each. She watched him sip his whisky. 'Chin-chin, old sport,' she said, and raised her glass to her lips.

'Where are the twins?' asked Boots.

'Up in their rooms, doing their homework,' said Polly. 'As befits a boy and girl who wish to follow in their father's footsteps and become wise and clever.'

'Who thought that one up?' asked Boots. 'Whoever did, I forbid it. Better for sons and daughters to carve out their own way of life than to try to emulate their fathers. Fathers generally are far from clever, and wise only after the event. They escape falling over their own feet only with the help of their wives.'

'Save my soul,' said Polly, 'your modesty alarms me. Gemma and James are fortunate enough to have a remarkable father, and if either of them takes on only your ability never to flap, I'll be happy for him or her. As it is, they're both coping with the kind of things that affect all young people.'

'Such as?' said Boots.

'Well, Gemma, as you know, has made up her mind that tall, dark and handsome men only appear to young ladies who wait, and James has developed the useful gift of avoiding commitments.'

'Very sensible at his age,' said Boots.

'Very,' said Polly. 'You and I, old love, can thank the gods that our twins aren't giving us the problems that I think Emily is going to give Rosie and Matt. By the way, what did Lizzy have to say?'

'That she had a visit from a neighbour who brought her flowers and an offer of help whenever she needs it,' said Boots, and went into a more detailed exposition. Polly asked if he knew the man.

'I only know his name is Witchet,' said Boots.

'Witchet?' said Polly, a gleam in her eye. 'Is there anyone living called Witchet?'

'This one is Sidney Witchet,' said Boots, and

Polly might have fallen about if it hadn't meant her gin and tonic would fall with her.

'Sidney?' she said. 'Sidney Witchet?'

'We all have our disbelieving moments, old girl,' said Boots. 'Enjoy yours.'

'Well, I ask you, old bean, Sidney Witchet?' said Polly.

'I knew a man in the army by the name of Peregrine Windybank,' said Boots.

'Good grief, is that possible?' asked Polly.

'Everyone called him Curly,' said Boots.

'How did he come by Curly?' asked Polly.

'He was bald,' said Boots. 'I've a suspicion that Mr Sidney Witchet is likely to become a new card in Lizzy's life, although I don't think she knows it. Or would even want to know it.'

'Save her,' said Polly.

'Lizzy,' said Boots, 'is quite capable of saving herself. Further, I wouldn't dream of interfering.'

'Saving dear Lizzy from anyone by the name of Sidney Witchet couldn't be called interfering,' said Polly. 'Not under any circumstances.'

'Nevertheless, I shall stand aside,' said Boots, quite sure that Lizzy could see Witchet off if the gent got too close.

It was Emily's dad, Matthew, who next had the pleasure of hearing a young baritone voice

568

when he picked up the phone at eight that evening.

'Hello, it's Brad here – who's that?'

Matt, as much in the picture concerning this character as Rosie was, said, 'Are you the young man who kept my daughter out late last Saturday evening?'

'It wasn't late, was it?' said Brad, sounding youthfully untroubled. 'I mean, it was nothing like three in the morning. Hey, could you be Em's dad?'

'Not could be,' said Matt. 'I am. So let me take this opportunity of reminding you of what my wife told you last evening, that Emily is a mere thirteen, and any time past ten in the evening is late for her to be out. Ten past eleven is too late.'

'Mister, you're serious?' Brad now sounded astonished.

'I've never been more so,' said Matt.

'Hey, man, that's sensational. I guess it's tough being a parent. Anyway, can I talk to Em?'

'She's watching television, but I'll ask,' said Matt, acknowledging that even at only thirteen, Emily had a right to make certain decisions for herself. He called her. In response, Emily yelled back from the living room.

'What's up, Daddy?'

'There's an acquaintance of yours on the phone. He says he's Brad. He'd like to talk to you.'

'Oh, him.' Emily raised her voice again and yelled, 'Tell him I'll see him at the dance next Saturday evening. I don't want to talk now.'

'If you heard that,' said Matt down the phone, 'you'll know the answer to your request was no.'

'Little Prairie Cloud no feeling too good?' suggested Brad, one of whose heroes was Geronimo. 'Oh, well, she's still a great number. Could I talk to her ma instead?'

'Would you like to repeat that?' said Matt.

'I talked to her last night,' said Brad, 'and I figure she's great too. Sounded as if she could rock around the clock all night. That's style, man. Could she spare five minutes for another talk?'

'Don't push your luck, sonny,' said Matt, 'keep your head and stay alive. Goodbye.'

'Hey, man—'

But the phone was dead, and Brad's evening had turned out blank.

While Rosie listened with interest to Matt's recital of the phone conversation, neither Giles nor Emily were diverted from their enjoyment of the television programme until their father reached the point when Brad, turned down by Emily, had asked if he could speak to their mother instead.

'Tell more,' said Emily.

'Tell all,' said Giles, grinning at his mum.

'I can hardly wait myself,' said Rosie, whereupon Matt let them all know that Brad considered Little Prairie Cloud, Emily herself, to be a great number surpassed only by Heavenly Cloud, her mother. Giles fell about, Emily had fits, and Rosie regarded Matt with a mixture of suspicion and amusement. Matt played the final card by informing her that Brad reckoned she could rock around the clock until breakfast time with the best of the dolls. That put the whole family, including Rosie, into hysterics, which meant that Matt had garnered something uplifting out of a phone conversation irksome at times.

'All this, Rosie, reminds me that there's an old Dorset saying,' he said.

'There always is,' said Rosie, 'but can we be spared on this occasion?'

'No, let's have it, Dad,' said Giles.

Matt recited.

'Down by Dorset in the west,
Dads be helpful, but mums be best,
And when the tinkers do pass by
They'll take mums dancing on the sly.'

'That's as cock-eyed as all your other Dorset sayings,' said Rosie, 'but tinker fits.'

'Fits who?' asked Giles.

'Young Mr Impertinence,' said Rosie. 'Emily, keep your distance from him.'

'Stop fussing,' said Emily, whose vision of life embraced wider horizons than were good for a girl of only thirteen. But then in this day and age, other young girls felt they were already adult enough to run their own lives. This included the freedom to go to pop concerts every night, including Sundays. 'Brad's not evil, Mum. More of a laugh, really.'

'A scream, apparently,' said Rosie drily.

'Come dancing with us on Saturday evening, Mum,' said Giles, 'and you can find out for yourself.'

'I'm touched by your offer, Giles,' said his mum, 'but I think I'll give it a miss and stay home with your dad.'

'Lucky old Dad,' said Giles.

Chapter Seventeen

The following day, Sammy drove to Southend-on-Sea, taking Rosie and Rachel with him, as promised. Southend, on the Essex bank of the Thames estuary, did claim to be 'on-Sea', and no-one had ever lodged a legal complaint, so it lived merrily on as a seaside holiday resort for London cockneys year after year. Highly prized were the town's shellfish, particularly its cockles and mussels, and the cockneys' love of fried fish and chips was abundantly catered for. So was their liking for funny hats printed with catchphrases such as 'Kiss Me Quick' or 'Chase me, Charlie'.

Southend pubs did a roaring trade in the evenings, and in pre-war days many a rosy-faced female party had been caught doing a knees-up while rolling back to a boarding house. Come to that, such goings-on still happened. In the Kursal, a place of entertainment well patronized in the evenings, visitors could ride carousels or much livelier contraptions, participate in a coconut shy, have their fortunes told or guess their own weight in return for a prize. It was always very jolly, and on any fine evening, the shrieks of ladies trapped in speeding machines that played havoc with their dresses could generally be taken as signals of dire distress. Not that this kind of SOS ever resulted in a rescue. No, under the delighted eyes of male spectators, they had to endure the full ride for which they had paid.

'Elsie, what happened that we had to pay for being on show like that? I've never blushed more in all me life.'

'Well, I tell yer this much, Glad, I dunno why we let Albert and Ronnie talk us into it in the first place. Now everyone in Southend that ain't short-sighted knows the colour of our bank holiday knickers.'

The day was fine, the weather still hot, the crowds and players at Wimbledon in for a sweltering time, and when Sammy reached Southend the colourful holiday scenes, touched with summer's warm light, at once smote the eye in happy fashion. Not that the resort was crowded. That wouldn't be the case until July and August, the school holiday period, when the boarding houses would be full to over-flowing with London families. In these post-war

574

years, the place was as popular as it had ever been.

The time was ten twenty. They had left early in order to give themselves a few enjoyable hours in the town, along with an inspection of the acquired shop. It being the first time Rachel and Rosie had seen Southend, they took in all they could as Sammy slowed and found a parking place in the main esplanade, which overlooked the beach and the sea, or, more correctly, the swirling waters of the Thames estuary. Still, it seemed like the sea. Sammy and his passengers alighted. Rachel and Rosie resumed their survey of the scene, that of strolling visitors, a cheerful promenade, a man leading donkeys down to the beach, and shops whose wares were on outside show. Such wares seemed, at first glance, to consist mainly of painted buckets, castle-building spades, funny hats and beach towels. These represented popular holiday offerings.

'Sammy,' said Rosie, 'it seems a happy place.'

'Southend,' said Sammy, 'has never been known to sulk, even on wet August bank holidays. But it does get a bit ratty if anyone suggests its sandy beach is made up of Thames mud. Come on, let's have coffee before we go and look at our holiday-wear shop.'

That was what they were there for, to inspect

the dress shop acquired by the property company for the benefit of Adams Fashions. The present proprietors, a young couple, would hand over the premises at the end of June. Running it with local staff from July through to September represented a new development for the company, that of entering the summer-wear market particular to seaside holiday resorts. Some shops in some resorts, such as Brighton or Blackpool, could make a small fortune from mid-June to mid-September.

Sammy had parked opposite a cafe called Sailor Joe's, and he headed straight for it, followed by Rachel and Rosie, both of whom looked nicely attired for the outing. Sammy had said they didn't need to dress up, that Southend wasn't as fashion-conscious as Ascot or a Buckingham Palace garden party, but neither Rachel nor Rosie would have dreamed of dressing down. For that matter, Sammy himself didn't believe in any female woman looking like a jumble sale, and accordingly Rachel in a stylish dress of a creamy coffee colour and Rosie in elegant light blue were highly acceptable to his critical eye. They also aroused the interest of a couple of old-age pensioners, male gender.

'There's a bit of all right, Fred. Two bits, you could say.'

'I ain't looking too hard, Bert, or I'll have one of me turns.'

'Go on, chance it. It wouldn't be a bad way to go, giving your mince pies a genuine treat. They're prime, them ladies.'

'I'd go up and give 'em me compliments if I was twenty years younger, but I ain't, so I won't.'

Sammy reached the cafe and opened the door. He held it for Rachel and Rosie, and they entered. The place was surprisingly attractive for a cafe. Most were plain and practical. This one was nicely appointed, and on the tables only cruets were visible. There were no bottles of ketchup keeping company with other condiments, and there were no table stains that needed cleaning.

A number of customers were present, including two young men and two young ladies at a table for four. While enjoying coffee and fruit buns, they were indulging their collective sense of humour. Their witty sallies and gusts of laughter were running around the cafe like titters around a court. With other customers in a genial conversational mood, the atmosphere was lively without being raucous. Rachel noted a waitress service, unusual in the general run of practical establishments. Sammy, once he had seen that the ladies were seated at a vacant table, excused himself for a moment.

'I'm just going to have a word with Sailor Joe,' he said, 'I knew him when he had a whelks stall down East Street market.'

'I have a permanent impression that all the people you knew in old Walworth ran a whelks stall in the market,' said Rosie.

'Whelks happened to be highly popular, along with jellied eels,' said Sammy. 'Order coffee for me when the waitress arrives, would you?'

'With a buttered fruit bun?' said Rachel, studying the menu.

'Good idea, it's been a long drive,' said Sammy, and took himself to the counter, behind which stood the proprietor, a large middle-aged bloke in a white apron and a chef's hat. 'Watcher, Joe,' said Sammy, 'how's business?'

Joe Plummer, known as Sailor Joe in his Walworth days because of his rolling gait and his shipboard talk, fixed a searching eye on the man in a light grey suit, trilby in his hand. A happy grin arrived.

'Well, blow me across the briny,' he breezed, 'if you ain't Sammy Adams as ever was.' He reached over the counter and shook hands. 'How are yer, matey?'

'Still up to me eyes,' said Sammy. 'How's yourself and how's the missus?'

'I'm shipshape,' said Sailor Joe, 'but Maggie's

putting on a bit of weight. Too many tasty vittles coming out of our galley. Still, her waistline don't stop her doing her afternoon bingo at thruppence a card.' He glanced across at the table where the waitress was taking an order from Rachel. 'Susie looks like she's changed a bit,' he said.

'Eh?' said Sammy, then realized an explanation was necessary in order to let Sailor Joe know he didn't have a mistress, and that he hadn't brought one with him. In any case, a Southend landlady could spot an immoral intention as soon as the guilty parties arrived on her doorstep. Straightaway she'd send them packing. Sammy's explanation was accordingly hasty but clear. It embraced the purpose of his presence in the town with two members of his staff. Sailor Joe looked intrigued.

'It's a fact?' he said. 'You're taking over Warner's Wardrobe?' That was the present name of the shop, which name Sammy was going to change to Adams Fashions. Adams Fashions had style and gave a bit of class to a label, and he knew there was no reason why a bit of class shouldn't go down as well in Southend as in Torquay. There were people everywhere who knew quality was more lasting than the cheap.

'Yup, it's a fact, Sailor,' he said.

Sailor Joe showed another grin.

'So you're going to operate in my harbour? Welcome aboard, shipmate,' he said, at which point the waitress arrived behind the counter to prepare two trays, one in respect of Rachel's order, and the other in respect of a new customer.

'One ham sandwich, Joe,' she said, 'with mustard.'

'Got you, Queenie,' said Sailor Joe. 'Give us a minute, Sammy.'

'See you again before we leave,' said Sammy, and rejoined Rachel and Rosie. They were chatting away in easy fashion, enhancing the lively atmosphere of the cafe. All was redolent of the summer day and of vibrant Southend, and the sudden sounds of fire engines racing by outside seemed all part of the bustling day rather than an intrusion.

'Here we are,' said the waitress, arriving with a tray. From this she set out cups of coffee with saucers, sugar bowl, jug of milk, a dish of buttered fruit buns warm and fresh, with plates, dessert knives and paper serviettes. All of which confirmed Sammy's belief that if a cafe could promote a bit of class, so could a dress shop.

A yell of laughter rang out from the witty quartet. Infectious, it made other customers smile.

'Someone's happy,' said Rachel.

'They're on holiday from Barking,' smiled the waitress, 'and enjoying themselves.'

'I don't know Barking,' said Rosie, 'is it enjoyable to leave it behind?'

'Seems like it,' said the waitress, departing. She stopped to speak to a new customer as he came in. Sammy, Rachel and Rosie all heard him say, 'Woolworths, so I was told.'

Everyone looked up, and Sailor Joe said, 'You telling us those fire engines were heading for Woolworths?'

'So I heard,' said the new customer.

'It's all hands to the pumps, then,' said Sailor Joe.

A lady member of the quartet said, 'My dear old mum grew up on nothing over sixpence.'

'Well,' said one of the young men, 'it looks like it's all going up in smoke. Come on, finish coffee and let's take a shufti.'

The four were up and away a minute later, all keen to see a branch of the famous high-street store ablaze. Sammy, Rachel and Rosie remained to enjoy their coffee and buns at leisure. When they did leave, Sammy exchanged a few more friendly words with Sailor Joe, who supposed he'd see him regularly once he'd set up his shop, and that from the cut of his jib he was obviously worth a bob or two. Sammy said that if Sailor was referring to his suit, it was one he'd just redeemed from Camberwell pawnbrokers.

'Pull the other one, me wooden peg,' said Sailor Joe.

Sammy, accompanied by Rachel and Rosie, left with a grin on his face. He always enjoyed a bit of repartee with old associates.

'Right, ladies,' he said, 'this way to the shop.'

'We're not going to race down to the fire at Woolworths?' said Rosie.

'I'm leaving it to the fire brigade,' said Sammy. 'Let's head for the shop.'

They began their walk in the bright sunshine, the shop in question being located in a side street some way down. Rachel and Rosie did a little window-gazing here and there, and Sammy did not hurry them. There was no need, and further, the idea was for the ladies to explore Southend. He himself peered ahead from time to time.

'What are you looking for, Sammy?' asked Rachel.

'Well, as I recall,' said Sammy, 'Woolworths is down there somewhere, but there's no sign of a fire or fire engines. I can see smoke, but it's well to the left.'

'I can smell it now,' said Rachel.

'There, look,' said Rosie.

The smoke was drifting lazily above buildings to dirty the sky, and something made Sammy pick up the pace.

Ten minutes later, and still in company with Rachel and Rosie, he was part of a crowd watching firemen directing their hoses to douse the last of any burning embers of Warner's Wardrobe. Woolworths my aching foot, thought Sammy, that bloke who mentioned it in the cafe had a fit of mishearing.

The shop was a drenched, smoking ruin, equipment and stock all consumed. Mrs Phyllis Warner, wife of the owner, Bill Warner, was talking to Sammy. She was tearful as she told him she had no idea how the fire started, but thought it might have been due to a woman customer who went into the cubicle to try on a dress. She was smoking a cigarette.

'Thinking back, Mr Adams, I'm sure she didn't have the cigarette when she came out. I'm terribly upset, for Bill and myself, and for you – it's ruined your plans.'

'They're up the spout all right,' said Sammy, grimacing. Only a short while ago, the bright atmosphere of the seaside town had warmed the cockles of his heart. Now, everything relating to the main purpose of his visit lay under collapsed ruins and drenching water. Ninety-nine cor-blimey curses, he thought.

'What about the insurance, does it cover fire?' asked Rosie.

'It's a fact it does,' said Sammy. The property company had taken over the insurance cover on the day purchase was completed, with the priviso that Warners could have up to the end of June to sell what they could of their stock. 'But I ask meself, Rosie, how much of a consolation is that at this particular moment? And I answer not much. Still, I'll feel better in a month's time. There's always someone more unlucky, someone who's forgotten about insurance cover.'

The hoses were shut down then, and two firemen made a close inspection of the blackened ruins. The crowd began to break up as people drifted away.

'Mr Adams, I'm terribly sorry,' said young Mrs Warner.

'I share your headache,' said Sammy.

'Fires do happen,' said Rachel, 'but my life, this one has really wrecked the premises. I should be upset? I am, especially for you and your husband, Mrs Warner.'

'I must go home and phone Bill,' said Mrs Warner, her tearfulness on the brink of a breakdown. 'You'll contact the insurance company, Mr Adams?'

'I'll talk to my son and his co-director as soon as I get back to the office,' said Sammy. 'They'll be in touch with you, since part of the deal was that the insurance would cover cost of any ruined or stolen stock, and that we'd pass the reimbursement to you, right?'

'Bill and I will be grateful you agreed to that clause,' said Mrs Warner. She eyed the smoky ruins of what had once been a dress shop catering for the kind of visitors who were always looking for bargains rather than anything expensive. The fact that the shop had been sold and she hadn't long to go as its proprietress seemed of little consolation to her at this moment. A sigh escaped her, and then, with some murmured words of goodbye to Sammy and his companions, she turned and left.

'We should be sorry for her and ourselves for this kind of day, Sammy,' said Rachel.

'Right on,' said Sammy, grimacing again. He took a last look at the blackened ruins, from which the final wisps of smoke were escaping, then had a word with the fire brigade's chief officer, letting him know one of his firms, Adams Properties Ltd, owned the shop, such as it was right now. He was told that only an official investigation could determine the cause of the fire, and that the owners would be advised of the findings. 'Well, I've had other corblimey upsets in my time, Chief, so I daresay I'll get over this one.'

'All in a day's work for us, sir,' said the chief officer.

'Good luck,' said Sammy, and left, in company with Rachel and Rosie. They were both very sober.

'What do we do now, Sammy?' asked Rosie. 'We're hardly in the mood to go paddling or to wear funny hats.'

'Well, we need something to take away the nasty taste of burnt smoke,' said Sammy. He looked at his watch. Eleven forty. 'I know just the place, a pub that'll serve us a plateful of shellfish, together with rolls and butter. It'll also serve wine to you girls and a tankard of its best brew to me. D'you fancy the prospect? We'll take our time and head for home afterwards.'

'Lead on, Macduff,' said Rosie.

'If I'd been born a Macduff,' said Sammy, 'I'd be wearing a Southend kilt.'

Chapter Eighteen

Sammy and the ladies arrived back at the Camberwell offices at mid-afternoon, enabling Rosie to get home before her son and daughter returned from school. She was always adamant about that.

Sammy and Rachel looked in on Boots to give him the news of the fire. Boots expressed sympathy for their spoiled outing, but was philosophical about the event.

'Well, it's just another shop, Sammy, it's not your family home, or mine. Or Rachel's.'

'Thank you for that thought, Boots,' said Rachel.

'Hold on,' said Sammy, 'things ain't as casual as that. We've got to wait for the inquiry to tell us how the fire started, then sort out the insurance and consider whether we rebuild the shop or sell the site. Right now, there's no prospect of opening up until next year.'

Boots thought about all that.

'Sammy,' he said, 'don't we have an agreement with the Warners to reimburse them for loss of stock in the event of burglary or a fire prior to our taking over?'

'Is that a question or a reminder?' asked Sammy.

'Yes, we do have that agreement, Boots,' said Rachel.

'We all thought it a fair clause,' said Sammy.

'Well, I wonder,' said Boots, 'what happens if the investigation discovers the fire was started deliberately? That would point to arson and the Warners.'

'Look, I haven't spent the morning getting a headache just for you to give me another one,' complained Sammy.

'My life, Boots,' said Rachel, 'are you implying that the Warners may have lit the bonfire themselves in order to earn the reimbursement from the insurance company?'

'It'll be from us,' said Boots, 'after the insurance company has paid up, but of course it won't pay a penny if the fire was started deliberately.'

'That's it,' said Sammy, disgusted, 'you've definitely given me a headache on top of the one I've had since this morning. No, listen, I know the Warners, both of 'em, and I'd swear they're as honest as Chinese Lady and her vicar. In any case, you're only talking about a figure that wouldn't amount to more than a few quid. Well, comparative, like.'

'Very true, Sammy, if the Warners' claim for lost stock turns out to be modest,' said Boots.

'That's a point,' said Sammy.

'So is the possibility that the loss of stock was self-inflicted by the Warners,' said Rachel. 'We'll need to look carefully at the amount they claim. My life, Sammy, if arson is proved, the insurance company won't pay a penny, either for lost stock or ruined property.'

'Rachel,' said Sammy, 'it's bad enough listening to Boots, without you putting the wind up me as well. I'm going to have a word with the property company's joint managing directors.' He was referring to his son Daniel, and Boots's son Tim. Together, they had turned the property company into what Sammy called an asset with rounded corners and no sharp edges, which meant highly profitable and a valuable contributor, along with Adams Enterprises and Adams Fashions, to the personal prosperity of every family member who worked for the companies or had shares in them. Sammy, as the founder of the business, modestly accepted the largest percentage as his due, despite the fact that Chinese Lady frequently told him he'd turned out to be an implorable profiteer – she meant deplorable – and she could only hope no-one else in the family would turn out the same.

Tim and Daniel listened to him retailing the happenings in Southend, and what Boots had implied in regard to the Warners. Tim said his dad must have been looking on the black side of things for the first time in his life. He thought that perhaps at sixty, the old lad was losing a bit of his bottle. Sammy at once said that if Boots lived to be a hundred, he'd still have all his bottle, and would take it with him when he did go. Tim said it simply wasn't worth the risk for the Warners to have fired their stock themselves. They'd get very little out of it. Sammy said they were his sentiments entirely, but there was always the chance of something dubious about some shop fires. Anyway, the next step was to contact the insurance company, which induced Daniel to unconsciously echo Rachel's declaration that not a penny would be paid unless the investigation into the cause of the fire came up with the right answer.

'Don't I know that?' said Sammy. 'Anyway, have a dicky bird with them. Let them know about the fire and ask for a claims form.'

'Dad, you're teaching us to suck lemons,' said Daniel.

'Well, I had some of that myself in me

younger days,' said Sammy. He brightened a little. 'Still, Southend wasn't all bad news. Rosie, Rachel and self enjoyed some nourishing cockles, mussels and shrimps at a pub that poured me a tankard of its best brew. All right, then, I'll leave the pair of you to start the ball rolling in respect of the fire.'

'Much obliged,' said Tim, smiling.

'And never mind your sorrows, Dad,' said Daniel, 'you look in great shape.'

'I don't know how I've managed that,' said Sammy from the door. 'Not considering I've had the kind of day I want to forget.'

Over supper with Boots and the twins that evening, Polly said it wasn't often that Sammy, in his business career, had been stopped dead in his tracks.

'On this occasion,' said Boots, 'it's not Sammy, it's the company. The Southend shop prospect is now flat on its back in the middle of the town.'

'I've never been to Southend,' said Gemma, by way of a mild complaint.

'I could say the same,' said James, 'but I won't.'

'The fact is,' said Boots, 'if there's any suggestion of arson, there could also be a suggestion of collusion between the Warners and the company.'

'I say, old thing, that's a bit pessimistic,' said Polly.

'Dad, collusion's a crime,' said James. 'Under certain circumstances, that is.'

'That's pessimistic, you gloomy boy,' said Gemma.

'Hear, hear,' said Polly, 'except I exclude gloomy boy. And let's banish pessimism. This family has managed to do without it ever since you and James were born.'

'What about the time when Daddy had chronic dandruff and we all thought he'd have to shave his head and go about bald?' said Gemma. 'It was gloom all the time.'

'That was when you were nine,' said Polly, 'and it wasn't Daddy's head, it was Uncle Tommy's, and he didn't have to shave it. Your Aunt Vi cured the problem by giving him a medical shampoo every night for weeks.'

'Good old Aunt Vi,' said James.

'Further,' said Polly, 'I would never allow your father to develop anything as frightful as dandruff.'

'But what about if it crept up on him when you weren't looking?' said Gemma.

'I'd rely on you and James to give it the old one-two,' said Polly.

'Where'd you get that from?' asked James.

'Well, dear boy,' said Polly, 'it could be the

old heave-ho, not the old one-two. Whichever it was, I think I heard it on *The Goon Show*.' *The Goon Show* was a hugely popular radio programme. It featured four comedians, Michael Bentine, Spike Milligan, Harry Secombe and Peter Sellers, every one of them as zany as a cross-eyed parrot, and so excruciatingly funny off the cuff that they frequently departed from their script. 'Yes, I'm sure it was a Goon thing,' murmured Polly.

'Mummy,' said Gemma, 'if it came out of *The Goon Show*, it's just a big laugh.'

'Oh, well, never mind, ducky,' said Polly, 'it all sounds better than a discussion on the Southend shop fire, and I'm sure we've all helped to make your father more cheerful about the future.'

'I'm sure myself, that with my kind of family I'll never feel the need to leave you. I won't emigrate to Australia,' said Boots. 'Or Canada. Or New Zealand.'

'Or even Clapham Common,' said James.

'It's a promise,' said Boots.

'And so say all of us,' sang Polly, James and Gemma in concert.

'What's next?' asked Boots, noting that the repartee hadn't interfered with anyone's appetite. Sliced choice ham, with a mixed salad and hot new potatoes, had vanished from every plate.

'Oh, yes,' said James, 'what's for afters, Mum?'

As usual, their daily maid, Flossie Cuthbert, had prepared the supper before leaving, and Polly had only needed to serve it. However, she did know what the dessert was.

'Peaches with ice cream,' she said.

'Great,' said James.

'Goody,' enthused Gemma, and no-one said anything about the fact that they knew the peaches had come out of a can. One couldn't always get fresh and luscious imported peaches.

'And what do you say, Boots?' smiled Polly.

'What's one more shop?' said Boots.

At a little after eight, Giles Chapman answered the ringing phone.

'Yes, hello?' he said.

'Who's that?'

'Oh, I just live here,' said Giles. 'Might I ask who you are?'

'Hey, Buster, you're not the brother of that doll name of Em, are you?' asked the Teddy boy who called himself Bradley Thompson.

'I've got a sister called Emily,' said Giles, 'but I don't know how much of a doll she is, just that she talks too much when the radio's on.'

'Do us a favour and bring her to the phone to

do some talking to me, would you, man? I'd like a cosy chat with her. Tell her it's Brad.'

'Wait a bit and I'll see,' said Giles. He put the phone down and went into the living room, where his parents and Emily were watching a television programme on the life and death of an African lion. 'Emily, it's your funny friend again, Brad Whatsisname. He'd like to have a cosy chat with you.'

'I'm sure he would,' said Rosie, 'and I forbid it here and now.'

'Tell that precocious young man that Emily's too young for the kind of caper he's got in mind, and that she is not going to speak to him this evening,' said Matt.

With which message Bradley Thompson had to be content, although he assured Giles that come Saturday evening he'd rock around the dance hall with Em until closing time.

'You make it sound like a pub,' said Giles.

'That'll be the day, man,' said Brad, 'when your sister and me can legally prop up a bar.'

'In the Last Chance Saloon?' suggested Giles.

'You bet,' said Brad, and Giles hung up.

'Honest, I just don't know why everyone fusses about Brad,' said Emily as the family watched the doomed lion begin its last attempt to oust stronger rivals. 'Or treats me as if I'm only six years old. But anyway I wanted to see this telly programme all the way through, and if I hadn't said so before, which I know I have, I'll see him at the Saturday dance.'

One of a certain man's favourite ways of acquiring what didn't belong to him was to go to any of London's main railway terminals, buy a platform ticket and wait for a train to come in. He would then make a quick sortie along the platform, using keen and greedy eyes to spot anything passengers might have left behind, usually in an overhead rack. Whenever an item was noticed, he'd take a quick look around to make sure no railway official was watching, then dart into the compartment and snatch what was there for the taking. Mostly it was something like an umbrella, a parcel or a man's hat. Parcels could turn out to be nice surprise packets, while umbrellas could always be passed on to hawkers in street markets, for something like a bob a time. The hawkers, of course, would sell them as second-hand goods in first-class condition, which some of them often were.

Recently, on separate occasions, he'd come into nefarious possession of a very smart umbrella, a superior raincoat and a bowler hat. He was minded to visit one of London's busy Sunday markets to barter them for a quid or two. Instead, however, he decided to pay a return visit to a certain house near Herne Hill, south-east London. Yus, he'd do that, and maybe pick up a useful item or two. Well, he owed the woman of the house a bit of misfortune. He'd suffered painful headaches for weeks ever since the morning when she'd bashed him with a saucepan. Bloody cow. It was people like her that made life difficult for a bloke whose last job as a Government-directed farmhand had come to a finish at the end of the war. Well, after all that suffering as sweated labour, up at dawn and out in the fields for a back-breaking twelve hours every day, he was finished for any other work. For years now he'd had to live hand to mouth, like, and didn't get any help or sympathy from them toffee-nosed people at the employment agency, except an offer to put him in the way of starting a new career as a navvy. He always asked if they were offering to pull the shutters down on his suffering life.

That's it, he thought, that's what I'll do. I'll try that house again, even if only for the pleasure of paying that woman out for what she'd done. She needed to be out shopping, of course, and with luck, she might be.

So he set out from his grubby room in a dosshouse on a bright but chilly morning.

'Where are you off to at this time of the morning?' asked the bloke who acted as warden.

'To see an old friend.'

'Didn't know you had any.' The beery warden grinned. Well, it was something to see Dodgy Dan going forth wearing a fine bowler, a posh raincoat, and carrying an umbrella. Usually he looked what he was, a tramp on the make. Still, no questions of a meaningful kind were ever asked of the inmates. So off went Dodgy Dan, free as air.

His get-up, of course, meant that outwardly he was very unlike the tatty old figure of before. No-one who had seen him on that previous occasion would recognize him now, even if he hadn't bothered to shave for a couple of days or so.

The scene in Kestrel Avenue, near Herne Hill railway station, was peaceful in the well-known way of lower-middle-class suburbia. That is, there were no hollering street kids kicking a ball about, and no rent collectors hammering on the doors of defaulting tenants. The only movements of any note were those of a housewife carrying a shopping bag, and of a car coming out of a drive to turn in the direction of Herne Hill. From the far end of the avenue, a respectably dressed man on the corner was watching.

He saw the car turn right into Herne Hill, whereupon he entered the avenue to follow in the footsteps of the woman with the shopping bag.

She was well ahead of him, but he made no move to catch her up. Indeed, when she too turned right into Herne Hill, he stopped at the gateway of a particular house. Looking around, he noted the convenient absence of people out and about, then made his way up the drive to the front door. He knocked, and, while apparently waiting for an answer to his summons, turned to take a look up and down the road. All was still clear, and with no-one responding to his knock, he used the side path to walk round to the rear of the house.

He moved slowly and silently up to the edge of the kitchen window. He hesitated a moment, then leaned to look through. It was immediately clear to him that the kitchen was unoccupied, which, on top of the fact that his knock had not been answered, convinced him there was no-one at home. Setting the umbrella aside, he drew a crowbar from the deep pocket of his raincoat, only to tense and stiffen as he heard someone knocking on the front door. Although the sound did not reach his ears loudly, it was all too recognizable as a demanding rat-a-tat. He stayed where he was, unmoving. He thought he heard footsteps on the path then, and he certainly heard a voice.

'Excuse us, missus, are you there hanging out a bit of washing in the sun? Parcel for yer.'

Dodgy Dan scurried into the nearest hide-away, the garden shed. A postman, coming round by the side path, took a look at the garden and the empty washing line, decided the lady of the house was definitely not at home, and left. Dodgy Dan re-emerged and ventured to put himself at a point on the side path from where, craning his head, he was able to observe the morning scene again. He saw a post office van moving away, while across the road a housewife was putting an empty milk bottle on her doorstep. That done, she went back into her house and closed the door.

The coast was clear again, but Dodgy Dan waited a few more minutes before going to work.

Meanwhile, Mrs Patsy Adams, American daughter-in-law of Sammy and Susie Adams, was driving to the shops and the local post office. Suddenly she slowed down and brought the car to a stop. Oh, shoot, she'd forgotten the letter she'd written to her good old pa last night. It needed an expensive stamp and an air-mail sticker, and then posting. She turned the car round and drove back home.

Entering the house, she went straight to the kitchen. The letter, she knew, was on the kitchen table. About to pick it up, she became aware of an unfamiliar noise, a creaking and straining of the back door. She yelled.

'Who's there?'

A bowler hat appeared at the left-hand edge of the kitchen window. She didn't recognize the hat, but she did recognize the face beneath it, a swarthy face, unshaven and bristly. Startled eyes peered into hers, then the bowler hat turned at speed and Dodgy Dan, a greasy old piece of work-shy humanity, made a run for safety towards the back wall of the garden.

Patsy, hollering in good old American fashion, unlocked and wrenched open the back door, seized the nearest weapon and ran out in punitive pursuit. She caught the bloke as he was scrambling up and over the ivy-covered brick wall. She struck. A heavy, old-fashioned wooden rolling pin assaulted his purloined rain-coat exactly where it covered his backside. He bellowed with pain, and again when a second strike landed quite ferociously. He fell over the wall, which wasn't part of his escape plan at all. The tarmac surface of a path came up and bruised him horribly, which, on top of the pain in his injured male behind, caused him to emit a hoarse cry of agony. Also, the bowler hat fell off. A shout reached him from the other side of the wall.

'Stay there, you punk! I'm coming after you!'

He didn't wait to find out whether that was true or not. Despite his injuries, he upped and bolted, even though every yard he covered hurt him disgustingly. It was all too much like that first time, when she went for him with a saucepan. Bugger this, he thought, what a cow. Females like her ought never to have been invented. This is the last time I want anything to do with her and her shack. She ain't fit to know. She's cost me an arm and a leg. Well, a prime bowler hat and a nearly new umbrella. It ain't my day.

Patsy, returning to her kitchen, spotted an umbrella on the path, obviously left behind by the injured party. She then noticed the edge of the door was scarred from wounding treatment by a jemmy or something similar.

'Who'd have thought it?' she asked herself. 'When I was young and naive, I used to think this little old island was full of eccentric but harmless old buffers with moustaches. I didn't know a thing about thieving old tramps in bowler hats. I guess there's always something new to learn about everything.'

*   *   *

She had a story to tell Daniel when he arrived home from his office. He listened, then inspected the scarred door and asked her if she'd called the police. No, she hadn't. She didn't think she needed to, since she was sure there wouldn't be a third visit from the great and lousy unwashed.

'What makes you sure?' asked Daniel.

'Well, Daniel old boy,' said Patsy, taking off Aunt Polly, 'I guess I didn't hit the blighter hard enough the first time. I know I did today, the second time. He won't be able to sit down for a jolly old month. Oh, and we've won an umbrella and a bowler hat, so chin-chin, old top.'

'Get you, cookie,' said Daniel. 'I'll have the door seen to. But next time stop to think what might happen if the great and lousy unwashed turns on you. I'm dead against anything happening to my favourite wife. I mean, favourite wives aren't on sale in London markets at bargain prices.'

'I guess not,' said Patsy, 'but behind a closed door you might get one for fifty dollars. That's if you won't mind her being about ninety, with dentures and a wig, but good references.'

'Somehow,' said Daniel, 'I don't think I'll swop one like you for someone like that.'

'That's it, thrill me,' said Patsy.

Chapter Nineteen

Charlie Ellis had an instinctive affinity with a camera. His professional name was Morton Fraser, and his studio was in the West End. That is, in a room above a shop in Soho. He had good contacts, mainly Continental. With the assistance of a ferry, he usually took the negatives across the Channel himself. A fellow couldn't always rely on the post office not to nose into a packet destined for Denmark and marked 'Holiday Snapshots'. Some interfering GPO blighter had caused Charlie to be informed that the export of obscene material was illegal, and that he was liable to prosecution for attempting it. Be warned, that was the message.

If photographs of a model doing a cute striptease in her hot kitchen while baking a cake were obscene, then the law lords of Great Britain were silly old buggers. Fortunately, once across the Channel a bloke didn't run up against that kind. The law lords of the

Continent had a broader outlook, and a mistress or two in some cases. As for Continental men, they were highly appreciative of eye-winking ladies of a photogenic kind with no inhibitions in front of a camera, and no objections to decorating spicy French magazines. They particularly appreciated the UK variety, especially those who could, in their looks, be classed as English roses.

Charlie had just found a perfect example. Well, no, he couldn't claim that credit. That belonged to a photographer name of Amos Anderson, who had a studio in some London backwater called Camberwell Green, and did weddings, portraits and kids. And as a sideline he did pin-ups, mostly of girls in swimsuits. Charlie knew Amos. They'd studied photography at the same polytechnic. In later years, he'd told Amos more than once that his kind of studio work was all right, but after a lifetime at it, ten to one he'd still be riding on buses instead of having his own limousine.

Now, however, Amos had found a real earner in the shape of a piece of local talent called Maureen Brown. He'd photographed her as everybody's girl next door, but with a saucy touch to the poses in the way of a breeze-blown dress. Result? He'd actually got the photographs published in a national daily and elsewhere.

Further photographs of her had popped up in weeklies and magazines, all credited to Amos Anderson. Each one made Charlie feel that Continental eyes would see the girl as a typical English rose.

Metaphorically licking his lips, he eventually phoned his old polytechnic buddy.

'Good morning, Anderson Studio here,' said Amos's lady assistant. 'Can I help you?'

'Yes, you can put me through to Amos. Tell him Charlie Ellis, an old friend, is calling.'

'Ever so sorry, Mr Ellis, but he's in the studio at the moment. He has a sitter.'

'Well, good for him. As soon as he's free, would you ask him to give me a ring?' Charlie quoted his phone number.

'Yes, I'll ask him, Mr Ellis.'

Amos rang back half an hour later.

'What's brought you out of the woodwork, Charlie?'

'Glad you asked, mate. How's business? Making your fortune yet?'

'Not yet,' said Amos.

'Told you years ago weddings don't rate an apartment in Monte Carlo or even a seaside shack in Sussex. Listen, I'm interested in this girl you've found, the one you've labelled as everybody's girl next door. Smart touch, that. And you've used a genuine pin-up angle with

606

the flirty dress and the leg showing. Start her off with that before we get into real money with swimsuits. Listen, where can I find her?'

Amos, not in the same league as Charlie, seeing as he was basically a decent bloke with a sense of what was fair, if businesslike, baulked at that request. He knew Charlie Ellis as a gifted professional but with the kind of Continental contacts that meant he turned out photographs fit for export but unfit for home consumption. He was always sailing close to the wind. Amos was pretty sure that what he had in mind for Maureen would end up in the naughty magazines of Holland, Denmark and elsewhere. She'd be paid well, but it wouldn't do much for her career in the UK. As things stood she was earning steady money, which he paid to her out of the sale of her photographs. Maureen was under contract to him. He'd been sharp enough to see her potential. He now informed Charlie that Maureen was exclusive to himself, and he was keeping it so.

'Now, now, Amos, come on,' said Charlie, 'you can lend her out to an old friend, can't you? I'll pay you a fee, of course, and you wouldn't stand in the way of her earning her own fee from me, would you? Just give me her phone number and then later on we'll talk about what she can earn for you and me both.'

'Not if she's going to end up glazing the eyeballs of every dee-oh-em on the Continent,' said Amos, dee-oh-em standing for dirty old man. 'And in my book, her earnings come from poses that don't give her the wrong kind of label. Clean earnings for her and me I like, don't I?'

'Course you do, Amos, course you do,' said Charlie. 'Where would we be without the little darlings?'

'I'd be where I am now, wouldn't I?' said Amos. 'With my usual earners.'

'I'll be fair to the young lady and to you,' said Charlie.

'Being fair ain't going to include making Maureen stand on her head in a party frock, no, man,' said Amos. He went on to say that Maureen came of a respectable family, and photographs of her for permissive Continental publications were out as far as he was concerned. So no, he wasn't going to give Charlie her phone number, her address or permission to sell any photographs of her, not unless he saw them first.

'Here, hold on,' said Charlie, 'I know she's under contract to you, but shouldn't you give her the option of deciding for herself. But all right, okey-dokey, you've got a point. I'll let you see the contacts first, then, and if I could say fairer than that, I'd be everyone's Father Christmas.'

'Mrs Anderson and self don't do Christmas,' said Amos, a follower of Moses. 'But I should trust you?' Charlie had made his own point in saying Maureen had a right to decide for herself, providing Charlie would guarantee straight poses and no dubious stuff. 'Can I trust you?'

'Course you can, Amos, course you can,' said Charlie. 'Don't you and me go back to the polytechnic as student mates with only pennies in our pockets? Come on, what's her phone number? I could find out from some other source, y'know, so do me the favour.'

'I'm thinking about it,' said Amos. The most important thing was for him to make sure he definitely saw the contact sheets himself before giving permission to sell any of the photographs. 'All right, you give me sight of the contacts as soon as they're ready.'

'Promise,' said Charlie.

'All of them,' said Amos, 'and my fee for giving you permission to photograph her will be five guineas, which is fixed and non-negotiable.'

'That's tough on me, but all right,' said Charlie. 'We can all earn some useful lolly on your girl next door, and I do mean lolly and not peanuts.'

★   ★   ★

609

Maureen took two phone calls later that day. The first was from Amos, who told her that a photographer from town, Morton Fraser, would be contacting her with a view to arranging a sitting. Maureen responded with enthusiasm. Being a glamorous pin-up model was great. Amos said make sure he doesn't pose you in a way your parents wouldn't like. Some photographers who concentrated exclusively on glamour, he said, asked more of a girl than was decent. Maureen rushed in to say oh, she wouldn't ever do anything exotic in front of a camera. She meant erotic, but exotic sounded in keeping, so Amos let it go and assured her he was going to vet all the shots before he allowed Morton Fraser the legal right to sell any.

'Morton Fraser's a posh name,' said Maureen. 'Is he posh?'

If Charlie Ellis is posh, thought Amos, I'm baby Moses in the bulrushes, which I know I'm not.

'No, he's not posh, Maureen, just a good photographer with a lot more outlets than I've got. You're earning a few guineas fairly regular at the moment, and Charlie will—'

'Charlie?'

'Mmm?' said Amos. 'Oh, yes, that's his middle name but he doesn't use it profession-ally, which I wouldn't myself if it was mine. It

610

ain't got enough dignity for a professional man. Anyway, he'll help you earn more than a few guineas at a time, and if I didn't think he would, I'd have turned him down. Looking after your interests is a serious responsibility of mine, and don't we know it?'

Maureen said she was happy at the way he looked after her, and that Morton Fraser sounded ever so promising. What she would like, she said, was to see herself on the front page of a classy magazine. Amos said a cover girl, eh? Not half, that's what we'd both like, he said.

'Crikey, you bet,' said Maureen.

'Well, we know, don't we, that a model who's made a front cover is a model who's close to regular top earnings,' said Amos. 'So when Fraser gets in touch with you, play a bit hard to get. That'll up the ante.'

'Oh, I'll look after my interests,' said Maureen.

Her second call was from Charlie himself, who came across as a very friendly-sounding bloke and who introduced himself as Morton Fraser, West End photographer.

'West End?' said Maureen, thrilled. 'My manager, Mr Anderson, mentioned you worked in town, but he didn't say West End.'

611

'Haven't you heard of me?' asked Charlie, letting his tonsils sound surprised.

'Well, no, I can't say I have,' said Maureen. 'Mind, I could've done, except it's sort of escaped me.'

'I forgive you,' said Charlie. 'But I'm sure you've seen photographs of Rank film starlets in your newspaper or magazines.'

'Oh, yes,' said Maureen.

'Well, every time you've seen one, you've been looking at my kind of work,' said Charlie.

'Crikey, I've seen some of those starlets on the front cover of *Filmgoer*,' said Maureen.

'If I photographed Diana Dors tomorrow, it wouldn't be the first time,' said Charlie, on easy terms with a porkie.

'Diana Dors? Oh, crikey, imagine that,' said Maureen. Diana Dors was a bit more than a starlet. She was well on her way to becoming the UK's favourite blonde bombshell. 'Mr Fraser, are you phoning about giving me a sitting?'

'So I am, girlie,' said Charlie. 'How will next Tuesday suit you? Say two in the afternoon at my studio?'

Maureen said that would suit her fine, and how long would the sitting be? Charlie suggested it could well be two hours, and Maureen asked what the fee would be per hour. Charlie said he'd

612

pay her five guineas for the session, which delighted Maureen considering Amos had told her some photographers only paid one guinea an hour. She ventured to ask this West End professional who had photographed Diana Dors if Mr Anderson would also receive a fee, seeing she was under contract to him. Charlie said she and Amos, and he himself, were all expected to earn something from the sitting.

'Oh, who do you expect to sell the photos to?' asked Maureen, thinking of the front covers of famous magazines like *Vogue*.

'Not to a tuppenny-'apenny comic,' said Charlie. 'But first let's see how the pics turn out, right? Next Tuesday, then, at two?'

'What kind of outfits d'you want me to bring?' asked Maureen. 'I've got some lovely dresses.'

'Don't you worry about that,' said Charlie, 'I'll supply the costumes from me studio wardrobe, every item clean and laundered. You just bring yourself, eh? Good-oh.'

But Maureen asked what kind of costumes did he have in mind? Charlie said highly fancy and very chic. And Maureen said she was in favour of anything chic, as it helped a model to look high-class. Apart from her latest poses in a sweater, all her sittings for Amos had required her to do leggy shots, since that was how he had first brought her to the attention of some newspapers and magazines. Sitting on a gate with the breeze lifting her dress. Amos said every girl next door ought to have legs like hers, but liked the fact that hers alone were special.

'Oh, all right, Mr Fraser, I'll be at your studio at two next Tuesday afternoon,' she said. 'What's the address?'

'It's Old Compton Street,' said Charlie, and gave her the door number.

'I don't think I've ever been in Old Compton Street,' said Maureen. 'It's in the West End, is it, like you mentioned?'

'Is it?' said Charlie. 'It is, and no more than a stone's throw from good old Piccadilly Circus. Nor is it here today and gone tomorrow. From Monday to Monday, every day of the year, it's where it is now, next to Shaftesbury Avenue, and if I could say fairer than that I'd be everyone's guide to the bright lights.'

'Oh, I know Shaftesbury Avenue,' said Maureen.

'Then I'm glad for both of us, girlie,' said Charlie.

Over the phone, they parted company on very sociable terms, each looking forward to meeting the other next Tuesday.

Of course, Maureen's parents, Cassie and Freddy Brown, wanted to know all about their daughter's latest booking, and when she told them it was to be with a real West End photographer, they both wished her luck, except that Freddy spoiled it a bit by asking what an unreal West End photographer was like.

'Is that supposed to be funny, Dad?' said Maureen.

'No, just something I thought I'd ask,' said Freddy.

'Well, now you can answer it yourself,' said Cassie. 'Maureen and me both like a laugh.'

Neither she nor Freddy had had any objections to Maureen giving up a boring old office job to become a pin-up model. They both took pride in her looks and her figure, and went happily along with her dreams of becoming as popular as a Rank film starlet, or as glamorous a cover girl as Diana Dors. Diana Dors always seemed to photograph with a saucy twinkle in her eyes and lots of uplift. Still, saucy pin-up girls had been part of the social scene since the heady barrack-room days of the Second World War, when American soldiers and sailors pinned up photographs of Betty Grable, the Hollywood film star, and men of the British Eighth Army adopted the German Afrika Korps's dream girl, Lili Marlene, as their own pin-up in the shape of an artist's impression.

So Maureen was in good company, really.

'D'you know how much you'll be paid for the sitting?' asked Freddy, who liked to feel sure she'd always receive her fair dues.

'Five guineas,' said Maureen.

'Bless my dear old dad,' said Cassie, 'that's as much as some workers earn in a week.' Her dear old dad, known as the Gaffer, still lived with them, and had taken to spending part of his pension playing bingo regularly at the local hall. 'That pleases you, Maureen, I'm sure.'

'Oh, not half, Mum,' said Maureen, 'and think what I might earn if Mr Fraser helped me to become a cover girl. Well, he must have the right kind of contacts, being a well-known West End professional.'

'Is he well known?' asked Freddy.

'He told me he was,' said Maureen.

'I don't think I've heard of him,' said Freddy.

'Nor me,' said Cassie.

'Well, he was a bit surprised when I told him I hadn't heard of him meself,' said Maureen. 'I expect he meant well known in the West End, and we're Walworth.'

'I've been Walworth all my life, except when I was in Burma with the old 14th,' said Freddy.

'Oh, we're proud of you, Dad,' said Maureen.

'Both of us,' said Cassie, 'and my dear old dad too.'

'I wasn't asking for compliments,' said Freddy. 'Still, you can all put something extra in my stocking come Christmas. Anyway, Maureen, you go ahead next Tuesday and then let me and your mum know how it worked out.'

'Righty-oh, Dad,' said Maureen, chuffed at developments.

Chapter Twenty

It was Matt's dubious pleasure to pick up the phone that evening and to hear that Emily's Teddy boy was on the line again.

'Hi there, it's Brad here – can I talk to Em?'

Matt let the phone shift from his ear for a moment while he regarded the instrument as if he was losing faith in its usefulness. Then he spoke.

'Brad there,' he said, 'this is Emily's father here, and I'd like to know if we're to expect a phone call from you every evening for the next ten years.'

'Hey, man, is that what you'd go for?' said Brad.

'It's what's bothering me,' said Matt, 'and I'm not sure it isn't bothering Emily.' As soon as the phone had rung a minute ago, she had said if that was Brad, tell him she was busy doing her homework.

'Believe me, Mr Chapman, sir,' said Brad, 'I

don't go in for bothering people. I'm a genuine good guy, and both my parents like me. I could grow on you, given time, like. So can I talk to Em?'

'My daughter,' said Matt, 'is busy doing her homework. After which, she'll be just as busy making a dress for her favourite doll.' That wasn't actually a prize porkie, but an attempt to capitalize on the fact that Emily had made a dress for one of her dolls when she was nine, and that she was still only thirteen.

'No kidding?' said Brad. 'Well, man, I grew up with a teddy bear myself, and I think it's still somewhere around in my family's shack. But listen, are you telling me that my sugar baby actually does homework? School homework?'

'My daughter is not your sugar baby,' said Matt, 'but yes, I assure you she really does do school homework. What do you do?'

'Plumbing.'

'Plumbing?'

'Sure,' said Brad, 'glad you asked. Well, strictly, I'm an apprentice. Mister, you positive I can't talk to Em?'

'Quite positive,' said Matt.

'OK.' Brad sounded philosophical. 'Saturday evening, then.'

'Do me the favour of co-operating with my

son to make sure Emily is back home by not later than ten thirty,' said Matt, with a touch of parental severity.

'Ten thirty?' said Brad. 'That's no time. Still, early birds can still swing.'

Burn my Sunday shirt, thought Matt, plumbers' apprentices weren't like this one in my day. They were too busy fetching tea for the plumber to make phone calls, and too simple to make weird ones.

'Goodnight, young man,' he said, and hung up.

'Hello there,' said Rosie, when he rejoined her in the lounge. Giles and Emily were in occupation of the living room, doing their homework. Giles was industrious as a scholar, while Emily thought society ought to have invented a more entertaining alternative to schools. 'What kept you?' asked Rosie.

'A plumber's mate,' said Matt.

'A plumber's mate?' Rosie smiled. 'Is that something to do with the precocious Teddy boy?'

'The young gent informed me he's apprenticed to a plumber,' said Matt.

'I'm glad to know there's something in his favour,' said Rosie, 'since I had the impression that his main activity was standing on street corners.'

'Well, he told me he's a good guy, and that both his parents like him.'

'Really?' Rosie was amused but not a little sceptical. 'Well, I beg you, Matt, not to let him into the house if, instead of making phone calls, he rings our doorbell.'

'Better if you hadn't said that,' murmured Matt, switching on the radio, 'it's tempting Providence.'

The following day Mr Austin Cobb, manager of the claims department of the relevant insurance company, telephoned the offices of Adams Property Company Ltd and asked to be put through to Mr Tim Adams. Connected, he informed Tim that the insurance company would send an official to work in concert with the investigators of the fire. He also said a claims form was on its way, but that there was little point in completing it until the cause of the fire was known.

'Thought you'd say that,' said Tim. The fire and the destruction of the Southend shop was less of a headache to him than to Sammy. He considered only an earthquake under his living-room floor could spoil his daily delight in the fact that Felicity's blindness was gradually curing itself. All the years when the world had been a blank to her were coming to an end, and against that a shop was only a shop to a firm that already had a dozen. However, Uncle Sammy seemed to have taken the loss and the implications personally. 'Mr Cobb, how long do these fire investigations take, do you know?'

'The time taken varies. It's always governed by circumstances. You understand, Mr Adams?'

'Yup, I understand only too well,' said Tim. 'But I'd be obliged if you'd keep in touch.'

'If you're asking for a daily bulletin, it's against the rules.'

'I learned when I was still young that there are rules and rules,' said Tim.

'Of course,' said Mr Austin Cobb, 'so shall we say a bulletin once in a while?'

'That's fair,' said Tim.

'I'll be in touch, but it's certain that in the event of the cause of the fire being acceptable, settlement will still take time.'

'I'll bet Christmas,' said Tim, 'and who's going to quarrel with that? Only Mr Sammy Adams, our managing director.'

'I've heard of the gentleman.'

'So has everybody here in Camberwell,' said Tim, and closed the conversation on a cordial note. He'd won a small concession from the manager of the claims department, and that was as much as he could hope for. He let his co-director Daniel know of this, then went to talk to Sammy. Sammy wasn't so much concerned with bulletins as with the fact that the powers-that-be were going to turn over every spot of ash in the burnt-out shop. It meant, he said, that the cause of the fire was considered suspicious.

'Uncle Sammy, you know better than that,' said Tim. 'All destructive fires have to be investigated, and no insurance company will settle a claim until the cause has been discovered.'

'Well, I do know it, sunshine,' said Sammy, 'and I'm much obliged to you for reminding me. No, my big worry is if the investigation rubs off on us and some interfering newspaper hound turns it into a story. You know what editors are like, they'll print anything that smells a bit. My dear old ma, Lady Finch, won't let any paper into her house except my stepdad's *Telegraph*. That way she doesn't have to read about things like some bloke in Croydon turning into a woman. She'd throw up at that kind of stuff. I tell you, Tim, what with the headache that kept me awake when the garment union was threatening a strike, and now this new headache over who done what in respect of the fire, it's not been my year.'

'Well, hard luck, Uncle Sammy,' said Tim, 'but I don't think you'll go under, whatever happens. You've survived too many crises to let this one turn you grey. Which reminds me, d'you realize that you, Uncle Tommy and Uncle Boots don't have a single grey hair between the three of you?'

'Nice of you to mention it,' said Sammy, 'and might I point out that it's due to all of us being healthy, hardworking and honest since we left school. Of course, personally, I could say that being up to my ears in work every day is what keeps my loaf too busy to grow anything but me natural hair.'

'Grey hair's natural,' said Tim.

'Yes, but you know what I mean,' said Sammy. 'Now, about the insurance company and our claim. Keep after them.'

'Will do,' said Tim, 'and I'd better get back to my desk now.'

'For any special reason?' asked Sammy.

'Yes, I'm up to my ears,' said Tim. Sammy watched him leave and thought there goes a chip off Boots, the old block. And at thirty-six, he looked not unlike his dad at that age.

The phone rang in the Chapman family's home that evening.

Rosie twitched.

'Can it be?' she asked.

'Him?' said Giles.

'Him,' said Rosie, whose maternal instincts cautioned her to protect Emily from the advances of the Teddy boy who had phoned every evening so far this week.

'I'll go,' said Emily, 'otherwise there'll be more fuss.'

As soon as she picked up the hall phone, a well-known voice reached her ear.

'Brad here – who's that?'

'Me,' said Emily.

'It's you yourself, you doll?'

'Yes, and what d'you mean by phoning us every night?' demanded Emily.

'I've got this urge to talk to you,' said Brad, 'and I've got to do it over the blower on account of not being invited to drop in by your ma or your pa. I guess parents live in a different world, I guess they're all still waltzing or foxtrotting. That sure is sad, baby.'

'Don't call me baby—'

'Sugar doll, then?' suggested Brad.

'Not that, either,' said Emily, 'and stop talking like Frank Sinatra. And don't try to get me on the phone every night, because it's playing on my mum's nerves. She's beginning to twitch each time the phone rings.'

Brad said he was sorry to receive that piece of news because he was sure her ma was pretty nice, even if she was still stuck on waltzing.

Emily said not to keep phoning, then. Brad said he'd like to write to her once a day instead of phoning, except that his writing wasn't all that hot. Emily said to remember she'd only seen him once, last Saturday, and because of that she didn't need to be written to, whether it was hot or cold. Brad said she was real cute for her age, and was it true she was only thirteen? Emily said she was actually nearly fourteen, and would be when her birthday arrived in August.

'Well, that's great, baby,' said Brad. 'We'll go places one day. By the way, how's your pa's plumbing?'

'Do what?' said Emily.

'I could come and look it over if it's a mite screwed up in places, like you've got a toilet that won't flush properly,' said Brad. 'Me and plumbing, we're already buddies. I'm getting to know all the wrinkles, and I sure would be pleased to look at your pa's system and let him know if anything needs the expert attention of Jeremiah.'

'Who's he?' asked Emily.

'The plumber I'm apprenticed to,' said Brad. 'A genuine guy, except he's another one who's still into waltzing.'

'Forget plumbing and my dad's system,' said Emily, 'and meet me at the dance on Saturday. That's all.'

'Hey, give us a break, Em, I'm—'

'Goodnight,' said Emily, and hung up. She returned to the family in the living room.

'It was him?' said Rosie.

'It's not my fault he keeps ringing,' said Emily. 'Oh, he made an offer, Dad. He offered to come and look at your plumbing in case it wasn't working properly.'

'Your mother has instructed me never to let him into the house,' said Matt. 'The boy's a wrecker of nerves.'

'Still, he seems to be getting on well in his plumbing job,' said Emily, 'and he's a great rock 'n' roller.'

'So there you are, Dad,' said Giles.

'Matt,' said Rosie, 'I've a feeling that the young people are taking us over.'

'Burn my Sunday socks,' said Matt, 'is there a future for you and me, Rosie?'

'Only if we don't give in,' said Rosie.

Chapter Twenty-one

Saturday, and Phoebe and Philip were on the way home from their honeymoon. They'd enjoyed a lovely week, including the fascinating aspect of getting to know each other as well by night as they knew each other by day. Well, what else would the world have expected of them as newly-weds? However, Philip had to report back to his squadron on Monday, and Phoebe, happily, was to go with him, for the housing officer had arranged for them to occupy married quarters. Philip had said this would be in the form of a house, one of several available to married couples. Phoebe was talking about that now, which reminded him to remind her of what he had already told her, that she wouldn't have to worry about being suddenly overwhelmed by housework, because she'd be receiving help from his batman.

'Well, imagine that,' said Phoebe amid the rhythmic sound of the smooth-running train that was carrying them to London. 'It would be like having a servant while I'm still young and active instead of old and arthritic.'

'Just the job,' said Philip, 'so we'll hang onto him. We have to remember that at your age and under present circumstances, you never know when you might need someone to lend a hand with the Hoover.'

'Why?' said Phoebe, too entranced by love's purple horizons to be as quick on the uptake as she usually was.

'It does happen to wives,' said Philip, and Phoebe did catch on then.

'Oh, help,' she said.

However, she wasn't the only Adams bride who had called theatrically for help at some time or other. Adams bridegrooms were an adventurous lot.

Saturday evening, and the dance at a hall in Brixton was swinging, the young people rocking and jiving. Dance halls generally were becoming the haunt of the young, and only rarely on Saturday evenings were there occasions when an old-fashioned band played old-fashioned music for old-fashioned couples. The latter weren't necessarily aged, but even a husband and wife in their mid-twenties were counted as old hat if they still preferred the foxtrop to jiving.

The band this evening was hot stuff, made up of four young men and a young woman vocalist who owned a powerful pair of lungs. She belted out the numbers, the microphone trembled, and the sounds bounced back off ceiling and walls, adding continuous echoes to the recreational buzz.

Giles was swinging it with Cindy Stevens. Cindy, in her assertive way, was intent on drawing him into her exclusive circle of boyfriends who would, in a manner of speaking, eventually bow down to her. Giles, however, while thinking Cindy the tops in looks and style, wasn't the kind of young bloke who didn't mind being one of a crowd. This evening, for instance, Cindy had two other boys waiting for her to notice them. Giles, accordingly, was inclined to side with the non-committed.

'Giles, you're great, and you're swinging great, d'you know that?' she said.

'Pardon?' said Giles. It was difficult to hear, especially with the vocalist belting out one more number. He and Cindy had to shout at each other. 'What was that you said?'

'I said you're going great, Giles, you're the best.'

'It'll probably be a wet Sunday tomorrow, then.'

'What d'you mean?'

'Didn't you say there was rain coming from the west?'

'Would I say that? No, I said you're the best.'

'Pardon?'

And so on. It tangled up the dialogue, which suited Giles.

Emily, meanwhile, was jiving with young Bradley Thompson. Away from the four walls of her home, and her parents, she was more responsive to the Tony Curtis lookalike. They'd established a rapport based on hitting the rhythmic factor together, and Brad, who always had a lot to say, even when it was difficult to be heard, let Emily know in loud tones that she was the classiest ladybird of all time.

'You've got style, babe, as well as the same name as my grandma.'

'What? Oh, your grandma. Well, never mind her, I wasn't named after her.' Emily was fully aware that she'd been named after Uncle Boots's first wife. He was her grandpa actually, but she never called him that, and nor did any of her cousins. He was simply everyone's uncle, and she was pretty sure he wouldn't fuss about her social life, not like her parents did. He didn't fuss about anything, actually. 'Oh, watch your feet, d'you hear me?'

Her Teddy boy's feet were flying about.

'Come on, let's swing, Em,' he said, bawling

the words into her ear as he stepped up the rhythm.

'Don't go mad,' yelled Emily. He was all moving limbs and hips, the music and the beat sending him over the top. Still, it was infectious enough for her to match his gyrations.

They were surrounded by other dancers, the girls passing in and out under their partners' upraised arms and swinging their hips joyfully.

'I've got music in my hoofers, so go, baby, go,' said Brad.

'There's not enough room,' said Emily.

In the packed dance hall, all the young people needed more space.

'Give it a go, doll,' said Brad.

'Excuse me, mate,' said a vigorous bloke, 'you talking to mine?'

'Yours?' said Brad.

'My private doll. You don't want yer leg broke, do yer?'

'You bet I don't,' said Brad, noting that the private doll, a blonde, was closer to him than to her partner, such was the way the crowded hall jumbled people up. 'Believe me, I'm talking to nobody but my own ladybird.'

'Eh?'

'It sure is a great shindig,' said Brad, and went rocking with Emily, who told him he was bound to fall down a hole if he kept talking all the time. Brad said a load of silence always made him feel the cops were at his door and about to charge him with robbing a bank. Well, anyway, he made a gifted partner for Emily. His sense of rhythm matched hers, and that was something worthwhile in any boy. Too many of them couldn't shake a leg without falling over.

Not far from them, James and Gemma were going it with a girl and boy respectively. Gemma was alight with enjoyment, eyes sparkling, skirt swinging. James's partner was a girl he'd only just met. Or, rather, a girl who'd fastened onto him. James didn't mind. He took life, events and people as tolerantly as his dad. From time to time he cast a glance at cousin Emily and her Teddy boy partner. James had been asked by his mother to help Giles make sure that Emily was home by ten thirty, and thus save his Aunt Rosie a touch of the twitches. Giles himself was also keeping an eye on Emily to make sure she didn't suddenly disappear.

It so happened that at fifteen minutes to ten, Brad suggested to Emily that they leave now so that she'd be home as early as any parents could dream of. He'd mentioned, he said, that parents had a bit in common with the dodo, and it sure was best to keep them happy before they were only history.

'I don't want to leave yet,' said Emily.

'How about if we took a taxi ride to your ranch?' said Brad.

'Do what?' said Emily, using her elbows to make space for her swinging hips.

'I'm flush,' said Brad, 'I picked up my pay yesterday afternoon. It wasn't a fortune, but it wasn't peanuts, either. Well, plumbers' mates are valuable to plumbers, and if a plumber's got his own business, he'll slip you a dollar or two. So how about a taxi ride, babe?'

The thought of a ride in a taxi instead of on a crowded bus won Emily over, and she left the hall after first letting Giles know that Brad was taking her home this minute, and in a taxi.

'God's honour?' said Giles.

'Yes,' said Emily.

'Sure,' said Brad, and Giles felt tickled by the possibility that his mum and dad were going to come face to face with Emily's Teddy boy. It wouldn't, he supposed, be something they'd welcome, although it might give his dad a chance to let Brad know in no uncertain terms that his relationship with Emily wasn't what her parents wanted at this time in her life.

The fact was, of course, that like many parents, Rosie and Matt weren't too much in favour of the burgeoning social changes that were giving young people an overblown sense of their own importance, and leading them into foolish or reckless behaviour.

'Well, good heavens, Emily,' said Rosie a little later, 'you've made up for last Saturday.' The time was ten twelve. 'Is Giles with you?'

'No, he'll be home at his usual time,' said Emily. 'But Brad's here, he brought me home in a taxi. Come on, come in, Brad, and meet my mum.'

Brad entered the hall, and Rosie did indeed come face to face with Emily's Teddy boy, whose dark shiny quiff was undisturbed by the evening's exertions. His light brown thigh-length jacket was single-breasted and fastened by one button only. His double-breasted fancy waistcoat of maroon bore gleaming brass buttons. The collar of his white shirt was adorned with a dark brown bow tie, and his dark brown drainpipe trousers clung to his legs all the way down to his crêpe-soled suede shoes. However, he had surprisingly pleasing features, which cancelled out the suspect aspects of his outfit. His smile indicated he didn't feel in the least nervous. Rosie decided to be welcoming.

'Good evening,' she said.

Brad was taking stock of Emily's Ma. He hadn't expected to see a quite lovely woman with massed hair the colour of golden corn, and blue eyes that could mesmerize a guy in two shakes of a gee-gee's tail. She didn't seem at all the kind of woman to come down hard on her daughter for being a bit late home. No, she looked a knockout. Brad judged her to be about thirty-five. She was actually forty-two. He himself was sixteen. Coming to, he said, 'Good evening to you too, lady.'

'So you're Mr Bradley Thompson,' smiled Rosie, recognizing his voice.

'Lady, I don't go with mister, call me Brad, and I've got to say it's great to meet Em's mother. I kinda like mothers, I've got one of my own, and she's a real sweetie most times.'

'There are other times?' said Rosie, with Emily looking on.

'Only when she knows Aunt Totty is going to call,' said Brad. 'Aunt Totty kinda rubs Ma up the wrong way, and Ma's a mite difficult to live with then.'

'Who'd have an Aunt Totty?' said Emily, and took herself abruptly off to enter the living room and let her dad see she was home early, and therefore no-one need fuss.

'Well, Brad,' said Rosie, 'come in and meet Emily's father. He'll be happy to know you brought her home in a taxi.'

'I guess she's worth a cab now and again,' said Brad, 'she's a great girl and a great rocker.'

'And a young schoolgirl.' Rosie's reminder was gentle but pointed.

'It hardly notices,' said Brad airily, and followed Emily's striking mother into the living room.

For the next several minutes he made himself known to Emily's parents. If they thought his Teddy boy outfit was a bit bizarre, they were pleasantly surprised by his social graces. His habit of using American terminology was accepted by Rosie as part of his obvious desire to be noticed. Matt thought it the sign of a young man hooked on Hollywood Westerns. But for that matter, all kinds of people of all ages liked Westerns.

Emily played a looking-on role, and from time to time her expression conveyed a rebuke to her parents on the lines of 'There, now you can see why you don't have to fuss.'

After ten minutes, Brad was offered a cup of tea or coffee before departing. No, thanks all the same, he said, but his ma would have something for him, like a slice of pork pie and a glass of barley water.

'You can digest a slice of pie before you go to bed?' said Matt.

'No problem, mister,' said Brad. 'Ma's pies are digestible any time of the day. She's a natural in the kitchen, and could make a name

637

for herself running a cookery class. Well, I guess I'll say goodnight now. Been real homely, meeting you both, and any other Saturday when I'm hoofing it with Em, I'll see she gets to her front door in good time.'

'Don't get smart,' said Emily, and saw him out. On the doorstep he bent and gave her a kiss. 'And don't take me for granted,' she said.

'I'll call you,' said Brad.

'You'll drive Mum and Dad dotty if you phone next week as much as you did this week,' said Emily, at which moment Giles appeared. He grinned to see Brad and his sister.

'OK?' he said.

'Sure,' said Brad, 'a great evening, and I kinda like your parents. So long, Em, so long, man.' Off he went.

'What a character,' said Giles.

'He's all right when he's not talking too much,' said Emily. 'Listen, you're getting a bit close to Cindy Stevens, aren't you?'

'Well, she's grown up in pretty good form,' said Giles. He closed the front door and went to show himself to Rosie and Matt, with Emily following. His parents told him about their meeting with Bradley Thompson, and how he had arrived with Emily in the full regalia of his outfit. They didn't seem as if they'd met a bit of a layabout, which was what they had thought he might be. And they'd been quite impressed by his good manners, even if he did talk like a cowboy. Rosie said the young man had proved quite likeable, and Matt said he might well become an asset to civilization once he dropped his Teddy boy outfit off London Bridge and passed his plumbing exam.

'He won't drop his outfit off any bridge,' said Emily, 'he'll live with it for years. Crikey, don't you know Teds feel they belong to a club, and clubs can last for ever, can't they?'

Rosie had a sudden mental picture of Bradley as a bridegroom, all togged up in his long jacket, his drainpipe trousers, a waistcoat like a purple sunset and a wedding-day shine to his quiff.

'Well, for his own sake, I hope he grows out of it,' she said.

'Anyway, Mum,' said Giles, 'you and Dad didn't find him such a bad bloke?'

'In future,' said Rosie, 'I'll do as I usually do, reserve my judgement on people until I've actually met them.'

'There you are, Emily,' said Giles, 'Brad's been approved by Mum and Dad as your boy-friend.'

'No, he hasn't,' said Matt, 'he's on probation until your sister's out of her school uniform and either at university or in a job.'

'But I'll be fourteen in August,' protested Emily.

'That's no age,' said Matt, now a heavy-handed father but a cautious one. 'There's an old Dorset saying.'

'There always is,' said Rosie, 'and how many times have I told you that every one's a shocker?'

Ignoring the opposition, Matt recited in his native county's accent,

'Down by Dorset, so they say,
Perky chaps roll in the hay,
Enticing girlies every day
To join them in their saucy play.'

Emily giggled.

Rosie said, 'That's the daddy of all shockers, but I think it means keep away from boys who talk like cowboys, Emily.'

'Brad's just a laugh,' said Emily. 'I thought you could see that while he was here.'

'Well, you can go dancing with him,' said Rosie, 'but your dad and I still want you home by no later than ten thirty on your dance nights.'

'But like I mentioned, I'll be fourteen soon,' said Emily crossly.

'Yes, very young,' said Matt.

'I'm going to bed,' said Emily, 'it's no fun down here.' And off she went without saying goodnight, leaving Rosie wondering how it was that she and Matt were troubled by a rebellious daughter. The answer, she thought, lay in the fact that many modern teenagers were beginning to regard parents as out of touch with developing trends.

Chapter Twenty-two

The following day, Sunday, saw Nigel Killiner and Linda promenading again in Ruskin Park. He found it easy to talk to her, and in the sunshine of the afternoon, she found it easy to listen. After a while, however, Nigel encouraged her to tell him all about herself. What were her favourite recreations, for instance?

'Oh, I don't have what you call recreations,' she said, the flared skirt of her summer dress lightly whispering. It was no more given to making itself loudly heard than Linda was herself. 'I mean I don't play tennis or anything like that, and I don't go on country rambles. I help my mother with the cooking sometimes, and listen to gramophone records on the radio.'

'You're a home girl,' smiled Nigel, looking pleasantly relaxed in an open-necked beige sports shirt and navy blue slacks. He was bare-headed, and the widow's peak of his black hair was well defined. It gave his comfortable look a tidy appearance. 'I read somewhere that home girls get full marks as housewives.'

'Really?' said Linda. 'I might get to be a housewife one day, so tell me more.'

'I would,' said Nigel, 'if I knew more about home girls and housewives, and a lot less about cheeky schoolkids. It's my sincere opinion that most of them should never have been born.'

'Oh, that's a bit hard on them,' said Linda, enjoying the stroll, the park and the company she was keeping. Nigel really was entertaining, and despite what he had just said, she could imagine there were moments in class when his pupils were either tittering or laughing at his sense of humour. 'You make allowances for most children being naturally precocious, don't you?'

'If I didn't,' said Nigel, 'I'd end up as a cross-eyed patient in a home for the deranged.'

'How sad,' said Linda, smiling. Nigel reciprocated. Round the park they strolled, and round again, along with other leisurely promenaders, and Linda wondered if Nigel was beginning to regard himself as her beau. She was ready to have him do so, even though this was only the second time they'd been out together. Bless me, she thought, have I met my fate or does he just like walking and talking in a park on a Sunday? Certainly, neither last week nor this week had he suggested taking her dancing or to a cinema or a theatre. Of those pastimes, she felt Nigel, as a schoolteacher, would opt for a theatre, which a lot of people would consider a bit more cultural than a dance hall or a cinema.

'Penny for your thoughts,' said Nigel, and she realized she'd been musing for a couple of minutes.

'Oh, I was just thinking it'll be teatime soon,' she said.

'Good point,' said Nigel, 'let's go to the tea rooms.'

Linda said they didn't need to do that, because when he took her home he could stay for tea, like he had last Sunday. Her mother had said so. Nigel said her mother was very hospitable, and he'd be delighted to stay.

At this point, two boys, both about ten years old, approached at a run, their smothered mirth suggesting they had just teased a girl or two. On they came, and one glanced at Linda and Nigel as he rushed by. He called, 'Oi, Killy, where'd yer get yer filly?'

'Who's a clever bloke, then?' called the other.

Both boys kept going and disappeared, leaving Nigel to make the kind of comment Linda expected.

'There you are, Linda,' he said, 'that's a

definite example of two young specimens who should never have been born.'

'Oh, well,' said Linda, 'you can't stop boys catcalling. Most of them have their rowdy years.'

'What d'you say, shall I walk you home now?' asked Nigel.

'That's a very sudden offer,' said Linda, 'but I suppose it's time we did think about leaving.'

So they walked to the gate, from where Linda caught a glimpse of the two boys. They were pointing at Nigel and laughing. I suppose it is funny to them, she thought, a schoolteacher walking me round the park, like boy meets girl. Nigel, however, took no notice of the pair, apart from saying he'd sort the terrible twins out at school tomorrow. Linda asked were they twins? Yes, said Nigel, in that both of them were a pain to everyone else.

They left the park to walk to Linda's home. There Nigel was given a hospitable welcome by Annabelle and Nick, who were quite happy for him to stay to tea. Annabelle was happy because a schoolmaster was the epitome of respectability, and Nick was happy because Linda was. It was obvious she was enjoying the prelude to what might become a romantic relationship. Society might be changing, but some young women still thought in romantic terms.

So tea was served in the open air of the sunny garden. The conversation flowed, Nigel again encouraging Linda to put in her tenpenny-worth, and Nick, a football fan, talking about the local amateur club, Dulwich Hamlet, until Annabelle reminded him this was the cricket season, and football was out of order.

Linda ventured to tell her parents that two of Nigel's pupils had catcalled him in the park.

'In the park on a Sunday afternoon?' said Nick with a broad grin. 'That'll alarm the park-keepers. They'll think about smothering the kids for the sake of peace and quiet. It's always been that way in Ruskin Park. As far as I know, they've never allowed any kind of high jinks, especially on a Sunday. What will you do to those kids, Nigel?'

'Smother them and save the park-keepers a job,' said Nigel good-humouredly, and that raised a laugh.

Annabelle took covert note of the developing relationship between Linda and her school-teacher friend, and she thought how well matched they were, the amenable nature of her daughter complemented by Nigel's easy approach to life and people.

The chink of cups and saucers, the appeal of home-made scones and cake, and four people all in tune with the sunny afternoon, made for very pleasant moments. By the end, Nigel was as comfortably ensconced as if he were one of the family. Before he left, he asked Linda if next Sunday, for a change, she'd like to go with him to Hyde Park. Linda enthused at the idea, and said that in Hyde Park they could count on the absence of rowdy kids from his school.

'That's a point,' said Nigel.

'But what about young rowdies from other schools?' she asked.

'Don't tempt Providence,' said Nigel.

That evening, Joe Chambers asked his wife Lily, not for the first time, if she had something on her mind. It was, he said, making him feel he wasn't there. Lily came back with the riposte that more often than not he actually wasn't there, he was either doing overtime or playing darts.

'Overtime pays,' said Joe. 'Come on, there is something on your mind, so give.'

'Well, if you must know,' said Lily, 'it's my housekeeping money. I've been sure for some days that somewhere or other I either lost a ten-bob note or had it pinched. Mind, I don't know how it could've been pinched because it was in me purse and me purse was in me handbag, and no-one could've got at any of the money unless they pinched the purse out of me handbag, but it's still there.'

'You sure the ten-bob note was there in the first place?' said Joe.

'There, I thought losing it might upset you,' said Lily, and continued with her fairy story. 'I've been worrying about it since it happened, and it's not doing my peace of mind much good.'

'Well, cheer up and start living again,' said Joe. 'What with your wages and mine, plus a bit of overtime, you don't need to make yerself sick over ten bob. It's not as if you lose it every week. Forget it, eh?'

'Oh, all right, thanks,' said Lily. 'I didn't like having to tell you because it makes me look careless, and after all ten bob is ten bob, not fourpence. Still, if you think I needn't worry, I won't, but I'll be a lot more careful in the future.' She carried on in this vein, swamping Joe with words, most of which began to go in one ear and out the other, while all the time her mind wasn't on any ten-bob note, but Mr Sammy Adams. It was no good, she'd fallen in love and something had to be done about it. Lord, if only she could be sure she wouldn't be interrupted if she spoke to him in his office again, then she'd have a go.

She looked up as her flow of words, all for Joe's benefit, dried up, and what did she see?

She saw Joe with his head on his chest, fast asleep, the *News of the World* on his lap.

Husbands. What got into them that they couldn't talk to their wives?

Monday morning, and Sammy and Susie were at King's Cross railway station with Phoebe and Philip. Sammy had made the journey in his car so that he and Susie could see the young people off to begin their new life. The train was in and waiting, emitting little puffs of restless steam as if impatient to get going. Phoebe was by no means impatient herself. She was facing up to the wrench of saying goodbye to her adoptive parents in the knowledge that her home would no longer be with them. Like Rosie, the adopted daughter of Boots and his first wife Emily, Phoebe had known years of caring love, the kind that fully compensated for an unhappy beginning to life.

'I'll write lots,' she said, her eyes visibly misty.

'And there's always the phone,' said Susie.

'Do we have the phone?' asked Phoebe of Philip. She looked engaging in a light summer coat and a pillbox hat, and he looked like every girl's lanky dreamboat in his RAF uniform and cap.

'Yup, we have the phone,' said Philip, 'and we pay the bills.'

'Oh, phone bills are never much,' said Phoebe, 'and anyway, I can reverse charges when I phone Mum and Dad, can't I, Dad?'

'Be my permanent guest,' said Sammy, who knew when a financial outlay was worthwhile. He had a bit of a lump in his throat, while Susie was as misty-eyed as Phoebe.

'Phoebe kitten,' said Philip, 'I think we'd better do our boarding act. The train's due out in a few minutes.' He had a first-class railway warrant for both of them, and had already taken their luggage to the relevant compartment.

'Oh, I suppose we'd better,' said Phoebe. She gave way to emotion then by closely hugging her parents in turn, and hanging onto each of them for a few seconds. Her goodbyes were somewhat muffled. So were Susie's. And Sammy had to cough to clear his lump.

'Good luck, pet,' he said. 'Good luck, Philip.' He shook hands with his new son-in-law.

'Thanks a bundle to both of you for giving me Phoebe,' said Philip, and kissed Susie before shepherding his bride onto the train. The platform was clearing of passengers, and the guard had his flag and whistle at the ready. As

Phoebe entered the compartment she had a sudden attack of nostalgia for the life she was leaving behind. She let down the window, put her head out and smiled wet-eyed at Sammy and Susie, who were close by.

'Love you, Mum, love you, Dad,' she said huskily.

'It's always been mutual,' said Sammy, who had another lump in his throat as Susie reached and touched Phoebe's hand.

A whistle sounded, the engine blew steam and the train began to move. Philip and Phoebe were both at the compartment window, waving to Sammy and Susie.

There they go, thought Sammy.

It's their own lives now, thought Susie.

We've seen them all go off to their own homes, said Sammy to himself. Daniel and Patsy, Bess and Jeremy, Paula and her Italian heart-throb, Jimmy and Clare, and now Phoebe and Philip. I feel sort of deprived. He took off his hat and waved it as the train slowly disappeared and took Phoebe and Philip with it.

'Well, they're on their own now, Sammy,' said Susie.

'Susie, how old are you?' asked Sammy, as they left the platform.

'Gentlemen don't ask ladies their age,' said

Susie, 'especially not in public.' They were skirting numerous individuals weaving about in different directions. London railway stations always provided telling examples of how arriving and departing people could get mixed up with those merely waiting.

'Well, between you and me in private, Susie,' murmured Sammy, 'you don't look like anyone's middle-aged mother. No, more like a female woman of thirty, for which I admire you considerable.'

'Thank you, Sammy,' said Susie, 'but what's on your mind, if it isn't Phoebe?'

'Well, I was thinking, Susie, are we still young enough to start another family?'

People hurrying into the station turned their heads to look at two people coming out, a well-dressed man and a nicely dressed woman. The woman was laughing aloud.

In public.

Sammy drove Susie home, then went on to the Camberwell Green offices. Once there, he asked Tim and Daniel if they'd received any kind of official letter about the fire. The answer was no. Tim said it was a bit soon, anyway, and Daniel said the only official letter he wanted to arrive on his desk was the one advising them that the fire had started accidentally and they could therefore rightfully make their claim on the insurance company.

'I couldn't agree more,' said Sammy, 'you're a bright lad, Daniel.'

'I could point out I'm now thirty,' said Daniel, 'but I won't in case you don't believe it. Did Phoebe and Philip catch their train on time?'

'In good time, actually,' said Sammy.

'How was their honeymoon?' enquired Tim.

'Don't ask me,' said Sammy, 'send them a postcard care of the RAF and ask for an answer.'

Chapter Twenty-three

At the offices on Tuesday, Sammy and Boots were inspecting the conversion job that would turn the ground-floor shop and storeroom into a canteen and an extra office. The work was in its final stages, and Sammy and Boots both liked what they saw, the canteen invitingly bright and spacious, and the kitchen and counter clean and gleaming. Boots said he'd be happy to lunch there from time to time, but would keep mainly to his ingrained habit of enjoying a beer and a sandwich or a salad at the pub opposite.

'Well, I've got a habit of having to go out for business lunches now and again,' said Sammy, 'so would you mind telling me what ingrained means?'

'That one gets stuck in a groove,' said Boots.

'I thought so,' said Sammy, 'but I wouldn't use ingrained meself. I'm not educated enough. I'd just say what you just said, that I'm stuck with it.'

'So am I,' said Boots.

'Who's playing a comic?' asked Sammy. 'By the way, Rachel has found a woman who'll be assistant to the cook. It's all going well, no headaches at all – no, button up, I shouldn't have said that, it's a sure way to muck up progress.'

'Touch wood, old lad,' said Boots, and Sammy touched the main door. He wasn't keen on inviting trouble or any kind of a headache. He'd lived uneasily during the days when a strike was threatened, and he was now having to live with the consequences of the Southend fire. What else had given him a headache? Oh, yes, that peculiar female bookkeeper, Mrs Lily Chambers, a little while ago. Pity about her peculiarity, because she was a good worker.

He made his way upstairs to his office, and of all things, who should be waiting at his door but the funny female herself.

'Oh, good morning, Mr Sammy,' trilled Lily, 'I was hoping to see you as I've got something to show you.'

'A dubious bank statement?' said Sammy, as he entered his office.

Lily, following him in, closed the door and said, playfully, 'Oh, no, nothng like that. It's this.' She placed a Marks & Spencer carrier bag on the desk, reached into it and drew out something black and silky. She shook it out and Sammy found himself mesmerized by what it was, a black nightie trimmed with lace. 'Isn't it sexy?' said Lily, hoping there would be no interruptions.

'What's it doing in my office?' asked Sammy, squaring up to the necessity of giving her another talking-to.

Lily sighed, let her eyes go soulful, and whispered, 'Wouldn't you like to see me in it, Mr Sammy?'

'Where?' asked Sammy, as she placed the nightie against her female figure. The item was sexy all right. 'Yes, where?'

'Oh, we could go to a country hotel one evening when my husband's playing darts,' said Lily, proving that because Joe left her alone so much she'd gone potty.

'I'm not going anywhere,' said Sammy, setting aside good humour to make himself understood, 'but you'll be walking the plank if you carry on like this. I'm happily married, and I don't need any piece of sugar in a black nightie. The idea embarrasses me considerable. What's got into your brainbox, might I ask?'

'Mr Sammy, I'm in love,' said Lily.

'No you're not, and anyway it's not allowed, and I ain't in favour,' said Sammy. 'Put that nightie away and forget having a bit of what you fancy with me or any other bloke except your old man. Does he know about your problem?'

'No, course not,' said Lily, 'he's got his darts and I keep me problem to meself – oh, except now I'm sharing it with you.'

'Leave off and be your age,' said Sammy. 'And stop looking at me as if I've just been turned into a fruit bun. Go back to your work and make it your only interest in office hours. If you don't, I'll have to do what I won't want to do, and that's give you your cards.'

'Mr Sammy, you wouldn't do that, would you?' Lily looked upset, very. 'You wouldn't give me the sack, would you?'

'If you don't put that nightie away and out of sight,' said Sammy, 'it'll happen here and now.'

'Oh, that sounds awful hard on a girl,' said Lily.

'You're not a girl, you're a woman and your old man's wife,' said Sammy, 'and you're also a good bookkeeper. It's better you live with that than some cock-eyed idea about what you'd like to happen in a country hotel. Are you with me, Lily?'

'Oh, Lor',' said Lily, 'I didn't think it would come to this, Mr Sammy.' The black nightie was drooping forlornly, and Lily herself wasn't exactly at her brightest. 'I didn't think you'd talk about giving me the sack.'

'Well, I am, and I will if you don't get your head in order,' said Sammy, pretty sure that to be kind he had to be tough. He knew she enjoyed her job, and a threat to hand her a week's notice had every chance of scaring her out of her dotty notions. 'Now, go back to your desk and behave yourself.'

'Yes, all right,' said Lily, dreams of romantic high jinks crushed by this, the second time Mr Sammy had spoken to her in an unsympathetic way. She walked to the door, the nightie back in its bag, and she couldn't help thinking this was the one time when there had been no interruptions and yet it had all ended in a wounding negative.

However, once she was back at her desk, a succession of book entries played their soothing part, and the black silk nightie lay unseen and unspoiled in its carrier bag.

Joe was in when Lily arrived home from her job. He'd been working an early shift. Usually, on early shift, he stayed to do overtime. He hoped it would help them to save enough for a car. Not many postmen had a car in addition to a wife.

'Welcome home, me love,' he said, 'I've just made a pot of tea. Like a cup? Yes, course you would. Sit down and I'll pour you one.'

Lily blinked. She seldom received a welcome

like this. Her suspicions pointed her at a reason.

'Oh, I know what this is all about,' she said, 'you've got another darts match tonight and you know you're going off for the evening. Don't you care about leaving me alone so much?'

Joe poured the tea, put one knob of sugar in the cup, and pushed cup and saucer along the kitchen table in the direction of his wife.

'Come on, Lily,' he said, 'sit down and drink this. It's nice and hot and fresh. And listen, about darts—'

'I don't want to hear nothing about any darts,' said Lily, but she sat down. 'Darts are all you live for.'

'Only three times a week,' said Joe.

'Yes, and your overtime or your late shift at other times make sure I hardly ever see you of an evening,' said Lily. But she took a sip of the hot and welcome tea.

'Well, I want you to know I'm giving up darts,' said Joe.

'You're what?' said Lily.

'I'm resigning from the pub team,' said Joe.

'I don't believe it,' said Lily.

'I've been thinking,' said Joe, 'and I've decided it's up to me, as your lawful wedded, to spend more time with you. I went into Palmer's shop on me way home and ordered a television set on hire-purchase terms that won't do no harm to your housekeeping money, even if it sets us back a bit on getting a car. It'll be delivered and set up tomorrer. And tomorrer evening, you and me can sit and have our first telly evening together. How about that, eh, Lily?'

For about twenty seconds, Lily was lost for words. Then she said, 'We're going to have television and you're not going to darts any more?'

'That's it,' said Joe. 'Except for late shifts and when I'm doing a bit of evening overtime, I'll be watching the telly with you. As for me beer, I'll stock up with a few bottles of light ale.'

'What's brought all this on?' asked Lily, now making much of her cup of tea.

'I told you, I've been thinking,' said Joe, 'and I've concluded, Lily, that you're more important than me darts. It's a poor man who can't enjoy evenings at home with his better half, specially if he can still enjoy his beer.'

'I just don't know what to say,' said Lily, 'except are you sure you're all right and not feeling a bit queer, like?'

'I'm fine,' said Joe, 'and I don't have any quarrel with me thinking. So how d'you feel about things now?'

'I can hardly take it in,' said Lily. But she was conscious that Joe's words were softening the blow of being finally rejected by Mr Sammy. 'Well, having a television and you home most evenings is a bit of a surprise, I can tell you, but it's a nice surprise.'

'That's my girl,' said Joe. 'Listen, what's in that carrier bag?'

'Pardon?' said Lily.

'What is it, something you've bought for yourself?' asked Joe.

'Well, I'm glad you asked,' said Lily. 'It makes a nice change, being asked about me personal shopping. Yes, it's something I bought for meself.'

'Let's have a shufti,' said Joe.

'All right,' said Lily. Present circumstances being an improvement on what had gone before, she took the nightie out of the bag, stood up and draped it over her front. Joe visibly goggled.

'Eh?' he said.

'Like it, do you?' said Lily, feeling a whole lot better.

'Saucy sailors,' said Joe, 'it's a black French nightie. Lily, you going to bed in it?'

'Not now, not right now, but later,' said Lily.

'Not too much later,' said Joe. 'I mean, I can hardly wait, can I?'

'Well, I'm blessed,' said Lily, 'you're remembering I'm alive, Joe Chambers.'

Sammy, meanwhile, had said not a word to anybody about Lily Chambers being definitely off her rocker. He thought keeping it under his hat best for both of them, in the hope that what he had said to her this time would finally cure her of her desire for a bit of what she thought she fancied in a country hotel. Imagine her coming out with that in working hours.

Women. Mother O'Grady, what a funny lot they were. Except Susie, of course. And Phoebe had never been off her rocker. It had been a pleasure, having her and Philip at home for the weekend, even if a bit gloomy watching her disappear on that train yesterday. He hoped she'd like married quarters and not come up against too many rules and regulations. In the army, navy and air force, everything had to be done by numbers or regulations. It was a wonder that Boots's time in the army hadn't turned him into a filing cabinet.

Chapter Twenty-four

Tuesday afternoon.

In a photographic studio above an Italian grocery shop in Soho, Miss Maureen Brown, known to pin-up fans as London's girl next door, was getting ready for her sitting under the auspices of Mr Morton Fraser, whose real name was Charlie Ellis. The dressing room, brightly lit, was a welcome treasure trove, with its rich supply of all kinds of fine-quality cosmetics laid out on a dressing table. They enabled Maureen to ensure her make-up was perfect.

The first outfit awaited her. It was right up to the mark fashion-wise, a full mid-blue skirt, stiff petticoats, a black bodice-style top with a plunging neckline, black nylons, a white half-bra and frilly white panties. Everything was new, so Maureen had no qualms about wearing any of the items. She changed in front of a lovely full-length wall mirror, a great help in ensuring she was satisfied with her look. Her ponytail hairdo went perfectly with the outfit, although the plunging neckline of the top and the skimpiness of the half-bra revealed more of her bosom than she had bargained for. But she was not prudish about it. She supposed that while Amos liked to focus on her legs, of which he was proud, Mr Morton Fraser was going to help her show off her figure, of which he was admiring. On her arrival, he'd said he was dee-lighted to see her and to classify her as a 36–24–36 girlie. She asked how did he guess? Experience and sensitive eyesight, he said.

When she was ready, Maureen entered the studio. It was spacious, but the only furniture was a small corner table on which stood cartons containing rolls of film, a central round-topped table and an old-fashioned sofa with red and gold upholstery. There was also another full-length wall mirror to enable her to check her appearance from time to time. Mr Morton Fraser – Charlie Ellis – received her with hearty acknowledgement of her turnout.

'Girlie,' he said, 'you're great and we're going to have a great session. Sit your fair self on that table.'

'Sit on it?' said Maureen.

'Sure. Plant your derrière on it and cross your ankles.'

Maureen did as he wanted, and the session

664

began. He posed her this way and that, making the most of her legs before moving in on her tantalizing cleavage. The glamour came from her, and the studio soundtrack from him, for he talked all the time to let her know how photogenic she was. Maureen was sure the bodice-style top with its plunging neckline was committing her to the kind of poses new to her. The wall mirror confirmed it. Still, she was in the mood, a glamorous-minded mood. After all, cleavage was ultra glam, even if it wasn't quite in keeping with a girl next door.

He posed her next on the sofa, and in a kind of languid, feline way that made her look like an old-style Hollywood vamp, except that her outfit was far from old style. He began to take close-ups of her plunging neckline.

'Fantastic – great – super-duper – love it – don't go away – stay like that – got you.'

'Crikey,' said Maureen, 'I don't know what my dad's going to say about these kind of photos.'

'Take it from me, girlie,' said Charlie, 'it's your photographers and pin-up fans who'll make your career, not your dad.'

Maureen accepted that. She was, in any case, under the spell of a real West End professional. Her bus ride to Soho, her walk down Old Compton Street, and the fact that she actually

665

had an appointment in the heart of London's glamorous playground, all planted the seeds of excitement. Well, Old Compton Street wasn't like Camberwell Green, where Amos had his studio, it was much more intriguing. Even the people seemed different. She'd noticed several Italian-looking characters, all of whom wore black trilby hats and shiny shoes, and one or two very flashy-looking women of indeterminate age. She wasn't so naive that she didn't know Walworth people would have called the latter tarts or old pros. Still, you couldn't deny everything had atmosphere, whereas the only places of interest in Camberwell were the Camberwell Palace theatre, two cinemas and a Lyons teashop.

After the sofa shots, her real West End professional photographer asked her to change into a second outfit of blue jeans and a red-and-white checked shirt, together with a half-bra the colour of golden wheat and a cowboy's hat. Maureen asked if jeans would look glamorous.

'They will, girlie, they will,' said Mr Morton Fraser, 'providing you don't do all the shirt buttons up, if you get me.'

'Oh, I get you,' said Maureen, 'it's more cleavage shots.'

'In your case, lovey, more is plenty, and plenty's not what every girlie can lay claim to.'

So she went back to the dressing room and changed outfits. She left the top three buttons of the shirt undone, did an unnecessary repair job to her make-up, put on the felt Stetson, regarded herself in the long mirror and returned to the studio, where Mr Morton Fraser again received her with enthusiasm.

'Well, here's a glad picture of a girl cowboy,' he said. 'All we need now is a horse.'

'Don't tell me you've got one here,' said Maureen.

'What I will tell you is that while we've got you, we don't need any gee-gee. See that chair, Gloria? Sit on it like a cowboy.'

'Gloria?' said Maureen. 'I'm not Gloria.'

Mr Morton Fraser shook his head at himself. A model who called herself Gloria was a do-it-all for the Continentals, one of his regulars.

'I'm not all there,' he said, 'I'm intoxicated, believe me, by how cute you look in that cowgirl outfit. Anyway, sit on that chair like a cowboy, eh?'

A pine chair with a low back had made an appearance. Maureen sat down on it like a cowboy, facing the back and planting her legs on either side of the seat. A new succession of poses began, all aimed at proving how cute a cowgirl could look in an unbuttoned shirt, a skimpy bra and a Stetson hat. The low back

667

of the chair left her shirt and cleavage un-
impeded, and she had the Stetson tipped back
to ensure no shadow darkened her face. Mr
Morton Fraser's enthusiastic verbosity accompanied every click of his shutter.

'I tell you no lie – that's the tops – love it, love
it – what kept you away from me, girlie? Turn
your head a little to the right – good on yer –
beautiful – take a bow.' And so on.

Maureen was used to a photographer's
verbiage, the kind that was supposed to make a
model feel she was the one he'd been waiting for
all his life. Even so, it was always helpful,
especially coming from this larger-than-life West
End bloke.

Having satisfied himself that he'd taken all
the shots he wanted of her as a cowgirl, he sent
her back into the dressing room to change
into her third and final outfit, an off-shoulder
low-cut evening dress of midnight blue, with a
narrow waist and flared skirt. The bra, matching the dress, was built-in, with the result that
the upper curves of her well-developed bosom
hardly hid their light under the midnight blue.

'Oh, help,' she murmured, studying her
reflection in the mirror, 'I hope he doesn't pose
me in a way that'll make me fall out. Oh, well.'
She made adjustments to the dress, to her hair
and to the dress again.

In the office, where three of the four walls sprouted filing cabinets, the photographer's assistant was busy cataloguing contact sheets. He looked up from his desk as someone entered.

'Afternoon,' said someone, 'I'm Amos Anderson. Is Charlie busy?'

'Mr Morton Fraser, if yer don't mind,' said Curly Harris, the assistant.

'Oh, Charlie's an old friend of mine, ain't he?' said Amos. 'He's spoken of me, I expect.'

'What did you say your name was?' asked Curly, dark, foxy and protective. This bloke could be a copper. Coppers in Soho were always poking their noses into some legit business. Well, any business was legit if it had customers.

'I'm Amos Anderson, a fellow photographer.'

'You're him?' said Curly. 'It's one of your models he's busy with just now, right?'

'I'm Miss Brown's manager,' said Amos. 'I'd like to see how she's getting on. My privilege. Can I go through?'

'OK, but knock first,' said Curly.

Amos went through to the studio. On the door was a notice in heavy black capitals.

KEEP OUT AT ALL TIMES

Amos knocked. He was there for a very specific purpose, having had second thoughts this morning about Charlie Ellis and the way he earned most of his bread.

'Whoever that is, bugger off,' called Charlie.

'It's Amos.'

'Eh? Look, I'm busy.'

'I know. I'm only here to see how you're getting on with my best model.'

The door opened, and Charlie thrust his head out.

'I'm doing great, she's doing great, we're both doing great, so what's your problem, old buddy?' he asked.

'No problem,' said Amos genially, 'I'd just like to sit in on a couple of shots, and see what she's looking like. I should have a personal interest in her promotion to a West End studio? I do, you bet.'

'All right, come in for a couple of ticks,' said Charlie, 'I'm just about to photograph her in classy evening gear. She's got a prize figure.'

'Yes, 36–24–36,' said Amos, and entered. Maureen was still in the dressing room, so he looked casually around. He noted the furniture and the corner table on which lay about a dozen completed rolls of film, some cartons containing new film, and, to one side, three more completed rolls. He further noted the full-length, highly polished wall mirror.

In came Maureen, looking stunning in the evening dress, the built-in bra giving her noble uplift. Amos had to admit she was glamour personified, with all the advantages of her nineteen tender years.

'Well, look at you, Amos, where did you come from?' she asked.

'Just passing by, so I thought I'd drop in and see how you were getting on,' said Amos.

'Well, that's ever so nice of you,' said Maureen, 'and I think I'm getting on fine. Am I, Mr Fraser?'

'Great,' said Charlie, 'you're top of the bill. And that outfit is just the job, and not half. I'll pose her conventional to start with, Amos. You take a seat on the sofa for a couple of minutes.'

'Sure,' smiled Amos, although he knew he'd been given his marching orders. Charlie didn't want anyone ferreting around, especially a fellow photographer. He posed Maureen standing, the round table behind her, her hands on its edge, her body leaning slightly backwards. This enhanced the uplift. Amos, seated on the sofa, smiled again. Charlie knew his stuff. Maureen looked like everybody's favourite pin-up for sure, the evening dress real flattering to her figure.

A knock on the door preceded Curly's voice.

'Hey, Mr Fraser, there's a client wanting to see yer.'

'I'm busy, he'll have to wait.'

'I know you're busy,' called Curly, 'and I

wouldn't be interrupting yer, only the client's come a long way and he's a regular.'

'Oh, right,' said Charlie, getting the message. 'Excuse me for a couple of shakes, Maureen, there's some clients some of us can't keep waiting. Amos, you're going now?'

'I'll follow you in a tick, won't I?' said Amos, coming to his feet. 'I need to get back to Camberwell pretty quick, anyway.'

'Right,' said Charlie. He gave Amos a look, and he glanced at Maureen. Both smiled in return, and out he went to see to the client who'd come a long way. From Amsterdam.

'Don't ask questions, Maureen,' said Amos. 'Just tell me what's on the other side of this wall mirror.'

'The dressing room,' said Maureen, 'with a matching mirror.'

'That's a fact, is it?' said Amos, and made a quick inspection of the dressing room. He noted the mirror, and then made a keener inspection of the one in the studio. He knew what it was all about then, a two-way contraption with a concealed button which, when pressed, would turn the studio mirror into a window. Charlie Ellis was down in the dirt. It was a disgusting practice, keeping models unaware that he was photographing them when they were dressing and undressing. And they remained unaware,

672

for such photographs were sold abroad by Charlie, and never seen in the UK. Amos wished he had never met the man. 'Change into your own clothes, Maureen,' he said.

'What?' said Maureen. 'But me and Mr Fraser, we're not finished yet.'

'Yes, you are,' said Amos, 'and if you need an explanation, little lady, just see this.' He found and pressed the hidden button, and the mirror became a window that revealed the brightly lit dressing room.

'Oh, the rotten swine,' breathed Maureen, 'no wonder he put me in different outfits so's he could watch me changing.'

'I hate to say so, but I think it amounted to more than a peepshow,' said Amos. He pressed the button again, and the window became a mirror once more. 'We're leaving,' he said, 'so go and put your own clothes on.'

Maureen, flushed with fiery anger and not a little humiliation, rushed into the dressing room. Amos looked again at the corner table on which lay about a dozen spools of completed film, and three to one side. He slipped the three into his pocket, and replaced them with three from the large number, of which there were actually fourteen. Charlie had done his pin-up work at length, and Amos didn't doubt that the contacts would all be acceptable.

Out came Maureen, ready and willing to leave. Quietly, Amos took her by the arm and they left the studio, bypassing the office and the subdued sound of voices, to make a silent way down to the exit at the side of the Italian grocery. Outside, in the busy street, Maureen drew a deep breath.

'Amos—'

'Wait till we're in my car,' said Amos, 'it's parked in Shaftesbury Avenue. I should be glad I decided to look in on your sitting? I am.'

'So am I, even if it means I won't get my fee of five guineas,' said Maureen, still flushed and angry.

'We'll see, we'll see,' said Amos. 'I wasn't born yesterday, was I, and nor were you.'

Chapter Twenty-five

On the way to Camberwell in his car, Amos explained exactly why it was necessary for Maureen to have nothing more to do with Charlie Ellis, who called himself Morton Fraser but was far from being a gentleman or even a reputable professional.

'In my pocket,' he said, 'I've got three rolls of film, which I suspect are shots taken of you through that two-way mirror while you were changing outfits. It's best you know that—'

'But if you knew he wasn't what he ought to be,' said Maureen, still very upset, 'why did you agree to me sitting for him?'

'I did think he was going to play straight with you, didn't I?' said Amos, driving with care towards Waterloo Bridge. Motor traffic in the West End and the City was far more intrusive than pre-war. 'About lunchtime today I had second thoughts. I began to worry, didn't I? Get up to Soho, I said to myself, and see what's happening with my girl next door.'

'I'm glad you did worry,' said Maureen.

Amos said that as soon as he saw that studio wall mirror and three rolls of completed film set aside, he had his suspicions. But he didn't want to create uproar, not on the premises he didn't, and decided it was best to do a quiet bunk with her when Charlie's absence offered the opportunity. She wouldn't have liked a stand-up set-to with everything being shouted out. That would have added to her embarrassment, wouldn't it? In his opinion, went on Amos, not half it wouldn't. Maureen said she was grateful to him for coming all the way to the studio to find out what was happening. But was he sure the three rolls of film really did have shots of her dressing and undressing?

Driving over the bridge, Amos said no, he couldn't be sure, so he was going to develop them and find out. If they turned out to be illegit photos of her, he'd destroy them.

'And I'll have a short word with Charlie, won't I?' he said.

'I think he's going to come after you,' said Maureen, as they entered Waterloo Road and headed for the Elephant and Castle junction. Post-war developments of bomb sites made their mark on the eye. 'I think he might turn out quite nasty, especially if you're wrong about the photos.'

'I've got instincts, ain't I?' said Amos. 'You bet I have, as well as knowing a bit about Charlie and how he earns the butter on his bread.'

'What d'you mean?' asked Maureen, not too knowledgeable about what some photographers could really get up to. But she was coming to realize that the highly dubious could exist along with the reputable. 'Yes, what d'you mean, Amos?'

'I mean, Maureen, that if these shots are what I suspect,' said Amos, 'then Charlie would have sold them to a Continental publisher of naughty girlie magazines, the kind that are banned in the UK, and you would never have known anything about it.'

'Oh, the rotten beast,' said Maureen, 'and would he have sold the decent shots to UK mags?'

'You bet,' said Amos, 'he had you looking like a hundred guineas in that evening dress. That wasn't for the sake of kidding you, he had legit earnings in mind as well as the other kind.'

'What upsets me as well as those mirrors,' said Maureen, 'is losing out on the five guineas.'

'I'll see to things, don't worry,' said Amos, feeling for her blush-making afternoon and her bitter disappointment. 'So we won't give up on that five guineas, you bet we won't. We might even up your dues.'

'Get more, you mean?' said Maureen. 'But I bet he's not going to pay me a penny now, not after me walking out on him.'

'We'll see, we'll see,' said Amos. She was back on her home ground as he entered Walworth Road, since she lived in Wansey Street, close to the town hall. 'Would you like me to drop you at Wansey Street?'

'No, I want to come to your studio with you,' said Maureen, 'because I've got a feeling you're going to develop those films as soon as you get there.'

'So I am, Maureen, so I am, ain't I?'

But when they reached his studio, his lady assistant, who was about to leave, since the time was just after five thirty, said that the phone had been ringing repeatedly for the last half-hour, and each call had been from Mr Ellis. Would Mr Anderson please ring him now? Amos said he'd see to it at once, and his assistant left. No sooner had she disappeared than the office phone rang. And it sounded like an angry ring. Amos looked at the instrument.

'You'll have to answer it,' said Maureen.

Amos picked it up.

'Anderson's photographic studio here,' he said, 'can I help you?'

The response was a tidal wave of foaming threats and oaths from Charlie, all on account of Amos having the gall to remove a model for no given reason while his back was turned, which was a bleedin' breech of professional etiquette and the law as well. For said act he could be sued down to the last coin in his bank account.

'And don't think it won't happen. What the hell did you think you were bleedin' doing?'

'I'll ring you and let you know,' said Amos. He had to get those films developed before he had the necessary ammunition to fire at Charlie, and that depended on whether or not the films were what he suspected they might be. He'd made a mental note of the fact that Charlie hadn't mentioned there were some missing. He hadn't noticed, obviously. 'Yes, I'll let you know in the morning.'

'You'll let me know now, you hear, you bugger?'

'Tomorrow morning,' said Amos, 'and don't try calling me any more, the phone will be off the hook. Sorry, Charlie.' And he put the receiver back to cut the call before placing it on the desk, where it lay looking as if it had fallen out of bed.

'What did he say?' asked Maureen.

'Nothing for your ears, m'dear,' said Amos. 'Now, you take it easy while I get busy in the darkroom.'

'Shall I make us some tea?' asked Maureen. She knew where everything was.

'What a great girl,' said Amos tenderly. 'One lump of sugar for me.'

Sometime later, in the office, he showed her several of the negatives, of which there were thirty-six in all. Maureen held them up to the light, since Amos had not printed any contacts. He wanted nothing to do with seeing the shots in stark black and white, not even as small two-by-two-inch contacts. Stark was the word all right, if the negatives were anything to go by. His eye was sharp and practised.

'Oh, Lor',' breathed Maureen. Just three or four negatives were enough to make out that she'd been photographed while undressing. In another one she was sure she was down to the nuddy. 'I'd never have believed anyone could take such a rotten advantage of a girl. He's disgusting.' Maureen was flushed again, very much so. 'Amos, what're you going to do with all these negatives?'

'First, I'll talk to Charlie tomorrow morning, won't I?' said Amos. 'Then at the right time I'll burn them.'

'You're not going to make prints, are you?' said Maureen. Amos gave her a sad look. 'Oh, sorry, Amos, you wouldn't have gone to all the trouble you did if you— Well, you know.'

'Look in again tomorrow morning about coffee hour,' said Amos, 'then I'll let you know how much Charlie is going to pay you for your time and trouble.'

'You think he'll do that?'

'Yes, I think so.'

'I'll get my five guineas?'

'More, I hope.'

'You'll frighten him?'

'I'll blackmail him.'

'Amos, you'll do that?'

'All's fair in war, ain't it?'

'Blackmail as well?'

'You bet, not half,' said Amos.

The phone call next day didn't take all morning. Amos had Charlie with his back to the wall in two minutes flat, which was pretty good going where fly Charlie was concerned. He was told he not only had to pay Maureen ten guineas or else, he also had to pay her twenty per cent of what he earned selling the straight pin-ups, again or else. Or else what? The negatives, said Amos, would be shown to Maureen's dad.

'You're a traitor to your profession, you bleeder,' breathed Charlie.

'And you, Charlie, you grieve me,' said Amos. 'You don't have any ethics or principles, and you know it. In view of which, I want a legal guarantee from you that you'll pay up.'

'Or Daddy's going to find out, is he?' That was a sneer from Charlie.

'Daddy will,' said Amos, 'and what you'll find out is that Daddy's got muscle.'

'Do I get those negatives back?' asked Charlie, rocking quite a bit.

'Is that a serious question?' asked Amos.

'Don't you have any principles yourself, you punk?' bawled Charlie. 'You nicked those films.'

'So I did, and it's your hard luck, ain't it?' said Amos. 'That's all for now. Just make sure I get that guarantee.'

'Sod you.'

'Or else,' said Amos, and closed the conversation.

When Maureen arrived at coffee time, Amos took her into the studio away from the ears of his receptionist, and told her that he'd talked to Charlie, and that Charlie was going to settle at ten guineas for the sitting and twenty per cent of what he earned for selling the straight shots.

682

'Amos, honest?' Maureen glowed.

'Honest,' said Amos, 'and I'm personally advancing you five of the ten guineas this morning. After all, it was my doing that sent you to Charlie.'

'Crikey, I'm thrilled about the money,' said Maureen, 'but I'd still like to dot that Charlie beast one in the eye.'

'Did you tell your parents anything?' asked Amos.

'Not likely,' said Maureen, 'or my dad would've gone out and bought a shotgun. I kept quiet about that mirror, I just said I hoped me poses in different outfits would come out great and get me on a front cover.'

'Wise girl,' said Amos, 'we don't want shotguns sounding off, do we? Shotguns are noisy. And damaging.'

'Oh, not half,' said Maureen. 'Amos, I'm ever so grateful for all your help.'

'I should turn a blind eye? Not on your life,' said Amos, and handed her five one-pound notes and five shillings as the promised advance on what she could expect to receive from Charlie.

'Oh, thanks ever so,' said Maureen, 'I'm feeling better now, Amos.'

'Good,' said Amos, 'feeling better is what we both like.'

Chapter Twenty-six

'Hi, sugar.' Brad was on the line.

'Mum said it was you again.' Emily was at the other end.

'She's a cookie, your ma,' said Brad.

'Don't you do anything of an evening except make phone calls?' asked Emily.

'I sure don't,' said Brad, 'I only call you, and it's more than worthwhile if your ma answers first. What a lady. Anyway, doll, what're you doing right now?'

'I'm just finishing my homework,' said Emily.

'School homework again?' said Brad. 'That's sad, baby, considering you're ready to make your mark on civilization. Say, when d'you leave school?'

'I'll be going on to higher education when I leave my present school,' said Emily. 'My parents think I'm just about bright enough for university.'

'Hey, baby, that's for eggheads,' protested

Brad, 'and you're no egghead. You're built for living.'

'Yes, but parents always have the last word until a girl comes of age,' said Emily. 'Most girls have to do what they're told, just as if they're still children. And parents always expect us to behave like they behaved a hundred years ago. Change passes them by, poor things.'

Brad said that sounded painful, and something he wouldn't have expected of her ma, who looked great enough to be able to rock around the clock with the best of guys and dolls, like he'd mentioned before. Emily asked if he had a fancy for her mum. Brad said that seeing she herself was the most fanciable doll in the UK, he didn't need to answer her question. It was just that her ma looked something special, considering she was a parent. Parents usually look old, he said. Emily said it wasn't that they looked old, it was more to do with them thinking old.

'I get you,' said Brad. 'Still, if yours feel you ought to try for university, I wouldn't say that was old thinking. More like good thinking.'

'Crikey, you said it was only for eggheads a minute ago,' protested Emily. 'Now you're talking as if you're on the side of parents.'

'No, I'm on your side, sure I am,' said

cowboy Brad, 'which is why I'm giving you the lowdown. Yep, I'm telling you university will mean you'll get to be more than a plumber's mate.'

'What's wrong with being a plumber's mate?' asked Emily.

'OK, I guess, if you get to be the plumber,' said Brad. 'But I wouldn't have minded having your chance to go to Eton.'

'Not Eton, you dummy,' said Emily, 'you mean Oxbridge. Besides, I want to make my own decisions about my life, and anyway, I can't stay here gassing all night. Bye for now, see you at Saturday's dance unless you're going to a Tommy Steele shindig with my mum.'

'Leave off about that and talk more to me,' said Brad, but there was no response from the other end of the line. Emily had hung up and gone back to her homework.

In another family home, Polly, while waiting for the nine o'clock news on the television, was asking the twins exactly what they thought of the odd young man who was apparently their cousin Emily's current dancing partner. She knew of the Teddy boy only by way of their mention of him.

'He's all right,' said James. 'I mean, he doesn't go in for robbing banks, just some cowboy talk, like cousin Daniel does at times, when he's talking American with Patsy.'

'His clothes are a bit freakish,' said Gemma.

'Freakish?' said Boots. 'Daniel's?'

'No, not Daniel's,' said Gemma. 'We're speaking of Emily's Teddy boy. But he seems all right to me.'

'What is meant by freakish?' asked Boots.

'Freakish, dad, means unusual,' said James.

'Boots,' said Polly, 'our children are doing shuddering things to the English language.'

'Might I point out, Mum,' said James, 'that in your time you did your particular thing, like calling fussy elderly blokes frightful old kippers?'

'She still does,' said Gemma.

'Change the subject,' said Polly. 'No, switch the television on, James, and let's catch the news.'

That did little good, for the main bulk of the news concerned what was known as the Cold War, the antagonism existing between the Western democracies and the Soviet Union bloc. Accusations and counter-accusations of espionage were never-ending, and since the whole thing had been going on almost from the moment the Second World War ended, boredom was now the principal reaction of many people to any mention of it.

Gemma said she'd go to bed unless she was

allowed to turn the set off. Boots said he'd prefer a silent set to his daughter's absence. Polly said asking for the news to be switched on was sometimes a ghastly mistake, so if James would care to switch it off, perhaps more could be told about Emily's Teddy boy. He was, after all, the first of his kind who had brushed up against Grandma Finch's redoubtable family.

James switched the set off. 'Well, there are a lot of them about. Perhaps everyone will end up wearing their clothes.'

'I don't think your headmaster will,' said Polly. James was attending Dulwich College. 'I won't. And your father certainly won't.'

'Mum, you can't buck a trend, you have to let it happen,' said James. 'Dad might be persuaded.'

'Daddy a Teddy boy?' said Gemma, and yelled with laughter. 'That'll be the day.'

'Take it from me, little lady, I'll fight any of it that appears in my wardrobe,' said Boots.

'What does Emily's odd friend do?' asked Boots. 'Or is he still at school?'

'He's apprenticed to a plumber,' said James.

'A plumber?' said Polly.

'Yes, he's a plumber's mate,' said Gemma.

'Well, if he qualifies,' said Boots, 'he'll be joining a band of blood brothers that our plumbing systems can't do without. As your mother will tell you, all a good plumber asks for is a pot of tea and the price for the job. By the way, James, are there Teddy girls as well as Teddy boys?'

'James, don't answer that,' said Polly, 'because if you do I'm afraid I'll have a sleepless night worrying about what Gemma will look like dressed as a Teddy girl.'

Young Mr Albert Thompson, who called himself Bradley, had no idea at all that his arrival in the life of Miss Emily Chapman was making him the talking point not only of her family, but the family of cousin Gemma.

At this moment, in company with a band of Teddy boy brothers, he was in Leicester Square. Moving as one in theatrical fashion over the pavement, they were showing off their feathers, much to the amusement and interest of a group of foreign tourists out to enjoy the atmosphere of the West End. On the whole, that was all a Teddy boy asked for, the public's admiration of his rig-out, although some nervous people were inclined to regard his exaggerated sartorial look as a sign of delinquency, the kind that posed a threat to law and order, and their personal persons.

To someone like that, Brad would have said something like this: 'Gee, man, cool your blood pressure.'

The following morning, Lizzy had a caller. Opening her front door, she found Mr Witchet on the step again, another bunch of colourful sweet peas in his hand and a neighbourly smile on his friendly face.

'Good morning, Mrs Somers,' he said, lifting his hat in a gesture of courtesy, 'how are we today?'

'I can't complain about my health, thank you, Mr Witchet,' said Lizzy, standing four-square at her open door in an instinctive posture that defied entry.

'Splendid,' said Mr Witchet. 'Might I be so bold as to offer you these sweet peas fresh from my garden?'

Lizzy could not refuse without being ungracious, so she said, 'That's very kind of you, Mr Witchet, they look lovely.'

'My pleasure,' said Mr Witchet, and handed her the bunch of fragrant blooms. 'May I ask how life is treating you now?'

'I'm managing, if that's what you mean,' said Lizzy, the sweet peas held close to her bosom, their scent delightful. 'Well, one has to manage.'

'Any little problems?' enquired Mr Witchet, portly self face to face, as it were, with Lizzy's comely plumpness. She had given up trying to reduce her figure, and accepted the fairly comfortable spread of middle age, since it was by no means excessive. 'I'd be happy to be of service at any time, Mrs Somers, which I might have mentioned before. Well, being a widower, I do have a special sympathy for widows and any of their problems.'

'Well, thanks, but like I told you, I don't have any problems that my family can't see to,' said Lizzy.

Mr Witchet nodded understandingly, his occupation of the doorstep again inviting a 'come-in' response.

'Might I be bold enough to offer to do any shopping you require?' he said. 'It must be an ordeal for you, I'm sure, facing up to the shopkeepers and their solicitations. It means a daily reminder of your loss, and I remember that for quite a time after me dear wife went I tried to avoid being reminded of it day after day.'

'Oh, I don't shop daily,' said Lizzy. A sound issued from her kitchen. Her kettle was whistling. 'Oh, there goes my kettle, Mr Witchet, it's boiling. Do excuse me— Oh, what's that?' The whistling had stopped, and a sharp little clattering noise reached her ear.

'Allow me, Mrs Somers,' said Mr Witchet, latching onto the opportunity to be of service as he stepped smartly past Lizzy and sped into her kitchen. Steam climbed to the ceiling from her newfangled electric kettle, the lid of which lay on the floor. He switched off the electricity supply and pulled out the plug. Then he made an inspection. The kettle was hot and empty. 'My word,' he said, as Lizzy entered, 'just as well we heard the noise, Mrs Somers. The kettle's boiled itself dry. The whistle should have sounded minutes ago. It's faulty.'

'I should have turned it off before I answered the door to you,' said Lizzy. 'Now look, my kitchen ceiling and walls are wet with steam.'

'Don't worry, my dear,' said Mr Witchet, 'we only need to open a window and let in some warm fresh air. As for the kettle, I'll take it home with me and see if I can spot the fault and put it right. I do pride meself on knowing a bit about these modern devices, which is all self-learned. Were you boiling water for some tea?'

'No, to make myself a cup of instant coffee,' said Lizzy. 'I'll have to use my old gas kettle.'

'No, sit yourself down,' said Mr Witchet, 'this has been a shock to you. These electric things are a bit complicated for ladies. Nothing like our old-fashioned stuff, eh, Mrs Somers? Allow me to boil your old kettle and make you your coffee while you take a rest. Go on, I insist. It's no trouble, and what are friends and neighbours for, I ask, in times of need?'

He talked Lizzy into a mind-soggy acceptance of his presence, his help and his provision of instant coffee for both of them, which they drank in her parlour. She had always referred to her front room as the family parlour, for that was what she'd grown up with in her Walworth days. It was instinctively shrewd of her to have Mr Witchet end up there, since the parlour had a much more formal air than her living room or kitchen.

All the same, Mr Witchet made himself at home without too much effort, causing Lizzy to wonder what excuse or reason she could find for getting rid of him. Not that he was an awkward old misfit. No, he had plenty to say about the problems of life for widows and widowers, and the odd ways of certain neighbours. Did Mrs Somers know, for instance, that Mrs McCorkindale of number sixty-two worked behind the bar of a pub in Brixton every evening, and that she dressed for the work in very fancy get-ups?

'No, I didn't know,' said Lizzy, thinking that Mrs McCorkindale, well into her forties, was a bit past togging herself up in fancy costume. 'What does Mr McCorkindale say?'

'According to my hearing, not much,' said

Mr Witchet. 'Well, since commercial television opened up a couple of years ago, he watches the ITV programmes every night and all weekend. His next-door neighbour, Mr Clements, says he's developed staring eyeballs, which I venture to suggest, Mrs Somers, is quite comical. More coffee, might I ask?'

'No,' said Lizzy, 'no, thank you, and don't let me keep you.'

Not until the parlour chiming clock struck twelve noon, however, did her friendly visitor take himself home, along with her new fangled electric kettle, and a promise to bring it back as soon as he'd repaired the fault, which he was confident he could on account of having a bit of a gift for such things.

Lizzy wondered how to keep him from crossing her doorstep when he did return. Her kettle, yes, she could let that back into her house, but she would rather not entertain Sidney Witchet again. He might be well-meaning, but he was definitely not her cup of tea. For that matter, there would never be anyone who could take the place of Ned.

Imagine Mrs McCorkindale working as a Brixton barmaid, and in fancy get-ups too. No-one could have looked or acted more respectable than that lady when she was out and about in the Denmark Hill area. But in Brixton these days, apparently, one just couldn't tell what some people could get up to. She'd even heard that Rosie's daughter Emily was actually going dancing there with one of those funny-looking Teddy boys.

Later that day, when Boots dropped in on his way home from the office, Lizzy told him how Mr Witchet had finished up in her parlour.

'That actually happened, did it, Lizzy?' smiled Boots.

'Well, like I've just told you, it wouldn't have happened at all if my electric kettle hadn't blown its lid off,' said Lizzy. 'Next thing I knew, there he was, in my kitchen making coffee and then in my parlour drinking it. What's going to happen when he brings that kettle back?'

'Tell him the neighbours have started to talk,' said Boots.

'Well, yes, so I will,' said Lizzy, 'what a good idea, Boots. That's bound to send him on his way.'

'He may need a little push as well,' said Boots.

'I don't like being unkind to people, especially if they think they're being helpful, but I'll have to give Mr Witchet a bit of a push if I feel I need to,' said Lizzy. 'Listen, lovey, I've been hearing things about Rosie's Emily, that she's actually taken up with a Teddy boy, and her still at school, would you believe.'

'Well, the twins have given Polly and me some information,' said Boots, 'and as we understand it, it seems that Emily and this lad get together at Saturday night dances.'

'Well, I don't know much about Teddy boys, except I heard they're not very respectable,' said Lizzy. 'And it's not as if I could phone Rosie or Matt and ask about the one Emily's friendly with. It would be like poking my nose in, which makes me remember we were always brought up to mind our own business.'

Boots, who rarely lost sight of the humorous aspects of life and people, said, 'Well, Lizzy, if our revered mother finds out Emily goes dancing with a Teddy boy, the heavens will fall. I'll wager she rates Teddy boys on a par with delinquent young Bolsheviks.'

'Oh, Bobby's told me they're not as weird as they look,' said Lizzy, 'they just like dressing up, he says. Oh, d'you know what Mr Witchet told me about a neighbour, Mrs McCorkindale?'

'No, I don't know,' said Boots, 'and I don't think I know the lady, either.'

'Well, she's always looked and acted very respectable,' said Lizzy, 'but it seems she does a bit of fancy dressing up as an evening barmaid in a Brixton pub.'

'Is that sensational?' asked Boots.

'No, not actually sensational, I suppose,' said Lizzy, 'but a bit of a shock because she's over forty and she's got married daughters.'

'Well, earning some lolly as a dressed-up barmaid could be counted as enterprising, I suppose,' said Boots. 'And good for a spot of gossip.' He smiled. 'I daresay Mr Witchet could let you know more about the lady and her Brixton outfits, given the chance.'

'He's not going to get any chance,' said Lizzy.

'That's the style, Lizzy, fight the good fight,' said Boots. 'Ned will be right behind you.'

'I'll always be sure of that,' said Lizzy.

Over drinks when he arrived home, Boots acquainted Polly with the details of Mr Witchet's successful entry into Lizzy's parlour. He painted the picture in light-hearted style. Polly demurred.

'Boots, you old horse chestnut, your sense of humour is out of order in this case,' she said. 'Your sister Lizzy is still a grieving widow, even if she doesn't show it as much as she did at first.'

'I wouldn't argue with that,' said Boots. 'We all still miss Ned, but there's something a little amusing about my sister's electric kettle going pop at a moment when the helpful widower was on her doorstep.'

'Utter disaster,' said Polly, 'and it's up to you to help her deal with the Witchet blighter before he takes up permanent residence in her parlour. Great mothballs, think what that could lead to. I demand appropriate action from you.'

'I think we can leave all necessary action to Lizzy,' said Boots. 'It won't be in the form of cutting the bloke dead. She's too nice to be as unkind as that. She's more likely to see him off by telling him the neighbours are talking about him. I suspect he doesn't want to be bracketed with Mrs McCorkindale.'

'Who on earth is Mrs McCorkindale?' asked Polly. Boots gave her the details, and she laughed so much that the twins came running down from their rooms to find out why their dearly beloved mother was having hysterics. They thought their father's explanation was on a par with rhubarb.

The ground-floor conversion job had been finished at the Camberwell Green offices, and the opening of the staff canteen was officially heralded by a speech of welcome from Sammy. He'd asked Susie if it should be him or Boots.

'I'll admit,' he said, 'that Boots, being

educated, is probably better at speechifying than I am.'

'Sammy,' said Susie, a light in her eye, 'much as I adore Boots—'

'Now, Susie,' protested Sammy, 'how many times have I told you it's not fitting for you to adore any bloke except me?'

'Be that as it may, Sammy,' said Susie, 'you'll make the speech, just like you did when Bert and Gertie Roper retired from the factory. You founded the whole business, you put all the profit-making ideas into it, and you thought up the conversion. The speech is your privilege, and anyway, Boots is the last man who'd push himself forward.'

So in the virgin atmosphere of the bright and shining staff canteen, Sammy addressed the multitude. That is, some thirty-odd staff, with just the switchboard girl left on duty. He said the management was pleased to offer its workers up-to-date amenities, such as what was usual plus a recent drying-out room for wet coats on rainy mornings, and now this canteen, which, he hoped, would feed them good lunches without giving them indigestion. So would they kindly note that the chef, Mrs Mary Tindall, wouldn't be dishing up any lumpy suet puddings. On which cue young Mary Tindall presented herself, complete with kitchen apron and chef's hat. Applause rang out, as well as one or two relevant questions.

'Will you be doing sausages and baked beans?'

'Sorry, I'm a chef, not a can-opener.'

'Will you be serving prunes with hot custard for afters?'

'Only by special request.'

Sammy, resuming his speech, said it wasn't compulsory to use the canteen, but he'd give it a month to see what the general figures for usage were. Mrs Tindall could then settle into providing for the average amount of food required, which would do away with a lot of leftover consumables and also look after the overheads. (Smiles of understanding travelled round the listening staff.) Oh, in respect of costs, Sammy went on, they all knew they'd only be charged nominal prices for their lunches, and now they might like to know everything on this first day was free.

'Spoken like a real gent, Mr Sammy.'

'Love it, Mr Sammy.'

'Happy day, Mr Sammy.'

And so on.

'Finally,' said Sammy, 'as today's the one and only first day, we're all lunching together. That's excepting Freda, who's looking after the switchboard and taking down phone messages.

For which, when she comes down to lunch herself, she can have a second helping of fruit pie, which I understand from Mrs Tindall is on the menu. After today, however, half of us will lunch between twelve and one, and the other half between one and two. The management couldn't afford for no work at all to be done for a full hour, especially if our competitors found out. Some competitors don't have any manners. That's it, then, enjoy your lunch with the compliments of the management.'

That was a signal for all present to give Sammy a ringing round of applause, then to see what was on offer on the day's chalked-up menu and to line up for counter service.

Sammy, Boots, Rachel, Rosie, Tim and Daniel, the management, in a natural gesture of what was right, brought up the rear.

Subsequently, an excellent meal was enjoyed by all, and both Boots and Sammy not only complimented the chef, they also complimented Rachel for finding her and hiring her.

'I should be happy for all of us?' said Rachel. 'I am, especially as she'll be with us for at least two years. That's a definite promise.'

'Definite promises,' said Sammy, 'happen to be a welcome change from all that's fell apart or gone down the drain this year. I've nearly been ill from me heartburnings and headaches.'

701

'Be of good cheer, Sammy, you're still on full charge, still on your feet,' said Boots.

'Yup, you're still alive, Dad,' said Daniel.

'I'm wondering,' said Sammy. 'Rachel, d'you think you could ask our valuable chef if there's any fruit pie left? I think I fancy seconds.'

Chapter Twenty-seven

On Saturday evening, Emily again spent most of her dancing time in company with Brad, which flattered him. Well, although she was still a schoolgirl, he could see she really did have all the makings of a great cookie. Rocking together, they were a smash hit with each other, and the only time Emily saw fit to disagree with him about anything was when he again suggested they should leave a little before ten in order to get her home well before ten thirty.

'No, I'm going to stay on for a while,' she said, 'it won't matter if I'm a bit after ten thirty.'

Brad said he'd more or less promised her parents to get her home well on time, and a bit after ten thirty would ruin things for him. Emily said that was his hard luck, especially as he'd made the promise without consulting her.

'D'you want to land me in the doghouse?' said Brad. 'If I get you home late, that's where your ma and pa will put me, in the doghouse, and without handing me a bone. So come on, baby, let's hoof it to the bus stop.'

'No taxi this time?' said Emily.

'Man, I'm short of bread this week,' said Brad, 'I had to divvy up for this new waistcoat.' His new waistcoat was purple and gold, and highly noticeable. Accordingly, it pleased his idea of trendy plumage and it drew attention. Emily thought it great, and said so. 'OK, then,' said Brad, 'no taxi tonight, so let's hit the trail on a bus and get back to the ranch pronto.'

Emily sulked for a minute or so, then said, 'Oh, all right,' and they detached themselves from the crowded floor. She caught sight of Giles, waved to him and indicated Brad was taking her home.

Giles, ready to follow on, bawled, 'OK, sis, got you.'

On the bus, she asked Brad if he'd ever been to Brighton. Brad said yes, his parents took him when he was ten, and he remembered living it up for the day in old-fashioned style, like going on the pier, having a trip in a boat called *Saucy Sally*, and eating fish and chips on the beach. He asked Emily if she'd been there herself. No, she hadn't, she said.

'I hear *Saucy Sally* has been pensioned off and that the place is now up and coming,' said Brad.

'I'll find out if I do go there,' said Emily.

Brad delivered her home to her parents well in time again, and they invited him in for a cup of tea and a slice of cake, which he accepted on this occasion. Rosie said nothing about the fact that his new waistcoat hurt her eyes, and Matt refrained from mentioning that his quiff had reached a memorable height.

It was when she and Matt were preparing for bed that Rosie said, 'Can that young man be true, Matt?'

'Not to look at,' said Matt, 'but apart from his waistcoat, he could be quite sound. He's keeping Emily up to scratch time-wise.'

'I feel there's something brewing in Emily,' said Rosie.

'Growing pains?' said Matt.

'Ask me another,' said Rosie.

Sunday in Hyde Park. July had brought breezy conditions that stirred the laden top branches of trees and caused well-dressed women to clutch at their hats. Old-fashioned hatpins were no longer in vogue.

Mr Nigel Killiner, strolling with his young lady, Linda Harrison, wore no hat. Neither did Linda. Hats for young men were out of fashion, and hats for young ladies were mostly seen only on special occasions. The breeze plucked at

Nigel's hair without altering the shape of his widow's peak, but it was playing havoc with Linda's untrammelled locks. They blew about her head and face. She laughed as she swept them aside.

'It hasn't been like this in our walks round our local park,' she said.

'You mean this isn't Ruskin Park weather,' said Nigel.

'Oh, the sun's out, and I'm not asking for more,' said Linda. 'I don't mind colliding with the breeze. If there are any cobwebs in my hair, they're being blown away.'

'You've got beautiful hair,' said Nigel, casting an admiring glance at the fair if wayward tresses.

'Well, thanks for saying so,' said Linda.

The crowds were turning London's premier park into a panorama of colour, life and movement. Its atmosphere was always that much more vibrant on Sundays.

'I must say I'm fond of parks,' said Nigel.

'Yes, I think you are,' said Linda, watching some young people dashing about. The fresh and sunny day, and the handsome park itself, did, she thought, invite energy to have a go. 'You're fonder of parks than cinemas or dance halls, Nigel?'

'I prefer the open air,' said Nigel, 'especially

in summer and especially with someone like you. But cinemas, yes, I know the kind of fascinating entertainment they offer, so would you like to see a film with me next Saturday evening?'

'I really would love to see *High Noon*,' said Linda, 'it's on at the Camberwell Green cinema all next week.'

'I've heard of that film,' said Nigel.

'Yes, it stars Gary Cooper and Grace Kelly,' said Linda, 'and it's the second time round in Camberwell. I suppose, as a teacher, you go in more for museums than films.'

'With you,' smiled Nigel, 'I'll be delighted to go in for *High Noon* next Saturday evening.'

'Oh, flattered, I'm sure,' said Linda.

'By the way,' said Nigel, 'I've spoken to my landlady about you, and she's agreed that as you're respectable and don't go in for high jinks at low dives, I can entertain you to tea in my rooms next Sunday afternoon. It'll be in return for having Sunday tea with you. Would you like to come?'

Linda said she'd love to see his lodgings, anyway, and to stay for tea. What was the address?

Nigel gave her the details, and Linda thought that at last something more personal than a walk round a park could be in the offing. She was still willing to be Nigel's steady. Would his landlady stand outside his door, however, listening to make sure nothing unrespectable was going on? She asked the question. Nigel laughed and said well, actually, the old girl would be out visiting her sister all that day. Would Linda mind about that?

'Not if I can trust you,' said Linda.

'A hundred per cent,' said Nigel. 'Come on, let's go to the tea rooms now and catch a pot of tea and a currant bun.'

Which they did, and very enjoyable it was too. Afterwards, Nigel took her home and they regaled her parents with an account of Sunday afternoon in Hyde Park before Nigel left to go home to his lodgings. He had some work to do on next week's lessons, he said. A teacher's spare time was never completely spare. There was always something getting in the way, such as working out a system that would make it easier to teach arithmetic to backward school-kids. But he said so long to Linda and her parents in his usual easy manner, as if awkward schoolkids were really no bother at all.

During the evening, Annabelle, Nick and Linda watched television's most popular show, *Sunday Night at the London Palladium*, hosted by an ex-Army comic, Tommy Trinder. Some of its acts featured new stars of wit and modernity, as well as established stars of the fading music-hall world. The latter needed to be on top form to sustain their old-style acts, for their general popularity was falling way behind that of television presenters like Trinder and the increasingly popular Bob Monkhouse. Any Palladium number that featured Britain's blonde bombshell, Diana Dors, was received uproariously.

On this Sunday evening the show, as usual, went with a swing and a gallop. Many households owned television sets, and most watched the Palladium spectacular on the commercial channel, ITV. It was putting the BBC's Sunday nose out of joint.

While enjoying the show, Linda's mind frequently turned to next weekend and a possible new development in her relationship with her favourite schoolteacher.

Chapter Twenty-eight

It was Tuesday morning when Lizzy discovered that a knock on her front door heralded Mr Witchet calling again. She noted at once that he had brought back her electric kettle. This domestic appliance was actually one of the last items Ned had bought for her, telling her that its whistle would always alert her to its boiling point. In the hands of Mr Witchet, Lizzy felt it looked out of place. However, she didn't want it to remain faulty, and if he'd mended it, she'd be grateful. She liked using it daily in simple memory of Ned and the thoughtfulness behind his purchase.

'Ah, good morning, Mrs Somers, here we are again,' beamed Mr Witchet.

'And with my kettle, I see,' said Lizzy. 'Have you mended it?'

'I'm pleased to say yes,' said Mr Witchet, looking the part. Self-satisfaction always sat happily on his countenance. 'I do have a little gift for mending this, that and the other. In fact, of course, as you probably know, my most paying gift was the repair of clocks, watches and all kinds of timepieces, including, I'm proud to say, some very old and valuable Swiss cuckoo clocks that belonged to various customers of mine. If you happen to own one of these and you ever find it faulty, I'd consider it a privilege to repair it for you as an act of friendship. Well, of course, that applies to any clock – or watch – of yours that needed looking at, especially as I know how much the correct time means to those of us who live alone.' Mr Witchet paused to let Lizzy digest this opening speech and its message of good neighbourliness and possible honourable intention.

Lizzy, who had suspected his intention from the beginning, said, 'Well, I think everyone likes to know what the correct time is. I mean, the wrong time isn't much good to anyone, is it? But thanks ever so much for mending the kettle.' She took it from him. 'It was one of the last presents Ned gave me, so I'm grateful.'

Mr Witchet beamed.

'Shall we test it?' he asked, looking ready to step in. His portly outline was in the forward position in a manner of speaking.

Lizzy, glancing over his shoulder, gave a start.

'Oh, dear,' she said.

'What's wrong?' asked Mr Witchet.

'I think Mrs Palmer's curtains moved,' said Lizzy, drawing back from her open door in what seemed like an attempt to efface herself.

'Beg pardon?' said Mr Witchet.

'Yes,' said Lizzy, knitting her brow in worry, 'I think she's noticed you from behind her curtains, I think perhaps you're being talked about.'

'Talked about? Me?' Mr Witchet looked startled.

'I expect it's only a rumour,' said Lizzy, casting another glance and doing her best to appear upset for him. 'But I did hear Mrs Palmer's been talking.' Which was no lie. Mrs Palmer was known to talk every day, just as everyone else did, apart from those unfortunate souls born dumb.

'She's been talking about me?' said Mr Witchet, casting his own uneasy glance at the curtained windows across the way.

'I expect it's only a rumour,' said Lizzy again. 'But she might have noticed you knocking at my door just recent.' Half of her was now behind it. 'Oh, dear, she might also have noticed how you call on other ladies.'

Mr Witchet's healthy complexion paled slightly.

'But only to make a little gift of vegetables or suchlike,' he said.

712

'I expect it's being invited in that Mrs Palmer might have noticed,' said Lizzy. 'Some people gossip about that sort of thing in an unChristian way. I'm sure nothing's ever happened that's been unmentionable. Still, I'd best not invite you in. Mrs Palmer might still be looking to see if I do.'

Mr Witchet quivered.

'Yes,' he said. 'I mean no – that is, yes, I see. People gossiping. I never – well, we don't want that – no.' He proved then that although he liked to be regarded as upright and reputable, qualified to talk about his neighbours, he didn't at all favour being talked about himself. Flapping a bit, he removed himself from Lizzy's doorstep with the haste of a man who had no designs on the widow, none at all. He accompanied his departure with several agitated words. 'Yes, I'd better go, Mrs Somers – your good name and mine – most upsetting – I wouldn't like to think . . .'

His voice, slightly hoarse, trailed off.

'Goodbye,' called Lizzy, most of her respectable self well behind the door now. Her word of farewell and her cautious effacement plainly implied she'd prefer it if Mr Witchet didn't come back and get both of them talked about.

Boots had been right. His sister had known the best way of keeping the widower from her door, leaving herself content with her memories of Ned.

On behalf of Maureen, Amos Anderson received a cheque for ten guineas from the chastened Charlie Ellis, together with a guarantee of straight dealing. He also sent contact sheets of the acceptable photographs he'd taken of Maureen. Nice, thought Amos when he noted how Charlie had brought into being the distinctly appealing nature of her cleavage. One had to hand it to him. He knew how to pose a model.

Amos banked the cheque and phoned Maureen. When she subsequently arrived at his studio, he gave her what was still owing to her, five guineas, and told her that Charlie would definitely divvy up in the event of selling any of her photographs, the straight ones. Maureen was delighted at having received a full ten guineas. Not only was the amount handsome, it also went more than a little way towards curing her feelings of mortification.

'Amos, d'you think he might get me on a front cover?' she asked.

'A front cover we'd like, you bet,' said Amos. 'Here, take a look at the contact sheets.'

Maureen took a look, and a second look.

'Crikey, is this me?' she asked.

'If Charlie sold one of these for a front cover,' said Amos, 'it could match you with a Rank starlet, or even Diana Dors.'

'Diana Dors?' breathed Maureen. 'She's me dad's favourite pin-up after me mum.'

Amos coughed.

'Your – er – your mother does pin-up poses?' he said.

'No, course she doesn't, you daft thing,' laughed Maureen, still entranced by the contact sheets. 'It's just what me dad calls her. Well, she's always been attractive-looking and still is. Mind, I think she thinks Diana Dors is a bit fast, like.'

'The lady's very photogenic, though,' said Amos.

'Oh, yes, I know,' said Maureen, thinking of Diana's glamorous image as she regarded the photographs of her bosom, which was un-heralded so far, apart from a couple of sweater shots sold by Amos to a magazine. 'Imagine that man Charlie Ellis giving himself a posh name like Morton Fraser when he's just low and common. Still, I must say he's made me look very sexy in me dressy poses.'

'With a bit of a saucy touch?' said Amos.

'I never thought about being saucy as well as sexy,' said Maureen, 'but I don't think Mum and Dad will kick up a fuss. They're both broad-minded.'

'Broad-minded is good, ain't it?' said Amos. 'Don't you worry, I'll see that no photographer ever gets you to step over the mark. You'll still be everyone's girl next door, even in outfits like Charlie supplied.'

'Oh, that's good,' said Maureen. She had achieved her ambition of becoming a pin-up glamour girl, and it wouldn't actually ruin her life if she never overtook Diana Dors. Just the front cover of a posh magazine like *Esquire* would do.

'Linda,' said Nick Harrison to his daughter over breakfast on Wednesday morning, 'you know you mentioned to me that Nigel was taking you to the cinema on Saturday evening?'

'Yes, did you tell Mum?' asked Linda.

'Not until he got out of bed this morning,' said Annabelle, looking at her husband as if he'd made a mess of the day. 'He forgot and you forgot that we're all due to attend your Uncle Boots's birthday party. He'll be sixty-one on Sunday, but of course, he and your Aunt Polly are giving the party on Saturday.'

'Oh, Lord, yes, I did forget,' said Linda.

'You and me, we're both for it,' said Nick. 'But I can't stay for a beating, I don't have the time. I'm off to the office.' He was a senior partner in a City firm of accountants.

716

'Don't panic,' said Annabelle, 'you're forgiven. But you'll have to cancel your date with Nigel, Linda.'

'Silly me,' said Linda, 'I should have remembered about Uncle Boots when Nigel and I were talking about arrangements for next weekend.' She made a face. No-one in the family missed Uncle Boots's birthdays. No-one wanted to. 'Oh, I know, I'll go to Nigel's lodgings during my lunch hour today and leave a message with his landlady. I'll cancel next Saturday's date and say I'll still see him on Sunday afternoon for tea.'

'Good idea, pet,' said Nick, on his feet. 'So long now, Lady One and Lady Two.' He gave his wife a peck, his daughter a peck and then left. The necessity of reaching the station on time took priority over further breakfast-time chat.

'Yes, you must cancel your cinema date with Nigel, Linda,' said Annabelle.

Linda looked wry.

'I know that, Mum,' she said, 'so I'll definitely go round to his lodgings at lunchtime.'

'It's a shame you've got to cancel,' said Annabelle, who was altogether in favour of Nigel as a candidate for keeping Linda happy ever after.

'It's my own fault,' said Linda, 'I should have remembered, and anyway, I expect I'll only be postponing the invite, and as it's on account of Uncle Boots's birthday, it's postponement in a good cause.'

At lunchtime, she made her way to Bessemer Road. It was a fifteen-minute walk from her copy-typist's job in an office near Camberwell Green. She found the address Nigel had given her. It was halfway down Bessemer Road, one in a row of terraced houses, and not far from his school. She knocked in expectation of bringing his landlady to the door. His landlady, she was sure, would accept the message and pass it on to him.

She waited. No-one came. She knocked again. No answer. His landlady was out, obviously. From the direction of the school she heard the noise of pupils in the playground, enjoying their lunchtime break. Well, of course, the best thing she could do now would be to go to the school and ask if someone could fetch Nigel.

She walked there and arrived at the closed but openwork iron gate. Through it she saw the young boys of this primary establishment, leaping and larking about amid a cacophony of noise. Linda smiled, remembering her own lively days as a young, scatterbrained pupil. Schoolkids always let themselves go at break times. She noted a boy, one of the few not making a name for themselves at jumping and hollering. She called to him and he came to the gate with a grin on his face. It didn't go away as he looked up at her. She thought him about ten, and belonging to the well-known fraternity of perpetually grinning boys.

'What's up, miss?' he asked.

'I wonder, could you get a message to one of your teachers?' asked Linda.

'I could, as long as it don't mean letting off a firework,' said the boy. 'You get sent home to your dad if you do, and your dad belts you.'

'It's nothing to do with fireworks,' smiled Linda, 'it's to do with asking Mr Killiner to come and talk to me. I need to speak to him.'

'Mr Killiner?' said the boy, his grin diminishing a bit.

'Yes, he's a teacher here, isn't he?' said Linda.

'Yes, but he's not in today, he's gone to his sister's funeral. She went and died last week.'

'Pardon?' said Linda.

'Yes, last week, poor woman,' said the boy. 'It upset old Killiner. Well, for a teacher, he ain't a bad bloke.'

'I don't think we can be talking about the same man,' said Linda.

'Well,' said the boy, his grin back in place, 'I

know who I'm talking about. Old Mr Killiner, our geography teacher.'

'What d'you mean by old?' asked Linda, confusion stirring.

'I dunno his real age,' said the boy, 'but he must be near on fifty.'

'That's not the Mr Killiner I know,' said Linda, and she described Nigel in detail.

'Oh, him,' said the boy, his grin broader. 'That's Walter Kilby. He's not one of our teachers, he's the caretaker. Me dad says that in America they call them janitors. Me dad reads a lot of American stories. Anyway, that's what Mr Kilby is, our caretaker, and he's in the boilerhouse just this minute, making sure the boiler's in good condition when we all come back from our summer 'olidays. Here, miss, is he the bloke you want to talk to? Has he been gamming you in that posh voice he puts on sometimes?'

Linda, trying to come to terms with what this grinning young ape was telling her, took several seconds to find words. Then she asked if this Walter Kilby called himself Nigel Killiner sometimes.

'I dunno about that,' said the boy. His grin disappeared and was replaced by a furrowed brow. It suggested youthful concern for this nice young lady. 'Here, you ain't sweet on him, are you, miss? Only he's a married man, y'know, except they say he ain't seen his wife for a year and more.' The furrowed brow gave way to a knowing look. 'He ain't been leading you up the garden, has he?'

Linda, her disbelief painful, was tight of voice as she asked the boy if he would go and fetch the caretaker. The boy suggested in turn that he should take Linda to the boilerhouse, where she could talk to the bloke on the spot, instead of at the gate. Linda, gathering herself, said yes, she'd like to do that.

The boy opened the gate.

Chapter Twenty-nine

Mr Walter Kilby, who sometimes called himself Nigel Killiner, was sitting on a packing case, munching on a lunchtime sandwich. He was dressed in blue dungarees and a cap. A shadow fell across the sunlit doorway of the boilerhouse, and someone looked in. He glanced up.

'I'm seeing you, Simpson, you little tyke,' he said in a northern accent. 'Push off, will tha?'

'Here, don't be like that,' said Simpson, the grinning boy, 'I've brought you a visitor. There you are, miss, there he is.'

'Thank you,' said the visitor.

Out stepped Simpson, and in stepped Linda. Walter Kilby's jaw dropped.

'What the . . . ?' Words failed him.

'Surprised?' said Linda, her cool expression hiding her sense of betrayal.

'What're you doing here?' asked Kilby in what Simpson had referred to as his posh voice.

'I called to find out if I could talk to a teacher by the name of Nigel Killiner,' said Linda, dreams of romance all in bits. 'But it seems I was asking for the wrong man. You're not a teacher, and you're not Nigel Killiner.'

Kilby came to his feet, looked at his sandwich and then glanced around for a dumping place. He chose the packing case and laid the sandwich on it. He was taking time to compose himself.

'Oh, well,' he said eventually, 'just a little deception. It isn't as if I don't work at the school.'

'What was the point of saying you were a teacher and using someone else's name?' asked Linda, illuminated by the light from the open door, but feeling the reverse of bright.

Kilby spread his hands.

'I ask you honestly,' he said, 'how would your parents have taken it if I'd introduced myself as a school caretaker, and with a name like Wally? The Denmark Hill area is littered with middle-class snobs and names like Nigel and Andrew.'

'Oh, really?' Linda had lost her blinkers. 'You'd know about snobs, of course. But who's worse, snobs or married men who go about acting unmarried?'

'Well, bugger the person who let that cat out of the bag,' said Kilby.

723

'Your father's not a stockbroker, of course, and your sister's not at university, I suppose,' said Linda. 'Exactly where d'you come from, a school for smart alecs?'

This smart alec shrugged, smiled a little disdainfully, recovered his wits, and then, in the broadest of Geordie accents, confirmed that his real name was Walter Kilby, that he came from Newcastle, where he'd been an office clerk, that his father was a shipyard worker, and his sister had a husband and three kids. He had moved south, and taught himself to speak like a Surrey stockbroker in the hope of landing a well-paid job with nothing very much to do. But he hadn't been able to get anything better than this work as a school caretaker, after being sacked by an advertising agency for not living up to his qualifications, which he admitted weren't his own. As for his wife, well, there was an example of marrying in haste and repenting at leisure. She lived in Chatham and he hoped she'd stay there for ever, seeing 'she were always fonder of sailors than of me.'

Linda had to listen to all this through what to her was the tangled web of his Geordie accent. At the end, she asked him what he had had in mind for her.

'Oh, some Sunday afternoons on my sofa,' he

said, reverting to his acquired refined tones. 'You'll have noticed I didn't attempt to rush you. I was taking my time. I like taking my time in that respect.'

'Well, dear me, how thoughtful of you,' said Linda, her cool sarcasm admirable considering she was fuming. 'Am I just one of a long line of girls who've been on your sofa?'

'Not a long line, believe me,' said Kilby. 'Let's say you're about the third.' He was fully recovered from the unexpected, accepting that the game was up as far as his intentions towards Linda were concerned. 'I haven't lived too many years yet.'

If his arrogance and shamelessness were breathtaking to Linda, worldly women might have found him diverting.

'How long do you think you'd have lasted with me before I found you out?' she asked.

'Long enough, I hope,' said Kilby, and Linda had a mental picture of herself being seduced on his sofa on a Sunday afternoon. It made her feel sick with herself for being taken in. Looking back, she could see now that he'd always been too good to be true. She remembered the moment in the park when some kids catcalled him. One had shouted, 'Oi, Killy.' No, she'd assumed he had. Killy for Killiner. But it had been Kilby, of course, and it had put the man out of his smooth self for a moment or two.

'Mr Kilby, I think you're wasting your talents as a caretaker,' she said. 'I think you should be on the stage. That's where all people like you can pretend to be what they're not. Goodbye.'

'Sorry and all that,' said Kilby, 'and give my regards to your parents.'

He watched her leave, then picked up his half-eaten sandwich, looked at it, shrugged and began to finish it.

Linda had an uncomfortable time recounting her tale of disillusionment to her parents that evening.

Annabelle, suffering for her daughter's very personal let-down, was furious that they'd all been taken in. Nick said that at forty-four he'd have thought himself far too old to have fallen hook, line and sinker for the kind of bait offered by a bloke he ought to have guessed was all of fishy. But his own personal feelings, he said, were nothing compared to what Linda's must be.

'I just feel sick, full stop,' said Linda. 'I'm going to spend the next few days sticking pins in myself. It's what I deserve for being a prize simpleton.'

'If you're a prize simpleton, I'm the original

village idiot,' said Nick. 'No, I'll bet the feller's fooled all kinds of people in his time.'

'Well, I hope none of us will let this ruin our lives,' said Annabelle.

'Or even our weekend,' said Nick.

'And certainly not our time at Uncle Boots's birthday party,' said Linda, and put Walter Kilby firmly out of her mind.

Nick reflected on the fact that he and Annabelle had been only too ready to accept the man as a possible suitor for Linda. Linda, modest and retiring, had never had a really close man friend. Nick very much hoped that Walter Kilby would come to a bad end, such as falling into the school boiler when it was hotting up.

He mentioned to Annabelle the next day that the best and quickest cure for Linda's smack in the eye would be the entrance into her life of a really decent bloke, say at Boots's birthday party. Annabelle pointed out that Linda was off all young men, and suspicious, in fact, of the breed as a whole.

'Hell,' said Nick, 'we don't have a daughter already set on remaining a spinster all her life, do we?'

'I wish you men wouldn't call unmarried women spinsters,' said Annabelle. 'It's a very unappealing word.'

'Believe me, I didn't invent it,' said Nick.

'I'll bet some man did,' said Annabelle, 'and I'll also bet he invented the word bachelors for unmarried men, which sounds much more pleasant than spinster.'

'Don't look at me, Annabelle,' said Nick, 'I didn't get to know a thing about unmarried women until I met you. Then I was amazed at what your lot were capable of. Talk about mesmerizing a bloke, I was hooked from the beginning. And still am.'

'Oh, very funny,' said Annabelle, but she smiled. If she liked to be the one to make the decisions, she also liked the fact that her husband wasn't argumentative about it. 'Anyway, don't try bringing home one of the young men from your office for Linda. It won't work, Nick, she won't fall for it.'

'I feel for our girl,' said Nick.

'We both do,' said Annabelle, 'and I hope the school boiler blows up when that man Kilby is stoking it.'

Which echoed Nick's idea of a suitable end for the bloke.

'No, I can't come to the dance on Saturday, after all,' said Emily into the phone, 'I'm going to a family birthday party.'

'Gee whiz,' said Brad, 'how unreal can a

family get? A birthday party with tea and cake, and shrimps and winkles? Man, is that sort of thing still alive?'

'Don't think I don't share your opinion,' said Emily, sounding as if she was on the way to becoming a social Bolshevik by the time she was fourteen. And that was only a month away. 'But this party's for the birthday of my uncle, who's really special. When I get married, which I'm not actually bothered about, it'll either be to someone like him or no-one at all. So I'm going to his party. Well, if I refused, my parents would drag me.'

'Parents again?' said Brad. 'Not that I'd strictly complain about yours.'

'All right, I know you fancy my mum,' said Emily.

'She's out on her own,' said Brad.

'I'll tell her you said so. Anyway, I shan't be seeing you until Saturday week, which is a fortnight before we all go on holiday to Dorset, to stay with my dad's sister. It's where my mum served in the ATS during the war, and where my dad ran a garage and taught Land Army women to drive tractors. He and Mum are talking about a walk down memory lane. Can you believe it?'

'Oh, well,' said Brad, 'I figure that most people over thirty live in the past. But it's not actually antisocial, just kinda quaint.'

'When I get to be over thirty, I'll still be myself, just as now,' said Emily. 'Anyway, that's all for the time being, so goodnight.'

'So long, baby,' said Brad, and they rang off.

Chapter Thirty

By six thirty on Saturday evening, Boots's sixty-first birthday party was in full swing, the handsome house in East Dulwich Grove packed out with friends and relatives. Even Vi's mother, old Aunt Victoria, was there. She had deserted her constant companion, her television set, to attend the party, although she had tucked herself away in a corner armchair, where Vi looked after her wants, and Boots arrived to ask after her comfort. She said she was having a very nice time, but wasn't everything getting a bit loud?

'Afraid so,' said Boots, 'and it'll probably get louder. It so happens that the party's being run as it was last year, by James and Gemma, with Gemma's record player well to the fore in a little while.'

'Oh, my goodness,' said old Aunt Victoria.

'I feel the same,' said Boots.

A little later, buffet food was being consumed,

and James was watching Cindy Stevens making herself interesting to the seventeen-year-old son of nearby neighbours. James knew he himself had been temporarily relegated to the also-rans, along with cousin Giles. Cindy was always searching for the absolutely perfect boyfriend, so James minded relegation not at all. He was pretty sure that as far as an absolutely perfect boyfriend was concerned, he'd never make the grade with any girl. A feller could be thankful for that. Well, think of having to live up to that kind of a label. He wondered what had happened to Cathy Davidson, who'd been living with her mother in Paris for a couple of years now. She was probably going great with a French boy.

James turned his attention to cousin Linda. He'd never known her so vivacious. In a small group of people helping themselves to food, she was the life and soul, which was a bit unusual. Linda was normally a nice quiet girl. Not actually a wallflower, simply not pushy. But she seemed full of gusto this evening.

'Hello,' said a voice in his ear. He turned. Cousin Emily was beside him, her plate of food now history. 'When's the music going to start?'

'When Gemma's ready,' said James, relieving her of her empty plate and putting it on the buffet table.

'We're not going to have to wait, are we?' said

Emily, looking young and appealing in a party dress of white with blue polka dots, but sounding a bit disgruntled.

'I think it'll be any minute now,' said James.

'Well, I hope so,' said Emily, 'I could be doing more exciting things, you know.'

'You can go and do them, if you want,' said James. 'Dad won't mind. I mean, you've put in an appearance and he'll settle for that.'

'Oh, your dad's great,' said Emily. The highlight of the party so far had been the few minutes she spent talking to Uncle Boots, who'd paid her compliments and been as droll as ever. 'I suppose you know Cindy Stevens has found a new boyfriend? She's over there with him.'

'Yes, it's Malcolm Jeffries from across the road,' said James. 'I introduced them.'

'Serve you right, then,' said Emily. 'Crikey, look at cousin Linda enjoying herself.'

Linda was laughing her head off over some joke that had just been told. Nick glanced at her from across the room. He knew, as Annabelle knew, that their daughter's high spirits were a facade hiding her unhappy feeling that a smooth talker had made a fool of her.

At that moment, Linda gaily interposed herself between Cindy and the boy from across the road.

'Here, d'you mind?' said Cindy.

'Oh, Cindy,' said Linda, bent on a rescue act, 'would you take a glass of wine to your mother? She's over there, by the fireplace.'

'Well, I just don't know what's wrong with her legs,' said Cindy, but she adored her German stepmother, Anneliese, and detaching herself from her new interest, she took a glass of wine to her.

'What's this?' asked Anneliese, in company with her husband, Harry Stevens, and their close friend Boots.

'Linda told me to bring you a glass,' said Cindy.

'Well, thank you, darling, how very nice of you and Linda too,' said Anneliese, at which point up came Giles to request five minutes of social chat with Cindy while she was still wondering if she'd been hoodwinked or not.

Linda, having saved Cindy's new interest from being overwhelmed, wished him good luck and moved to talk animatedly with cousin David and his wife Kate, up from their dairy farm in Kent. Annabelle glanced, wanting to keep an eye on her over-vivacious daughter.

Suddenly, the first amplified strains of music flooded the residence. In the adjacent lounge, Gemma had the volume control of her record player turned to maximum as a galvanizing

734

introduction to one of Bill Haley's ever-popular numbers, and as a guarantee that the music wasn't lost on the people elsewhere in the house.

'Have the Martians landed?' asked David, and Linda explained through the waves of sound that her Uncle Boots's birthday parties had been run by Gemma and James for the last three years.

In the dining room, Chinese Lady had arrived beside Boots to let him know she wasn't altogether in favour of this arrangement. 'Gemma is a dear girl,' she said, 'and no-one could say she isn't, but I just don't know why you let her play her records so loud.'

'Gemma says it's to give everyone in the house the benefit of being able to hear and to dance to the beat,' said Boots. Some young people were already swinging.

'Yes, but I don't understand what she's playing,' said Chinese Lady. 'Don't you and Polly have some nice records like "The Blue Danube" and "When Irish Eyes Are Smiling"? Gemma could put them on her gramophone.'

'All our old wax records are stored in a cabinet,' said Boots, 'and if Polly or I let them see the light of day, the twins would probably leave home. Fashions change, old lady.'

'I can't hear a word you're saying,' complained Chinese Lady. Young people were rocking and rolling. Emily was going it with

735

James, and looking as if her evening had its fun factor.

At the Brixton dance hall, Brad was swinging the evening away with Alice Fairbanks, a close schoolfriend of the absent Emily.

'Imagine letting some old birthday party get in the way,' grumbled Alice, fourteen, and as pert as Emily herself. She was known to some relatives as a spoonfed brat.

'Come again, baby?' said Brad, whose preference was for Emily.

'I wasn't talking to you,' said Alice, 'and watch your elbows, will you?'

'No problem,' said Brad, tucking them in a bit. 'What did you mean, get in the way? Get in the way of what?'

'You'd like to know, I bet,' said Alice. 'Why d'you wear such loud waistcoats?'

'I like them, that's why,' said Brad, as the band came to a temporary halt. 'Come on, cookie, give. Let's hear you spout.'

'Well, don't tell anyone else,' whispered Alice. The whisper was essential, for ears were everywhere, along with the bodies they belonged to. 'Me and Em were going to Brighton from this evening till tomorrow night.'

'Hey, give me a break, baby, I can't swallow that,' said Brad.

'Well, what a shame,' murmured Alice, 'but it's a fact. Em was to tell her parents she was staying with me, and I was to tell my own parents I was staying with her.'

'Oh, yeah?' said Brad. 'And where were you going to put up in Brighton, the Majestic Hotel?'

'No, with a cousin of mine,' said Alice.

'So why all the plots, then?' asked Brad. He could have asked why all the lies?

'My parents don't like my cousin,' said Alice.

'Why?'

'They said she does shoplifting, but I don't believe it,' said Alice. 'Parents make up stories about people they don't like. Look, stop asking questions, will you? It's all gone wrong, anyway, with Em choosing to go to a dreary birthday party instead. Come on, you Ted, let's dance.'

Brad followed her into the rhythm of the number while thinking about Emily. What a cookie. Someone had to take hold of Em before she gave her mum and dad a heart attack. He could tell them, of course, to watch out for what their daughter might get up to with her dotty friend Alice. No, Em wouldn't like him to do that, she'd call him a lousy telltale or hit him with something like Lonnie Donegan's washboard.

He'd simply have to keep tabs on her, for her

own sake and for the peace of mind of her parents, especially her mum, a geat cookie who could knock spots off more than a few dolls, even one fresh out of Hollywood.

For all the gaudy nature of Brad's waistcoats, under them beat a sound heart.

The party was well on its way, and Boots and Polly were in the hall, saying goodnight to Tommy, Vi and Vi's mum. Tommy and Vi were taking the old lady home before the lateness of the hour and the musical vibrations became too much for her.

'Thanks for a great evening, Polly,' said Tommy, 'and I only hope, Boots, that by Monday we'll get official word that the Southend fire was started by accident.'

'Well, word should come through sometime in the near future,' said Boots, and Tommy nodded. Vi's mum mumbled something.

'Happy birthday for tomorrow, Boots,' said Vi, and then she and Tommy disappeared into the night with her mother. Boots closed the door.

Polly said, 'Your old Aunt Victoria may look fragile, but it's my belief she and your mother will last for ever. They both belong to a lasting generation.'

'So do you,' said Boots, at which point Linda

came into the hall, intent on getting Boots to swing with her. She was still keeping up an air of vivacity.

'Uncle Boots,' she said amid the noisy revelry, 'would you like to come and rock with me?'

'Come again, poppet?' said Boots, and Linda repeated her offer, but in louder tones, with Polly smiling knowingly. She was always well aware that Boots fascinated young ladies, inside or outside the family. Boots, having now heard Linda's invitation to dance, said, 'At my age?'

Someone knocked on the front door at that moment, but such was the sudden increase in the volume of sound that even Boots, Polly and Linda didn't hear it. So the knock came again, loud enough this time to be heard.

'A late arrival?' suggested Polly.

'I'll see who it is,' said Linda. She walked to the door, and opened it. A young man in a check shirt and blue jeans gazed at her. He looked a little awkward about his presence on the doorstep.

'Sorry and all that,' he said, 'but me and my parents have just moved in next door, and they'd like to know what all the noise is about.'

'Oh, sorry,' said Linda, 'but it's a bit of a loud birthday party. Are you and your parents asking for us to tone it down?'

'We'll do our best,' said Polly.

'I'm not asking for that,' said the young man, taking note of Linda looking a knockout in her party dress. 'I thought, in fact, that—' He coughed and tried again. 'I actually thought of asking if I could join in as a new neighbour. It'll be a nice change from moving furniture about, which I've been doing most of the day.'

Linda, being once bitten twice shy, made a quite calculated study of the young man. He coughed again and ruffled his hair in a fit of embarrassment.

'I see,' she said.

'No, it's all right, forget it,' he said, 'it was a bit of a cheek, anyway.'

'What's your name?' asked Linda.

'Alec Gibson.'

Linda turned her head and glanced at Boots. He smiled and nodded. So she opened the door wider and addressed the young man in welcoming fashion.

'Come in, Alec Gibson,' she said, 'come in and meet the Adams family. You can't miss them, they're all over the place.'

It was six weeks later when Rachel, needing a word with Sammy, entered his office.

'Sammy,' she said, 'I should tell you something I don't wish to. I must.'

'Go ahead,' said Sammy, looking up at her

740

from his capacious old desk. 'I'll do me best to grin and bear it.'

'It seems,' said Rachel, 'that a couple of months ago our canteen chef and her husband celebrated their first wedding anniversary in style.'

'So?' said Sammy.

'High on champagne, they forgot themselves,' said Rachel, 'and it means Mrs Tindall isn't going to be with us for at least two years, after all. Sammy, she's giving notice.'

'Eh?' said Sammy.

'If you know what I mean,' said Rachel.

Which Sammy did, and which, on top of other happenings, convinced him that this definitely hadn't been one of his better years.

Still, there was always tomorrow.

THE END